Willow Grove Abbey

Willow Grove Abbey

An Historical World War II Romance Novel

THE FIRST BOOK IN THE 'SOMERVILLE TRILOGY'

MARY CHRISTIAN PAYNE

Published by TCK Publishing

ISBN: 1631619993
ISBN 13: 9781631619991

Dedication

*To My Darling Jim, Who Never Stopped Encouraging Me to Write,
and Waited Thirty Years for This*

Table Of Contents

Prologue   ix

Chapter One   1
Chapter Two   16
Chapter Three   26
Chapter Four   43
Chapter Five   57
Chapter Six   70
Chapter Seven   82
Chapter Eight   94
Chapter Ten   121
Chapter Eleven   127
Chapter Twelve   140
Chapter Thirteen   156
Chapter Fourteen   168
Chapter Fifteen   191
Chapter Sixteen   199
Chapter Seventeen   208
Chapter Eighteen   221
Chapter Nineteen   230
Chapter Twenty   244
Chapter Twenty-One   266
Chapter Twenty-Two   274
Chapter Twenty-Three   297
Chapter Twenty-Four   306

Chapter Twenty-Five 317
Chapter Twenty-Six 332
Chapter Twenty-Seven 346
Chapter Twenty-Eight 367

About The Author 375
One Last Thing... 377

$\mathcal{P}rologue$

1917–1935

Lady Sophia Somerville

When I shared a room at *The Ashwick Park School* with Edwina Phillips, she often referred to my years growing up at *Willow Grove Abbey*, my family's ancestral home, as a *Cotton Candy* existence. At that time, it seemed senseless to compare my life to a sweet confection. Later, as I compared the milieu of my upbringing to other young women at *Ashwick Park*, I realized that I did indeed live a privileged life. However, that was valid only when viewed from afar, which was Edwina's vantage point. She saw the Somerville family and its' seemingly charmed circle exactly as my parents had so carefully planned. Outsiders were unaware of our family's deeply held secrets. The tidy flowerbeds, expanses of manicured lawns, beautifully appointed rooms, and priceless objects d'art at *Willow Grove Abbey* disguised the tumult and discord that often reigned within those stone walls.

While persons who knew me casually envied what appeared to be my idyllic lifestyle, speaking of my family in reverential tones, while the truth was much less appealing. Because of my family's diligent attention to appearances, there was no chance that anyone would have believed the truth. My father, Nigel, the Earl Somerville, considered the quintessential English Lord, was genteel and soft spoken, with a kindly word for everyone. More than one wife throughout the countryside wished that her husband could be like my handsome, revered father. People said that he did not have an enemy in the world, and that was undoubtedly true. He'd learned early in life that reputation was of prime importance. Armed with the esteem of his fellow man, and the power that comes from being extraordinarily wealthy, Nigel Somerville was free to follow his own devices, and to do so without a conscience.

Alternately, my mother, Pamela, Countess Somerville, thought to be an exemplary Lady, was a dual-sided puzzle. None of us understood her. She kept her strange personality traits well hidden from the public. Tall and slender, she carried herself with regal bearing and was the epitome of well-mannered decorum. On the other hand, she displayed periodic eruptions of abusive rage, which were ghastly scenes of carnage. Once ended, the family never spoke of them again. One moment, she would be in an expansive mood, seemingly happy and content. Then, in the blink of an eye, her mood deteriorated into explosive anger, followed by despair. During those times, she hurled vicious words at whomever happened to be in her path. Her words were like arrows, piercing hearts and leaving scars, just as real as if they'd penetrated flesh. The wounds took a long while to heal. Many never healed at all. Words spoken during *rages* significantly altered the course of all of our lives. And words were not the only things she hurled. When in the midst of a rage, anything within her reach was fair game for what we children termed a 'smash fest'. The term was spot on accurate. She threw and smashed everything within her grasp. Those wretched scenes never took place in any sort of public arena, at least not until much later in my life. To those outside of the family, Mummy was grace and charm personified. However, inside of the 'charmed circle,' she was often a guttersnipe.

From the time I was only fifteen years, Mummy began to harp about my finding a husband immediately upon turning eighteen. Whether I found a gentleman attractive, or even kind, had no relevance. She frequently taunted that I was no great beauty, and that I should never turn a man away because of *his* appearance. Supposedly, she did not believe in marrying for love. However, that was confusing because she consistently maintained that she'd adored Papa from the moment she set eyes upon him. The primary factors I was encouraged to consider in my search for a prospective husband were heaps of money and social status. There was no question that my future spouse was to be from a noble family. He would preferably be a Duke. I was often reminded that I did not resemble

Mummy in any way, and that she had been a sensational beauty when my age. The truth is that I was really quite attractive…Some even said beautiful…but, I had a highly distorted image of myself. How could I not have?

Upon the death of his father, Papa learned, to his great dismay, that my Grandpapa had squandered nearly all of the family fortune. Papa enjoyed his bachelorhood well into his thirties, so he was close to forty years of age when his father died. It was then that he realized he would need to find a mate, and that she would have be someone who could provide a plentiful dowry. He did so rather quickly, as time was of the essence. That's when he discovered Mummy. She was Pamela Jane Wickes and, as the child of a commoner, had no title until she married an Earl. She grew up in the small village of *Awre-with Blakely,* where her father was a prosperous landowner. Her aspirations were much loftier than her lineage, however. Mummy was arrestingly beautiful, with icy blue eyes, an English rose complexion, and a haughty air. She immediately bowled Papa over with her charms. As a result, he married her shortly after they met in 1910, before he saw her shadow side. In fact, she often boasted that he asked for her hand in marriage on their second assignation. He must have thought that she was the answer to his prayers, as she brought a substantial dowry and beauty as well. Similarly, she must have believed that Papa was the Prince Charming she had awaited, for he offered entry into the nobility, which all of her father's prosperity could not buy. She cared immensely for the title and trappings that marriage to nobility offered, and was never shy about making her status known. She was only eighteen years of age at her marriage. Papa was twenty-two years her senior, which was not unusual in those early years of the twentieth century.

Willow Grove Abbey, my ancestral home, was considerably different from my school roommate's Tudor cottage. The *Abbey* still stands in the Parish of *Bedminster- with- Hartcliffe,* near Bristol, in the County of Somerset. Once a bustling hamlet, with many shops, time has reduced it to a few small cottages and a pub. Nevertheless, after nearly eight centuries, *The Abbey,* with its ancient stone gables, towers, mullioned windows, and slate roof survives. It dates to the thirteenth century Once a Benedictine nunnery, at its dissolution Henry VIII granted it to John Somerville who turned it into a private home. There was an Italianate garden, with formal areas set on three levels, including parterres, balustrades, and a summerhouse. In addition, there was a small arboretum and a conservatory. It is no wonder that I adored such a Shangri-La, with its full staff of servants, exquisitely polished mahogany, and fresh flowers in each room. In 1931, it was the most beautiful place in the world to me. In many ways, it still is.

We Somervilles were not famous. At least, not renowned, in the manner of film and stage stars of the day. It is certainly true that within *certain* circles in Great Britain people *knew* who we were, if only because we were of the landed gentry. My father was brilliant in business matters, and might have achieved success in whichever endeavor he chose. Nevertheless, he did not *earn* his title, nor the riches that accompanied it. Rather, a King or Queen bestowed it upon a distant relative for service rendered to the Crown. It found its way to Nigel Somerville because he was an eldest and only son. Due to that act of fate, he inherited not only his father's title, but of greater importance to me, our beloved home.

The Somerville family owned enormous woolen mills, renowned as far away as America, under a company umbrella known as *Somerville, Ltd.* Papa expanded the mills, profited greatly, and rebuilt the family fortune, with the assistance of Mummy's dowry. He also held a seat in the House of Lords. As a result, the Victorian way of life was by no means dead at *Willow Grove Abbey,* while I was growing up. Our family was one of the fortunate few who clung to the old lifestyle, maintaining a staff of servants that was, by some standards, quite excessive. There was a housekeeper, kitchen maid, upstairs maid, downstairs maid, chauffeur, valet, caretaker, footmen and several garden laborers, as well as a nanny who looked after Blake, Andrew and me, when we were children.

I am the youngest in the family, five years behind Blake, my eldest brother. He was my hero, but I was nothing of the sort to him. An athletic, wiry child, he grew into a strikingly handsome adult. Moreover, he was a *hellion.* Papa used to say that if Blake ever managed to acquire an education there would be no end to what he might accomplish. However, nobody really believed that he would reach that momentous occasion. Blake's hair was very dark, as was Papa's, but he had inherited Mummy's wintry blue eyes. He'd also inherited her disposition. Tall and well built, he exuded self-confidence and arrogance. There were infrequent times when he demonstrated the affection and attention that a younger sister craves, but his cruelty towards me was by far the rule. Mostly, I simply tried to avoid him when I was a young girl. He was sarcastic and critical, which brought about feelings of terrible inadequacy. Whether he inherited Papa's lack of conscience, or learnt his behaviour from watching performances of his mother, Blake often frightened and intimidated me. He frequently told me how unattractive I was, and because he *was* my hero, I believed his every word to be Gospel. My parents never contradicted or corrected him, which leant even more credence to his comments. I never stopped loving him, but most certainly did not always like him. He hurt me greatly and left lasting scars. Blake married while still at Oxford, and had two children by the time he was aged twenty-four, a son, also named Blake, and a darling little girl named Pippin. I adored both of them, and loved being an Aunt.

Drew, my second brother, four years my senior, was a charming youngster who grew into a fetching man, with chestnut brown hair, perpetually falling onto his forehead. His hazel eyes and a sweet, crooked smile gave him a boyish appearance. Drew was always more comfortable in a pair of old corduroy trousers and a well-worn jumper, than a trimly cut, Seville-Row suit. I absolutely adored him, and still credit him for helping me mentally survive an often turbulent and miserable childhood. He was my only source of comfort, for many years. On more than one night, he sneaked into my bedchamber after bearing witness to sounds of muffled cries. He would stroke my hair and wipe away tears, saying that I was a most special, wonderful girl, and that he hoped one day to be fortunate enough to marry someone very like me. Those were the rare times that I heard words of kindness and compassion. Drew *did* marry as soon as he finished Oxford, and his wife, Annie was a lot like me…small, dark haired, and kind hearted. We became dear friends.

Like Blake, I favor my father in appearance. Our Mediterranean appearance, unusual in Great Britain, is the result of my Grandpapa having married an Italian Countess whose name was 'Sophia Isabella Conforti', hence my own name. For obvious reasons, my childhood years at *Willow Grove Abbey* were an anomaly. On the one hand, there were truly hideous experiences. Yet, it was also a golden time, if only because of the love I felt for the pastoral setting of our home. I learnt, at an early age, to immerse myself in books, and by nature, I was a solitary youngster. Nothing pleased me more than a lengthy stroll over the grounds of *Willow Grove,* accompanied by one or more of my cherished terriers; or an afternoon spent sitting beneath the old, knurled tree in the ancient churchyard of the Chapel of St. Edward and St. Mary. There, among the ash, willow, and birch trees I spent countless hours, reading *Charles Dickens and The Bronte sisters,* or scribbling in my journal. The Chapel of St. Edward and St. Mary was attached to my ancestral home by a cloistered walkway. Because the dwelling had once been a Benedictine monastery, it made perfect sense that it would have its own private chapel. It was uniquely lovely, with hand carved wooden pews, and a very ornate alter. There were also exquisite stained glass windows at the front of the Apse, and on both sides.

By the time I emerged into the wider world, it was 1931. I'd survived over fourteen years being *Lady Sophia Somerville,* with accompanying privileges, secrets, sins, and peculiarities. It was in that year that my parents allowed me to attend *The Ashwick Park School in* Kent. My brothers had been at Eton, and then Oxford, but no Somerville female had ever attended public schooling. However, after women won the right to the vote in 1928, my parents began to discuss whether I should receive additional formal education. Papa felt that further learning was going to be necessary to meet the demands of a changing world. Similarly, Mummy was much in favor of continued schooling, but her reasons centered upon meeting the proper people, and finding a suitable mate. Thus, my parents reached the decision that I would attend *Ashwick Park,* well known for its education of females, including several Royals.

It was there that I met Edwina Phillips, by sheer happenstance, when the school matched us as roommates. From the first, we were both certain that our friendship was predestined. I was petite and dark haired; shy and introverted; conventional and lacking in self-confidence. Edwina was blonde, buxom, extroverted, unconventional, brimming with self-confidence. She was entirely unfazed by her stint at boarding school. Strangely, such a combination made us wonderfully compatible. Of course, neither of us had the slightest notion that our destinies would forever be entwined, nor that our simple meeting on a crisp, sunny, September afternoon would become an enormous watershed moment in both of our lives.

There was a clear vulnerability about me, and I was definitely aware of it. Although schooled in the art of social graces, with the best of manners and extensive knowledge of etiquette, I oft times felt like a fraud. Amusingly, I have been told many times through the years that my aura of bashfulness and timidity add immeasurably to my charm. If one but knew the entire story of my childhood, the latter would cease to be an oddity. But few persons were privy to such information. All the public knew was that I was Lady Sophia Somerville, the daughter of the Earl and Countess Somerville, highly esteemed members of the British aristocracy, said to be a delightful family.

There was no question that my lack of self-esteem was a direct result of my parents' inability to meet any of their children's emotional needs. Mummy was incapable of complimenting any of us, or showing belief in our abilities. I have no recollection of her ever saying 'I love you.' In that regard, my parents matched perfectly, since my father possessed similar shortcomings. An aloof man, he was inexorably slow to praise. However, he did not exhibit the horrific anger that Mummy so frequently displayed. Thus, he became the more trusted parent. He was the one to whom we children gravitated, and we all adored him. He often smoothed the path between us and our mother. Still, the majority of the time, Papa seemed to be more child than husband, more sibling than father. However much he was the preferred parent, blessed with an even temperament, I realized quite early into adulthood that he was completely devoid of scruples. Nevertheless, in my very young years, I viewed him as a Savior. I believe that both of my brothers also suffered feelings of inferiority, but they kept that fact well hidden. Blake was a rebel, who stuffed anguish profoundly inside, and gave the impression that he was incapable of emotional wounds, which of course was nonsense. Drew, on the other hand, was very sensitive toward others, and had strong moral values. But, oft times he seemed lost, with no one available to give him direction. He grew up with a personality much like mine, and a strong bent toward being wary and distrustful of others.

Edwina was the quintessential free spirit. She definitely danced to the beat of a different drummer, and in no time, I grew to adore her. With her luminescent blonde hair and intense blue-green eyes, I considered her my *'shining friend'.'* Her family lived at Bury St. Edmunds in Suffolk, and could not have been more different from mine. The Phillips lived in a modest home. Her father was retired from his job as a small business owner. He did not have a title and had never served in Parliament. The only commonality we shared was the more advanced ages of our fathers. George Phillips, Edwina's father, was twenty-eight years older than Edwina's Mum. Papa was twenty-two years older than Mummy. Edwina was the youngest of six children. Her siblings did not have the advantage of boarding school, although the family was not poor. Her opportunity to go away to *Ashwick Park School* had more to do with her father's wish to avoid the chaotic teen years, than any sincere desire to see his daughter well educated.

No matter how much Edwina teased about my privileged upbringing, the truth was that *Ashwick Park* became the real *cotton-candy* experience in both of our lives. *Ashwick Park* provided tranquility, consistency, laughter, and security. We followed a daily routine of classes and study, but we also paid attention to the rules, in order to avoid the wrath of the headmistress, a middle-aged Dickensian woman named Miss Kiskadden. The school promoted the philosophy that women could accomplish anything they set their minds to, a concept unheard of at that time. Although I never totally subscribed to such a belief, I did grow to have more faith in myself. Alternately, Edwina believed nothing could prevent the achievement of her goals. She had not needed *Ashwick Park* to tell her that. She embraced the school code with all of her being. Her heart was set upon becoming a world famous clothing designer. On occasion, I, too, fantasized about some sort of career. However, I never seriously considered such a future. A husband and children were the time worn choices for Somerville females.

Toward the end of our initial year at *Ashwick Park*, I began to spend an occasional holiday with Edwina's family. It was the first I had ever seen of the inner workings in a very different sort of home. I initially noticed the overwhelming amount of effusive compliments that Mrs. Phillips heaped upon her daughter. Edwina was encouraged, inspired, fortified, supported, and given confidence. I never once saw my friend criticized or spoken to in a disparaging tone. There were no harsh words; compliments flowed like water from a fountain; no shouting, and always time to sit down and have a long chat with Edwina's mother, who insisted that I call her 'Thelma', and not 'Mrs. Phillips'. I felt awkward doing so, and finally settled upon '*Mum Phillips*.' Edwina considered her a fount of wisdom, always patient and kind, even when circumstances called for firmness. She possessed the same *joie de vivre* as Edwina.

Edwina's assortment of brothers and sisters were gone from the home. One brother, Eugene, had married his primary school sweetheart, and managed a bookstore in London; Another, Orville, had immigrated to Canada. Fiona, the eldest girl, was a nurse. Another sister, Violet, taught school. Edwina's closest sister, Grace, married a well-to-do banker, and lived in the States. She had a magnificent home in Greenwich, Connecticut and was the one they all seemed to envy, albeit with pride. While I met most of them, I never knew them well. Although initially I thought the Phillips family were a bit of a strange lot, slowly I began to make comparisons between Edwina's family and my own. It soon became apparent that the Somervilles were the ones who were odd. It was a rather rude awakening.

Edwina and I swooned over the Prince of Wales, considering him our *ideal man*. We hung his framed photograph, attired in regimental dress uniform, in our room. We danced the *Jitterbug*, smoked cigarettes, sneaked an occasional nip of pink gin, and laid awake into the wee hours listening to tunes on the *Victrola*. It was a magical time, when life consisted of dreams that always seemed possible, and happiness that might truly be forever. We formed a pact early on, whereby we would always tell one another the truth. I learnt to trust Edwina implicitly; a rare thing for a girl like me, who did not trust easily. It was trust that created our strong bond of friendship, and betrayal that tore it apart. However, that came much later. Our biggest concerns at that time surrounded clothes, parties and boyfriends, rather than whether the Nazis might invade one of their neighbors. Or that one of us might fall in love with the wrong man. That also came later.

After four carefree years, our time at *Ashwick Park* ended in 1935. We prepared to leave with a combination of excitement and trepidation. By then we were closer than most sisters. I'd shared nearly every confidence with Edwina, and she with me. My dear friend knew of my mother's horrific *rages*, my feelings toward my brothers, and Papa's numerous weaknesses. She also knew that I was timid but resilient; solemn but witty; quiet but outgoing, and quite the most naive person on Earth. On that last day in our dormitory room, I threw my arms about Edwina.

"I truly can't think what I'll do without you. You've been the sister I never had."

"Oh Sophia, we'll still be close as sisters A bit of distance won't matter. I expect you'll visit me in Paris regularly," she replied, hugging me with dear friendship. Edwina's acceptance at the renowned *Esmod International School* in Paris, to study fashion design, was about to bring enormous change to both of our lives. Her childhood dream was becoming reality. Someday she hoped to work for one of the great fashion houses: *Worth, Chanel or Mainbacher*. I envied her a bit, but clearly understood that it was my lot in life to find the proper mate.

"Yes, I intend to visit Paris until I find the 'suitable husband'" I answered, laughing. "Then I'll be tied to hearth and home." The '*suitable husband*' was a cliché we had coined at the beginning of our friendship. It referred to my mother's desire for me to find the proper man, secure a proposal of marriage during my eighteenth year, and marry soon after. I had just turned eighteen. Thus, my long-awaited debutante season was upon me.

"Just postpone that as long as possible, Luv. I don't think you're at all ready to settle down in the country, raise a passel of children, entertain at fancy Balls, and put up with the same man every day for the rest of your life."

"No" I answered. "I find that scenario most unappealing, although in my heart of hearts, I can't imagine going off to Paris to seek a career, as you're about to do."

Edwina vowed to have scads of love affairees before she settled for one man. She said that she would fall in love with a destitute, Parisian artist, share his garret, and pose for her portrait in the nude. The concept was surely risqué, but I didn't think less of my dear friend because of her willingness to live without regard to restrictions. While we didn't always agree, our promise was to be honest with one another. Neither took offense if there was a difference of opinion. We were school girls then, and young, so the differences of opinion were not profound.

Chapter One

SATURDAY, 25 MAY, 1935
A BALL

I made my debut at a Buckingham Palace garden party, where all of the season's debutantes bowed. I spent months and months practicing my deep curtsy, which culminated in a graceful walk backwards, away from their Majesties. It was not as easy as it appeared. Edwina laughed uproariously as she assisted during the rehearsals. My gown was a truly delectable creation. I'd never had one remotely like it. I honestly felt like Cinderella when I slipped it over my head. The world-renowned designer, *Worth*, had fashioned it. An extraordinary confection of white, silk organza, quite simple in line, it was sleeveless, with a full skirt, seed pearl bodice, and jewel neckline. I carried a white fan and wore a gem-encrusted headband with an enormous white plume. At my neck were the Somerville Pearls, which my parents had given to me upon commencement from *Ashwick Park*.

I felt dreadful that Edwina couldn't participate in that grand occasion. There was so little that we didn't share. However, we both knew, and accepted, that the Presentation was one of the few times that my position in the nobility would separate us. The rigid class system in Great Britain seemed so terribly antiquated to me. Nevertheless, it was mandatory that I adhere to the rules. If I had made any attempt to circumvent them, there would have been a ghastly *rage* on the part of Mummy. There *were* several happenings during the upcoming Season in which Edwina *would* be sharing; punting on the Thames, Ascot, archery contests at Strawberry Hill, point-to-point at Cowdray Park, and numerous weekend house parties.

Those were just a few. Nevertheless, Presentation at Court was the highlight and the beginning of the season.

It was a perfectly splendid spring day, made even more memorable because the Prince of Wales held Court. Although he seemed a bit distracted and weary, he was terribly dashing and charming. All of the girls that season were madly in love with him. I was no exception. He was every bit as handsome as his photos. My rehearsals in preparation for the presentation ensured that my every move was perfection. I was terribly relieved when that portion of the day ended. My usual shyness melted away, as I sipped champagne and accepted compliments. There were other girls present with whom I was acquainted. Most were also graduates of *Ashwick Park*. I had never become exceedingly close to anyone except Edwina, which was a clear indication of my preference for solitary pursuits and one-on-one friendships, as opposed to 'running with the pack. I looked forward to the forthcoming Ball which my parents would be hosting at *Willow Grove Abbey* the following evening. Edwina *would be* present on that occasion.

When the evening of the Ball arrived, I was even more excited than I had been about the Presentation. My second gown for the Debut Ball even surpassed my Presentation dress in beauty. It was created by Madeline Vionnet, a renowned French designer. It was crafted from white organza and the sheerest, fine tulle. Its' delicacy was underlined by appliqued velvet swallows scattered across the skirt. It was absolutely ethereal. I felt like an angel. There were two hundred invitations sent out, and nearly all responded that they would be attending. The guest list consisted of my parent's wide number of social acquaintances, as well as their more intimate friends. And, of course it included my own friends. I received many, many baskets and bouquets of flowers that were banked near and around the place designated for me to receive my guests, next to Mummy. I carried the small nosegay made up of white rosebuds and white violets, which my father had presented to me. The guests began arriving at about half after ten, and I stood by Mummy and received until midnight. We were at the end of the Ballroom, furthest from the entrance, and as each guest arrived he or she was 'announced'.

The enormous Ballroom at the *Abbey* was festively adorned with splendid floral displays, spilling out of large Grecian urns. The color theme was pink and white, and the predominant flowers were roses, lilies, peonies, and white violets. The air was fragrant with their mixed scent. A string quartet had been engaged and was stationed in one corner of the lavish gold and white room. They were an addition to the exquisite white Grande Piano, which was a permanent fixture in the *Abbey's* ballroom. My parents had spared no expense. This was, after all, the first social introduction of their only daughter, and it announced to the world that I was available for marriage. Mummy had dreamed of such an evening all of her life, and undoubtedly had begun its planning while I was still in my pram. A sumptuous supper preceded the Ball, and individual, round tables were set about the grand dining room covered with snow white linens and the finest silver, china, and sparkling crystal. Each displayed an elaborate silver fountain of flowing champagne. The supper followed the reception of my guests, and I felt thankful to have that chore behind me. I'd grown rather weary of elderly gentlemen making remarks such as "You don't mind, my dear, if I tell you how sweet I think you look?" or "May I say what a lovely frock you are wearing?" I was looking ahead to the elegant feast that awaited, and the lessening of formality, since I would be surrounded by just close friends. My own table was somewhat larger than the others and was made up of my most intimate friends and their dinner partners. It was proper form for me to go to supper with a partner who had spoken for the privilege many weeks beforehand. My partner was Owen, Marquis of Winnsborough. His family owned one of the largest estates in England, *Winnsborough Hall,* which he would one day inherit, along with his father's title and holdings. The Somervilles and the Winnsboroughs had been acquainted with one another since Owen and I were children. Mummy never made any secret that Owen was her choice as a suitable husband for me. He was kind enough, but certainly not my idea of a prospective spouse. He was considerably older than I was and something about him reminded me of a spaniel, or perhaps a bloodhound. He had sandy, thinning hair, and a long upper lip. His face was topped by brown, droopy eyes. In addition, he was not overly tall and of slight frame. Nevertheless, I was polite to him, and felt at ease, since we had known one another for so long. The others at my table were Edwina and her partner, Anne Johnson and her beau, and another *Ashwick Park* friend, Margaret Radcliffe, and her partner.

Edwina looked radiant. Her taste had developed over the years, and she was much slimmer than when we had first met. While not truly thin, she was curvy. She designed her own clothing and it always had a distinctive flair. Her ball gown, which was ecru taffeta, had a sweeping skirt of cascading ruffles and large, balloon sleeves. It set off her figure, and worked well with her eyes. She had let her hair grow to pageboy length, and it was platinum in color. I thought she was dazzling, and I did overhear some of the other girls making envious comments to the effect that Edwina's gown was sensational and very chic.

I have to admit that I felt truly beautiful for the first time in my life. Many alluring girls attended, and I perceived most to be as attractive, or more so than I was. But, the attention I received was astonishing. My dance programme filled immediately. I found myself swirling about the floor with first one, and then another, of the eligible bachelors present. Owen was, of course, the most frequent gentleman requesting my attention. I allowed him to pay compliments, bring champagne and pencil his name on my dance card. However, I was not thrilled each time I saw that he would be my partner. Edwina absolutely could not bear him and did little to hide her antipathy. She said out-and-out that he was a pompous Arse. Poor Owen possessed little sense of humor, and for all of his upbringing, didn't seem to know how to romance a lady. He gave the impression that he was somewhat tongue-tied in my presence. I found his mannerisms effete. Even so, my parents were present, and I had no intention of starting a row due to some imagined or real slight, with respect to Lord Winnsborough.

I danced so much that my feet ached. Finally, the crowd began to thin as the clock approached the 3:00 a.m. mark. I was completely enervated, and praying for a breath of fresh air and peace. Thus, I silently slipped through the French doors leading from the drawing room to the terrace. I knew that it was not the 'done' thing, and hoped that no one would notice my absence. Especially my parents. I was finally alone for the first time since that morning. It was heavenly to enjoy a moment of silence. While the string quartet played softly in the background, I stood by the stone balustrade, trying to commit to memory the beauty and perfection of the night.

Suddenly, a man, whom I didn't remember ever having seen before, appeared at my side.

"At last, I have the opportunity to meet the lovely *Lady Sophia*," he commented.

I was startled, turning to see who had spoken. He was tall, slender, broad-shouldered and exceptionally good-looking. The light was dim and I could only hazard a guess as to his features. Nonetheless, it was clear that he was very handsome.

"How did you learn my name?" I stammered.

He leaned against the balustrade, placing his right hand on the stone railing. "This occasion is in your honour, after all, and even if it weren't, you are certainly the 'Belle of the Ball'. I've been hoping that I'd have the chance to meet you personally. It was certainly impossible to get near you to request a dance."

"What a nice thing to say, even if it is a bit of an exaggeration. Have we met?" I asked, while searching my memory. *Surely he must have queued up in the receiving line. How in the world could I have missed him?*

"I know your brother, Blake. We were at the same schools. I'm also acquainted with your brother Drew. But, no, I would certainly remember if I'd met *you* before. I didn't get an opportunity to go through the receiving line, as my arrival was a tad late. I'm the guest of one of your invitees, Charles Dyer. My name is Spence. Actually, it's Doctor Spencer Stanton, if I'm to be perfectly correct."

Ah, yes. I knew Charles Dyer, or rather knew who he was. He was much better acquainted with my brother Blake. They had been at Oxford together. I'm not certain that I even knew that he had been invited to the Ball, but I was suddenly very glad that he had been.

"Doctor? Are you a professor then?" I asked. I was very, very intrigued. He seemed different than the rest of the young men present that evening…more mature…surer of himself.

"No. A medical doctor," he answered. I studied at Oxford, followed by medical school at The University of Edinburgh. I also did Cadet training at RAF Cramwell, Lincolnshire. I rose to Group Captain, but then resigned my commission to continue my studies. So, I've not had much time to spend at debutante Balls, he smiled."

"What an interesting life you've led, for such a young man."

He laughed. "I don't feel young. In fact, I'll turn twenty-five in a few weeks."

"That isn't old. It's a perfect age," I responded. "Are you practicing medicine in London, then?"

"No, nothing so grand. I'm filling in at a small medical practice in Twigbury, Gloustershire. I've always thought I might like to be a country doctor. This was a good way to give it a go. The man who I'm replacing has taken a sabbatical. He needed someone for a year's time." He removed his hand from the balustrade, and leaned back against the wall.

"And do you like being a doctor in Twigbury?"

"Quite. I'm new at it, but it seems a *fit* for me. So, then, how do you spend your time, Lady Sophia, when you aren't sweeping young men off their feet at fancy Balls? Are you a part of the gay young set who make up London's café society?"

"I've only just finished at *The Ashwick Park School*. I guess I'm rather old-fashioned, in that I haven't *any* experience with the gaiety of London nightlife and café society, as so many of the other girls here tonight have. I've led quite a sheltered existence. Even with having been away at school. They kept a keen eye on us at *Ashwick Park*."

"Ah, an *Ashwick Park* girl. I should have guessed. And, what of your plans now that you've left school?"

"I'll have to wait and see what life holds for me," I smiled. "I haven't any definite plans. Of course, the season is here, and that's supposed to be my immediate concern."

"So, there's no handsome Duke or Earl to whom you've been engaged since childhood?" he chided, gently.

"You're teasing me. No, nothing of the sort, although my mother would like there to be".

"Ah, the match-maker mother, then. There of many of those here this evening." He laughed, and I joined in.

"Yes, I know. It's all I've heard most of my life. Nevertheless, I intend to do my own choosing. I'm nowhere near ready to marry and settle down, when I'm still so very young.""I can certainly understand that attitude. You seem very young to be married."

"I think so too, but I can assure you Doctor Stanton, a lot of the girls you see here tonight, will be married within the year. You know that's the entire purpose behind the Presentation and the Debut Ball. Actually, it's all rather embarrassing. I'm sure you were made to take dance lessons when you were a boy, just as we girls were. Remember how excruciating it was to wait and see if a girl would want to accept your invitation to dance with you, or, in my case, to wait to see if a boy would ask me to dance?"

"I doubt that you had too many excruciating moments waiting to see if you would be asked to dance," he laughed.

"Well…perhaps that's a bad example. But, you understand what I'm saying. Here are all of these debutantes, lined up for everyone to see, hoping to be selected by the man with the most promising future. And, furthermore, all of the gentlemen, are assessing which debuting girls have the most promising dowry."

Spence nearly bent over laughing. "Sophia, you're hysterical. What a perfect description of a debut Ball! It's so true."

"Don't misunderstand. I've had a good time. I love my dress, and all of the flattery. But, my parents have spent a fortune to try to attract the proper man. I'd much rather be searching through brochures for University courses."

"Do they know that?"

"Heavens no. They'd think I was bonkers. There are certain things expected of young ladies. This event is one of them. Perhaps someday women will stop all of this nonsense and expense, and get on with their lives after school. A nice graduation party would be fine. However, it's the fact that the whole thing is created to entice a man into marriage that I find ridiculous. It's fraudulent."

"I've never met anyone like you. There doesn't seem to be an artificial or pretentious bone in your body."

"Oh, if my parents were here with us, I'd have to recite the so-called party-line. You know what I mean. I'd simper, be coy and sweetly ask you to refresh my drink." I giggled.

"I find *you* very refreshing."

"Thank you, Doctor. I'm just being honest."

"If you were looking through college brochures, what would you want to study?"

"Probably Psychology. It's not a typical field for a girl, or even a man. But, people and their actions have always interested me. I've read a lot on my own. I'm fascinated with Freudian theories, and those of Carl Yung."

"Well, that's simply amazing. I'm terribly interested in psychology too. Of course, in medical school I had courses in that area. They were some of my favorite. I've entertained ideas, from time to time, of going back to school and getting an advanced medical degree in that discipline."

"That's interesting. I'd like to talk to you more about it. I'm certain you know a lot more than I do."

"Perhaps. We might arrange that. I'd be very interested in talking with you more too. Besides that, I find myself very attracted to you."

"That's a rather bold statement to make, just having met me."

"Yes. But you seem to like honesty. Are you offended because I find you attractive?"

"No…not really. It's just that no man has just come out and said it before."

"Well, then it seems to me that we should get along quite well, because you're the only lady I've ever met who's so honest and forthright."

"That's probably true," I laughed. "Gosh, I wasn't always like this. I used to be very shy and awkward around men. Perhaps all of the champagne I've had tonight has made me bold. But, I don't really believe so. I have a very strong belief in honesty. To tell you the truth, I've grown up in a family that oftentimes has trouble with the truth. Perhaps I've gone overboard in the other direction,"

"I like your honesty. It's a good trait, and makes it clear right at the beginning if a man is wasting his time or not."

"How do you mean, 'wasting time?"

"Just that. I suspect that if you'd prefer that I not bother you, you'd simply politely excuse yourself. Or, if you didn't want to see me again, you'd tell me."

"Yes, that's right. But, I *would* like very much to see you again."

"Right. Lady Sophia, you've cast a spell upon me."

"Please stop calling me *'Lady'* Sophia. My name is Sophia. Actually, it *is 'Lady'* Sophia, but everyone calls me just *Sophia*," I said, raising my head, and finding that I was staring directly into his sapphire blue eyes.

He had a comeback for everything I said. I remember thinking that he possessed an unforgettable face, the kind that stood out in a crowd. It had more to do, perhaps, with an attitude than anything else. His steely, sapphire-blue eyes were straightforward. They had a kind of mesmerizing hold when engaged in conversation. I could never have denied that I was attracted to him.

"May I call on you tomorrow?"

"Yes." I replied, surprising myself with such rapid acceptance. "However, I won't be here at *Willow Grove*. My brother Drew has a townhouse in London. I'll be staying there with him and his wife for the season. It's' just across from Kensington Gardens, at Number Ten, Lancaster Gate. Will that present a problem for you?"

"No. Not at all. I have the entire week free. I was planning on being in London. I'll stop by at two o'clock, if that's suitable for you? Are your parents going to be in London for the season, as well?"

"Papa has to look after business interests, so he comes and goes. Drew is studying Theology there, and Mummy spends time in the city, as well. They'll be remaining here at *Willow Grove* after tonight, so they won't be at Drew's house tomorrow. Drew's wife, Annie, is splendid. She's been very gracious about allowing me to spend time at Lancaster Gate, not minding playing hostess to my friends."

"She won't object to my calling?"

"No, of course not. The purpose of my being in London is, after all, to have gentleman callers."

"There's your refreshingly honesty again." he laughed, shaking his head. "Right. Then. I'll see you tomorrow afternoon. We'll have tea together at some elegant spot."

"That sounds marvellous, but now I really must get back to the party, or someone will embark on a search, wondering what's become of me."

I fleetingly questioned whether I should have accepted his invitation quite so readily, but he was, after all, an old acquaintance of Blake's, and there was no doubt that he was a gentleman. Besides, he was extraordinarily good-looking. I'd never had tea with a gentleman at 'an elegant spot.' He escorted me back into the ballroom, where my brothers had just discovered my absence. My parents were going through the ritual of saying 'goodnight' to guests. Then, I was certain they would retire. I tried to gauge by the number of persons queued up to say their farewells. That would give an indication of how long they'd still be present in the Ballroom. I hoped that they might meet Doctor Stanton.

I felt a stab of sadness come over me, even though I was exhilarated about my conversation with Spence. My exquisite Ball was coming to an end. I likened my feelings to the way Cinderella must have felt at midnight. Drew and Blake were looking a bit frantic when I re-entered the room, escorted by Spence. Their expressions were ones of relief, mixed with surprise, when they saw me with him.

"Good Lord, Spencer Stanton. I never thought to see you at a function like this. I'd heard that you'd buried yourself in a country village, dispensing elixirs and the like," exclaimed Blake. "

"True, but even country doctors can use a bit of amusement now and again. I'm a guest of Charles Dyer. Do you remember him from Oxford?" He smiled, showing lovely, straight white teeth a rarity in our country.

"Yes, of course. Rather a boring chap, if I recall," Blake replied, with a sheepish grin.

Elizabeth, Blake's wife, nudged him in the ribs, and chided.

"Blake, really! What a beastly thing to say."

Elizabeth was Blake Jr. and Pippin's mother, whom Blake had married while still at Oxford. Lately it seemed that they weren't getting along tremendously well. Blake, of course, had a strong desire to control his environment and everyone in it. Elizabeth was the complete opposite. She too was extremely honest. That didn't always please Blake. Mummy had told me, in confidence, (which meant that she'd told it to the whole world) that Blake had met a young lady in Scotland, on a business trip for Somerville Ltd, and was quite smitten. I wondered if he was embroiled in an affaireee. If so, I could have slapped him, for I adored Elizabeth. One thing I knew for certain. If Blake was carrying on an extramarital affaireee, and Elizabeth found out, she would leave him in nothing flat.

The conversation in the ballroom continued.

"Charles Dyer has a country house near Chipping Camden. I accompanied him to your parent's Ball as a sort of favor, although it's beginning to look like the favor was his to me," Spence said. "Charles fell from his horse while hunting, and had a bad break, so he's not able to drive. Train travel is difficult as well, so I agreed to drive him."

"And, now you've met and charmed our little sister," Blake smiled. "I don't believe you've met my wife, Elizabeth, nor my brother, Drew Somerville and his wife, Anne."

"Yes, Drew and I *have* met. I believe it was at an Oxford gathering." Drew nodded in agreement. All of the men exchanged handshakes. Spence took Annie's gloved hand and kissed the fingertips. He repeated the same act with Elizabeth. "It's a pleasure to meet you," he answered. "And, yes, I've met Lady Sophia, but I believe it's she who's charmed me."

"Just keep in mind that she's our *sister*," Drew laughed. "I assure you, it wouldn't be wise to tangle with my parents or with us where Sophia is concerned."

"I've only honourable intentions," Spence grinned. "She's consented to see me tomorrow. Have either of you any objection?"

"None whatsoever. I'd rather have you show her about London than some of the fops I've seen hovering over her this evening," Blake answered. Of course, he was referring to Lord Winnsborough. I felt like a child. *Who were my brothers to offer any objection regarding whomever I chose to see?* However, I'd been well schooled at never showing displeasure in front of others, so I remained passive.

"Then, we'll meet tomorrow, Lady Sophia," Spence said, taking my hand and brushing it with his lips. "I'm looking forward to it."

I blushed. "You promised to call me 'Sophia.'" We were in the lighted ballroom and I was able to see how truly handsome he was. I'm certain that I trembled at the thought of seeing him again.

"So I did," he answered. "I just wanted your brothers to know that I *am* aware of the correct form for addressing gentry." He chuckled and so did they.

"She's been 'Sophia' from the day she was born," Drew replied. "Don't stand on form with us, Spence."

He laughed heartily. "Sophia' it is, then," he added, with a fond look in my direction. "I promised to see that Charles gave that leg a rest before the night is gone, so I'd best keep my word," he continued. "Drew and Blake, I'm awfully glad to have seen you, and of course to have met you, Anne and Elizabeth." He turned, saying, "Sophia, I'll see you tomorrow."

Once he'd departed, I had a hundred questions for my brothers, but didn't want to seem inappropriately curious. They weren't fools. I was certain that both already suspected my strong interest in Spencer Spanton.

"Sophia, a word of caution," Blake warned. "Spence is a good chap, but you *do* realize that he won't meet with Mother and Father's approval?"

"Why ever wouldn't he?" I asked, truly unable to understand such a statement.

"No title, no land, no inheritance. A nice fellow, and a bright one too, but he's not of the nobility."

"Blake! I've never heard you talk this way! My Goodness, he must have *some* means. After all, he has an excellent education. And in addition to being a doctor, he was an officer in the RAF."

"Sophia, I don't mean to imply that Spence is a pauper. He comes from good people, if I remember correctly. It's just that his parents were killed in some sort of accident, and what inheritance he received was used on his education. You know very well that our parents would consider a physician in the same vein as one who practices a *trade*."

"Good Lord Blake! He isn't a rag picker. Mummy, herself wasn't a noble, until she married Papa. I cannot imagine that he wouldn't be acceptable to *any* family. On top of that, it takes a lot more intellect to be a physician than it does to be a land owner."

"He might be acceptable to *most* families. Nevertheless, when it comes to marriage, you know our parents. They'll expect you to marry at the same social status or much higher."

"What foolishness! Mummy has told me all of my life how unattractive I am. Now, she and Papa think that someone of the gentry should choose me? Why on earth would they, when, according to them, I'm lacking in all of the grace needed to attract a 'suitable' man? Anyway, I have only just met Spencer, and you're already speaking of marriage! That is *so* typical of this family. He seems very nice, and very much a gentleman. I certainly shall see him if I want to. So what if he's not nobility? Neither is Edwina, and *she's* my best friend on earth."

Annie spoke next. "Oh Sophia. Don't you know by now that your mother is horrifically jealous of you? You're beautiful and charming. She would give anything to have been like you, when she was your age. She wants to live her life again, through you. Don't listen to any of the nasty things she says. None of them have a whit of truth. Doctor Stanton seems divine to me. I'm glad you agreed to see him again."

Elizabeth chimed in. "Let's face it, gentlemen, the doctor is absolutely stunning. I know I'm speaking of my mother-in-law, but what Annie said is correct. It really kills your mother to see anyone young and pretty having fun, and not toeing the line when it comes to marriage."

Elizabeth had a lovely smile, and twinkly eyes. She was small, like I was, with perfect skin and lovely hair. We all thought that she was terribly witty. I had known Elizabeth since primary school. We had shared many wonderful times. I was glad when Blake married her and now I had dreadful concern about whether their marriage was going to last. Blake was dreadfully difficult to live with. Elizabeth didn't let him treat her with the same nastiness that has always been his stock in trade with women, it seemed possible that she would someday throw up her hands and leave.

Drew smiled. "Annie and Elizabeth are absolutely correct. Please don't allow Mother's wicked tongue to mar your self-image. Anyone with a brain can see the enormous splash you made tonight. I doubt that would have been the case if you were so unattractive. That's pure rubbish, Sophia. You know that it's just the 'done thing' to be sarcastic in this family. You're my little sister. I'm very proud of you. He put his arm around my waist and pulled me close.

Elizabeth agreed. "I married Blake *in spite* of his family." We all laughed at again at her comment. Elizabeth's father *was* a well-known landowner, and a breeder of fine horses. However, she had not been a Marchioness before she married Blake. Annie was not of the peerage either. She'd never seemed overly impressed with English titles.

"Do you think this nobility thing is so much nonsense, then?" I asked.

"I personally do. I think people are less and less inclined to worry about such things these days," Annie replied. "Just look at the circles the Prince of Wales travels in", she smiled.

"Yes. Spence seems as fine a person as Mrs. Simpson," added Elizabeth. That was a bit of sarcasm, because everyone knew what was going on in Royal circles. Annie and Elizabeth were referring to the information that it was well-known that the Prince was obviously enamored with a twice-married, American woman. "My parents would never object to someone like Spence. They'd find him eminently suitable," Elizabeth continued.

"Well, he's obviously a good person. Imagine devoting your life to healing sick people? I shall see him if I want to" I repeated.

"I didn't say he wasn't a good person," Blake responded. "Of course, you should see him. This isn't the Victorian age. I just think you need to be aware that there'll be objections if you ever entertain thoughts that go beyond friendship."

"Oh Blake! This is the most ridiculous conversation. Mummy and Papa have never objected to any of my friends."

"Your friends haven't been potential sons-in-law. I don't have anything against Spence, Sophia, but he just isn't a member of the nobility."

"Blake, I'm just eighteen. I'm not worried about whether Dr. Stanton belongs to the nobility. How many times do I have to say it? I'm not even remotely thinking in terms of marriage to anyone."

Edwina appeared at that moment, flushed from hours of dancing and coquetry. She always had scads of young men wanting to dine with her, and take her dancing. The fact that she was not in the market for a husband definitely heightened her appeal. Men were undoubtedly relieved to be able to socialize with a woman who was not angling for a wedding ring.

"Did I hear the word *marriage* escape your lips, Sophia? Surely, you haven't found your *'suitable man'* so quickly. There's far too much fun to be had this season to settle so soon."

"No, *Goose*. Drew is the one who is talking about marrying me off, simply because I made an engagement for tea with a gentleman."

"An engagement for tea? Hmmm. How intriguing? Is he someone I know?"

"I don't think so. His name is Spencer Stanton. He's a doctor. A physician, actually."

"A physician! Gracious, Sophia. Be careful! Just think of all the things he must know about the female anatomy," Edwina laughed.

"Edwina, I daresay, you're as bad as Drew and Blake. Doctor Stanton seems very nice. I'm only going to tea with him. Blake has me married, playing a country doctor's wife in a Cotswold cottage."

"Actually, dearest, I think that sort of life would suit you very well. I think you'd find it far more appealing than acting as mistress of some ancient country house, with a pack of servants to order about. If you *do* find the good doctor irresistibly attractive, you mustn't care whether the Earl or Countess would go *bonkers*. It's *your* life, Sophia, not theirs," Edwina stated firmly.

"Quite right," echoed Drew. Now, let's enjoy a last glass of champagne and drink to Sophia's newly declared independence.

Chapter Two

MAY 26, 1935
AFTERNOON TEA

Of course, I had no way of knowing how prophetic that conversation would be. Promptly at two o'clock the next afternoon, Spencer Stanton appeared at the door to Number Ten Lancaster Gate. Annie, who had the task of chaperoning me during the upcoming season, answered the bell, ushering him into the parlor. I was sitting in front of the French doors, which opened onto the attractive garden. It was a lovely, warm spring day. The roses were blooming in profusion. Their scent, mixed with day lilies, peonies, and lilacs filled the room. I wore a simple white, voile dress, embellished with a pattern of pale yellow sprigs. I'd brushed my hair until it shone, and parted it on the left side, securing it with a small gold and topaz clip. My natural curls bounced just above the shoulders. I felt quite attractive.

The look in Spence's eyes when he entered the room indicated that I wasn't mistaken. Nor was I disappointed with him. He was, quite simply, the best-looking man I had ever seen. His hair was very dark, and those splendid sapphire-blue eyes, which had so entranced me the previous night, were even more intense in the daylight. His strong chin had a deep cleft, and he had perfect teeth, as well as dimples in his cheeks. The combination created a dazzling smile. I would be lying if I said that I wasn't utterly smitten. He was even better looking than I'd remembered. It seemed as though my pulse was beating very irregularly when he walked into the room. I was afraid I wouldn't find my voice.

"How lovely you look today, Sophia. Last night's late hour doesn't seem to have taken any toll, he smiled.

"No, I slept rather late, actually. It was awfully nice to be lazy."

"Yes. I don't have that chance very often. I never know when a patient might ring me. It always seems as though persons tend to need a doctor in the dead of night."

"I suppose that could be annoying."

"Not so much annoying as inconvenient. Especially when one is truly looking forward to a good night's rest. However, it's part of the profession. We train for it, so I'm accustomed. At the moment, however, I'm on holiday, and savoring every moment, particularly the eight hours of uninterrupted sleep."

"May I offer you a glass cup of tea, Doctor, or perhaps a Brandy," Annie interjected?"

"No, thank you. In fact, I've arranged for tea at the Royal Hotel for Lady Sophia and myself. We had best be going, if we're to be on time for our reservation at two forty-five."

We left the house, making our way to a gorgeous yellow auto parked at the curb. It was a 1935 SS Jaguar Tourer. "What a splendid auto," I remarked, knowing very well that the compliment would please him.

"Do you think so? I saw her in a showroom window and lost my head. It's true that I needed a reliable vehicle to carry me round on patient visits. Nonetheless, I'm fully aware that something less ostentatious would have been adequate."

"It's perfect. I can see why you lost your head," I replied. It was obvious that my compliment had pleased him. I *did* truly mean what I said. The auto *was* lovely. In fact, I'd never been inside of a Jaguar. During the drive to the hotel, which was only a few blocks, I sat back, luxuriating in the comfort of the leather interior. When we arrived at the Royal, Spence drove up to the entrance, and a uniformed door attendant helped me step from the vehicle. Spence handed the keys over. Together we made our way into that wonderfully elegant, structure, standing on the banks of the Thames. I felt very chic and worldly, as I took his arm. The head waiter escorted us to a round table for two in the *Elizabethan Foyer*. In a pavilion, in the middle of the room, a harpist accompanied afternoon tea. We were seated at a lovely table with elegant, gold-leaf chairs.

"Do you come here, often?" I asked, as I settled in, placing my gloves to the side, as well as my handbag.

"I must confess, it's my first visit. I'm trying to impress you, Lady Sophia." He smiled

"You're succeeding, Doctor Stanton," I bantered. "I've never been here either." I felt very much at ease with him. We both chuckled.

"Are you always so honest?" he continued.

"I try to be. Sometimes women have to play silly games where men are concerned. I learned that at a young age, having older brothers. I always thought it was foolish to have to pretend. For instance, I was instructed to act as though I was less skilled at sports than a male opponent, lest I offend his masculine pride."

The waiter brought a first course tray of four different sandwiches. They were small, finger sandwiches, with no crusts, and they were delicious. He also brought an array of exotic teas. We selected those which we wished to drink. After he departed, we resumed our conversation.

"So, if we played tennis, I wouldn't be forced to patiently toss you gentle serves and keep my boredom to myself?" he asked, smiling.

"Not on your life," I replied. "In fact, I consider myself quite a splendid tennis player. Don't expect me to request gentle serves, nor for me to return them to you." I grinned.

"Men can be such bloody fools where women are concerned," Spence remarked.

"I'm surprised to hear you criticize your sacred fellowship," I teased

"I like your honesty, Sophia. It's a good trait. I told you that last night. Truth is truth." He spoke with significant pauses, his words sounding well thought-out. His smile, slow to appear, gave him a boy-who-just-ate-the-pie look. He was unlike anyone I'd ever met. He seemed humble, gentle and intelligent.

"Being forthright is something I learned from my best friend," I continued. "When we first met at *Ashwick Park,* I was rather guarded and wary with others. She's very much the opposite. I've grown to admire that trait. You'll like her. Her name is Edwina Phillips."

The waiter reappeared and filled our teacups. The service at the Royal was remarkable. Next, the second course appeared. It was a tray of two different scones, plain and fruit. To go with the scones was fresh clotted Devonshire cream, as well as lemon and strawberry curd.

"I believe I was made aware of Edwina at your Debut Ball last night. She caught Charles Dyer's eye. She's quite an effervescent lady," he said, while spreading lemon curd on a fruit scone. "But, not nearly as attractive as you are," he added.

"You must be joking! I find Edwina stunning. I think she's dazzling. I always refer to her as my *shining* friend."

"She's certainly very outgoing; but I don't much care for her type. She is a bit dramatic for my taste. Brash, if you will. I find you infinitely more fascinating."

His words were truly puzzling to me. "I find Edwina to be one of the most alluring women I've ever known. She has such…such *joie de vivre*. She reminds me of fine champagne. So sparkly, and in love with life. I'm merely, well…I suppose I *am* pretty, in a certain way, but not shining."

"There are numerous ways to shine, Sophia. Edwina *is* like champagne, with her silvery hair and boisterous manner. But, you, my dear, are like fine wine. To me beauty is a combination of outward appearance, wit, charm and inward kindliness. In other words, I believe you just might serve well as the epitome of loveliness."

"Me! The epitome of loveliness! I wish my parents could hear you, Spence. They would be certain that you're after my dowry. I do thank you, however. I also look forward to you knowing Edwina better. I believe you'll find her enchanting. She has marvelous wit, and there's a very deep generosity about her. One simply has to be familiar with her."

"I'm sure if she's your best friend, I'll find her charming. I'm assuming from the comment you just made that you intend for us to be seeing more of one another, if you expect me to meet Edwina."

"Ah. You caught me. I suppose that must be what I meant."

"Why do you say your parents would think me a fortune hunter for saying that you're the epitome of beauty?

"Because they've told me all of my life that I am not very attractive, and that any man who showed the slightest bit of interest in me would probably be a fortune hunter."

"You! Not very attractive? That's absurd. Sorry Sophia, but they should be horsewhipped for putting such despicable ideas into your head. "Don't you realize that you're a gorgeous, breathtaking woman?"

"Spence. Are you serious? I can't tell if you're teasing or not. No, I do not think I am a gorgeous, breathtaking woman. I don't even feel like a woman. I feel like a self-conscious, little girl a lot of the time. This is one of them. I have no experience with flirting. I'm not very sophisticated.

"My dear lady. You have a greatly distorted image of yourself. We need to rectify that. I don't intend to make you over into a narcissist, but you need to have a more realistic view of yourself. However, I must admit that sometimes a lack of sophistication can be utterly charming. So, then, Sophia, tell me about yourself. I really know very little. You're Blake and Drew's sister, your father is Earl Somerville, owner of Somerville Mills and a member of the House of Lords, you have just finished at *Ashwick Park,* and yesterday was your Presentation at Court."

I selected a scone from the tray and spread it with strawberry curd. "Ummmm. This is positively delicious," I exclaimed. The scone *was* so marvelous. It nearly melted in my mouth. I swallowed, resuming the conversation.

"There isn't a lot more to know about me. Isn't that rather pathetic? My whole life can be summed up in four sentences, and two of them describe me in terms of being someone's sister and someone's daughter."

"I suspect there's a good deal more to know if one chooses to look. What's your passion?"

"My passion? I'm not sure I know what you mean?"

"Everyone has a passion for something in life. I have two, flying and medicine."

"You mean like Edwina, who's going to Paris to be a designer? I don't believe I have that sort of passion. I wish I did. I think it would be marvelous to be consumed by something. Perhaps Art, Music, or Writing. Or, as in your case, Medicine. Did you always know that you loved Medicine?"

"I always knew that I wanted to help people, and had a curiosity about nature and science. So, I suppose it's logical that those two interests became a passion for Medicine. Have you ever tried putting two or three of your interests together, trying to determine what career fits them the best?"

"No. That might be fun. Let's see…I love to write…and I love animals, particularly small dogs. I also love history. What do you make of that, Doctor Stanton?"

I have a perfect career for you. Trace the history of dogs back to their earliest origins, and in an understandable format, write a book explaining how wolves from millions of years ago, became the poodles of today." He smiled, and raised his eyebrows, as if to say, 'what do you think'?"

My eyes widened and I laughed. Gosh. That isn't an awful idea. It would call for a lot of research, but, you know, it could be done. I could call it something like "When Did Poodles Roam the Earth?"

"There ,do you see how easy it is to combine interests into a passion?"

"Well, I shall think some more on this. It's rather intriguing. To change the subject, you mentioned last night that you have a practice in Twigbury. Did you grow up there?"

"In Twigbury? Good Grief, no! It's a very tiny village. I suppose there are people who have and do, but, as I told you last night, an older physician, whom I've known for quite some time, wanted to take a sabbatical and we arranged for my taking over the practice for a year. I grew up near Bristol."

"Bristol is very close to my home. Just a few kilometers. I love it there. Actually, I love anyplace on the sea."

"Yes. My family home wasn't far from the water, near Abbott's Leigh."

"We were almost neighbors! Isn't that coincidental?"

"I don't believe in coincidences, Sophia, he smiled. "I believe in Far-sightedness. Fate, if you will. Our living in such close proximity is one of those *serendipitous* happenings, as was our meeting at your debut Ball. I've always believed that things are meant to be."

I returned his smile. "I believe in that too. You're speaking of destiny. Therefore, you think that we were destined to meet. For instance, Edwina and I think that we would have met whether or not we had ever gone to *Ashwick Park*. Nevertheless, not everything can be predestined, do you think? If that were true, then nothing would be an accident. Is that what you believe?"

"I believe that man has free will, able to choose whichever path he wishes. However, one path will lead to his destiny, and is the correct one to take. Some people make mistakes, and take the wrong path. Nevertheless, we don't live in a perfect world. Anyway, when it comes to people falling in love, finding their soulmate, then I believe it will happen, no matter where you are or what you're doing. When the time is right. What happens from there depends upon choices that both parties make."

"So, you believe in soulmates? I'm not certain that I do. I often think that there are many persons one could love."

"Sophia, I believe that we can err and take the wrong path, thinking that we've discovered our soul mate. That could be a heart-wrenching mistake. I believe there's only one true soulmate for every other. That perfect person, with whom you feel an affinity from the moment you meet. The one God intended for you."

That comment was one of the dearest I'd ever heard. *'The one God intended for you.'* No one had ever expressed such a view to me. I scarcely knew how to answer him.

"I'm older than you are, Sophia," he continued. "I've thought I found my soulmate many times, particularly when I was much younger." He placed his hand over mine. "However, I'm now beginning to think that those would have been utterly wrong paths."

I felt the color rise in my cheeks. *Oh Lord. Is he serious, or is this just the flirtatious way that men behave?* I was pathetically naïve. "Spence, if you're implying that you think *I* could be your soul mate, I'm…well of course, I'm terribly flattered. But…But, we scarcely know one another."

"Sophia, I don't mean to frighten or upset you. As I said, I'm older than you are. I just know that I feel an attraction for you that's rare, at least for me. I have known my share of women. No one has set sparks alight inside of me like you do. However, I don't want to rush you, or to give you false impressions. I'm finding myself in a bit of a quandary," he replied.

I looked down at the table, not knowing how to respond. My heart was throbbing. Thank Goodness, the waiter once again returned. This time he bore a third tray…a selection of chocolate fancies. *Gracious, when does this end? I thought.*

"We shall be here until midnight, with the waiter still presenting trays of delicacies' to us!" I spoke my thoughts aloud. Spence and I both broke into low laughter. We looked like two misbehaving children.

"Your eyes make my heart do somersaults," he suddenly murmured.

I wanted to tell him that I felt the same way about *his* eyes, but was uncomfortable with the turn the conversation was taking. He sensed that, making an obvious attempt to change the subject. Clearing his throat, he lighted a cigarette and poured me another cup of tea, before re-filling his own cup.

"Right. Shall we talk of something else? Perhaps it's too soon for me to be telling you these things. I'm not usually so forward on a first outing with a young lady. You see the influence you're having upon me?" He winked at me jokingly. "But, enough of that."

I lifted my eyes, and took another sip of tea "I notice that you speak in the past tense when you refer to Abbott's Leigh? Have you no family there anymore, then?"

"No. Both of my parents died in a beastly accident, when I was fifteen. It was a boating accident. They were in a high-powered craft.... but I was already off at school, so I suppose you could say I really didn't have a home after that. I just spent school holidays with assorted relations."

"That sounds terribly tragic. And, have you no brothers or sisters?"

"No, but many aunts, uncles, cousins, and other persons who are family, so I've never felt alone."

"Are they in Abbott's Leigh?"

"No, as a matter of fact, most are in Ireland."

"Ireland? Do you mean they're Irish?" My heart plummeted to my toes. I could just picture my mother's face.

"Yes. My mother was Irish. She was born and raised in County Cork. My father met her on holiday after he finished school. She was a nurse. Her family name was Ryan. That's my second name. Spencer Ryan Stanton."

I was a bit uncomfortable about asking the next question, but felt that I had to know the answer. "I don't mean to be ill-mannered, but does that mean you're a Roman Catholic?"

"Yes, that's what it means, Sophia. Is that a dreadful thing to be? He smiled, and his eyes twinkled.

"Oh, no. Not at all. It's just that, we…my parents are…You might say a bit narrow when it comes to the subject of religion." I was completely aghast, trying hard not to show it.

"In other words, they don't approve of Catholics."

"To be honest, I've never known a Catholic. I mean, I suppose I have *known* some, but not really well. I just know that Mummy is quite rigid in her views on certain subjects. Religion is one of those."

"Am I to be barred from the door then?" he asked, in a jocular manner.

"Of course not. I can't imagine that they would ever be rude to someone I cared for."

I was not so certain. My mother was demented on the topic. I had heard her go into ghastly rants about 'Papists.' I played about in the tray of chocolate fancies, selecting one that looked particularly tasty. I honestly had very little appetite left, but needed something to divert attention from the subject at hand.

"Does that mean you care for me, Sophia?"

"Now you're teasing again, Spence. As I said, I scarcely know you."

"And I scarcely know you, but I believe I care for you." He seemed so utterly sincere, and I felt that I already knew him well enough to be able to ascertain whether or not he was playing with my emotions. I could have sworn on a Bible that he was being exceedingly honest.

"Well, I believe I *could* care for you. Shall we just leave it at that for now," I countered, with a smile.

"Perhaps, just for now," he teased.

We were interrupted a final time, when the waiter presented us with the fourth course…a selection of cakes…Carrot, Fruit and Lemon. Ours eyes met, and once again we fought to suppress laughter. Both of us were filled to the brim, but we politely accepted the offering, sampling a bit of each cake, and proclaimed them outstanding.

What a glorious afternoon! I couldn't believe that it was already five o'clock. The time had flown by. I knew that my experience of tea at the *Royal* was one I would treasure forever. I already knew that there was no way that Spence and I would 'just leave it at that.' He was very proper when he took leave of me back at Ten Lancaster Gate, but he *did* ask me to accompany him to the theatre the next evening. I was ecstatic beyond words at the knowledge that he wanted to see me again so soon. Of course, I readily accepted his invitation. He was dreamy, and I couldn't believe that he actually found me intriguing. He could have had anyone in the world, and yet for the moment at least, he appeared to want me.

Could I trust him? That was my primary concern. My parents had raised me to be very wary of what they termed '*Fortune Hunters*' or '*Opportunists.*' The message they were attempting to convey was that any man who might show interest in me would be doing so because of the possibility of monetary gain. I couldn't imagine that someone like Spence could possibly love me for myself, no matter how much he protested.

Chapter Three

Summer, 1935

The Last Georgian Summer

The memorable tea at the *Royal* was the beginning of everything. Everything that meant anything to me for the rest of my life. The following night we attended the St. James Theater and saw '*Mask of Virtue*', which had opened to rave reviews in May. We had a lovely evening, and when we arrived back at my brother's home, Spence once again asked to see me the next night, and every night thereafter, until he was forced to return to Twigbury, and his medical practice. Even after that, I saw him every weekend.

We did not kiss until we had known one another nearly a month, but I was mad with desire to do so. We took a picnic to Hyde Park. Spence ordered a delicious basket of delicacies from Fortnum and Mason. There was caviar, liver-pate, cold chicken, assorted cheeses, fresh fruit, biscuits, and dilled parslied potato salad, along with a bottle of Pouilly-Fuse Chardonnay. It was a glorious June day, without a cloud in the sky, and just enough breeze to keep it comfortable. We talked while eating our lunch, of everything from politics to the types of literature we liked. Mostly we found that we agreed on every topic, except that I preferred the earthier Geoffrey Chaucer in my literary tastes, which caused Spence to laugh aloud. We moved from that topic, to that of soulmates again, and love. The wind ruffled his hair, and the sun shone upon his skin, which had turned golden from time spent out of doors that summer. He wore a white linen shirt, rolled at the sleeves, and light weight summer trousers in pale beige. I must have resembled a copy of the famous artist Benson's painting *Summer*

Girls, dressed as I was in white muslin, trimmed with lace at the high collar and cuffs. My heart caught in my throat when he said that he knew with certainty that he had found his soulmate.

"Oh Spence," I smiled in return; "I do feel as though I have known you forever. Isn't that strange?"

He took a last sip of his wine, and placed the glass back into the picnic basket. Then, he turned to me and took me into his arms. Birds sang in the trees and a nanny pushed a pram on the graveled pathway. I could hear the voices of children playing in the distance.

"No, it isn't strange, Sophia. It's exactly as it should be."

He gently pulled me close to him, and placed his lips upon mine. I had never been kissed like that before. I felt so close to him. I began to understand what Edwina had meant when she spoke of passion. "Sophia, I believe we have known one another forever. You are exactly as I knew you would be. You even have old, soul eyes."

"What are *old soul'* eyes?" I asked, still in his arms, hoping for another kiss.

"Eyes that look like they have lived many lives, and have experienced many emotions." He played with a lock of my hair, and kissed me again with heightened passion. I felt butterflies in my stomach. One kiss led to another, and I told him, between kisses, that he took my breath away.

As the summer moved swiftly by, I felt that I needed *more,* although I could not have defined what *more* meant. I just knew that our kisses were leading to something. He truly did render me speechless. He confused me at times, because one moment he acted as though he could not get enough of me…. Of my kisses…. Of holding me. Then, he would suddenly end an embrace, as though he had remembered that it was not appropriate behaviour. I did not know how to assess his actions. The most logical explanation was that he was concerned because we were from such opposite ends of the spectrum, when it came to social class, and because of the difference in our religions. I wondered if my position in the upper classes worried him. It was all so terribly confusing. I could see no Earthly reason for a problem arising from the fact that he did not own land, and didn't have a title. I respected him far more than anyone I'd ever met, and knew that, if anything, he would have preferred that I was just a simple girl, from a middle class upbringing, and not a member of the nobility. That particular part of the equation played no part in the feelings we had for one another. The worrisome aspect was whether my parents would view the matter as we did. It was hard for me to understand why Mummy had not been of noble birth, and yet was perfectly acceptable as a wife to Papa, yet in reverse circumstances, Spence wasn't a proper choice for me. It made no sense, but many of the peculiar positions my parents held, on various matters, never did make sense. There was no question in my mind that Spence was looking ahead to a future that included much more than simple picnics in the park and theater openings. So was I. While I had vowed upon graduation from *Ashwick Park* that I was not going to immediately settle for the 'suitable man', marry young, and settle down to being a wife and mother at a tender age, my meeting Spence had radically altered my views. I could think of nothing that would please me more.

I had not told my parents that Spence was Catholic, nor that his mother was Irish. I suspected that Drew had been right in May, when he'd warned me not to develop any serious feelings for Spence. My parents were going to be furious at his lack of a title and wealth. The additional fact that he was an Irish Catholic would probably make them apoplectic. In fact, I'd not even divulged that information to Drew or Blake, knowing that it would only lead to a repeat of the discussion we'd had on the night I first met Spence. Neither of my brothers had a bigoted bone in their bodies, but Mummy and Papa were an entirely different matter. I suspected that those difficulties weighed heavily upon Spence as well.

However, no amount of warning, schooling, or upbringing had taught me how to overcome feelings of the heart. I simply continued to grow ever fonder of him, as our relationship grew. No one had ever made me laugh the way he did, nor shown such interest in my thoughts and feelings; no one had ever made my heart race the way it did as I glided with him across a dance floor. I couldn't describe the feelings that were surging through me. Sometimes I felt that I could walk on water, and sometimes, for no reason whatsoever, when I heard a sweet love song, or walked in the garden on a warm, sunny day, I suddenly burst into tears. Edwina told me that it was true, first love, with all of its pathos and longing. I had never felt it before. I'd not told Spence that I loved him, nor had he said those words to me, but I *knew*.... Simply *knew*.... That it was only a matter of time. It was a romantic, idyllic summer, and I wished it might never end. Even though I continued to see others, most notably Owen Winnsborough, so as not to start tongues wagging about Spence, no one came close to touching my heart the way Spence did. I already knew that no one ever would.

Edwina left for Paris in September. I missed my dear friend greatly. However, because I was so consumed with Spence, her departure had less impact upon me than might otherwise have been the case. She settled into a flat near *The Esmod School,* in the ninth Arrondissment, and settled into the life she had looked forward to for such a long time. We wrote often and she seemed very happy. Edwina was clearly living the quintessential Bohemian life. She had already made several friends, which didn't surprise me in the least. It was amusing for me to think of the changes that had taken place since the times when Edwina and I had giggled about Prince Edward in our room at *Ashwick Park*. Only a summer later, I found Spence infinitely more attractive than the Prince.

Summer gave way to autumn and the days were cooler. There was a nip in the air and the lush trees began their annual change to burnished gold, red and russet. I began to cajole and beg Spence to allow me to visit him in Twigbury. I was mad with wanting to go. At first, he seemed reluctant to agree to such a rendezvous, but finally acquiesced. Annie and Drew discussed the visit's appropriateness, and made the decision that they would accompany me as chaperons. We settled upon the weekend of November the first. We made plans for a stay at the *Twigbury Court Hotel*, a charming old fifteenth century Inn, well known in that ancient Cotswold village. I blessed them for being such a loving brother and sister-in-law, especially since they were willing to keep the trip secret from my parents. We decided that if my parents knew of the journey, it would only raise questions that I wasn't yet prepared to answer.

For some reason, I knew before we ever reached Twigbury, that the weekend would turn out to be one of the most important in my life. I couldn't have said why that was so, but I was certain it was. We drove from London on a Friday afternoon, arriving in Twigbury a little past five o'clock. By half after five, we were settled into our marvellous suite, which boasted that King Charles had once been its occupant. The rooms were delightful and grande. There was an enormous drawing room, with a huge stone window seat, overlooking the garden, grounds, churchyard, and stream. Furnished with breathtaking antique pieces, a large fireplace dominated that area. Two bedrooms connected to the drawing room, both with large, antique canopy beds, topped with thick, goose-down comforters. The bathrooms were large and Victorian, with mahogany encased tubs. The hotel itself was an imposing mansion. Tudor in style, it was run on country house lines. The Twig River formed the boundary of the picturesque grounds, and inside there was a comfortable, homey feeling. There was also a large, well-proportioned paneled lounge, with a huge open fireplace, leaded windows and an impressive main staircase surrounding a first floor gallery. As a final added touch, there was even an in-residence Irish setter, named *Teddy*. I found it thoroughly captivating. Spence was at the door within minutes of my call. I heard his exquisite, yellow roadster, as it drove up the graveled lane through the gates, which led to the main entrance. Peering out of the window I watched as he disengaged himself from behind the wheel, and strode toward the hotel. When I opened the door to the suite, he wrapped me in a warm embrace. Then he shook hands with Drew, and kissed Annie on the cheek.

"How splendid to have you here," he exclaimed. "I so seldom have visitors. I cannot tell you how much this means."

"It was a grande opportunity for us to take a weekend holiday. One forgets how nice the country can be," answered Drew. "Especially at this time of year".

"Would you like to dine here at the hotel, or we can go to the *King Charles Hotel*, just down the lane? I thought we'd drive over to Broadway tomorrow, and dine at the *Ashton Arms*."

"What a marvelous idea, Spence! I have always wanted to visit there. Can you believe I never have?" I exclaimed, sounding like an excited little girl, which was exactly the way I felt. *The Ashton Arms* was a venerable old coaching Inn with a reputation known throughout England. I'd heard of it since a youngster.

"Then we're going to remedy that," Spence smiled. "Why don't we begin right now by going for a walk? I'll show you where I have my medical practice."

Drew and Annie discreetly declined his invitation, clearly recognising that Spence and I cherished every moment we could be alone together. We found our way down the staircase, and across the flagstone floor leading to the outer doors. We walked hand in hand down the graveled road, past a row of ancient old cottages called Wellington Row. Then we continued on to the paved main street, which wound its way through the village of Twigbury. About a half mile further, we came upon a Cotswold stone building, with high-pitched eaves. It cut into the hillside across from herbaceous gardens, a local trout farm and a duck reserve. A natural spring rose there to feed the river Twig, in a picture-postcard setting. At once, I understood why Spence had decided to fill-in for the physician who owned the medical practice in Twigbury.

"Spence, it's breath-taking. I never expected it to be so lovely. This is where you work?"

He laughed. "Quite. I feel I'm a rather fortunate chap. As I'm doing paperwork at the end of the day, I stop and listen to the sounds of the river, and cannot imagine being anyplace else on earth."

I can see why. It's heavenly."

He took my hand and led me through the doors of the small structure that housed his office. Inside, all was a model of efficiency. There was a comfortable waiting area, three examining rooms, and an office, where sat a dark, polished desk stacked with papers and silver frames, holding photographs. I picked up one of the photos, examining it. It portrayed a stunning woman, with dark hair done-up in a *Gibson girl*, and a lovely smile. Spence was almost the spitting image of her. She was standing next to a handsome man, who held a small boy in his arms. It was clearly a photograph of Spence and his parents.

"What a handsome family," I remarked.

"Yes. My parents must not have been much older than I am now when that photo was made. I wish they might have lived to see my life today."

"They'd be proud of you, Spence."

"Do you think so, Sophia? My father was in the ship building business. I don't know if he would have been particularly pleased that I chose the medical profession. I suspect he would have preferred that I follow in his footsteps."

"Do you think you would have?"

"It's hard to know, isn't it? So often persons do what others expect of them. Most of the chaps I knew at school were following the family tradition. In that respect, perhaps I'm fortunate that I was able to make my own choices.... Select my own path. Don't misunderstand," he smiled. "I'm certainly not fortunate to have lost my parents at such a young age. I would much rather have entered the ship building business and had my father, than have been free to follow medicine as a career. You understand what I'm saying, don't you, Sophia?"

"Of course, Spence. That's an interesting way to think of it. I wonder what my choices might have been, if faced with a similar situation. Of course, women are so much more limited in their choices, aren't they?"

"Some are, some aren't, Sophia. Look at Edwina. Going off to Paris to pursue a career, just as adventurous as any man I've ever known!"

We were still standing next to Spence's desk. I finally placed the framed photo back into its place. "Well.... Edwina has always marched to her own drummer," I laughed. "But, most women aren't given a lot of options. From the time I started at Ashwick Park.... Actually from the time I was born.... It was clearly understood that there was only one path for my life to follow. I was to marry as quickly as possible after completion of my education. Certainly, the goal of the season is to find a husband. You know that. I detest the way that sounds. It's as though I'm telling you that I rather expect a proposal of marriage rom you. It isn't supposed to be stated aloud, of course, but there it is."

"Sophia. You are a treasure. Not another woman in England would say those words. Frankly, I adore your attitude. It takes all of the game playing out of it. However, you told me early on that you wished you had more options.... That you weren't ready to think of marriage so quickly. What would you do if you had options?" he asked.

"I'm not sure, Spence. I used to think I would love other options. I'm not certain of that anymore."

"Would you run off to Paris with Edwina? Share her flat, have scads of romances, learn to paint, or write grande novels?"

"Me? Heavens no. London is quite adventuresome enough for me. I have never had any desire to live in France. I adore England. I especially adore London. Not necessarily to raise a family, but now, when I'm young. I think it would be smashing to be a part of it all. Rather like Annie and Drew are doing. They won't be in London forever.... Just while he finishes Theology School. Then, they'll return to a country setting.... Hopefully *Willow Grove's* chapel." As we talked, we moved to the small, slip-covered loveseat in his waiting area. We sat there and continued our conversation. Spence put his arm across the back of the sofa, and over my shoulders.

"Would you have a stylish home in London, then, and throw lavish parties and Balls?" He was smiling at me now, as he knew that was not who I was, and that such an idea wouldn't appeal to me at all.

"I don't think so, Spence. I've loved all of the parties and Balls during the season, but I cannot imagine a steady diet of that sort of thing."

I paused. In a tremendously impetuous moment I murmured *"Perhaps I could be a country doctor's wife in Twigbury."* I murmured the words so softly that I couldn't be certain that he'd even heard me. I shocked myself when I spoke them. *How could I possibly have said such a thing?* He turned and stared intently at me, wanting to be certain that he *had* heard correctly. He was looking at me very keenly. I caught my breath and my heart skipped a beat.

"I'm sorry, Spence, That was very forward of me. Please overlook that I was so audacious," I implored, as color began to rise in my cheeks.

"Sophia, that isn't at all an audacious statement. You have only put into words what I've been longing to say. Nevertheless, there are impediments to my asking that question. I don't feel that I have the right. There are many things to discuss. There are your parents, religion, and the differences in our social class. I need to speak with your father and I've only met your parents in the receiving line upon my departure from your Ball. They were both quite genial then, but that was before they knew I might become a serious suitor for their daughter's hand."

"I know, Spence. I know." My heart was actually hurting.

"Sophia, I love you," he said, very directly.

I raised my eyes and looked straight into his.

"Then nothing else matters, because I love you too."

I was in his arms and we were no longer speaking. It was all touching, kissing, and holding. I could feel his arousal as he pressed himself against my body and caressed me. Surprisingly, that didn't frighten me, as I'd always thought it might. Our kisses became more intense, and I had an overwhelming desire to have him touch me. Once again, there was that familiar feeling that I'd come to know as a mad desire for something *more*. He gently laid me down on the sofa, raised my skirt above my hips, and put his hand on the inside of my thigh. I was not at all embarrassed, which came as a surprise. I had always been very, very reluctant to let any man touch me in an intimate way, never having done so. I'd listened to girls at *Ashwick Park* talk about sex, but, I'd never became involved in those conversations, other than with Edwina. Something about the subject was unseemly to me. Still, Edwina assured me that when a woman truly fell in love it made an enormous difference. I was snug against Spence, his mouth by my ear. Turning his head towards me, he whispered, "I want you so, dear Sophia."

His words seemed to be the final hurdle. Gently removing my undergarments, Spence groaned as his hand found the soft fur between my legs. I thought I would go mad with longing as he touched that forbidden place.... That place where I had never allowed anyone to touch me before. Spence caressed me gently. I kissed him with reckless abandon. He then unbuttoned my blouse, unhooking my brassiere. His lips were on my breasts. I began to sigh, and could hear my voice as though from far away. Suddenly, Spence broke away from me, and turned his head to the side, as though to clear his thoughts. As though to stop the mad rush of passion carrying us toward a firestorm.

"What is it?" I asked him. Don't you want me?" I was confused.

"Oh, Sophia, I want you more than I've ever wanted anything in my life. I'm just not certain that it's the correct thing to do."

"Spence," I cried, "We love each other. What can be wrong when two people are in love?" I had heard those very words from Edwina.

"Nothing, darling Sophia, but I don't want to hurt you, or to do anything you might regret later."

"You could never do anything to hurt me, unless you stop caring for me. I love you so much," I whispered.

He clasped me to his chest, and we kissed with fierce abandonment. He must have known that I was ready for him, in the way that only men *do* know such things. Suddenly, all hesitancy was gone. He was clearly mad with desire. He shed the remainder of his clothing, and we lay naked together. Skin against skin. Ever so gently, he began to thrust. Each time, I felt myself more ready to receive him. Suddenly, my body welcomed his. We were as close as two human beings can be. I felt a brief stab of pain, but ever so quickly, ecstasy replaced discomfort. Instinctively, I brought my hips up, to be as close to him as possible. He thrust repeatedly, until we reached a pinnacle of passion that I could never have imagined or described. We cried out to one another in joy, and were truly one.

When our lovemaking ended, we lay quietly in one another's arms, relishing the serenity. I didn't regret what had happened. I finally understood what my body had been longing for each time we'd kissed and held each other. I loved him. Nothing else mattered. Nothing else would ever matter. We lay there calmly, savoring the aftermath of passion. Spence was the first to break the silence. Lighting a cigarette, he propped himself up on one elbow.

"Sophia, we need to talk, darling," he murmured as he nuzzled my neck. "

Yes, I know," I answered, running my hand through his thick hair.

"I love you so, dearest."

"I love you too, Spence. So much."

"But we have some things to work out. I have many things to talk to you about."

"Well, is it the religion thing, Spence? Or, the silly class nonsense. I don't care about either. What religious belief do you have that I don't?"

Oh darling, I'm not sure there *is* very much we don't agree on. The Anglican Church formed from the Roman Catholic, because Henry the Eighth wanted to be divorced to re-marry. If it hadn't been for a tart named Anne Boleyn, there never would have been an Anglican church. Funny, how the entire history of mankind can turn on something so seemingly trivial. Who knows? Perhaps they were soulmates too," he laughed. "Pretty unlikely, however, since he had her beheaded, when he tired of her." I joined in the laughter. "At any rate, the beliefs are really quite similar, other than the fact that the Anglican Church doesn't acknowledge that the Pope is infallible. Of course the Catholic church doesn't allow divorce."

"I haven't any intention of ever getting a divorce," I answered. "That isn't even a concern. Would we have to marry in the Catholic tradition and would I have to promise to raise any children Catholic?"

"Yes.... Well, there are other things.... Certain rituals. It would be best if you converted. Not totally necessary, but ideally."

"I don't know if I'd mind that. I'm quite intrigued with the history and ritual of your church. Although I know so little about it, I have a keen desire to learn more. It appears to play such a significant role in your life."

"But, what about your parents? From what you've told me, there is not going to be a wondrously happy reception from them at the news that their daughter is seriously considering marriage to a Catholic."

"They'd mind, very much. Mummy would go into a gargantuan rage. I've no doubt."

I had described my mother's rages to Spence, as my trust for him steadily escalated throughout the months of our dawning love. Being a physician, he knew and understood better than some might. Nevertheless, no matter how much he helped me understand Mummy's rages, I was still deathly frightened of them.

"When you say that they would mind very much, do you feel that you could withstand their disapproval?"

"Spence, I've never thought about it. Mummy is the one who terrifies me so. You know she rules Papa with an iron glove. Mummy has shut a child out for much less serious infractions. The position of being Mummy's favorite child has a high turnover rate, I'm afraid." I ruefully laughed. "Nonetheless, I feel so madly in love with you that I believe I could withstand anything."

"I hate you having to face that, darling? I know you love them very much. Of course, I fully intend to speak to your father alone."

"Don't count on that, Spence. I don't believe there is any way that Mummy wouldn't insert herself into the middle of any conversation that you had with Papa.

"I'm not an easily intimidated man, Sophia. I'll make certain they understand that I 'm there because I know how dearly *you* love them, and how much you long for their approval. Nevertheless, I intend for them to clearly understand that I dearly love *you*, with all of my soul, and that I'm not leaving without their blessing."

"*I love them and hate them, Spence.*" I nearly shouted. I surprised myself with my vehemence. I'd never said such a thing to another soul; had never even said it to myself. I felt a bit of a traitor. No matter. It was true. "My parents' don't care a whit what I want from life. It seems that my entire purpose for existence has always been to please them in some manner. Everyone Spence, *simply everyone*, thinks Papa and Mummy the most charming couple on Earth. They *can* be so kind and generous. So charming. But they can also be…"

"I know, Sophia. It doesn't sound as if they've been ideal parents."

"They haven't, "I replied. "Spence, they're so terribly odd. Both of them. They *are* my parents, and of course I *do* love them. But I have yearned for their approval for as long as I can recall. If I didn't love them, I wouldn't care about their approval. No matter what I've ever accomplished, they've been snide and disparaging. I feel that I've spent my entire life doing cartwheels and backflips, hoping that they would show pride in me. I've never had any affection from either of them. Truly, never. My mother says some of the cruelest things imaginable. Really hurtful things. She's told me that I am not pretty…. Perhaps a bit above average, but certainly nothing compared to how lovely she was at my age. She tells me that I shall be fortunate if I ever find a man who loves me. Papa believes that the only reason a man would want me would be because of my dowry. Papa has never taken my side against Mummy. I've already told you about Mummy's ghastly rages. But, I've never really shared details. She smashes anything within her reach, screams, yells, and literally throws a tantrum. I have been slapped in the face more times than I care to remember. And…. Spence…. I've never said anything to you about *this*…. In fact, have never told a soul…. Not even Edwina…. But, when I was a young girl, Papa did some vile things to me. Really vile. Do you know what I mean?"

"Yes, I think I do. Are you saying that your father mistreated you sexually? I hope you aren't talking about incest?"

"No, not that. But, fondling…. Touching. Definitely inappropriate. I knew the things he did were wrong from the beginning. But, for some reason, I felt protective of him. More protective of him then of myself. I would never have told anyone…. Surely not Mummy. Isn't that sad? I obviously cared more about him than I did about myself. Even knowing it was wrong. What in the world would make a child act that way?"

"Sophia, are you certain that you might not have misinterpreted some bit of his behaviour?"

"No, no Spence. Please don't say that. I remember everything distinctly. All of this is just part and parcel of what *really went* on in our *highly respectable home.*"

"As to why you would act to protect him, instead of yourself? It's hard to know. I suspect that you had been raised in such a terribly dysfunctional environment that you actually believed it was more important that a parent's secret behaviour not be exposed, than to make certain you weren't harmed. Did anyone even tell you that his behaviour *was* immoral?"

"No. Absolutely not. And it was not mentioned in school, or anyplace else that I recall. Yet, I *did* know, beyond any shadow of a doubt, that it was improper. My primary concern was shielding Papa from Mummy's wrath. Somehow, I believed that if she found out, she wouldn't have protected me anyway. I think it would have been *my* fault, in some way. I'm just beginning to realize now that she was jealous of me."

"You *are* very perceptive, darling. I suspect had you told her, she would have made certain that you were sent away somewhere. I intend for us to tell your parents our wishes as quickly as possible. What you're telling me is absolutely foul behaviour. I'm glad you told me. It helps me to understand you better. This is not the way normal families behave. I don't want you to be upset, Sophia. This should be a happy time. Tell me when can I meet your parents? I want you to be mad with happiness."

"I *am* deliriously happy about *us*. Papa is receiving an award at a charity event in London in two weeks. That would be a splendid time to speak with him…. Well…. Probably *them*. Perhaps you could come to London for the evening. We could arrange the long overdue meeting. Do you think you could make the trip during the week? I just feel so strongly that once they've met you, they can't help but love you as much as I do."

"I wouldn't be too certain about that," he laughed. It matters not whether they love or even like me, to tell you the truth. All I want is their consent to marry you. I'm sure I can arrange to be in London in two weeks, darling. What night would that be?"

"Thursday. They'll be staying at Grande's. That's where the dinner is to be held. Blake and Drew will be present as well. However, is what I've told you going to create an insurmountable barrier between you and my parents?"

"No, precious girl," Spence smiled. "It doesn't endear them to me, but I'll just have to hide my feelings for your sake, knowing that speaking to them about their actions would be futile. This just makes me want to protect you all the more." He crushed out his cigarette and took me into his arms again.

"I just want it all behind me', I replied, burying my head on his shoulder once again, running my fingers through his hair.

"Did I hurt you, my sweet Sophia?" he murmured.

"No.... It was wonderful. I'm glad it happened. I feel as though nothing can ever part us now. We truly are one in every way."

"I never want to hurt you," he whispered, as he began to plant tiny, nibbling kisses on my neck. Silence followed. I could hear the splashes of the river outside, babbling as it flowed over the rocks. There were birds singing in the distance.

"Sophia. I want you to clearly understand that what just happened between you and me was the way it is supposed to be, because we are a man and woman in love. We plan on giving ourselves to each other for the rest of our lives. Your body is a precious temple, and nobody ever had a right to touch you in any way, unless you give them your permission. You do understand that, don't you?"

"Yes, Spence, I do now. But, to be completely honest, for the longest while I used to think that there really wasn't anything so terrible about Papa fondling me, because, after all, I was a part of him. I didn't think of myself as a separate entity, with my own boundaries."

"God, Sophia, it's amazing that you even have an identity of your own."

"I know, I'm aware of that." There was a long silence, while we both contemplated the strange behaviour that had taken place in my young life.

"Spence, why would we have to be married in your religion? I asked, changing the subject. Couldn't you become an Anglican? "To me, one religion is like another."

"Oh, Sophia, there's the rub. I truly believe in the Catholic Church. I believe it is the one, true religion. I don't believe I have any choice. If I were to leave the Church, I wouldn't be happy. The Catholic Church provides me with great comfort. I have deep faith and belief in it. I do hope that you don't think that I'm sounding selfish."

"I should never want you to do anything for me that would cause you to be unhappy," I answered, truly meaning it.

"The Church is a part of me, Sophia. It's my soul. When I was born, I was born a Catholic. In my heart, that's who I am. I don't have a choice in this. I have to live Catholic and die Catholic."

"Well, doesn't your Church consider it a sin to marry a non-Catholic?"

"The Catholic Church frowns upon mixed marriages. Nevertheless, with a presentation of reasons, a disposition can be given There are ways to make it acceptable. That is why I said that ideally you would convert. However, I wouldn't want you to do something you didn't believe in either. Do you see the dilemma?"

I was still lying next to him. I turned, placing my head on his shoulder and putting myself into a position so that I could look up at him and see the expressions on his face.

"I was never raised to be terribly strong in my religious beliefs. It was just the 'done' thing to attend chapel on Sundays. We didn't really live the church's teachings in our home. I suppose that's quite obvious," I laughed ruefully. "I cannot say that I'm very clear about what I believe. I've never studied religion. I know that the world is an astonishing place. It can't all be an accident. It simply cannot. It's so well ordered and well planned. So, I believe that I have some germ of belief planted in my soul, but as to denominations and the like, well…. I only know that I love you, and that we must be together.

He took my face into his hands. "Darling Sophia," he began, "please tell me that you will marry me. We'll manage the logistics concerning religion."

"Spence, I want more than anything to marry you, and of course I accept your proposal." We kissed once again, and he held me close once more. I reached up and traced the outline of his handsome face. Spence began to caress my breasts a second time. Slowly his hands moved again, to touch the warmth between my legs. And once more, desire arose. We ceased conversation, making love again, familiar with each other's bodies and committed to one another in our hearts.

The sun was low in the sky as we dressed and returned to the hotel. It was difficult for me to face Drew and Annie upon our return. I felt so extraordinarily different that I could not be certain it didn't show. I soaked in the tub, luxuriating in my newfound happiness, and dressed carefully in a new, royal blue woolen suit, purchased especially for the trip to Twigbury. We all shared a lovely evening dining at the *King Charles Hotel*. There was newfound intimacy between Spence and me. The evening ended with a nightcap in the drawing room of our *Twigbury Court* suite. Then, Drew and Annie retired to their room. Spence and I, having vowed not to repeat our amorous afternoon in near proximity to my brother and his wife, also concluded the evening.

Such vows did not hold for the entire weekend. It would have been foolish to assume that we wouldn't continue our journey of discovery, having once experienced the ecstasy of one another's bodies. The following day we planned a rendezvous in Spence's cottage, which was next to his office. Once again, Drew and Annie were most accommodating, announcing that they were going for a drive to explore the countryside. Spence collected me a little before noon, and we lunched at the hotel. Then we made our way back to his cottage, which was picturesque and engaging, with cob walls, a thatched roof, and a large baking oven at the foot of the chimney. I couldn't help but remember Edwina's comments about a thatched roof cottage in the Cotswolds being perfect for me. There were six rooms, including a parlor, two bedrooms, a dining space, a kitchen and a loo. It was obvious that a bachelor lived there, for the decor was sparse, and there was precious little of a personal nature. The older physician, who actually owned the cottage, had removed his belongings. Still, it was charming, if a bit sparsely furnished. An old four-poster dominated Spence's bedroom, topped with a lovely hand stitched quilt.

I found that the anticipation of lovemaking only heightened its intensity. When we were finally in the bedroom, with the door closed and shades pulled, I was fairly trembling with desire. We came together in a passionate embrace, and it was no time at all before we were completely unclothed and lying on the crisp, linen sheets under the quilt. I was much less hesitant than I'd been the first time, even eager to touch Spence….To feel his hardness….To stroke him and give him pleasure. I would never have believed that I could be feeling such desire. We openly expressed our love for one another, in delight and joy. When he entered me, it was absolute ecstasy. I knew that he shared the same emotions. We spent the afternoon making love repeatedly, each time reaching new heights of passion. Over and over, I would believe that we were both fully gratified, but somehow the desire always returned. Had it not been for the human body's natural need to satisfy hunger and thirst, we might never have left the tiny bedroom in that old, country cottage near the River Twig.

I was never the same after that weekend. If Spence had been the primary consideration before in my life, he was all-consuming thereafter. All I could think about was how much I loved him, wanted to share his life, and grow old with him. I could not wait to get beyond the hurdle of confessing my love for him to my parents, so that he and I might look forward to planning a future together.

Chapter Four

November 8, 1935

A Confrontation

I immediately rang my parents upon returning to London on Sunday evening. I did not want to make the topic of Spence an enormous *issue*, as I feared that they would attach more importance to it than I wished, before they'd had a chance to meet him. I was not so foolish as to think that because I loved Spence, all obstacles would magically disappear. There were certain to be voluminous objections. I *did* hope, however, that upon meeting him those objections would become less significant. I had two weeks to prepare myself for the charity dinner, but decided that I would meet with my parents before that occasion to tell them of my feelings for Spence. I felt that it would be wiser to broach the subject with them privately. I knew how emotional Mummy could become, and didn't want to expose Spence to an unpleasant scene.

The following weekend, I made a long-overdue visit to *Willow Grove Abbey*. Upon arrival, my mind was looking ahead to a life eventually spent there as Spence's wife. I'd begun to fantasize about a future in which Drew would minister to the congregation of St. Mary and St. Edward, Blake would oversee *Somerville Ltd.*, and Spence and I would settle into the idyllic life of country doctoring, perhaps in *Bedminster-with-Hartcliffe*. We could all live at *Willow Grove*. Spence knew of my deep love for my ancestral home. I knew that he would do anything to make me happy. The fantasy was lovely, albeit very unrealistic. There was certainly no reason to assume that my parents would be leaving *Willow Grove Abbey* anytime soon.

When I arrived at *Willow Grove,* my parents greeted me at the entrance. I had not seen them in weeks, as I'd repeatedly manufactured excuses to keep them from visiting London. Their presence would have meant that I couldn't see Spence, and seeing Spence had become the centre of my life. Both of my parents appeared to be in high spirits on that afternoon, for which I silently thanked God. I hoped theat would still be the case when my visit ended.

"You look splendid, Sophia," Papa exclaimed when he saw me. "Absolutely splendid. I can see that London agrees with you."

"Oh, Nigel, you men are so obtuse," Mummy responded. "It isn't London that agrees with Sophia. A whirlwind social life has put roses in her cheeks. Isn't that right, Sophia?"

I smiled, and felt a bit uncomfortable. "Well, partly right, Mummy," I murmured.

"Why don't you have Joseph bring your things in? Perkins can see that they are sent to your room, and Violet can set about unpacking for you? If you want to freshen up, Papa and I will be in the drawing room, so join us in there."

Joseph was our chauffeur and Perkins was our Butler, with whom Mummy and Papa could not have survived. He did a great deal of work and was one of the most important servants in our home. Perkins ordered all of the supplies, kept the household accounts and engaged both men servants and housemaids, parlor maids and even our Rose. Violet was our lady's maid. She had a great many duties, and was first rate. She was a hair-dresser, a good packer, and a fine needlewoman. She also drew Mummy's and my baths, laid out our underclothes, brushed our hair and dressed it. Actually, Violet was Mummy's lady's maid, but when I was at home, we shared her. Mummy had tried to persuade me that we should employ two lady's maids, one for each of us, because she felt that it was impractical for a debutante and her mother to share a maid.... At least during the height of the Season. I firmly refused such an excessive suggestion, nor would I agree to take Violet with me to Annie and Drew's house. I really felt no need for a lady's maid at all, and thought it a great affectation on Mummy's part.

The only person I really adored in the servant's realm was Nan, our housekeeper, who had been at *Willow Grove Abbey* since before I was born.

She had her own bedroom, bath and sitting area. All of the servants, including Perkins, came under Nan's authority. She supervised the entire house exactly as a very conscientious and skilled mistress would do herself. I worshipped Nan, and really considered her to be a 'second mother' to me. How I often wished that she *were* truly my mother! Nan had an innate kindness, and the patience of Job. It was sad that she had never borne children of her own, because I believe she would have been a superlative mother. She was always there for me during my growing up years, and I undoubtedly learned about love from her. She showed her affection for all of us in abundance.

I climbed the winding staircase to my old bedchamber, furnished in period French. There were twin beds, a dressing table and two matching armoires. The walls were covered in Fortuny fabric of pale, pink silk. Since meeting Spence, I'd become acutely aware of the fact that I'd always taken my opulent lifestyle for granted. My love for him made me aware that there were other places and ways to be happy. While my childhood home was uncommonly splendid, it would not have had much meaning if I'd had to face life without him. It truly didn't matter where I married him, or whether we could ever afford the kind of life I'd known. I only wanted to be his wife. I fluffed my hair, splashed cool water on my face, and slipped into a blue cashmere skirt and twin set. Then, I joined my parents in the drawing room. It was an elegant room, with bay windows, inset with softly cushioned window seats. The portieres were buttery yellow velvet, fringed in white, and they puddled to an Aubusson carpet, patterned with rose, crème and blue. A magnificent fireplace covered half of one wall. There were white sofas, yellow winged back chairs, and pale blue club chairs scattered about. Papa offered me a gin and tonic and I settled myself upon the sofa across from where both of my parents were sitting.

"Right, so, bring us up to date on happenings in London," Papa began.

"It's been a frightfully busy summer," I smiled. "I've had marvelous fun, and hope I haven't been too great a burden on Drew and Annie. They have been wonderful. I don't think I've missed a West End show, and I've attended all of the gallery openings."

"That's splendid" Papa smiled.

"Are you meeting many suitable people?" Mummy asked.

"I should think that everyone I meet is suitable, Mummy. I cannot imagine where I would meet any but suitable types," I teased.

"You know what I mean, Sophia" Mummy responded, in a not altogether light tone.

"I know, Mummy," I murmured, realizing my mistake, and assuming a more serious pose.

"I saw the Duchess of Winnsborough last week in Bath. She told me that Owen has been in London nearly the entire Season. Did you know that he will inherit his father's estate, *Winnsborough Hall*, in Gloustershire? In fact, his parents are prepared to gift it to him and a bride, and remove themselves to their second home, *Snow Hill*, as soon as he marries. *Winnsborough Hall* is one of the most splendid estates in the country, and he's very eligible, Sophia. Do you spend much time with him?"

"Yes, Mummy. You know that Lord Winnsborough and I are good friends. He has escorted me to several social functions, including Ascot. You recall, I'm sure, that he was my partner for supper at my Debut Ball. Unfortunately, he rather resembles a bloodhound, Mummy."

"Sophia, what a dreadful remark. Are you one of the *'great beauties on Earth'*? She asked, snidely. "The Winnsboroughs are lovely people, and he is highly suitable. I should like you to be nice to him. The Duchess hints that he has thoughts that go well beyond being your escort to parties, the theater, and Balls. I think there is an excellent chance that you will be receiving a proposal of marriage from him in the not too distant future."

I was stricken. Lord Winnsborough *was not* who I had in mind as a future husband. I was in love with Spence, and did not intend to consider any other man. I suspected that Mummy had been conspiring with Lady Winnsborough to match me with Owen, probably since my birth. It was time to set my parents straight about future intentions. Choosing my words carefully, I began.

"Do you remember that I've mentioned Spencer Stanton before? I believe you even met him in the queue at the end of my debut Ball. I don't think you could help but remember him. He is an exceptional stand-out."

"I do believe I met someone of that name and description. Is he talll and dark haired? Quite good looking?" Mummy answered. She took a large gulp of her gin and tonic.

"Yes. That is Spence, exactly." My heart speeded up.

"Are his people the Stanton's who own Stanton Hall in South Molten, Devon?"

"No Mummy. Spence's parents are deceased. They died when he was fifteen. The Stanton's in South Molten *could* be some relation, I suppose, but Spence was raised near Bristol, until he went off to Eton and Oxford."

"Where is his land, then?" questioned Papa.

Why in the world was it so important for people to own land? "He isn't a landowner, Papa. He's a physician. A very fine one. He has graduated the University of Edinburgh and is presently in a private medical scheme. In addition, he's a rather renowned RAF pilot."

"Doesn't have land? Has he a title?" asked Mummy.

"Well, in a manner of speaking he does. One he earned with a lot of very hard work. That of 'Doctor'," I replied, feeling very proud of Spence.

"Sophia, are you telling us that you are more than a friend to this title-less and probably penniless, physician?" Mummy asked, with an edge to her voice.

"That's what I'm telling you, Mummy. Only he is not penniless. He is in a private medical practice in Twigbury, and is doing wonderfully well. He's terribly busy with patients and they all adore him." I shifted around in my chair, trying to make myself more comfortable, because I felt that the atmosphere was growing more stifling as the conversation continued.

"Twigbury! Twigbury near Cirencester! In Gloucestershire? My God, Sophia. There's nothing there save a brewery, a duck reserve and a couple of hotels. When did you visit Twigbury?"

"Last weekend. Drew, Annie and I drove over and stayed at the Twigbury Court Hotel. Spence wanted me to see where he practices. It's a lovely spot, very quaint and old."

Mummy returned to the sofa. I could see that her mouth had turned white round the edges.

"Sophia let me be clear about this. Are you telling me that you are involved romantically with this doctor, who has no title, no land, no inheritance, no parents, and not very decent prospects? Who lives in a Cotswold cottage, in Twigbury, delivering babies and treating the croup?"

"I don't see it that way, Mummy."

"Tell us how you do see it then, Sophia?" asked Papa.

It was always abundantly clear that Papa had to agree with Mummy or face her wrath. I took a deep breath and gave it my all.

"Papa, I see Spence as a very decent man, with great intelligence and kindness. He has a strong love for humanity, is one of the most moral individuals I have ever known, possesses great, genuine integrity, and is warm and witty. He's also devastatingly handsome," I smiled, blushing. Taking another deep breath, I finished by saying: "But, perhaps, more than anything else, he loves me, not because I'm Lady Sophia Somerville, but for *myself.* He cares about my thoughts…. My dreams….I love him." I stopped, out of breath.

"I see," said Mummy, as she placed her drink on an inlaid French table, to the left of the sofa. "That was quite a speech. And has he asked you to marry him?"

"He's waiting until he can ask Papa's permission. But, yes, we have spoken of marriage."

"And what answer have you given him?"

"I've told him that I should love nothing better than to marry him, but that I have to speak with my parents. I want your blessing. I know you haven't met him, but I can assure you, he is everything that I say."

"That is my concern, Sophia."

"What do you mean, Mummy?"

"You are well aware that he is not suitable. I cannot imagine you having allowed this to progress beyond friendship. What in God's name were Drew and Anne thinking to encourage this?"

"They were thinking of my happiness."

"Oh happiness! Rubbish! Sophia, you are just a child, and don't have the faintest notion of what 'happiness' means. You will not find yourself so happy when you're working your fingers to the bone as a doctor's wife, never having nice clothes, never entertaining, worrying all of the time about money. It would never do. Moreover, what about children? How would you intend to provide for them?"

I was growing very irritated. I loved Spence and Mummy was making it sound like he was a sheep herder.

"Mummy, Spence is not a destitute person! He might not have the means that you and Papa enjoy, but we wouldn't starve, nor would our children. He is as well educated as any of us…. better educated than most."

"He may have education, but it's perfectly obvious that he hasn't any money. Are you thinking that you would be able to rely upon your family for financial assistance? I suppose he assumes that you would receive a large dowry?"

"That has absolutely never been discussed. I don't think Spence would accept any help from my family. I don't think that Spence needs or desires any help, as he's perfectly content and happy with his chosen profession, and with the style of life it provides."

"Sophia. You are showing your usual naiveté. Don't for a moment believe that your Doctor Stanton isn't quite impressed by your background. Surely you can't be so foolish as to think that he doesn't hold great interest in your dowry? Obviously, he would be dependent upon only his salary, if he does not find a wife who can provide a dowry to enable him to become a gentleman of means." *It was unbelievable that Papa couldn't hear himself. He was describing what he had done when he married Mummy.* "How often have your mother and I warned you that this could happen? Let's assume, however, that you are correct, and he really *does* love you for yourself. Would you be perfectly content and happy with his lifestyle? Somehow I do not think so." Even Papa's voice was becoming more forceful.

"I have spent a lot of time thinking about how my life would differ, in terms of social status and so forth. It just does not matter to me. I know I would make a very good physician's wife."

"Have you made up your mind to accept this proposal with or without our blessing, Sophia?"

"Mummy, I hadn't thought about that possibility. I had hoped I would have your blessing."

"I suppose you would want to have a large wedding in the chapel at *Willow Grove Abbey*. He hasn't any noteworthy family. How on Earth would it look in the *Times?*"

"I think we would both love to have a glorious, traditional wedding." I took another deep breath. "But it couldn't be at 'St. Edward and St. Mary."

"Couldn't be here? Why ever not? All Somervilles have been married in our chapel for eons. If he has no ancestral home, what difference can it possibly make to him?" Clearly, he is a 'nobody from nowhere'". Mummy was becoming quite angry, snide and rude.

"He's a Roman Catholic, Mummy."

There was complete silence. I could hear the ticking of the Piaget clock, and sounds of the servants preparing afternoon tea. A dog howled in the distance. Papa poured two more drinks for himself and Mummy. Tonic water fizzed in the crystal glasses. I hadn't touched mine. Papa cleared his throat several times. Mummy looked as though she was in shock. She spoke first.

"This is out of the question, Sophia. Totally, absolutely, out of the question. We did not raise you to become a Papist, nor to raise Papist children. My God in Heaven! This man is not, nor could he ever be our caliber. We must forbid you to ever see him again."

I began to weep, but of course, it did nothing to soften my mother's attitude. My father looked much the same. Mummy sat cold and silent. Papa didn't move.

"Sophia, we know that this hurts at the moment, and that it seems as though it's the end of the world. However, you will survive I assure you. When you have met and married a suitable man, someday you will look back upon this and understand that we were correct. You must trust that your parents know better in this kind of situation." Papa was trying very hard to say the proper words, but they sounded like he was reading from a book. I was discussing *feelings*, and that was something that neither of my parents understood.

I continued to sob. "But I love him. I love him with all of my heart and soul. I shall never love anyone this much again. If you don't give me your blessing, I shall die. At least, please meet him. He will be at your award dinner at Grande's. Just meet him and give him a chance. Please."

"You have invited him to be a part of a family affairee, knowing that he will not fit in…. That we would never find him acceptable. I am utterly disgusted with your behaviour. Because of what you have done, you have now ruined that entire evening for your father. I refuse to attend a social event with a Catholic opportunist."

"Spence is not an opportunist, Mummy. In addition, I have ruined nothing. It's you who are choosing to ruin the evening with your narrow mindedness." *I shocked myself with those words.* Nevertheless, I was so angry and frustrated, that my true feelings fairly spilled out. Mummy became completely irrational. I had never spoken to her with such a lack of respect.

"You *will* begin to act like a grown woman and this unfortunate episode will be put behind us. We expect you to start behaving like a blue-blooded aristocrat, and not a common trollop. I shall not brook hysterics over this matter, and do not want this man's name mentioned again in our home. He has caused grave upset and concern. He is obviously a trashy fortune hunter, and you are too irresponsible to see him for what he is. You are never to see him again. Is that clearly understood?"

"No, no! How can you say you love me and act this way toward me?"

"It is because we love you, Sophia," answered Papa.

Mummy's icy blue eyes were livid.

"Now, you listen to me," she shrieked. "It's time for you to begin thinking about what *you owe to us.* We have given you the best of everything. We have offered you every advantage, and more freedom than any generation of young woman before you. If you think you are going to repay us by marrying a Catholic, and embarrassing us, then you are very mistaken. Obviously, this is the first man who has ever paid you a whit of attention. I might have expected this from you. His church takes its orders from the Pope in Rome, and the Pope in Rome dictates that if you do not prove that you have pleased him enough to ensure that you live in a state of Grace, when you die, you will go to a ghastly place known as Purgatory. Purgatory is a sort of holding cell for those who do not have the credentials to make it into heaven. Wealthy Catholics will have to light candles to free you from Purgatory. Some people never are freed at all. I doubt that Doctor Stanton would know enough wealthy Catholics, so you would spend eternity in Purgatory. We certainly do not know any wealthy Catholics, so our connections could not even help you." By that time, she was pacing up and down the room, as her emotions escalated. In spite of her terrible upset, I couldn't help but be amazed at her seemingly endless knowledge about the Catholic faith. I wondered if anything she said was true. "How on earth can this person be Catholic?" she suddenly asked.

"What is his background?" I decided that I might just as well tell them everything. If there was going to be a *rage,* Mummy might as well have all of the facts."

"His mother is from County Cork, Ireland."

"Oh my God in Heaven," Mummy screamed. "An Irishman! My daughter married to an Irishman. "Sophia, the only nationality I despise more is German."

"But, why, Mummy? What is wrong with Irish people? I have always found them to be warm and sensitive. They are wonderful artists, poets and musicians. Ireland is, after all, a part of the Commonwealth."

"Irishmen are drunkards, adulterers, liars, braggarts, and scoundrels. Do you want to spend your life in a Dublin pub?"

"Spence is none of those things. Frankly, I doubt that he's ever been in a Dublin pub."

Mummy picked up a *Lalique* crystal ashtray and threw it across the room. It splintered into hundreds of tiny pieces, as it hit the marble on the fireplace. She was in a total rage. She ran about the drawing room, picking up items and hurling them; Ashtrays, Sevres figurines, the Piaget clock. She was screaming and ranting in a ghastly harangue. In the past, I had never fought back, nor even tried to defend myself. However, I had a very deep love for Spence and it motivated me. "Mummy," I began, "I'm a grown woman, and this is simply not fair. I have done nothing wrong. I have the right to see whomever I wish. I understand that you also have the right to form an opinion about any man whom I might care for, but you do not have the right to form such an opinion when you have never even met him. In my opinion, you are being bigoted and small-minded. Just be honest enough to look at the way you are behaving. Sometimes I really think you're not normal."

All color drained from Papa's face, and Mummy stood stock-still. No one in the family had ever spoken the truth aloud. It was simply not the 'done thing'. Suddenly, Mummy screamed, an almost inhuman cry. "All right! That is it! You have always hated me. I have always thought that, and now I'm certain."

I stood, and for the first time in my life, I didn't run. I looked my mother straight in the eye and spoke in an amazingly calm voice. "Mummy, that's simply not true. Everything I have done all of my life has been proof to the contrary, and you know that is the truth. I sometimes believe you feel hatred toward all of your children, and I don't, for the life of me, know why."

Mummy stood perfectly still. Her eyes bored straight into mine, for what seemed an eternity. Then, she slapped me across the face. My head literally snapped around from the force of the blow. I could not help but cry out, as it hurt dreadfully. Yet, I still refused to retreat and run, as I had done so many times in childhood. With tears streaming down, I said, "You can be so cruel. Why don't you want me to be happy?"

Mummy lost her mind. Picking up a basket of fresh fruit from an ornamental table, she bashed it over my head. Then she threw herself on the floor, curled like a small child in the midst of a tantrum, and screamed hysterically. I stood in horror. Meanwhile, Papa finally found his voice and managed to stammer his usual line, "Pamela, please …." Of course, it did absolutely no good. It never did. In fact, it had the opposite effect. It seemed to re-energize her. Leaping up, she grabbed the silver teapot and hurled it across the room at Papa. Thank God, her aim was off, and it missed hitting him by a fraction of an inch. Nevertheless, scalding hot tea flew all over the room. Some of it splattered upon my arm. It hurt dreadfully, but I just stood, rigid and immobile. I still have a small scar on my right wrist, where that damnable tea burned me. In addition, the Sterling teapot was severely damaged.

Finally, she was worn to a frazzle. She stood, shakily, and held tightly to the back of a chair. In a controlled voice she said, "We shall never speak of this person again, Sophia. This Irish scoundrel. Catholic trash. You are not the grown woman you think you are. You are only eighteen years of age, and without your parents, you do not have a farthing. I shall ring the Countess of Winnsborough and arrange for you and Lord Winnsborough to make wedding plans immediately. You *will* find him attractive and very suitable, and when he proposes marriage, you *will* accept. If these plans do not meet with your approval, you are free to leave the Somerville family immediately and permanently. Doctor Spencer Stanton will rue the day he ever met you and turned you against your family. Your father has powerful friends, Sophia. It would be tragic if Doctor Stanton lost his medical license, and was unable to practice his *trade*. I imagine there are scores of women walking the streets of London, who for a few Pounds' Sterling, would swear an oath that Doctor Stanton helped them end a pregnancy. Such an illegal act would not only result in the loss of medical privileges, it would result in a prison term." With that, she turned and ascended the staircase to her bedroom, slamming the door and locking it.

I knew that I had been defeated. My mother was not just mouthing words. Indeed, she would be very happy to find some way to ruin Spence's reputation as a physician. She had enough money and was malicious enough. She didn't see herself as heartless and cruel. In her mind, she was saving me from making a terrible mistake. I was angrier than I ever recall being. I couldn't remember ever having felt such rage. Perhaps a lifetime of suppressed emotion over so many similar tirades burst forth. Still weeping, I began to shout. "Papa, you wouldn't do such a thing, would you? Spence is a good person. Please, please don't make him pay a price for loving me."

Papa stood silently, not meeting my eyes. He looked helpless. It was clear that Mummy had his full support, and that I would do my mother's bidding or risk seeing Spence ruined. Mummy had accomplished her goal. I whirled toward my father, and through clenched teeth spoke words I had never believed possible. "You have never stood up for me in your life. Everyone thinks you are such a wonderful person. Well, you are not. You allow Mummy to belittle me, and you do it yourself. Especially if you think it will win her approval. You aren't half the man that Spence is. I even understand why you take her side. You are just like your children. You want her approval so terribly much, you will do anything or say anything to agree with her. *It is sick, Papa.* I'm ashamed that you are my father. You have hurt me dreadfully, all of my life. There is something terribly, terribly wrong in this entire family. All either you or Mummy cares about are appearances. If people really knew the truth about this family, we wouldn't be welcomed into any house in the land. I do not *want* to be a part of this family anymore. As far as I'm concerned, I hope I never set foot in this house again. Now, please just leave me alone," I cried. "I'm going to do exactly as Mummy ordered. I'm leaving the Somerville family. You and Mummy seem Hell bent on destroying me, and certainly Spence."

With that, I turned and raced up the stairway to my bedchamber, and began to throw clothing back into my case. Unbeknownst to me, there was much worse to come. Mummy had been listening to every word I'd shouted at my father. She rushed out of her room from across the hallway, and into my bedchamber. She held a pair of scissors. Grabbing a handful of the clothing that I was re-packing, she began cutting it into shreds. "If you are leaving the Somerville family, you can begin by not taking any of the expensive apparel we have provided for you, in an attempt to improve your *exceedingly average appearance*," she screamed hysterically. Her voice was growing hoarse from shrieking. I was transfixed by the spectacle of my mother shredding, cutting, and ripping. After she had finished her demolition, she threw down the scissors, and ran back to her own room.

There was utter silence in the house. I knew that my father would soon be desperately trying to bring Mummy to her senses. Eventually, he would coax her out of their suite with the purchase of some sort of luxurious gift. I suddenly realized that the entire foolish dance was becoming very tiresome. I turned and ran down the stairs to the entry door. I rang for Joseph, and asked him to take me to the station at *Bedminster-with-Hartcliffe*. This time there were no bags to carry. I bid a tearful farewell to *Willow Grove.*

On the train en route to London, I finally stopped sobbing, and tried to think what my course of action should be. The logical thing would be to return to Drew and Annie's, but I didn't want to have to relive the whole nightmare again. In addition, by the time I arrived it would be late. They had no idea that I was coming. I wanted desperately to speak with Spence. But, I knew that if I told him what had happened, he would insist upon talking to my parents. I did not want to subject him to the verbal abuse that was certain to accompany such a conversation. I also knew that he would tell me not to worry about Mummy threatening to sully his reputation. On the one hand, I wanted to run to him, let him hold me, and tell me that everything would be all right. I didn't care about ever going back to *Willow Grove Abbey.* I did not care if my parents disowned me. I only wanted to be Spence's wife. However, I also knew that it was unlikely that Spence would marry me under such circumstances. He was so honourable and decent. The idea of marrying someone whose parents thought him beneath their station would be anathema to him. Finally, I decided that I would take a room at the *Royal Hotel,* and contact Spence in Twigbury. I would ring him, tell him where I was, and ask him to come to me. Thankfully, and unbeknownst to Mummy and Papa, I *did* have a farthing. Much more than a farthing. My dear Grandpapa had set up a banking account for me before his death, and had warned me never to tell my parents. He 'd said at the time that he wanted me to have something that was all mine, in case I ever needed it. I wondered if he didn't suspect some of the turmoil that I lived with. It was not a fortune, but enough to see me through an emergency, and that moment certainly qualified as an emergency.

Chapter Five

NOVEMBER NINTH, 1935
A LAST VISIT TO THE ROYAL

As soon as I entered the room at The Royal, I placed a call to Spence in Twigbury. His receptionist answered and it was only a matter of minutes before his voice was on the line.

"Sophia?" Is that you? Is everything all right?"

"I needed to ring to tell you that I've left '*Willow Grove Abbey*', and am at the *Royal*....Have taken a room at the *Royal*," I stammered. "I need you to come here when you're able."

"Whatever are you doing at the *Royal*?"

I searched for the proper combination of words. "It's much too long a story to go into on the telephone, Spence. I'll explain everything when I see you."

"Is there anything wrong, Sophia? Your voice sounds strange?"

"No, I'm fine. A little tired, perhaps. When do you expect you could come to London?"

"Darling, I have a full load of patients tomorrow, but I'll leave as soon as I've finished with the last. I shall come straight to the Royal. I should think it would be about seven. Why don't you make reservations for dinner in the *Thames Room*, and as soon as I arrive we can dine?"

"That sounds splendid," I agreed. The thought of a lovely dinner with Spence in the place where our romance had begun revived my spirits. He was all that mattered to me. We would talk, and make plans to be married very quickly. I was certain that I could convince him that there was no need to speak with my parents. That it would be fruitless. I

knew that he loved me, and would agree to marry me in whatever manner I thought best.

"All right then, Sophia, I'll see you tomorrow evening."

"Yes, Spence. And darling…"

"Yes, Sophia".

"I love you."

"Dearest, I love you too. Goodbye until tomorrow."

I placed the receiver back into its cradle, dropping my head into my
hands. I had a ghastly headache. My entire life depended upon him. I'd
made the decision to give everything in the world up for Spence. I didn't
care. He mattered more than anything else, but nothing had turned out the
way I'd hoped. I readied myself for bed, and was so happy to be able to have
a lie-down. The room was magnificent, decorated in the Edwardian style,
with yellow draperies which began at the ceiling, and fell to the floor in
folds, and a bed fit for royalty, covered with a pale lavender spread. However
lovely my surroundings, I am afraid they were a complete waste, as I tossed
and turned all night, and by morning, saw things from an entirely different
perspective.

My previous hopes of spending a future with Spence had evaporated.
I don't know what I had been thinking. The more I pondered the situation
through the endless, sleepless hours, I knew that the only thing for me to
do was put an end to my relationship with him. Certainly, he would not
marry me without speaking to my parents. I must have been delusional to
ever have thought differently. He was far too proper and moral to do that.
Moreover, once he spoke to them, I had no doubt that my mother would
carry through on her threat to ruin him. Papa would not have any control
over her. I had to make certain Spence wasn't harmed in any manner,
simply because he had made the mistake of loving me. Somehow, I would
have to make Spence believe that I had changed my mind…. Had decided
that marriage to him would be a mistake.

I spent a dreadful day, waiting for the evening and Spence's arrival.
My chest felt as if it had a large stone sitting upon it. I went shopping,
and purchased frocks, and other needed apparel, as I had only what I was
wearing when leaving *Willow Grove*. It seemed a meaningless errand, and
not at all what it should have been. I purchased another day dress, and an

evening gown, as I needed something appropriate to wear for dining at the Royal. I selected a lilac-colored, silk evening gown, with scalloped cap sleeves and a V neckline. Dressing carefully for that last evening, I wanted him to remember that I had looked beautiful, which was ridiculous and vain. And perhaps even a bit cruel. But, that isn't the way I saw it then. I was thankful that Mummy had forgotten to take away my jewelry. At my neck and ears, I wore my pearls, which had been there when I left *Willow Grove*, and *I* styled my hair in an up-sweep, proof that I had no need of a lady's maid. At nearly half after six, Spence arrived. I met him at the door. He was so handsome, dressed in an impeccable dark, blue suit, and I wanted desperately to forget the horror of the scene at *Willow Grove,* and concentrate solely upon my love for him…Upon our future together. However, I knew that I must not let go of my firm resolve. He pulled me close when I met him at the door, kissing me with passion. I *loved* him so very much. I *did* begin to wonder if there might be some way to sort through the ghastly nightmare without having to relinquish Spence. It was so tempting.

"Well Sophia, this is quite a mystery. Your being here, at the *Royal.* Why aren't you at Drew and Annie's? I've been worried since your call. Is something amiss? You sounded somewhat peculiar on the phone."

"I'd just arrived from *Willow Grove*. I was a bit fagged out. I decided we needed to speak in private, and that it would be easier if I took a hotel room." I tried to keep my voice normal, when all the while, my heart was breaking. My mind was also whirling frantically, as I searched for some other path than the one I had chosen to take. *Surely there was another way?*

"I might have met up with you at *Willow Grove*. That way I could have met your parents, as well. I assume you didn't want me to do that."

"Not at this juncture, Spence. I felt that we should have some time alone, and Drew and Annie would have been home if I had gone there, so this seemed a good alternative." I reached up, and smoothed the back of my hair. He smiled warmly, and put a hand out to touch a tendril which had escaped the side of my upsweep. "I adore your hair like that. It reminds me of your debut Ball. It makes you appear very chic and sophisticated."

"Well, Spence, I think you know I'm hardly that," I laughed, trying to sound casual.

"I know nothing of the sort, dear Sophia. But, I agree completely with your idea about engaging a room here. Good thinking. I'm pleased you did. Do you want to talk here in the room or would you rather go down to dinner?" he asked with a smile.

"I'm famished, and have been looking forward to dinner in the *Thames Room*. Let's go down. We can talk over dinner." I was postponing the inevitable. When I told him my decision, the romance would end. He would leave. I would never see him again. I was still desperately searching my mind for an alternative. Upon entering the *Thames Room*, a four-piece ensemble was playing, and there were couples on the dance floor. The Maitre'd escorted us to a table by the French doors. Spence ordered Dom Perignon champagne, making it evident that he intended the evening to be a celebration of our love and commitment to one another. I decided to let him speak first. Then I would cruelly break his heart.

"Well, Spence. Have you had a busy week since I last saw you?" I asked, after we had ordered the champagne, and had each been poured a glass.

He placed his hand over mine on the table. "Busy and lonely I've thought of you every moment. I'm rather glad I was so covered up with patients, or the time would have gone more slowly. I'm so anxious to meet your parents, and get the beastly formalities out of the way so that we can begin planning our future."

I hadn't planned on getting into this part of the conversation so soon. I still hoped that at the last moment I would change my mind. But, there wasn't any feasible way to work it out. I knew that. There also didn't seem to be any way to prolong my speaking. I was just about to reply, when another couple appeared beside our table. It was an acquaintance from *Ashwick Park* and her beau. I wanted to die. This probably meant that we would have to invite them, at the very least, to have a glass of champagne with us. The girl's name was Charlotte Ross, and she was a schoolmate I did not especially care for. She'd always shown a disdainful attitude toward Edwina. However, etiquette required that I be civil to her.

"Fancy meeting you here," Charlotte commented. "I'm surprised we haven't run into each other more during the Season," She smiled.

"Yes, I guess we've attended different functions," I replied. "Charlotte, I'd like you to meet my good friend, Doctor Spencer Stanton." Spence was now standing, and he reached over and shook her hand. Then he turned to her companion. "Hello there, I'm Spence Stanton. And you are…?

The other gentleman extended his hand and shook Spence's, while stating that his name was William Young. In turn, Spence introduced me to Mr. Young. Then, just as I'd feared, Spence asked them if they would like to join us, and they readily accepted. It meant that my opportunity to speak privately with Spence had been postponed. I hoped I didn't lose my courage. The four of us sat down at the same table where Spence and I had been alone before. The waiter hurried over, bringing two more glasses, while also spreading napkins in their laps. Then, more champagne was poured.

"So, Sophia. What a lovely dress you're wearing. Is this a special celebration? I hope we're not intruding upon anything."

Charlotte placed a beaded evening bag on the table beside her, and removed her lace gloves. She was wearing a pale pink, silk evening gown, with large shoulders and puffed sleeves. I complimented her dress, as well. She was an attractive girl, with fair skin and red hair. She also had a long, willowy silhouette. If I remembered correctly, she was not of the nobility and I could ascertain no reason for her to be looking down upon Edwina.

My voice took on a nervous edge. "No, we aren't celebrating anything of note," I answered. Spence just drove up from his medical practice in Twigbury. We decided to have a nice dinner in the *Thames Room*."

"You have a medical practice in Twigbury? How gruesome! What on Earth do you find to do in such a hole in the wall sort of place?" She picked up her champagne flute and took a sip. I was astonished at her rudeness. Nevertheless, I knew that Spence could take care of himself.

"We don't share the same view of Twigbury, Miss Ross. I think it's especially quaint and really quite charming. I enjoy working there very much," Spence smiled. He turned to face William Young. "And, what is it that you do, William?" he enquired in a pleasant voice.

"I've just finished up at Cambridge. I'm taking a year to travel, and then will undoubtedly join my father in his law practice here in London."

In the meantime, Charlotte was studying Spence carefully. There is no question that she was intrigued by him. How could she not be? He was so extraordinarily good looking, as well as so self-assured and poised. She was obviously trying to ascertain what exactly *our* relationship was. She turned to me.

"Have you and Dr. Stanton known one another a long time?" she finally asked.

"Just since the beginning of the Season," I answered. We met at my debut Ball. You must have met him? I remember you being present".

"Yes, I was. But, I didn't spend much time socializing with you and your group. I have never cared very much for Edwina Phillips, you know. A lot of the girls at *Ashwick Park* felt the same way. She just isn't the sort of girl one expects to come upon at such a fine school. She really hasn't a great deal of class, you know."

"As you undoubtedly know, Charlotte, Edwina is my closest friend, so I'm afraid I cannot listen to any negative comments you wish to make about her. I think she fit in splendidly at *Ashwick*. We shared wonderful times together."

I was astounded at Charlotte's cheekiness. What she was saying didn't totally surprise me, since she and others had never been shy about showing their disdain for Edwina. My rather brusque comment seemed to have put her in her place, as she did not make an attempt to continue the conversation. My own opinion was that Charlotte, and whomever her friends were, were green eyed with envy over Edwina. Instead, she looked over at Spence, and said, "You don't look like a doctor. You look more like a professional polo player, or a dashing RAF pilot." She laughed, in a pretentious manner.

"I *am* an RAF pilot. I'm not certain about the 'dashing' part," he retorted

"You *are* an RAF pilot! I just *knew* it. You have the sort of rugged, but genteel look of a pilot."

Her partner, William Young, looked a bit embarrassed and irritated. I changed the subject.

"What are your plans for after the season, Charlotte? Are you continuing on with school?" I asked.

She was making a complete fool of herself

"Yes. Yes, I am, Sophia. I shall be attending drama school. You probably remember that I was in several theatrical productions at *Ashwick Park*." She spoke in breathy tone…. In a very dramatic manner. There was nothing 'real' about her.

"Yes, I do remember that. How exciting for you. I'm sure you'll be an enormous success," I replied.

The waiter brought menus to the table, and we all ceased conversation. "Do you wish to join us for dinner, my 'dashing RAF pilot' asked?"

Both William and Charlotte spoke at the same time. "Yes, we would love to," she said, as he announced that they had to be on their way. Charlotte looked at him rather disagreeably, but she *did* get up, when he pulled her chair out, and retrieved her evening bag and gloves. She seemed a bit rattled. "Well, it's been lovely running into you like this, and certainly marvelous to have met you Dr. Stanton. I suppose I *must* pay a visit to Twigbury some time, if someone as obviously urbane as you are finds it charming."

I suspect she thought he would tell her to ring him if she ever came his way, but he did not. He ignored her while shaking hands with William. I told her it had been nice to see her, and finally they retreated from our table. They exited the revolving doors in the black and white marbled foyer and I was relieved that they had left. What truly odious people! Or at least *she* was.

Spence laughed after they had left. "That woman has some sort of problem," he chuckled.

"She obviously has a 'thing' for *Royal Air Force* pilots," I laughed "I think you sent her heart racing."

"There is only one heart I am interested in," he replied, becoming serious once again. "Now, let's pick up where we left off. What were you doing at *Willow Grove Abbey*, and why did you want to speak with me alone?"

"I guess we do need to speak about that," I replied, afraid I was going to cry. "I've spoken with my parents about you."

"Sophia, my God! Don't keep me in suspense. What did they say? What did you tell them? Do you feel it went well?" I couldn't meet his eyes. Instead, I concentrated my gaze out of the window at the silent river, and the raindrops that had begun to fall. I remember thinking that even the sky was weeping. The band was playing a love song. The sounds of tinkling crystal glasses raised in toasts, of orders being placed, and of convivial conversations seemed surreal. There were several couples on the dance floor.

"Spence," I began, "How could we possibly have thought that this could be worked out? It can't be, you know." I looked him directly in the eyes, but then I had to turn away when I saw the look of shock on his face. I looked down at my plate, twirling the stem of the champagne flute in my hand.

"What are you talking about? What can't be worked out?" His voice sounded panicky, and his face was ashen. He lighted a cigarette. "What in heaven's name can't be worked out?"

"Our situation," I replied in a choked voice.

"What about our situation? I love you. That is not a *situation*. That is a *fact*. I know that you love me, too. So, whatever obstacles we face, they can and will be worked out." Spence was agitated. I could tell it was difficult for him to sit there at an elegant table in the *Royal Thames Room*, when he wanted to be pacing, or trying to hold me in his arms.

"It isn't that simple Spence. I've thought and thought about it." I tried desperately to maintain a facade of cool poise, but it was more difficult than I'd ever thought it would be.

"What do you mean 'you've thought and thought' about it'? I don't understand. Is it the religious thing then? Sophia, you really cannot be serious. I'm dumbfounded."

"Yes, our religious differences play a large part in my thinking. That and other things. The difference between our social classes also concerns me greatly. After I visited *Willow Grove*, I realized clearly that my way of life has been so profoundly different from yours. You know that, Spence. I've been waited on hand and foot since childhood. I have no domestic skills…. have difficulty even arranging my hair without a 'Lady's Maid'." *I loathed myself for those words.*

"Class Difference? When have you ever cared a whit about class difference? This sounds like something your parents might say. Is that what this is about? Are they upset because I'm not a landowner and titled? You aren't making a whit of sense. I've known you for quite some time now, Sophia, and you are not someone I would describe as helpless. You would function quite well without a 'Lady's Maid', or any other sort of servant for that matter. I know this is something your parents have put into your head."

"They're concerned, Spence. Their concern made me see things in a different light." I was being so terribly dishonest. It went totally against my nature. Several times the thought crossed my mind to simply stop the artifice and be honest with him. He knew very well that I was not telling the truth. I could see it in his eyes.

"Are you saying that I'm suddenly not good enough for you?" He now sounded completely astounded.

"No, no of course not. However, you *have* lived a very different life from mine. You have said that yourself. It doesn't mean that my life was better, only different. It's difficult enough for two people to make a go of marriage when they come from the same sort of backgrounds. In our case, there are so many impediments. I seem to have temporarily forgotten that I too have things I hold dear in life. I have always dreamed of being married in the chapel at *Willow Grove Abbey*, for instance. Never thought of marrying in a Catholic Church that I've never even attended, or worse still, a Magistrates Office."

"This is nonsense, Sophia. We could still be married in the Chapel. I'll find a priest who will marry us there. That's not an impossibility. It may take some searching, but I'll question every priest in England, if necessary." He kept re-arranging the salt and pepper shakers on the table in front of him.

"But, that's just it, Spence. You're assuming that I would *want* to be married by a priest. In addition, you're assuming that I would want to raise children Catholic. Well, I don't. My parents and I discussed this at length. I just could never believe as you do." My voice sounded very firm, and I thought that I probably should have studied drama at *Ashwick Park*, along with Charlotte Ross. I would have made a superb actress.

"What? What can't you believe? Help me to understand this change in your thinking." Now, he lightly pounded his fist on the table.

I shifted positions in my chair. My head was beginning to ache violently. "It's not so much a change in my thinking, as it is a dawning of reality. I'm not saying I don't love you, Spence. I do. I could never deny that. Nevertheless, I had a life before I met you. I have family tradition and my own heritage. Your religion would force me to do things I don't believe in."

"Such as?" He asked, raising one eyebrow.

"Well, such as having more children than I might want."

"Darling, I'm a doctor. There are ways to prevent unwanted children. I've already told you how I feel about that subject. Why are you suddenly making it an issue now?"

"Because if you truly believe in what your church preaches, you would not disagree with one of their fundamental teachings." It was hard for me to continue to come up with arguments for him. Especially when I didn't even feel that his beliefs were an obstacle to our being wed.

"I've told you before that I truly believe in most of the tenets of my religion. But, I also have my own beliefs. There is no way I would force *any* belief on you, if we didn't agree on it." He was being so terribly nice…. So accommodating. Of course, that was one of the reasons I had fallen in love with him, but his reasonableness made it extremely challenging for me to make any genuine case to him.

"No, but then we would argue. Moreover, the children we *did* have would have to be raised in your religion. Unless I went to church with you, we would not worship as a family. That would be important to me, Spence."

"You told me in Twigbury that you'd never been strong in any faith and that one denomination was the same as another. Now, you say that you couldn't worship with me?"

"Yes, I know. And, perhaps I could. However, Mummy and Papa told me of some other beliefs, which seem ridiculous to me." I was beginning to stumble and falter. Spence had an excellent memory, making it hard for me to continue my deception.

"Such as?"

"Such as having to eat fish every Friday, confessing sins, and Purgatory, which sounds ghastly. *I had reached a point where I knew that I was beginning to sound foolish.*

"Sophia, if I have ever known anyone in my life who will have a straight arrow entrance into Heaven, it is you. That belief helps Catholics to understand why they should follow the Ten Commandments. As far as

Confession goes, it is just a way for a person to know that their sins have been forgiven. It brings a feeling of peace, and for Goodness Sake, if you don't want to eat fish, you needn't eat fish!"

"I hate fish," I replied. I realized that my answers had deteriorated to those of a child.

"We can dine out every Friday, and you can choose whatever suits you. These are all rather trivial objections in my opinion. Sophia. For God's sake. Please think about what you're saying. We love each other. I'm older than you are, and I know how rare our love is. Please, please don't throw this away. I'm begging you. You are going to regret this for the rest of your life. Neither of us will ever love anyone else like this again. I'm certain of that."

I was certain of it too, but I could not tell him the truth. Mummy's words came back to me so clearly. It was as though she was sitting at the table with us. *"Spencer Stanton will rue the day he turned you against your family."* I had to get away. I had run out of inane excuses. I stood and stumbled from the table, feeling that I needed to escape.

"Sophia! Where are you going? Wait." Spence abandoned his chair, and rushed after me.

I scurried outside, through the front-entrance doors, desperately trying to clear my mind, and to hold fast to my determination. Of course, Spence followed.

"Sophia, give me your hand," he said rather forcefully, taking hold of my left hand.

"What are you doing?" My heart was hammering. He reached into the pocket of his trousers, and in one swift movement slipped a magnificent ring on the third finger of my left hand. It was a square cut emerald, bordered with diamonds, in a platinum setting. I was stunned. He clearly believed that any obstacles we might face would be dealt with. Obviously, Spence was blind to any possibility that the happy future he envisioned could not become reality.

"I love you, Sophia. I know that this ring can only be symbolic of my intentions. If I could, I would marry you tomorrow. I want to give you this ring tonight, so that we both know that we're committed in our hearts. Please accept it and stop these foolish arguments."

I put my head down and tried to brush tears away, but they just kept falling.

"Spence, whatever can you be thinking, or aren't you thinking at all? We can't marry. Need I shout it? Why are you pretending that this isn't the end of everything? For of course, it is."

"We love each other. I know you love me. I know I love you. Yes, there are impediments, but we can work them out. For God's sake, Sophia, don't say you can't be with me."

"Sometimes love isn't enough," I struggled to say, through my tears.

"I'm remembering the woman who loves the countryside in Twigbury and cannot imagine anything more wonderful than sharing a life there. Where is the girl who said that she is an eternal optimist?"

He was holding on to my hand and I desperately wanted to turn and throw myself into his arms.

"Spence that was a dream. I wasn't thinking clearly. You say we can face and overcome the obstacles, but you really have no idea of how that can be accomplished. I don't either."

"I don't know, Sophia. I *do not* know. I only know that I can't lose you." He looked frightened. I wanted to put my arms around him. However, I knew I couldn't do that. The memory of my mother's threats forced me to remain steadfast in my arguments. There was not a doubt in my mind that my mother would carry through with her vile threats. I had to keep that from happening.

"Sophia, God has blessed us with something precious. Don't you see that?" Spence pleaded.

Of course, I saw that. I had never felt such pain in my life. Had never before experienced such heartache. I felt that my life was over, and knew that Spence shared those feelings. It was hideous and beastly.

"Sophia, it's obvious that I can't expect you to give me an answer on any of this tonight. I haven't figured it all out in my head either. I just know that I love you. I shall never willingly let you go."

"No, No." I shook my head. "It *will not* work. I have thought and thought about this and I shall not change my mind. Please stop asking me Spence. You are just making this so much worse.... More difficult. It's hard enough. Do you think I like this? Do you think I wouldn't love to say that

I'm certain we can work it all out? But, I know that we cannot. Don't you see that? If you love me as much as you say you do, you'll stop torturing me and let me go. "

At least a vast part of that pronouncement was true, although the reasons for why I felt the way I did were a complete mystery to him.

Spence didn't speak another word. He took me into his arms, and kissed me, as he had never kissed me before. A kiss to last a lifetime. Then he turned on his heel, and strode away from the hotel, leaving me alone in the rain with the magnificent ring still on my hand.

Chapter Six

Dɛᴄᴇᴍʙᴇʀ, 1935
Bᴜʀʏ Sᴛ. Eᴅᴍᴜɴᴅs

As winter descended, I didn't return to *Willow Grove Abbey*. I went back to Drew and Annie's, never making any mention of what had happened during the previous weeks. I *did* ring my parents, and tell them that I had ended my relationship with Spence. I hated having to speak with them, but knew that it was necessary in order to protect Spence from any harm. They seemed satisfied with my decision, and acted as if nothing untoward had taken place. That was typical. My heart was crushed, but I tried valiantly to give the impression that I was my usual carefree, young self. I did not attend Papa's charity dinner. I made the excuse that I had a beastly headache, and stayed home in bed. I doubt that anyone missed me.

In early-December my normal energy seemed low. I was tired all of the time, and only wanted to sleep. I was beastly depressed, and attributed the fatigue to my black mood. Then one morning I awakened with a feeling of nausea and began to count backwards. I'd always been regular in my monthly menses. Suddenly the fact that there had been none since two weeks before that passionate November weekend with Spence, hit me squarely between the eyes. There had been none since mid-October. It was the first week of December. That meant I was three weeks late. It is still embarrassing to admit that I was really quite ignorant about such matters. I had no idea about what to do. The thought of visiting a doctor was frightening. I was terrified at the thought of enduring a physical examination, or having to admit that I'd had sexual relations outside of marriage. In 1935, that simply was not acceptable behaviour. The dilemma wasn't something I could talk about with Drew and Annie. I knew that they would only feel tremendous guilt at having been a part of what had become an ill- fated weekend in Twigbury. Telling Blake was completely out of the question. He would tell Spence immediately. Edwina was the only person I trusted to keep the secret. She also had knowledge that came from living a Bohemian existence, which put her in an excellent position to advise me.

She was home from Paris for a full month during a midterm holiday. Immediately, I prepared to travel to Bury St. Edmunds, and spend time with the Phillips family. I was so relieved at the thought of being able to talk about my dilemma. I was desperately in need of counsel. I hadn't seen Spence since that last tragic evening at the *Royal*. Many times, I'd come close to calling him, as I'd lain awake in the early morning hours thinking about him. I still had the ring, and knew that I should return it, but was also certain that Spence wouldn't accept it. Instead, I wrapped it in velvet, tucking it into a special corner of my jewel case. Someday, when the memories were not so raw, I intended to *make* him take it back. I knew that if I saw him at that moment, I wouldn't be able to bear it.

Bury St. Edmunds was one of my favorite villages in England, long before I met Edwina. It's located in the county of Suffolk, only two hours from London, so there was no difficulty connecting to Edwina by taking the train from the Capitol. Bury St. Edmunds was primarily a market town of old, and was famous for its brewing. I'd spent many joyous weekends there, while Edwina and I were at school, but I knew that this would not be one of them. Upon my arrival, Edwina collected me. We drove to our favorite small hotel, *Heaven's Gate*, for lunch and a good chat. Edwina looked wonderful. I hadn't seen her since her move to Paris, and there had been considerable change in my dear friend's appearance. She had cut her hair to an above chin-length bob, and fairly glowed in a white fur coat. She was still my *'shining friend'*. It seemed that she continued to grow more and more attractive by keeping her weight down, and developing an *au courant* sense of style. She commented that I looked well, too, but I didn't think so. There were circles under my eyes, and I was pale and drawn. I'd purposely worn a vivid green dress with matching coat, in an attempt to brighten what was a very blue mood. We settled ourselves at a table in the restaurant. The small hotel had been welcoming guests' since 1700, and it always presented a calming haven with fresh flowers, polished tables, gleaming mirrors and pale Edwardian prints. We traditionally went there when I was in Bury. I shed my coat and draped it over the back of the chair, as did Edwina.

"Well, Lady Sophia," how goes the search for the suitable man?" Edwina joked, as she lighted a cigarette, and settled in for our long chat.

"Not so well, Edwina. Things are not well at all," I answered. It was clear that I was under a great deal of stress and was feeing miserable. I twisted a small pearl ring around on my right pinkie finger.

"Oh Sophia! I *am* sorry. I was teasing. Whatever is the trouble? You seem more upset than I've ever seen you." Edwina quickly rearranged her expression to fit the obvious fact that she was about to receive unhappy news.

"I'm afraid I've made an awful mess of things. Just a terrible, terrible mess." I was holding back tears.

"How so?" Edwina asked. "Something has upset you fearfully. Is it your mother again?" Obviously, the first thing that came to Edwina's mind was that my upset had something to do with my mother. Of course, she wasn't mistaken. Nearly every time Edwina had ever seen me upset during our friendship, it had been due to some difficulty with Mummy.

"Yes. Well, I'm not certain where to begin. Of course you remember Spence?"

"Yes, of course. The dreamy doctor. Are you still seeing him? I thought him immensely attractive."

"Yes, well, of course he is. However, there are difficulties. Besides being *Catholic.… Irish Catholic* and not titled.… There is another gigantic problem." I was interrupted by the waiter's appearance, presenting a luncheon menu. There was a period of silence while we studied the menu and made our selections. I ordered a Shepherds' Pie and Edwina chose fresh fish fillet. After the waiter left with our order, we resumed the conversation

"What on earth are you referring to? Edwina asked.

"Edwina, I saw my parents last month and confessed my love for Spence. Spence asked me to marry him in November."

"That's smashing, Sophia! I thought he was perfect for you from the first time I met him. You have to be filled with joy. Why the sad face, then?"

"No. Wait, Edwina, let me finish. I talked to them, and told them everything. I told them that I loved Spence and that he loved me. I confessed that he is Catholic, Irish and untitled. Of course, it was a dreadful scene. I was prepared to walk away from them if necessary, as I'd made the decision that a future with Spence was the most important thing to me."

"Good girl," exclaimed Edwina, as she lighted another cigarette.

"Yes, well, unfortunately, I didn't count on Mummy's cruelty. She threatened to ruin Spence if I continued my relationship with him. She said that she would use Papa's power and their money to blacken Spence's reputation. That he would never be able to practice medicine again. She came right out and said that she would pay money to a *prostitute* to have her swear that Spence had performed an *abortion*. It was appalling." I put my head in my hands.

"My God, she *is* beastly. Do you really think she would do such a thing? Sophia, could she just be threatening you, to frighten you into submission? You know she'd be very capable of such a thing."

"There's no way to know. Mummy generally stops at nothing to get what she wants. You know that. Papa would not give me any support. I think it's entirely possible that she would do anything to stop me from making what she sees as a dreadful mistake."

So, what did you do?" Edwina's face took on a puzzled frown.

"I ended it with Spence. I lied, and told him that I'd thought everything through. That his religion was a horrible obstacle, and that I didn't want to marry outside of my own class." I uncovered my face, and looked at her with the dreadful depression I felt clearly showing upon my face.

"Sophia, you didn't!" Edwina threw her hands up in horror. Her cheeks, had become quite flushed.

"Yes, and there appears to be a new wrinkle in this mess."

"What more could happen?" Edwina asked, her blue-green eyes glistening with tears of sympathy. "I can't imagine how this could get any worse. I'd like to slap your mother."

"Edwina. I think I may be pregnant." I took a sip of water.

"No! Sophia Somerville! You?" One hand flew to her mouth and the other to her chest.

"Yes, *me,* Edwina. I'm scared to death, and don't know what to do. I so hope that you can help by giving me guidance. I feel like such a nit. "

"Are you sure about this Sophia? Perhaps you have worked yourself into such a twit that you have made yourself sick""

"Oh I wish that were so. I don't feel well. I'm sick in the mornings and extremely tired. I haven't had my monthly since before Spence and I were together at the first of November, and my breasts are very tender and sore. What do you think?"

"Well, that certainly covers most of the signs. You definitely must see a doctor. I assume you haven't yet, have you?"

"No, who would I see?" The only doctor I know is Spence, and our family physician in *Bedminster-with Hartcliffe.*" I was wide-eyed with fright.

"Yes, I see what you mean," she answered, biting her bottom lip. "Well, that is the first thing you *must* do. I can arrange for you to see a doctor here. He's wonderful. I've known him since I was a child. He won't be judgmental, I promise."

"Will you come with me? I simply could not do such a thing by myself. I feel so stupid."

"Don't feel stupid. More worldly people than you have found themselves in such a predicament. Let me ring the doctor's office this minute and set up an appointment. This shouldn't be put off, Sophia. Once you know for certain, we can discuss what choices you have."

Edwina excused herself and went to ring the doctor, while I sat alone at the table, wondering what was going to become of me. *Oh Lord... if I could only tell Spence. He would take care of me.... Would marry me.... Everything would be fine. However, my parents would intervene.... Would stop it. It was out of the question. Perhaps it would turn out to be a false alarm. I'd heard of girls who worried themselves into a frenzy, missing their monthly curse, and they were not pregnant at all.* Such thoughts ran through my mind the entire time Edwina was away from the table.

She returned and announced that the doctor could see me at three o'clock that very afternoon. Thus, we had time to eat lunch and relax a bit before the dreaded appointment. I was apprehensive but also terribly relieved to have a direction in which to point. I had been so topsy-turvy with fear, naiveté, immaturity, and ignorance that I hadn't known where to turn.

Three hours later, we left the doctor's cottage. He'd all but confirmed that indeed I was expecting a baby. He conducted a test to absolutely verify the pregnancy, but it would take a couple of days to yield results. However, he said that from the physical examination, he was virtually certain that I was pregnant about six weeks. I accepted the news more calmly than I might have imagined, but I'm certain that I was in shock. Edwina was still having trouble believing that I'd had sexual relations with Spence. Not that she was judgmental or critical.... Just surprised that it was happening to me.... Her virginal friend.

"Sophia, I don't mean to pry for the more lurid details," she said, as we walked back to her auto, "but I just never thought to see *you* in this kind of situation. How did this happen? Were you intoxicated?" she asked.

"Nothing of the sort," I laughed. "In fact, I was sober as a judge." Edwina began to drive toward her parent's home. "It simply *happened*, Edwina. I love him. He loves me. It only happened that one weekend."

"What rotten luck. There was just the one time?"

"Well. Just the one *weekend*. A few times. Several, actually."

"That must have been a rather interesting weekend," Edwina smiled.

I gave her a nasty look.

"Sorry, I didn't mean to be flippant, she smiled."

"It's all right. It *was* quite a weekend. I'll remember it forever."

I was looking out of the car window at the snowflakes that were beginning to fall. *What on Earth was I going to do? There was no easy answer to such a conundrum. I wanted the baby. After all, it was Spence's child. Naturally, what I really wished was that I could have his child and him as well. But, I still couldn't see how that could ever come about. Baby or no baby, my parents' were not going to accept Spence as a son-in-law. With this new wrinkle, they would probably contemplate charging him with rape! I would still be forced to adopt out the child. That was absolutely not going to happen. Never.*

Edwina's next comment broke into my thoughts. "You'll have a *reminder* of it forever, I'm afraid. How do you feel about this?"

"I don't know. I cannot imagine that I'm really going to have a baby. Spence's baby. That makes all of the difference, Edwina. This is *Spence's* baby, and it means that I have a part of *him* inside of me. I shall *always* have a part of him in my life. I'm happy about that."

"Doesn't this change things?" she asked, as she made a left turn toward her parent's house. "Don't you think you should tell him now? Surely your parents wouldn't forbid a marriage when there's a baby involved?"

"*Oh yes they would, Edwina!* I suspect they would pack me off to some faraway place, and invent a story about my studying abroad or whatever. They would probably force me to place the baby for adoption. I shall *never* allow such a thing to happen. Mummy and Papa absolutely cannot know of this."

"How can you keep them from knowing, Sophia? A pregnancy isn't exactly something you can keep secret forever."

"Perhaps I *could* pretend that I wanted to go away somewhere? Perhaps I could say that I want to move to Paris with you?" I reached over and nudged Edwina in her ribs. "That's a perfect solution."

"Sophia, that would be fine, and you know I would do anything to help, but at some point you would still have to explain a *child.*"

"Quite right. I'm not thinking straight. That won't do at all." I bit my cheek, as I've always been prone to do at stressful moments. "Well, then there's only one other solution."

"I'm, sorry, dear heart, but I'm not following you," she answered.

"There's only one other solution. I'll have to get married, and rather quickly."

"What do you mean?"

"I'll have to find a *suitable* husband very quickly. He will become the father of my baby."

"Sophia. Are you implying that you would let someone else think it is *his* baby?"

"That's precisely what I'm saying."

"Oh my God in heaven!" Edwina rolled her eyes. "Have you lost your mind? Sophia, men are not total idiots. They know how many months it takes to make a baby. If you were to try such a daft scheme, this imaginary husband will be certain to learn the truth when the baby arrives."

"I'll simply have to worry about that when it happens. Babies arrive early all of the time." I smiled, undoubtedly looking as though I'd now discovered the perfect solution.

"Sophia, you don't even know who the poor man is yet. This baby will be arriving *very* early."

"Oh, but I think I *do* know who the baby's father will be," I mused.

"Who on Earth….?"

"Mummy is very keen on my marrying Lord Owen Winnsborough. She has virtually ordered it. Perhaps I'll comply with her wishes."

I'm certain that I must have looked like the cat that stole the cream.

"Sophia. Owen Winnsborough? He looks like a spaniel." Edwina had a horrified look on her face, and nearly ran the auto onto the curb.

"I've always thought more like a bloodhound," I giggled.

"Sophia, I don't believe we're having this conversation. Are you serious?"

"Yes, Edwina, I'm very serious." And I was. It was snowing more heavily. I pulled my coat closer, as it grew colder in the automobile. My mind was working at top speed, as I tried to envision what the future held for me.

"Come. Let's go into the house," Edwina said, pulling up in front of her parent's modest home. "We can talk upstairs in my room." I was shivering. We entered the house through a side door, shedding our coats and boots. Thelma Phillips came out of the kitchen, wiping her hands on an apron.

"Hallo, girls. I've been playing in the kitchen. It's Catherine's day off and I decided to bake bread. Catherine was their cook. Do you want to sample a piece? It's warm from the oven."

"That sounds heavenly," Edwina replied. Her mother quickly disappeared into the kitchen and returned with two plates, piled high with warm bread and jam.

"We're going to my room for a long chat, Mum. Do you need our help with anything?"

"No, Sweetie, nothing. Enjoy your time together."

I couldn't help but think about how different Edwina's mother was from my own. If Mummy had been like Thelma Phillips, I could have told her everything. A mother like Thelma would never have objected to Spence in the first place. Edwina and I climbed the staircase and entered her childhood bedroom. We curled up on the bright lavender bedspread, continuing our conversation.

"All right, Sophia. If you're really serious about this idea of marriage to Owen Winnsborough, which I must tell you I'm not *at all* in favor of, then we should talk specifics."

"Yes. I know you're not in favor of it. It's not exactly what I ever envisioned, either. Nevertheless, you must admit, it *could* be the answer. I would be able to keep my baby. Spence would never know. The child would not have the stigma of illegitimacy, and Mummy and Papa would have no reason to cause Spence harm." I nibbled on a piece of warm bread.

"Yes. Those are all reasons to consider such a scheme. I'm just worried about *you*, Sophia. I hate the thought of you being married to a man you don't love, who may be enraged when he learns what kind of a lie has been perpetrated upon him."

"I don't care about me. I'm certain I can convince him that it's his child. I'll manage to be abroad, visiting *you,* when the baby comes! We won't tell Owen when it happens, and will let him believe that the birth date is later."

"Well…. It might work. It would have to be very well planned." Edwina rolled her eyes and sighed.

"Edwina, we *can* do it. I know we can," I cried, as I took her hands into mine. "You *must* help me. Say you will," I begged.

"Of course I shall. But, Sophia, have you ever had a *date* with Owen?"

"Yes. Actually, I have. We've seen each another on a regular basis since early summer. He called just last week and I saw him. We really *are* good friends. He is very interested in me. I have no doubt of that. I was still seeing a few other men during most of the summer, so my parents wouldn't know I was so keen on Spence, but Owen was definitely the primary one."

"Does Owen know of your relationship with Spence?"

"No, *Goose,* I'm not such a fool as all that," I said, playfully, hitting Edwina on the arm. "Do you think I have been telling other men how much I adore Spence? So, now, I need to turn my relationship with Owen into a *love match*, become engaged, and marry him, all in a rather short time frame."

"Quite a tall order, Sophia." Edwina looked skeptical.

"Well, it is, but not totally unheard of. After all, you know that the whole goal of the season is to snag a husband before it ends. Everyone knows that. I have grown up hearing it all of my life. You know that Papa asked Mummy to marry him on their second date, if you can imagine. They were married not long after. I'll just have to do it, too," I replied. "I'll begin by accepting Owen's invitation to the Christmas Ball at St. James Palace on the 11th of December."

"That should be a good beginning, but it's not far away, Sophia. Can you pull it off that quickly? That Ball is almost mandatory for nobility, isn't it? Perhaps he's made other plans by now."

"I can do it. Absolutely. Owen has made it perfectly clear that he is *smitten* with me. I suspect a romantic night at the Christmas Ball would go a long way toward a proposal. He asked me to accompany him to the Ball some time ago. I've never responded, but I think it's time that I did."

"It seems a bit late to me, but if you think it will work then you must do it. You must call him right this minute. If this is your plan, and you're absolutely certain that it's what you want to do, you mustn't waste any time."

"Quite right," I answered. "Hand me the telephone, Edwina," I pronounced, in a determined voice. I didn't know Owen's number, so I rang Drew, and was able to obtain it from him. Surely, he and Annie were perplexed as to why I would want the number of someone about whom I'd made rather disparaging remarks. However, Drew was quite nice enough not to ask. Then, I placed the call to Owen. A man servant answered on the second ring. The line was static, as it was a long distance call from Bury St. Edmunds to *Winnsborough Hall*, but I managed to hear well enough.

"Winnsborough Hall".

"May I speak with Lord Winnsborough?" I asked, in my most *aristocratic* voice."

"May I say who is calling, please?"

"Lady Sophia Somerville." I made a gagging motion to Edwina, and put my hand over my mouth to keep from giggling.

"One moment, Miss," the voice responded. I tapped my fingers nervously, on the top of an end table, while waiting for Owen to come to the telephone. The time for anxiety was over. I knew what I had to do. Finally his voice came on the line.

"Lord Winnsborough, here," he said.

"Owen. This is Sophia Somerville. I hope I didn't disturb you."

"Not at all, Sophia. I am delighted to hear from you. Quite delighted."

"How kind of you," I simpered. "I hope you'll tell me that you'll be delighted to escort me to the St. James Christmas Ball," I said, in a coquettish voice. "Have I waited too long to accept your invitation?"

"Why Sophia! No, of course you haven't. It would be an honour. I may have to do some rearranging of my schedule, but certainly, I would be proud to be your escort. I *am* rather surprised. I'd thought some other fortunate gentleman must have laid claim to you.... That I'd lost my chance."

"Nothing of the sort, Owen. I have just been so beastly busy, what with my close friend Edwina visiting from Paris. I'm afraid I have shamefully neglected you and I'm so sorry. Now that the silliness of the season is over, I'm of a mind to look to the future, and begin to lead a quieter life."

"I see," he replied. "I'm happy to hear that."

"Yes, perhaps we'll be able to spend more time together. I do so enjoy being with you."

"And I you, Sophia. You cannot know how happy your call has made me. By the way, *wherever are* you ringing me from? This connection is beastly."

"I'm at Edwina's in Bury St. Edmunds. I was telling her of the many splendid times we've shared during the past few months. I suddenly remembered that I'd never given you an answer about the Christmas Ball." Owen seemed thrilled to hear that Edwina and I had been discussing him in favorable terms.

"Shall we try to dine before the Christmas Ball? Perhaps take in the theatre?" he asked.

"Yes, I'd like that very much."

"I'm certain I'll be able to procure tickets to '*The Late Christopher Bean*' at the St. James, Theater. Do you think you might enjoy that," he asked.

"Absolutely, Owen. I've heard a great deal about it." *The truth was that I had seen the play with Spence when it opened back in September.*

"Have you any plans for the coming Tuesday evening?"

"No, as a matter of fact, I haven't," I replied.

Well, splendid. I shall send my car for you at seven. We shall dine after the theatre. I'll be at my flat in London."

"That sounds simply wonderful, Owen. I'm so glad I called."

"Yes Sophia. I am too. I'll look forward to Tuesday."

"Good night then, Owen," I replied, as we rang off.

Edwina was rolling on the bed in hysterics. It was a terribly serious, horrible situation, and what I had in mind was exceptionally Machiavellian. Yet neither of us could stop from seeing its humorous side. Perhaps we were simply trying very hard to make the best of dreadful circumstances. On the other hand, perhaps we were only young girls, who simply couldn't imagine anything truly, truly *horrid* happening in our lives. It had been so long since I had laughed. It felt good. We giggled, snickered, chuckled, and tittered until our sides hurt. Later however, when alone, I wept.

Chapter Seven

21 JANUARY 1936
A WEDDING

In the blink of an eye, I found myself engaged on the night of the St. James Palace Christmas Ball. Even I hadn't dreamed of such good fortune. But, after our planned evening at the theater, followed by dining at The *Picardy Lane Hotel's* opulent restaurant, I saw Owen every night thereafter. I made a visit to *Willow Grove Abbey*, because there was the necessity of telling my parents that if Owen asked for my hand in marriage, I fully intended to accept his proposal. I made it clear to my parents that I was only considering such action because of their stated wishes, and that under no circumstances was I in love with him. Furthermore, I let them know that I did not want a long engagement, and wished to marry as soon as possible.... That I did not want a lot of formality and fuss. They were so thrilled that I had finally 'come to my senses' that they argued little with anything else I had to say. Owen showed up for a chat with my parents, while I was there. He spoke to my father, and of course was granted permission to seek my hand. Then, the actual night of the Ball, he presented me with a large, quite ostentatious, diamond ring. It was not at all what I might have selected, but it really didn't matter. Diamonds were supposed to show that one's intended was of an economic class that could afford such a divine luxury. Thus, Owen had complied with societal expectations.

He never did tell me that he loved me, nor did he kiss me. It was all rather business-like. He explained that because we had known one another such a long time, and that our families were so well acquainted, he felt that we were extremely well-suited to one another, and that I would make a splendid mistress of *Winnsborough Hall*. He felt that I had all of the poise and dignity that such a position required, and that he would be proud for me to be the Duchess of Winnsborough. I suppose there were many girls my age who would have been bonkers over such a request, but I wasn't one of them. I'd known love with Spence, and there was no way that marriage to Owen could begin to match feelings I still harboured for my lost love. After the initial niceties were behind, his parents and mine took over from there. The only other item that we really had much say about was the actual date of the marriage. Owen and I agreed that a long engagement would be trying for everyone.... Owen, me, both of our families and all of our friends. There just seemed no sense in such a waste of time. Needless to say, the sooner the wedding took place, the better for me. We had already known one another for some eighteen years. So, there was agreement that we would choose a forthcoming date in 1936. I suggested January 21, which sent his mother and mine into a tizzy. It was pointed out that such a hurried date provided barely enough time to accomplish the assembling of a trousseau, making plans for a wedding trip, choosing decorations, sending invitations and selecting a menu for the wedding supper. In addition, Owen's family planned a pre-nuptial dinner on the evening preceding the wedding itself. However, I stood my ground. I reiterated over and over that I did not want a lot of fuss and frivolity. After much arguing back and forth, everyone agreed that I had a right to pick my wedding date, and so it was agreed upon. It was a Tuesday, which was not unusual at that time. Particularly for a smaller wedding. We set the time as two o'clock in the afternoon, with the reception following at *Willow Grove Abbey* one half hour later. Since the wedding was to be held in the chapel at our home, there was little need for consideration of the distance one needed to travel between wedding ceremony and reception. Drew agreed to conduct the ceremony, which added a personal touch.

On 20 January, 1936, we all gathered at *Winnsborough Hall* for the pre-nuptial dinner, hosted by the Duke and Duchess of Winnsborough. In retrospect, it set the tone for everything that followed. Just as we were about to be seated for dinner, the butler interrupted with the announcement that a telegram had been delivered. The Duke, looking a bit irritated, accepted the yellow envelope and tore it open. After scanning the contents, he cleared his throat and asked for everyone's attention.

"I have just received word that our beloved King George the Fifth has passed away," he declared. There was complete silence in the room as everyone absorbed the news. No one was especially surprised, as the King had been ill for quite some time. He had not been a young man. Nevertheless, as is always the case when a Monarch dies, the gathering that evening was galvanized into mourning. The ritual, pomp, and ceremony that is such an integral part of British life would follow. The families present that evening were personally acquainted with the King, so all of us were even more sincerely distressed. My parents had last seen him at his Silver Jubilee Celebration in 1935, which had marked his twenty-five-year reign.

The Jubilee had marked the calendar that year, and a service was held at St. Paul's Cathedral on May Sixth, followed by a private reception given by the Prince of Wales. It was near in time to my Presentation. My family had been guests, although I hadn't attended. I was just finishing up at *Ashwick Park*. It was incredible to think that the Prince would be… Was…. The King. He would be known as Edward the Eighth, and his reign promised a breath of fresh air to a generation which thought there needed to be some loosening of social restrictions. Nevertheless, it was with heavy hearts that those of us who were gathered for the pre-nuptial dinner received the news of King George's passing. We were keenly aware that it was a momentous, historic occasion. Certainly, it put a damper upon the wedding festivities. Everyone drank a toast to the deceased King, and then another to the new King Edward. With that, the evening progressed in an orderly, if somewhat subdued, fashion. That was the prelude to the big event.

Edwina had come from Paris and I was grateful, as I could be honest with her. We spent my last night as a single girl in my bedchamber at *Willow Grove Abbey*, chattering into the wee hours, as we had done so many times before at *Ashwick Park*.

"Sophia, it's amazing that everything you predicted in early December has actually happened. And in such a short time," Edwina said, as she slipped into the twin bed opposite mine. 'I'm happy, in a way, because I know that it solves so many problems, but it truly makes me ill to think of you married to Owen."

"I'm in a bit of shock myself. Can you believe that he asked me to marry him the night of the Christmas Ball? Even I hadn't counted on such luck. It wasn't even difficult to convince him to marry so quickly. He really wasn't interested in a large, ostentatious wedding at Westminster, or wherever, and he certainly didn't wish for a prolonged engagement. I'm doing the right thing, Edwina. I know it's not what I dreamed. However, it will work out all right. My baby will have a name. Owen will be kind to me. Moreover, if he is not the *Grande Passion* you envisioned for me, please find comfort in the fact that I *did* have a wonderful love story. You and I have always known that our futures would carry us along different paths. Of course I wish circumstances were different, but what's done, is done."

"I just wish that if you couldn't have married the man you loved, you might have been able to wait a bit. You seem so young to be burying yourself in the country with Owen Winnsborough. I should go totally mad if that's all I had ahead of me. "

"What might I have done? Even if the baby hadn't been a consideration, I wouldn't have wanted to return to *Willow Grove Abbey*, living unmarried, embroidering linens, and waiting for a *suitable* man. Do you remember teasing me about living my life as a *Jane Austen* heroine? Anyway, Owen and I have the flat on Sumner Street in London, so when I feel the need to escape, I shall always have a place to go. Moreover, don't forget, I *do* have something marvelous to look forward to.... The birth of Spence's child."

"I know, I know. I look forward to that as well. But.... But.... You write so well, Sophia. I always believed that you might do more with *that*, beyond simply scribbling in your journal."

"Perhaps I shall, someday. But, I can be married and write as well." I scrunched my feather pillow into a ball, and settled my head upon it."

"I remember you saying that when we first met at school."

"Yes, I remember that too," I answered, wistfully. It all seemed such a dreadfully long time ago, although in reality it was less than two years. I had only just turned nineteen on the fourteenth of January.

"It's hard for me to think of you as Lady Sophia *Winnsborough*, Edwina continued. "At least, it's a rather nice sounding name."

"It's hard for *me* to think of *myself* as a Winnsborough. I guess I'll become accustomed to it."

"Will we still be close friends, do you think Sophia? Our lives will be so vastly different. Goodness! You will be a Duchess!

No…Not immediately I won't. Not until the Duke and Duchess, Owen's parents, are deceased. I hope that isn't for a long while. They are very dear people. Until then, I'll be a Marchioness. I won't make you use my title though," I teased. "I'll still be referred to as 'Lady, and you've never called me that. Don't you ever dare," I laughed…. Only my last name will be different. Anyway, as to your question about our friendship. It's totally daft. You know that we shall *always* be the dearest of friends. You're like my sister. I cannot imagine what I would do without you. You silly girl. We had this conversation once before too, on our last day together at *Ashwick Park*. That time you reminded me that we would be seeing one another in Paris before very long. That never came to pass, but this time we're saying it again. Paris. Midsummer." I was referring to our plans for a summer holiday visit, which would coincide with the birth of the baby. I'd already broached the idea of a visit to Paris to see Edwina for a girl's only rendezvous, and Owen had not voiced any objections.

"We have to vow to never allow *anything* to interfere with our friendship," Edwina reiterated.

"Nothing will ever interfere with our friendship," I stated unequivocally.

"Isn't it amazing to think that the Prince is now the King?" Edwina mused, changing the topic. I knew that she was trying to search for something less anxiety-ridden.

"Yes. You know, I worry for him. He doesn't appear to be happy. I'm not certain he wants all of the responsibility that goes with being the monarch. Have you heard any more rumors of L'Affaireee Mrs. Simpson?"

"Oh, my Gosh, yes. Paris is fairly buzzing with that topic. I'm amazed at how ill-informed Londoners seem to be."

"I believe you know more about it than we in England do. It's because *Fleet Street* is keeping a lid on the whole affairee." The English newspapers had been maintaining a virtual blackout on news of the new King's relationship with Wallis Simpson, the twice married American whom everyone assumed he was having an affaireee with. I suspected that was why he seemed so blue.

"What of her husband?" I asked.

"The most recent jest I've heard is that 'Ernest Simpson is only too happy to *lay down his wife* for England'."

"Edwina! How dreadful! Can he really be such a *ninny*? I can't imagine."

"It takes all sorts, I suppose. Apparently, in the beginning, Mr. Simpson was included in the house-party weekends and nightclub gaiety, but recently he isn't even seen very frequently. She appears with the Prince…. Sorry…. The King, alone."

"Well, certainly, nothing can come of it" I daresay. He surely could never marry her, even if she were to divorce. It would never be allowed."

"Right you are there," Edwina responded. "It's a bit sad, actually. I mean, if he truly loves her."

"Yes, I suppose it is." There was a woeful tone to my response.

"Oh Sophia, how stupid of me! I *am* dreadfully sorry to be so insensitive. What was I thinking?"

"It's all right, Edwina. You cannot go through your life watching everything you say, for fear you'll wound me. Please understand that *I* made the decision not to tell Spence about the baby, and not to marry him. I still believe it was the correct decision. The only one I could have made. Yes, it's sad that things couldn't have been different, but I'm glad that I shall have his child. I won't ever be totally without him, don't you see?"

Edwina crawled out of her bed and moved over to mine. She hugged me until my ribs hurt.

"Oh Sophia! I am so amazed at your strength. It *will* work out. I'll be there to help. You'll have a lovely baby and all of this will have been worth it."

"I know," I murmured. Everything will be fine."

Edwina returned to her own bed, and we whispered "Good Night" to each other. Before long, she was fast asleep, but I never closed my eyes.

At two-o'clock on the afternoon of 21 January, 1936, Lord Owen Winnsborough and I took marriage vows in the Chapel at *Willow Grove Abbey* It seemed an amazingly short ceremony. Perhaps that was because

I was in a dazed state during the entire affairee. After pledging to live together in 'God's Holy Ordinance' until death parted us, in less than fifteen minutes we were husband and wife. I was a married woman.... Married to a man I did not love, and never would.

My wedding gown was white velvet. If I had allowed Mummy to have her way it would have been ivory satin, embroidered with thousands of seed pearls and covered with Alencon lace. Thank goodness, time did not permit such an elaborate design. Thus, I was able to have the dress I preferred. I also wore a Spanish mantilla veil, of lovely old lace, which had been given me by my Godmother when I was just a child. I carried a bouquet of white roses and lilies. Edwina and Annie were my two attendants, wearing deep primrose, velvet frocks, with long, draped skirts, loose-fitting bodices, and chiffon bishop sleeves. They carried white calla lilies and pink roses. It was a simple wedding, but top drawer. We adorned the chapel with rose and crème ribbons on every pew, along with large masses of roses at the altar. Owen looked as handsome as possible in his Morning Suit. However, I could not say that I felt anything special as I walked down the aisle on my father's arm.

Mummy was radiant in deep cranberry silk, wearing the rubies that Papa had purchased after her last *rage*, which had been the dreadful November scene. In fact, she had been spectacularly happy for longer than any of her children could remember. Blake and Drew joked that they would have forced me into marriage long before, had they known the effect it would have upon our mother. Edwina said that the Somervilles needed to have more weddings in the family, which, in retrospect, became a rather ironic comment. Engraved invitations went out, emblazoned with the family crest, and glorious gifts began to arrive. Mummy resembled a shopkeeper keeping detailed inventory. She kept a white leather bound book in which she itemized each gift as it arrived, and assigned a number to it. There were hours spent arranging each, in just the proper manner, showing it off to best advantage. I received heaps and heaps of Sterling silver, Wedgwood china, Baccarat, Waterford and Lalique crystal. I spent the last week before the wedding staying current with 'Thank You' notes. In between, there were teas and dinners. All of this kept me far too busy to think about anything else, which was a blessing. Although the guest list was small…Less than one hundred…. I was amazed at the number of gifts. Even persons who only received Announcements, which etiquette makes clear does *not* require the recipient to send a present, sent one anyway. It was rather fun to see the boxes arrive all day long.

My trousseau was extensive, and I was careful to select only those designs that were not terribly *form fitting*, in anticipation of the change my figure was about to undergo. It would be necessary to camouflage my condition for as long as possible. Thank Goodness there was no indication whatever of the pregnancy yet. If I were fortunate, that would continue for many more months. The dressmaker nearly lost her mind trying to assemble an entire trousseau in such short order, Mummy purchased *fourteen* peignoir sets for me. They ranged in color from virginal white, which Edwina and I secretly giggled about, to pink and yellow. My mother believed that a bride should have a negligee for every night of her wedding trip, and mine was to last two weeks. Edwina said that when she married she would have no sleepwear at all, and I quite believed her. However, Edwina would not be marrying Owen Winnsborough. With all of the grandeur, the whole affairee seemed like a theatrical production, in which I was the playing the *lead*. Unfortunately, when the curtain came down I would have to continue playing my part. I wondered if there were other brides who felt the way I did.

After the ceremony, all of the guests, both sets of parents, the rest of my family, and Owen and I proceeded from the Chapel to the main house at *Willow Grove* for a splendid wedding supper. An awning made a covered walk from the edge of the curb to the front door. At the lower end, Joseph, our chauffeur, stood opening automobile doors and giving return checks to the other chauffeurs and their employers. Inside the house the florist had finished, and an orchestra was playing in the Great Hall. Everything was perfection. We took our places in front of the elaborate arrangement of plants and flowers that had been prepared for us. I stood on Owen's right, and the bridesmaids stood to my left. Owen's mother also received next to my mother, while both of our father's circled about speaking with the guests.

After receiving congratulations and best wishes from all of our guests, we were seated at a large round table, along with our parents, bridesmaids,

and groomsmen. A lovely meal was served in several courses consisting of
Court Bouillon, Lobster Newburg, Supreme of Chicken, Peas, Aspic of
Foie Gras, Celery Salad, Ices and Coffee. Of course, in addition, there were
the finest champagnes. In the center of the Bride's table sat an elaborately
designed, iced wedding cake. It was banked with gorgeous displays of
white lilies and roses. It stood four tiers in height. There was much laughter
and lightheartedness, and even Owen joined in the revelry. I nearly forgot
for a moment that I was pregnant, which was, after all, the reason we were
all gathered together. I made an excuse about not feeling like drinking, in
order to avoid anything alcoholic. My parents were beyond exuberance,
and one would never have guessed that only a few months before, Mummy
had been curled in a fetal position on the floor of the Drawing Room,
throwing a horrific tantrum because of my desire to marry Spence.

Twenty-four hours later, on the night of my marriage, I found myself in a
suite of rooms at the *Half Moon Hotel* in Bath, with a man I scarcely knew.
I was uncomfortably aware that physical demands were soon to be made.
I'd tried to prepare mentally for the inevitable. Owen was far from sober
when we arrived. He'd drunk a rather large quantity of champagne at the
reception, which was undoubtedly *de rigour* for a newlywed man. I might
have been more able to face the realities of the night if I were equally
intoxicated. My condition prevented that. There was a bottle of champagne in our suite when we arrived. Opening it, Owen poured each of us
a glass. Then, he proposed a toast, and held me in his arms for a moment,
giving me a pathetic sort of kiss, with his lips closed. I pretended to take
a small sip, and set my glass down. I waited for a more passionate kiss, but
none was forthcoming. Believe it or not, Owen had never kissed me at all,
up to that moment. I didn't know what he expected of me. I bit my cheek
to keep memories of my intimate moments with Spence from roaring
back. Perhaps Owen was being considerate, not wanting to frighten me.
Perhaps he simply respected me enormously. I decided that the best course
of action would be to go to the bath, and prepare for what would surely
follow. I walked across the lovely parlor to where my overnight case rested,

and removed the first of my fourteen-peignoir sets. It was the white lace creation, festooned with pink rose buds.

Once in the privacy of the bath, I began to quiver. I was suddenly terribly nervous, and more than a little frightened. Although I'd had sexual encounters with Spence, and was pregnant, I still felt naive and uninformed. Naturally, the fact that I was not in the least attracted to my husband didn't help matters. In addition, I definitely knew that I had to make Owen believe it was the first time for me. Mummy had taken me aside the morning of the wedding, and asked me if there was anything I needed to know. I told her that I didn't believe so. She told me that I was to just lie still and let him do what he needed to do, and that it would be over quickly. She said that sometimes it felt rather good. I almost burst out laughing. Poor Mummy had obviously never enjoyed the passion that came with a love like I'd experienced with Spence. I ran the bath, filling the tub to near overflowing, and poured in my lavender oil. It felt heavenly to soak in that delicious tub, and it did help me to relax. I tried to envision my naked body as I imagined Owen would, and I was satisfied that he would be pleased. I was not vain, but knew that I could be quite desirable. Spence had proven that to me. The pregnancy had given me quite voluptuous breasts, but I still had a tiny waistline. In addition, my skin was creamy and smooth.

Stepping out of the tub, I rubbed myself dry with the soft, fluffy towel waiting on a nearby warmer. It felt wonderfully snugly. Then, I slipped the nightdress over my head, examining myself in the mirror. I *did* look rather fetching. I fluffed my curls, added a touch of lip rouge and put a dab of perfume behind each earlobe and on the pulse points at my wrists. It was imperative that Owen find me irresistible. I was about to conceive his child! I was occupied in the bath for nearly an hour. During that time I assumed that Owen was doing whatever it is that men do to prepare for a wedding night. Perhaps he was relaxing in the parlor, or pretending to relax, so as not to make me nervous.

When I emerged, I felt very ready for what lay ahead. Not anxious nor eager, but ready. However, all of my carefully made plans went awry when I saw Owen stretched atop the white duvet cover on the bed. He was still clothed in his formal attire, snoring loudly and lying at a diagonal angle, with an empty champagne bottle on the nightstand. I didn't know how to react. On the one hand, I was relieved, for it appeared that I could simply curl up and go to sleep, undisturbed. On the other hand, I felt like bursting into tears. I *had* to consummate the marriage. Time was of the essence. I suspected that Mummy, in the same circumstance, would have had a *rage*. However, I knew better than to start my marriage off in such a fashion. Besides, I was not temperamentally given to rages. At first, I thought he might awaken shortly, as it seemed likely that he had dozed off for just a moment. After all, it *had* been a long, tiring day. The previous night he had celebrated with his male friends until the wee hours. I decided to let him rest a bit longer.

Wandering into the parlor, I settled myself upon the camelback sofa. At first, I considered placing a telephone call to Edwina, but then remembered that my dear friend's plans had been to return to Bury St. Edmunds directly following the reception. She was undoubtedly still en route. As I sat there trying to decide what to do, feeling somewhat frightened, I experienced a strange fluttering in my abdomen. My hand flew to my mid-section, instinctively and protectively. I did not know what to make of such an odd sensation. Then, I realized that I was feeling *life* for the first time. Spence's child was reminding me of its presence at precisely the proper moment. It was a never-to- be- forgotten occurrence, and it brought reality home with colossal force. I had no more qualms about what I must do. Resolutely walking straight into the bed chamber, I gently shook Owen until he awakened. He came round slowly, but finally realized where he was and who was rousing him. I quickly helped to undress him, which he was quite incapable of doing for himself, and pulled the covers back. Making him get under them, I slipped in beside him.

Our wedding night bore no resemblance whatsoever to my passionate afternoons with Spence. Nor had I expected that it would. However, I *was* surprised at Owen's almost total lack of enthusiasm. I'd always been led to believe that men were bonkers about sex. At first, I assumed that the excessive amount of alcohol he'd consumed, coupled with fatigue, accounted for his lackluster performance. In this role, as in so many others I'd had to undertake, I was a consummate actress. I need not have worried about whether he would guess that I was not a virgin, for he seemed much more concerned with himself. However, for some reason, I felt as if he too might be acting. The entire *deed* was over very quickly, which suited me perfectly. The important thing was that from that day forward I would be able to claim Owen as the father of my child.

We continued to the south of France for the remainder of the wedding trip. If I'd been dreading the thought of frequent sexual demands, I need not have worried. Owen did not *touch* me again during the entire fortnight. No matter how inexperienced and naive I may have been, I was not a total fool. There was no question that his behaviour was abnormal. I was not about to question him though, since I was actually quite relieved at his behaviour, or rather the lack of it. Each night I disappeared into the opulent gold and marble appointed dressing room and bath in our splendid suite, and when I emerged, Owen was fast asleep. Thus, we settled into our routine of pleasant day trips to quaint, medieval villages, high in the hills overlooking Cannes and Nice. My favorite was St. Paul de Vence, and I bought a lovely painting of the town. We took shopping expeditions to elegant boutiques along the Promenade Des'Anglais, consumed sumptuous dinners in fashionable restaurants, took long strolls along the seawall, and then quietly returned to our suite at the *Paradise Cay* in Cap d'Antibes and retired. It was quite nice. Owen treated me with great deference and was even somewhat affectionate in public. Strangely, he did not act as though there was anything inappropriate about his behaviour. I wondered if perhaps no one had ever explained to *him* about the physical side of marriage, which was preposterous. I was grateful we had consummated the marriage on the first night or I would have been beside myself. As it was, I was actually able to relax. It had been a long time since I'd been able to do so. In such a fashion the wedding trip ended. We returned to England to set up housekeeping at *Winnsborough Hall.*

Chapter Eight

MARCH, 20-JULY20, 1936
AN EXPECTANT MOTHER

I began practicing the intricacies of managing a massive country house. There was such a large staff at *Winnsborough Hall,* that it took me quite a good bit of time to learn everyone's' names and duties. I had a social secretary who saw to the writing and acceptance of invitations, as well as entering into an engagement book every appointment made for Owen and me, whether it was an afternoon tea, lunch, dinner, dress fitting or doctor's appointment. She also audited all bills and drew the checks for them. Her name was Audrey Evans, and she was highly capable. Of course, we had a housekeeper, whose name was Mrs. Whittaker. She had been with the Winnsboroughs since Owen was a child, and was of immeasurable help to me. In no time at all, we found that we worked very well together. She had charge of the appearance of the house and of its contents; the manners and looks of the housemaids and parlor maids, as well as their work in cleaning walls, floors, ornaments, pictures, furniture, books and taking care of the linen. Besides Mrs. Whittaker, the most important member of the staff was our Butler, Morris. He had charge of the pantry and dining room, engaged all footman and was in charge of their work and appearance. Then there was Mary, who was in charge of the kitchen, and the undercook. In spite of all of this assistance, I still found that I had plenty of free time and I also learned that I greatly enjoyed the freedom and independence that came with being married, even though my husband was not who I'd dreamed he might have been.

In late March I traveled to London, under the pretense of a shopping trip. However, the true reason was to visit an obstetrician. I didn't elaborate to the London doctor upon the length of my marriage. I merely recounted the fact that I'd not had my monthly menses since mid-October. Upon examination, he verified what I already knew. He pronounced the due date as 2, August. He stated that I was young and healthy, and that he expected an easy pregnancy and routine birth. Once that ordeal was behind me, I eagerly looked forward to enjoying a few days of shopping in Knightsbridge, visiting with friends, and dining with Drew and Annie. It was the first time I'd stayed in the flat on Sumner Street. The neighborhood was excellent and the building very fashionable. Thus, I wasn't in the least frightened of being on my own in London, even though it was a new experience. I had such a good time on that short visit. I learned what it was like to enter a fashionable shop, and make my selection without ever having to worry about the manner of payment. All that was required was my giving the name 'Lady Winnsborough', and any purchases were immediately sent to *Winnsborough Hall*, and placed on account. I'd been used to similar service before, as Lady Sophia Somerville, but I was literally fawned over as *Lady Winnsborough*. I had never been impressed with that sort of treatment, but had to admit it was rather fun now. Annie and Drew hosted a lovely, small dinner party in my honour during my stay, where I was able to catch-up with a few old friends, and we also attended a new play that had recently opened, *'Blackbirds'*, at the Adelphi Theater.

After a week away, I was rather glad to return to *Winnsborough Hall*, ready to talk with my husband about my pregnancy. We had been married two months at that point, and I knew that it was time to inform Owen that he was to be a father. It was undoubtedly going to be the biggest shock of his life, which was not surprising considering the circumstances. Upon my return home, Owen and I sat in front of the fireplace in the drawing room at *Winnsborough Hall*. I began a conversation about my visit to London. I'd been there the entire week. We chatted about inconsequential matters, and I told him of various things I'd done during my trip. Then we discussed the upcoming coronation of Edward the Eighth, scheduled for 12 May, 1937. There was no question that the coming year would be one of grand festivities before the Coronation. We would be on the guest lists for many glittering events. When Owen finally paused in his discussion of the much-anticipated splendor surrounding the crowning of a new King, I seized the opportunity.

"Owen, dear, there's something I need to speak with you about, and it's extremely important," I began.

"What is it, Sophia?" he asked, looking at me as though he had only just realized that I was in the room. There seemed no point in mincing words. I had carried the secret for such a long time, and was delighted that the moment had finally arrived to unburden myself.

"I'm going to have a baby," I beamed.

Owen turned white and his voice shook. "What? You are what? What did you say, Sophia?"

"I said I'm…. Well, I mean, *we* are going to have a baby. You're going to be a father." I couldn't tell if he was pleased, angry, or perhaps a bit of both. He just sat there, looking like a bloodhound. "Owen. say something," I implored. He continued to sit in silence, shaking his head as if to clear it. "Owen. Please. Say something. Anything."

"I'm not certain what to say. Are you certain? I mean…. Have you seen a physician?"

"Well, yes, as a matter of fact, I have. I visited a very fine obstetrician while in London this past week. He confirmed it. There is absolutely no doubt, Owen."

"When…. How…. I suppose on our wedding night?"

"I suppose," I echoed. *As though there could have been any other time.*

"Well…. This is incredible. Just incredible. I daresay I'm bowled over." He stood and put another log on the dying fire.

"Are you pleased?" I asked.

"Yes…. Yes. It's just so unexpected."

"Well, I assumed you wanted children eventually. I know this wasn't planned, and that you said that we should wait until I was older, but truly Owen I'm very pleased."

"Yes, well…. Quite. That is the important thing, I should imagine. You will be the person to go through the birth of the baby. Naturally, I'm pleased at the thought of producing an heir."

"Or an heiress."

"Yes, I suppose that could be too," he responded, not altogether enthu-siastically. "When will this child be born?" He enquired.

"The doctor thought somewhere around the middle of October," I lied. I'd counted carefully and knew when the birth date would have been, if I had not already been pregnant four and a half months. I was planning the visit to Paris to see Edwina in mid-July, when Owen and everyone else would think I was pregnant six months. Edwina and I had every detail organized to perfection. "I shall go on my holiday to Paris in July, and be home in plenty of time to have the baby here at *Winnsborough Hall."*

"Will it be safe to travel, do you think?"

"Oh, dear, yes. This is 1936, after all! Women don't go into seclusion because they are expecting a child."

"Well, I'll leave all of that to you and your physician" he replied. "Feeling all right, are you?" He was finally starting to make comments that were more appropriate.

"I feel splendid. Very well."

"I'm glad.... I should feel beastly if I caused you to be ill."

"Don't be a *goose*. I am extremely happy to be having this baby. I want you to be happy too." I could not help but think of the reaction that I would have been receiving if I'd been telling the same news to Spence. I knew that there would have been kisses, hugs and exclamations of joy. "It will be such fun to re-decorate the nursery. I don't imagine there has been a baby here at *Winnsborough Hall* in a long while," I smiled.

"No, not since I was born. It will need refurbishing. I'll leave that up to you. Audrey will have my permission to draw whatever amount of funds are necessary to do it up properly."

"Thank you, Owen. That's very generous. I hope your parents will be pleased. Do you think so, Owen?"

"Oh, naturally. That is the entire purpose for marriage, of course. Especially in noble families. Parents always worry themselves sick over whether there will be an heir. I'm certain mine have. Yours too, undoubtedly."

"Well, if your parents have been worrying, then they can relax," I smiled. It wasn't easy to smile, since I was simmering inside. *That was certainly not the entire reason for marriage, as far as I was concerned.* I'd thought

Owen loved me, but now I began to think that an enormous mistake had been made. Perhaps his entire reason for marrying me had been to produce an heir. However, that made little sense to me either, since it was impossible to produce an heir, if one didn't plan on having sexual relations.

"Owen, I wish you would show a bit more joy at my news. This should be a splendidly happy moment."

"I'm sure I shall once I adjust to this news," he stated, in a rather mundane manner. "I'm just imagining how having a child will change our lifestyle. Of course, we shall have a nanny. I am not a great believer in parents being overly involved in their children's lives."

Conversely, I believed very strongly that parents should be *exceedingly* involved in a child's life. Nevertheless, I didn't argue with Owen. It was clear that fatherhood was not a role he relished with enthusiasm. I would deal with his preferences when the baby actually arrived. There was silence between us, and after a few moments he said, "Shall we go in to dinner?" as though nothing whatever had changed.

He maintained the same rather disinterested air throughout the summer, which was a bit puzzling to me. If anything, he seemed rather embarrassed by my condition. He would never put his hand on my abdomen to feel the baby kick or listen for the heartbeat. It hurt my feelings a bit when he stayed away from *Winnsborough Hall* practically all of the time, preferring to spend time in London. At times I even wondered if he had a mistress, since he certainly had no interest in me. While I had no interest in him physically, I knew that our relationship was simply not normal. Since it was my intent to spend the rest of my life with him, I sometimes became very anxious at the thought that we were destined to live more as brother and sister than husband and wife. I was only nineteen, and it perplexed me that he didn't seem to find me at all desirable. Eventually, I hoped to have other children as the years progressed, but saw scant chance of that to occur. I might have attributed his behaviour to my being pregnant, had there been any sign of sexual attraction *before* the announcement of my condition, but there had not been. I just did not know what to make of it, nor how to deal with it.

In May, we traveled to Scotland for Blake's marriage to Lady Susan Feemster, a Scottish girl he had met while on a business trip for *Somerville Ltd.* I suspected that they'd engaged in an extra-marital affaireee, but whatever the case, Blake was divorced from Elizabeth in short order. I felt dreadfully sorry to lose her as a sister-in-law. It goes without saying that my parents were delighted with Blake's choice for a second wife. The wedding reminded me of what I expect my own might have been, had I married the man I truly loved. Susan was resplendent in a white organza gown, and Blake seemed very happy. I was truly delighted for him, though I can't say that I was overly fond of Susan. She had a rather supercilious attitude, and gave off the impression that truthfulness was not her strong suit. I'd not spent a good deal of time around her, but she was quite 'full of herself', and prattled on about her supposed impressive heritage. I had already caught her in several lies about her lineage, as well as her education. Blake's two children by Elizabeth, Blake Jr., and Pippin, weren't present for the ceremony, which seemed somewhat odd to me. Later I learned that they had never even been told that the marriage was taking place. However, I *had* seen a change in my brother, and prayed it was lasting. Susan *was* attractive, in a tarty sort of way. She had enormous breasts, and was very blonde..... What we called in those days, 'bottle blonde.' Blake made quite rude jests about her firm, rounded 'bum', and I wondered if that wasn't the primary attraction for him. No matter. Mummy was at her best, since all of us children were properly married to suitable mates. I even speculated upon the possibility that the *rages* of my childhood might be past. If only memories could be erased so easily.

Blake and Susan left on a wedding trip to Italy. Owen and I returned to *Winnsborough Hall,* and the odd life that had become routine. Of course, I didn't speak of, nor give any indication to my family that our marriage was anything other than normal and happy. Everyone had been exceptionally pleased at the surprise announcement of my pregnancy. The last thing I wanted was any hint that we were living an exceedingly strange life. I was certain that my mother would blame me for the loveless union. We continued in such a manner, and I could not say that I was terribly unhappy.

I enjoyed having a home and discovered quite a knack for roses, as well as other garden flowers. I spent whole days working with the soil, feeling the warm sunshine on my skin, which never burned because of my olive coloring. It was delightful to be able to plan dinner menus each day with Mrs. Whittaker and it was pleasant to dress for dinner each evening in an enchanting gown, selected from the vast collection in my wardrobe. Owen and I often entertained other couples from the surrounding area. He was very generous with me. I had no complaints, but for the lack of a physical relationship …. And, the lack of love, which obviously, nothing could be done about.

Finally, on one of my monthly visits to the Obstetrician, I gathered my courage and asked if it was normal for my husband not to want physical relations. The doctor said that it wasn't unusual for a man to feel reluctant to perform sexual acts with a pregnant woman, and that most likely Owen was afraid of hurting the baby or me. He counseled me to be patient. I didn't tell him that there had only been *one* sexual encounter since our marriage, and that my husband didn't remember that single occurrence on our wedding night. I decided to hope that the doctor was correct, and not to say anything until after the baby's birth. I shall always wonder what might have happened if I'd stuck to my original plan, and waited until after the baby's birth to speak to Owen.

In July, I felt as though I'd reached a breaking point. Perhaps it had to do with hormones. I simply knew that something was definitely amiss. I needed to find out what it was. Owen was once again in London, and I was once again home alone. I would be leaving on my trip to Paris in just two weeks. I decided that I wanted to get things settled before I left. On impulse, I decided to surprise Owen at the flat on Sumner Street, where he was staying. If he was having an affaireee then I would deal with it. I didn't really care if he had a mistress, but felt that I had a right to know what I was facing, and what the future held.

I took the afternoon train to London, arriving about seven o'clock in the evening. I had no problem finding a taxi, and within a few moments was paying the driver, while the door attendant handled my overnight case. He knew who I was, so there was no need to ring the apartment to announce my arrival. I simply walked over to the lift, entered the number for our floor, ascended, and came to a halt in the black and white marble foyer of the apartment. In front of me stood the double doors leading into the parlor. When I opened the doors, I had no idea what to expect. There seemed nothing amiss. A small fire was burning in the marble fireplace and two half-empty snifters of brandy were on the tea table. It appeared that Owen had a visitor, but apparently they had left to dine. There was soft music playing on the wireless. For some reason, I felt shaky and all undone. However, I had perfectly prepared to put my plan into action, so in spite of my nervousness, I swiftly moved down the hallway which led to one of the three bedrooms. The master suite was at the end of the corridor, and I knew that Owen would be sleeping there. I chose the room closest to his, and settled myself in the sitting space overlooking Sumner Street. From that vantage I could see anyone who came or left the building. My patience was rewarded. For in less than three quarters of an hour I spied two figures emerging from a taxicab, and entering the building. All of my senses alerted when I heard the lift, followed by low laughter. Owen and his companion entered the flat. It was positively my husband's voice, and he was definitely not alone. I silently crept down the hallway, taking extreme caution not to make any sound that would alert them to my presence. The door to the parlor was partially open, and I could distinctly hear their conversation.

"Well, darling, I certainly enjoyed myself tonight, though it was beastly having to keep from touching you. There's the trouble with having dinner at elegant restaurants. They don't take kindly to overt affection," his companion's voice said.

"I know. I wanted you so badly all night; I thought I couldn't bear it," Owen laughed. Yes, dinner was lovely, but I'm awfully glad to be back here, where we can relax and enjoy one another."

"I was aware that you desired me, sweetheart."

Really? And what made you aware of it?"

"Darling, your trousers gave you away. I think the waiter must have noticed the *'bulge'.*"

Was this the man I was married to? My husband? He, who had never shown the slightest interest in anything of a sexual nature, was now bantering back and forth in a suggestive, risqué, manner. There was silence for a few moments, and it was obvious that they were embracing. I could hear movement on the sofa, and then the rustling of clothing.

"Ummmm…you taste delicious. I really am quite in love with you. I cannot bear the thought of seeing you so infrequently once that bloody baby comes. I don't see you enough as it is."

"I know. I know. We shall work something out. If you would only agree to my employing you at *Winnsborough Hall*, I could see you daily. Just think, every night we could be together. I would no longer have to make such frequent trips to London. It's going to become more and more difficult."

"But I would be sharing a house with your wife and baby, feeling second-rate. I couldn't take that, darling. Can't you just continue the trips to London after the baby comes?"

"I would like nothing better. However, my father is adamant that I spend more time at *Winnsborough Hall* once that little brat arrives. He feels that it's unfair for Sophia to be alone so much. Since my parents practically forced me to marry, I don't see why I should care at all whether Sophia is alone. On top of that, she obviously tricked me into this baby. I was so drunk. She took advantage of my condition."

"I know, darling," Owen's lover continued. "I know you would never purposely have chosen to have a child."

"Well, of course, that's the reason my parents wanted a marriage so badly. It seems to me that now I've done my duty, and am about to produce a bloody heir, they would leave me to my own devices. The problem is, they are absolutely *potty* over Sophia. It's getting harder and harder for me to keep our secret. I want to be with *you*. I want people to know about our love. I despise having to pretend to things I don't feel for Sophia. Moreover, I absolutely cannot bear the thought of making love to her. Yet, I suppose that eventually she will begin to whine and complain if I don't. Frankly, I'm surprised she hasn't already. It's a maddening dilemma."

I had heard enough. I entered the parlor and switched on the overhead lighting. Owen was lying naked on the sofa. Next to him was a very attractive, rather small, and extremely effeminate *young man*, also unclothed. I must admit that such a thing hadn't crossed my mind until I'd heard their voices.

"Hallo darling," I said, as though I'd come upon my husband at the breakfast table. My voice echoed in the silence. Both Owen and his lover were shocked and stunned. Owen's face turned ashen. Obviously, he had believed that he was alone with his friend. That was why they had chosen the flat over the more elaborate surroundings of an elegant hotel.

"Good God! Sophia! What in damnation, are you doing here? How did you get in?" Owen's voice had a frightened tone, as well as defensive. Still, he was clearly more embarrassed and wary than he was angry. He was trying to affect quite a manner of outrage, but the tremor in his tone gave away his fright.

"It might be more appropriate for me to ask what in damnation *you* are doing here, my dear husband," I replied. "As to how I got in....I am your *wife*, in case that has slipped your mind. I have a key. I didn't think you would mind putting me up for the night. It's obvious that I should have rung you."

"I .... I.... Didn't know you were planning a trip to London," Owen stammered. He pulled himself to an upright position, folding his hands in front of his private parts. But he was still unclothed. It had to be difficult for him to maintain composure, let alone attempt a show of outrage.

"Yes, I'm aware of that. It was rather spur-of-the moment." I didn't raise my voice or create a commotion. In fact, I was quite proud later that I behaved like a lady throughout the entire, ghastly scene. Perhaps that was because I felt so emotionally detached. There was nothing for Owen to say. The only thing he could not be certain about was how much I had overheard.

"What are you going to do?" he asked guardedly.

"Of course I'm extremely upset, Owen. I would suggest that we begin this conversation by ridding ourselves of the presence of this gentleman," I said, waving a hand in the direction of his companion. The young man sat trembling from fear, trying in vain to cover himself. The poor soul looked very eager to be as far away from Sumner Street, and even from Owen, as possible. Owen looked at him in an obvious attempt to express some sense of reassurance. He whispered that he would be in touch the next morning. The young man, whose name I never did learn, scurried away like a frightened rabbit. Zipping his trousers, and tucking in his shirttail, he disappeared into the lift. Later, when I related the ghastly scene to Edwina, ever after she referred to Owen's lover as '*Bulge*'. It was so like Edwina to see humour, even in such dreadful circumstances.

Owen and I were alone in the parlor. While I was deeply shocked, I also felt pity for him. He had quickly slipped into his trousers and shirt, and was attempting to regain a modicum of composure.

"You asked what I intend to do," I began. "Now I think we should discuss what *both of us* intend. It is clear that you don't love me…. That you are in love with another person. Under such circumstances, I cannot imagine that you would have any difficulty agreeing to an annulment. I believe it would be wise for me to pack my belongings and return to *Willow Grove* at once. I hope and pray that this shock doesn't affect my pregnancy. This baby means everything to me. Obviously, there can be no legal action until after the child is born. But, as soon as practical after the birth, I believe annulment proceedings should begin. You clearly married me under entirely false pretenses. I believe any Court of Law will see that this should end as swiftly as possible."

Owen sat on the sofa, listening carefully to my words. "I cannot imagine that you will have any difficulty admitting that you are the guilty party. I don't want to be divorced, and I don't imagine that you do. There is the possibility that one or both of us may want to marry again someday, and a divorce could be an impediment. I *am* concerned that both of our reputations be kept intact."

In truth, I was ashamed of my much-maligned tone of voice, but the situation called for outrage on my part. Once again, I was putting my acting abilities to work. I felt guilty making pretense of being such a wounded and wronged spouse. There was a good deal more to the picture than Owen realized. I felt overwhelmed at the chaotic morass of lies that had led us to such a place and time.'

"What of my family?" Owen asked.

"I have no desire to cause your family pain".

"Sophia, please. Please do not tell my family. It would kill them. I know you won't believe this, but I *do* love you. Not as I should, I know. Nevertheless, I do. I never wanted to hurt you."

"You said some quite nasty things to your friend before I intervened. Why did you marry me? You knew you could never be a proper husband."

"I'm dreadfully sorry that you overheard what I said. I certainly don't have any ill feelings toward you. My parents were hounding me to get married. It never ceased. You had always been their choice. I finally acquiesced. I suppose I hoped that marriage would make a difference." He was openly sobbing by then, and I began to weep as well. "I never wanted to be the way I am," he cried.'

I sank down on the sofa next to him. "Oh dear God, Owen. I cannot bear this pain for either of us. It appears that we both have endured parental ranting." I made a hasty decision and continued speaking. "I'm going to tell you the unbridled truth. Perhaps it will lessen the burden upon you."

He raised his swollen, reddened eyes to me, with a puzzled expression. "What unbridled truth, Sophia?"

"Owen, I haven't been truthful with you, either. First though, you must understand that I fully intended to be a good wife to you. I would have been faithful. I would have spent my life trying to make up for not being truthful. However, *I have* told lies. Dreadful lies. Owen, the baby I'm carrying is not yours."

He looked stunned. Not angry. Just shocked, and, I suspect, somewhat relieved.

"Not mine? Not my baby? Then whose? This is greatly confusing. Who? Who is the father, Sophia?"

"The father, Owen, is a wonderful man with whom I fell deeply in love last summer. His name isn't important. I wasn't able to marry him because my parents didn't approve. They felt he wasn't *good* enough for me. They threatened to ruin him if I went against their wishes. I was desperate when I learned I was pregnant. I wanted to keep the baby. The only way to accomplish that seemed to be to get married, rather quickly. You were there. I needed a husband. Moreover, just like your parents, *mine* had berated me endlessly about marrying you. It appears that neither of us was honest with the other. I can say that I do care for you, Owen. I've grown very fond of you, but I'm not *in love* with you. I shall never love anyone again the way I loved…. Still love…. My baby's father. I'm sorry, Owen. Sorry for the both of us." I felt tears welling in my eyes.

"Oh Sophia, what a muddle we've made of our lives." He brushed tears from his own eyes. "What are we to do? I don't blame you. I quite understand how being desperate can drive one to do things that aren't ethical. Not moral. Sometimes there doesn't seem to be much choice, does there?" Owen held his head down, and ran his hand through his blonde hair.

"No, I suppose not," I replied. "But, as is always the case, one lie leads to another, and another, and another until suddenly one doesn't know which way to turn. That's where we find ourselves now."

"Are you serious about wanting an annulment? Perhaps we could continue on in this vein, since we both have needs that are met though the marriage?"

I must admit that I was tempted. It would have solved so many difficulties. But I knew I couldn't go on living a lie. I was ready to have the truth known, and did not really care anymore what people thought. That included my parents. The only person whom I did not want to know the entire truth was Spence.

"No, Owen. That won't do. It was one thing when we were both playing a role, not knowing the truth that the other was hiding. I don't intend to be difficult. I shall be glad to tell a Solicitor that I'm equally at fault. I don't know if specific details will be called for, but I know that anything we say will be treated confidentially. There isn't any reason for your parents to know the truth. "

He raised his head, and looked at me with a wretched expression. "We both married as a cover to satisfy our family's badgering about marriage. In my case, I also needed to stop tongues from wagging as I approached my forties, unmarried. In your case, you had a child to consider. What do you want to do about the baby? Surely you don't want to admit that the child won't be a Winnsborough?"

"I don't know, Owen. I honestly don't care for myself. Truly I don't. However, my baby should not have to suffer because of my foolish choices.

You know the ramifications of producing a baby that society would label a 'bastard'. I cannot bear the thought that this child should suffer because of my idiocy. The baby is my most important consideration. I shall do anything to protect this tiny life."

"I have no desire to see that happen. I'll be happy to give the baby my name," he said, in a matter of fact manner. "Perhaps that will make up a bit for not telling you the truth about my sexual preference."

I was stunned. "Owen, how can you possibly say that? How could you want to do so, knowing full well that this child is not yours?"

"It's really quite simple, Sophia. I'm a homosexual male. I don't want to have a sexual relationship with a female or another sham marriage. I cannot live this way either. Yet, I *do* want an heir. I am the last in the Winnsborough line. My parents want that more than anything."

"But, my child would inherit from you…. I don't feel comfortable about that."

"How is that different than if I adopted a child? In addition, isn't that what would be best for the baby? He or she would have the best of everything, always….Would carry a fine name…..Would be well-respected."

"Owen, I feel as though I would be *selling* my child."

"No, no. I don't mean to sound that way. Surely, the baby would have the same advantages if raised a Somerville. However, I strongly suspect that you *have* enjoyed the independence from your family that marriage has brought, whether you've been happily married to *me* or not. Also, if society thinks that this baby is mine, there will be no questions about who the *true* father is?""

"That's true," I answered. I couldn't deny it. My mind was whirling so quickly. I finally wanted to do what was *right*. However, I wasn't at all certain what that was.

"What precisely are you suggesting, Owen?"

He sniffed, and wiped his nose on his sleeve. "I'm suggesting that we *do* go forth with an annulment after the child is born. I shall settle an appropriate amount of money upon you. You will never have to worry about being dependent upon your parents again. I shall give the child my name, with all rights and privileges. In return, I ask that you keep the truth about my sexual preference confidential between us. Sophia, I assume you know that homosexuality is a crime in England. If the truth were known, I could be arrested and even put to death."

"My God, Owen. Surely not. I didn't know that. I've always been led to believe that it is an illness of some sort."

"Yes, that's the prevailing opinion, but I have known that I was not interested in the opposite sex since I was very young. And, I never liked the traditional male pastimes, such as fox hunting, fly fishing, athletics of any sort. Actually I preferred quieter pursuits, like reading and playing card games. I don't think it's an illness, at all. I feel as though I am a woman trapped in a male body. I think that I began life this way. Certainly, no person would *choose* a lifestyle that was considered so loathsome. You understand that, don't you?"

"Yes, of course. But, I have never thought of a preference for the same sex as 'loathsome. I knew girls at school who were attracted to other girls, and they weren't loathsome. You know how well read I am….How much I adore history….. . I'm certain you're aware that as far back as *Alexander the Great*, there were known homosexuals. In ancient Greece it wasn't at all unusual. Some of the greatest artists and writers who have ever lived weren't heterosexual. Perhaps I'm different in that respect. I really don't know. But, of course, I would never have *purposely* entered into a marriage with you, had I known this. I'm sure that *you* can understand *that*. It just never crossed my mind, Owen."

"Certainly. I should never have married you. It wouldn't have crossed my mind either, if my parents had just left me alone."

"Owen, this is all past history. Now, we're at the point in time where we have to deal with what *is* reality, and I'm glad we've both been honest. We have to look forward, not backward, and I would never wish to place you in any sort of jeopardy. What grounds would you intend for the annulment?"

"Something innocuous. I'll place the guilt upon myself. I'll admit to marrying you under false pretenses. I'll say that your money was the motivating factor."

"Owen, nobody would believe that. If anything, your family has even more money than mine, and certainly as much *blue blood.*"

"I'll think of something. I need to refresh myself about the grounds that the Church of England allows for annulment. Couldn't we say that I lied to you about something? Anything but the fact that I'm a homosexual?"

I still felt a dreadful stab of guilt. It was bad enough that such a nightmare was unfolding. I hated the fact that Owen's parents might spend the rest of their lives thinking that a grandchild had been the result our ill-fated union. "I don't see how I could lie to your parents about the baby, Owen. That would be a cruel lie."

"Would it, Sophia? Is it better for them to know that they will never have a grandchild than to accept your child with joy? I understand what you're saying, but don't you think that it would be even worse to tell them that the baby they are so thrilled about is not any relation to them?"

"Perhaps we should think on this a bit more. It has been a dreadfully unsettling night. I think we both need to sleep, and then we can discuss this again with clearer heads," I answered.

"Sophia, please don't leave the flat. I shall go to my club. I don't want you traipsing about London at this hour. If you are going to return to *Winnsborough Hall*, I shall ring you. I swear I'll return within a few days. I want to see my Solicitor before I leave London. I shall figure a way to resolve this muddle. The important thing is that we agree that the marriage should end, and that we get on with our lives. "

"Yes, that's the important thing," I answered. "And, I *shall* stay here tonight. I'm exhausted, and need time to sort through this mess. But, I *shall* expect you at *Winnsborough Hall* by week's end."

He leaned down and kissed me lightly on the cheek. Strangely, I felt more comfortable with him than I ever had before. Perhaps that was because it was the first honest conversation we'd ever shared.

"Take care," he said. "I'll think on all of this. We'll speak again at *Winnsborough Hall.*" Then, without another word, Owen left me sitting in the parlor of the flat. I put my head down and sobbed, out of exhaustion, sadness and relief.

Chapter Nine

JULY 23, 1936
A WIDOW

I returned to *Winnsborough Hall* on the early morning train. Upon arrival, I rang Edwina and told her everything, including the truth about Owen's homosexuality. I felt a tad guilty when telling her, as I had just promised Owen that the subject would be treated confidentially. However, I was not about to lie to Edwina. I knew that I could trust her implicitly. It was not a great surprise to her anyway. In fact, she said that she'd rather suspected something of the sort. She asked if I wanted her to come over from Paris. I could see no reason for that, other than the obvious comfort that would result from not shouldering the burden alone. I knew that eventually when we were alone, I would explain everything further. I was just thankful that I had her.

Whatever I'd expected, it wasn't what I'd discovered in London. I was surprised that Edwina had thought such a thing. It was 1936, and those persons who had different sexual preferences weren't able to live openly, nor be honest about their desires. After the admission of his homosexuality, I finally comprehended Owen's behaviour and lack of sexual desire. I suppose I felt somewhat better knowing there was nothing I might have done to make him want me. It was difficult to muster up outrage at this eye-opener. After all, I hadn't been honest with him when we married. *Were his lies any worse than mine?* I knew that we would talk further, and was optimistic that we would find a solution. A myriad of thoughts ran through my mind as I tried to rearrange plans to adapt to the new situation. The fact that Owen knew when the baby was *due* certainly simplified everything. I would still have to go through the pretense of changing the date of birth, in order for both sets of parents to believe that the baby was Owen's. Nevertheless, if I didn't have to keep the *supposed* father from knowing the truth about when the baby was born, it would make the situation less complex.

Having revealed my secret to Owen, my other concern was how to tell my parents about the end of the marriage. I knew that they would be terribly upset, primarily because of the family name. It was likely that I would be the one at fault. Mummy, in particular, thought Owen was a perfectly splendid fellow. I kept repeating to myself that these things *did* happen in life, and that my parents were not babes in the wood. Nonetheless, I felt embarrassed for Owen, as well as myself. *How could I foolishly not have seen the truth? Why did society practice such ridiculous prejudices toward a group of people who were not harming anyone?* Surely, Owen and I could find another explanation. I sincerely believed that we could come up with a story that was not painful for everyone concerned.

However, three days later, all hope of such an outcome evaporated. I had just drunk a glass of warm milk, and was ready to retire for the night, when the telephone rang. It was authorities in London informing me that they had just pulled my husband's body from the Thames River. I was extremely calm on the telephone. Then, I hung up and fell to pieces. *What had possessed him to do such a thing? Why? We had discussed everything. We were ready to come to an amicable solution. Why? Why? Why?* I sank down on the settee by the telephone table, and tried to think. Mrs. Whittaker found me there a few moments later. I must have looked white as a sheet.

"Mum, are you all right? Is it the baby?"

"No, no, not that. But, something dreadful has happened. Lord Winnsborough has died. I must ring my parents and the Duke and Duchess. I shall need you to make certain the guest rooms are ready. I'm certain family will be arriving. I also think that we need to call the entire household together and tell them of this tragedy. Would you please ask Morris to come to me at once?"

"Yes, Mum. Of course," Mrs. Whittaker replied, tears welling in her eyes. "May I ask, Mum, what……. What happened?"

"He was found in the Thames, in London. I suspect he must have slipped and fallen. Perhaps he'd had a bit too much to drink," I lied. Mrs. Whittaker wiped her eyes on her apron, and I stood, putting my arms about her. "It will be all right. We shall get through this. I'm going to need your help, so please try to be strong."

"Yes, Mum, I will. It's what His Grace would want," she sniffed, as she headed out the doorway of the room to seek out Morris, and to set about preparing guest suites.

A few moments later, Morris appeared. Mrs. Whittaker hadn't told him what had happened, and had simply asked him to report to me in the drawing room. I told him what had taken place, and he was very stiff upper-lipped. Naturally, he was devastated, but it was not considered proper form to show any such emotion. He assured me that the entire household would be assembled in an hour, and that I could then make my announcement.

In the interim, I picked up the telephone and rang my parents. I stared out the window at the dreary rain. Thank goodness, Papa answered the telephone, as I certainly did not feel up to dealing with Mummy. My father listened quietly, and then said that he and Pamela would be at *Winnsborough Hall* as quickly as possible. I silently blessed him for not asking a myriad of questions. Owen's parents were next. I dreaded that call most, knowing it was going to devastate them. The butler at *Snow Hill*, answered. I asked for the Duke. I knew that it would be wiser to tell Owen's father, letting him tell Owen's mother. There was a brief wait, and then his voice came on the line.

"Your Grace, this is Sophia," I began.

"Well, Sophia, what a nice surprise," he responded.

"I have such dreadful, terrible news to give you," I said, as I began to weep.

"What is it, Sophia? Are you ill? Has something happened to the baby?"

"No. No. The baby is fine. I'm fine. But, Sir, Owen.... . Owen.... . Owen is dead." I had been standing by the telephone table, but I sank back down onto the settee.

"How can that be?" he asked, stunned. "Was there some sort of accident? Was he out riding without his hard hat?"

"No. He drowned in the Thames. Dear God, I cannot believe it."

"Do you mean to say that he drowned himself? Committed Suicide? My Lord, Sophia, is that what you're saying?"

"No…. . No one has said anything like that. The police in London called and told me that they dragged him from the Thames. They said nothing about suicide. They wanted to tell me where they were taking his body."

Where is he? Where, Sophia?"

"At the London morgue. He has to be officially identified, even though he was carrying identification."

"I suppose that's their routine," he responded, trying to gain control of himself." I'll take care of that, dear. You don't need that trauma."

"Thank you, so much. I appreciate that immensely," I sobbed.

"Sophia, what in the world happened, or do you know? Was he alone? Do you have any details at all?"

"Not many. I don't believe there was anyone with him. At least they didn't say. I suppose he could have been accosted and robbed and…. . And…. Murdered". *I did not even remotely suspect such a thing.* "On the other hand", I continued, "I don't know? Could he have somehow lost his footing? Might he have had too much to drink and slipped, you know?"

"I have never heard of anyone slipping and falling into the Thames. You say that he had his identification. That would have been in his wallet, which seems to rule out robbery. Moreover, even if that were the case, Sophia, it is summertime and the water should be quite a decent temperature. Owen was an excellent swimmer. Of course if he were drunk…. . Well…. . That would be another matter."

"Yes, "I replied, not knowing what else to say. There was silence for a moment. I continued to weep.

"Sophia, do you think he committed suicide? Tell me what you honestly think."

"I think it's a distinct possibility, Sir," I answered truthfully, though reluctantly.

"Do you have reasons for such suspicions?" He continued. "Was Owen distraught?"

I continued to sniffle. "Sir, I don't think he would want me to tell you," I murmured.

Sophia let me make this easier for you. The Duchess and I have suspected for quite some time that Owen is…. Was….. Homosexual. We have suspected it for years, but I suppose we hoped against hope that he would outgrow it, or that marriage would make a difference. I don't think it has. Do you believe that this has something to do with what has happened?"

"Yes….Yes," I wept. "I do. I had just learned the truth. ….Was in London two nights before, and surprised him at the flat with a young man. It finally explained many things to me. Our marriage has been most….. Strange. It hasn't been. ….Physical."

"Did the two of you have an argument that night? Was he terribly upset that you had learned the truth?"

"Of course he was upset, but no, actually, we didn't have an argument. Unbelievably, we had a civil discussion. We were going to work it out …. . Not, of course, continue with the marriage, but obtain an annulment. There were not bitter feelings. He was to see his solicitor in London the next day, and then he planned to come home, where we were going to talk it all out." I felt better telling Owen's father the truth. At least a portion of the truth.

"I see. Owen, of course, did not think that his mother and I knew about his homosexuality. I should have told him…. . Should have told you. We thought that when you became pregnant it proved that he could change….. . wanted to change. Nevertheless, from the moment he told us of the baby, it was clear that we had made a terrible mistake, encouraging him to marry. It was apparent that he was not acting as a husband who was happily expecting his first child. He spent far too much time away from *Winnsborough Hall,* for no good reason. Now, he's gone and we've ruined your life too."

"No, that isn't the case. I don't know what caused Owen to wind up in the Thames, and I may never know. However, I'm certain that it was not because I was going to have a baby. Yes, he was terribly worried that you would find out the truth, and I assured him that I would never say anything, so he couldn't have been worried about that."

"Well, I'm dreadfully sorry Sophia…… dreadfully. We loved him dearly. Of course, I'm shocked. His mother will be broken-hearted. However, there are things that I must do. Can't fall apart, you know," he stated with firm resolve, while clearing his throat. "You and I shall speak again at *Winnsborough Hall.* I must tell the Duchess. I need to make some calls, and a dashed trip to London. I assume you wish to follow family tradition, and have him interred in the cemetery on the grounds?"

"Yes……Yes, of course. Whatever you think would be appropriate. In addition, do you think we should notify the newspapers before there is too much speculation?"

"Yes, jolly good. I shall do that at once. Now, you just hold fast, until we are able to get there. Is your family coming?"

"Yes, I've spoken to them, and they are," I answered.

"Good show, then. Brace up, Sophia. Owen would expect you to be strong. We shall be there by tomorrow at the latest." I felt better when we rang off

Next, I rang Edwina again, and told her. There was a long pause after I said the words "Owen is dead."

"Dead? Dear God, Sophia, you didn't kill him, did you?" she asked, sounding very serious.

"Oh Edwina, don't be absurd. Of course not. It is just horrible and I am all undone. My parents will be here shortly, and I need your advice and strength."

"I'm sorry, Sophia. I didn't *really* think that. What in the world *did* happen?"

"He was found dead, floating in the Thames. Drowned."

"How gruesome. You weren't in London too?"

I told her exactly what had transpired since my last call to her. When I finished, Edwina said that she quite suspected he had committed suicide.

"But why? We talked it all out. I was not going to expose him. In addition, as it turns out, his parents have suspected this for some time anyway. His homosexuality was not a shock to them. Of course, he didn't know that."

"Nice of them to tell you," Edwina sarcastically replied.

"I know, Edwina, but, let's face it; I wasn't exactly honest with them, either. My greatest dilemma now is whether to let them go on believing that my baby is Owen's. That is what he wanted me to do. He said that he wanted the baby to have his name, but I don't feel right about it."

"I would do what Owen wanted you to do. If you renounce him as the father, it will open an entire assortment of problems. Everyone will want to know who the father is, and Owen's estate could be protested by his parents, if, as you say, he left provisions for you and the baby."

"But it seems so cruel to let his parents think that they have a grand-child..... A part of Owen when they don't. And, I truly don't care about the money, Edwina."

"Either way it's cruel, but Owen chose to do this, Sophia. I can't tell you what to do..... Only what I would do, but then we both know that you've always had more integrity than I," she laughed. In spite of the situation, I couldn't help but return the laughter.

"Oh Edwina, whatever would I do without you?" I said. "At every crisis in my life, you've been there for me."

"Don't worry; I'm sure my time will come, dear heart. In the meantime, don't you need me to come home and help now? Then, you can return to Paris with me, under the guise of needing to get away."

"That *does* sound wise, Edwina. I would so like to have you here for support. You know that Mummy is going to be beside herself when she learns this."

"Oh yes, I know that for certain. Perhaps the Catholic doctor would have been preferable after all," Edwina said snidely. "I'll throw a few things in a bag and be on the train tonight. Expect me tomorrow, Luv."

I felt much better after having spoken to her, knowing that I would have her presence during the coming days. Edwina was the only person who knew the entire truth. It helped enormously to know that I would be able to speak honestly now and again. After I concluded my conversation with her, the household was assembled, per my request of Morris. They were all gathered in the main Drawing Room, and I broke the tragic news. There were audible gasps, and many tears. Owen had truly been beloved by those who worked for him. The fact that he was seldom present at *Winnsborough Hall* made the work load much easier for the household staff, as well. I had grown fond of many of them too, and knew that my days at *Winnsborough Hall* would be numbered, although I didn't make them aware of that. I imagined that his parents would decide to resume their life at their beloved former home. I, in turn, would undoubtedly return to *Willow Grove Abbey*, at least for a time, after the baby was born. As I spoke to each servant, I remembered the day when Owen and I arrived home from our wedding trip, and all of them had queued up outside in the front of the mansion, to welcome their new mistress. We had only been married two weeks then.

When the Duke and Duchess arrived, Owen Sr. took me into the library, and we had a long chat. I decided, after much deliberation, to be honest about everything. I could only imagine that things would become more and more complex as time went by, if I continued with lies and deception. I believed that the Duke would honour my wishes not to tell Papa and Mummy. I was correct. His acceptance of the truth exceeded my expectations. He only chastised himself for haranguing Owen to marry. He also showed great annoyance toward my parents for not allowing me to marry the man I loved.

"We parents can be such damned fools," he said.

I couldn't argue. "I wish I could be open and honest about this to my *own* parents, but I'm afraid for my baby. I hope you understand. I assume you intend to tell the Duchess?"

"I am obliged to, Sophia. This is not the sort of secret one keeps from one's wife. Believe me, she will understand. There will be no problem. She will not tell your parents, if that is your wish. Whatever provisions Owen has chosen to make for you and the child will be perfectly acceptable to us, and if they are not adequate, then I shall make certain that things are made right." The Duke and Duchess were such dear people, and it was tragic that life had dealt them such a harsh blow. I embraced my father-in-law, and thanked him, giving assurances that I was not interested in any gain from Owen's death.

The next few days are still a blur. Everyone arrived at *Winnsborough Hall*, and the staff took over, making them comfortable. I was thrilled to see Edwina when she arrived, assigning her a guest suite adjoining my own rooms. Mummy was surprisingly well behaved, in spite of the fact that Papa chose to tell her the entire truth. I was amazed that knowing of Owen's homosexuality, my mother did not launch into a gargantuan rage. Instead, her primary concern was making certain that everyone understood that wedding gifts were *my* property. I could only smile ruefully when I heard her say that. I also imagined that she could have been feeling a tad guilty, since she had been so adamant that I marry Owen in the first place,

The funeral service was at the small village church near *Winnsborough Hall,* and the burial took place at the family cemetery on the grounds of the home. It was a dreary July morning, with pelting rain, and a dark, threatening sky. Many, many people attended, from all of the surrounding villages. Edwina arrived the evening before, and it was comforting to have someone there who knew all of the details of the past year. She looked stunning. Despite the solemnity of the occasion, I couldn't help but marvel at her continued blossoming since the move to Paris. She wore a very *au courant* black ensemble, and her platinum hair shone even more lustrously than usual on that grey day. She had let it grow longer, into a sleek pageboy again, and was wearing more cosmetics. Her lipstick was a very bright red, and rouge heightened her cheekbones. It made her appear more sophisticated…more Parisian.

I was vastly relieved when the last of the guests departed, and I was able to kick off my shoes, remove my beastly black veil, and have a lie-down.

Although most of the world thought I was nearly six months pregnant, in reality, I was nearly eight, and my feet had begun to swell when I stood for long periods. I was not terribly large, so it was easy to maintain the subterfuge. The Solicitor from London, who had been present during the ceremony, requested that Owen's parents, the servants, other family members and I meet him in the library for a reading of the Will. I dreaded it, but was relieved that my mother was not going to be present. The meeting held no interest for Mummy. She was busily wrapping china. We all filed in, and took seats across from the large desk that had been the Duke's since time immemorial. The Solicitor, a Mr. Seymour Smyth, made certain that we were comfortably seated before he began. He cleared his throat, and started to read the Will. Most of it was standard form about 'just payment of debts' and 'sound mind'. I let my mind drift. It was hard to think that any of it concerned me. There were numerous bequests to loyal employees and others to Godchildren and friends, as well as to charities. Then, I heard my name. That forced my mind back to matters at hand. It was written in very technical terms, but the upshot was that Owen had left me the flat on Sumner Street in London, as well as a sizable sum of money…more money than I'd ever dreamed of having. I was stunned. He also left me any items of joint ownership that I wished to have from *Winnsborough Hall*, and his *Pierce Arrow* automobile. There was a separate Trust established for the baby, of which I was to be custodian. He had been excessively generous. It was obvious that he *had* visited the Solicitor the day of his death, as he had said he was going to do. I realized that because of his largesse, I would never again have to return to *Willow Grove Abbey* and the despotism of my mother or the passivity of my father, unless I wished to. Tears streamed down my face, leaving shiny snail's tracks, as I thought of Owen's generous spirit, and of a life that had been wasted. He had been a good man, and a kind one. It seemed unfair that he couldn't simply have lived his life in the sunshine. Later, when I told Edwina of Owen's generosity, she irreverently said that he owed it to me. I did not agree with her, but we never argued about differing points of view.

As everyone was filing out of the library, Mr. Smyth asked me to remain a moment. I was puzzled, but of course sat back down, and waited until the room had emptied. "Now then, Lady Sophia, I have a letter here which your deceased husband asked me to give to you, if anything were to happen to him. I have no idea of the contents, and do not need to know them. Of course, when I take into account the date upon which I saw him, and when the provisions for the present Will were made, it is clear that he anticipated his impending demise. But, there is no reason for that to concern me." He handed me an envelope, which was clearly Owen's personal stationery, engraved with the Winnsborough Coat of Arms. Mr. Smyth busied himself lighting a cigar, and told me to make myself comfortable. I was to read the letter and if I had questions, Mr. Smyth would try to answer them. I opened the envelope and took out two sheets of the same engraved stationery. It was clearly in Owen's hand.

Dearest Sophia,

I know that this is not what you expected. I fully intended to come back to Winnsborough Hall, and work out our problems. I walked about London for hours, thinking and thinking .It finally became clear what I must do. I spent the following two days putting my affairees in order. I hope you can forgive me, and pray that God will forgive me my sins.

You will wonder why I chose this path. Please be assured that it had nothing to do with fear that you would make a laughing stock of me. You are a good, kind, loving lady, and I wish I could have been the sort of man who deserved you. When I thought it all through, it became clear that I have never been happy. The chances of that occurring in the future are remote. I was raised to behave in a moral manner, and the life I prefer is not considered moral. Whether married or not, I would have to go on living my life in the shadows. I am very tired of lies and games.

On the other hand, I believe that you can and will find happiness. It will be easier to do so as a widow, than as someone whom people whisper about in corners, wondering why your marriage was annulled. You will now be free to go on with your life, and your child will not have to deal with the confusion of having an absentee father. Eventually the child would learn the truth about me, and it could well destroy him or her. If I believed I could be happy, and that you and the child could be equally so, then perhaps I might have reached a different decision. However, I see nothing ahead for me. Please do not feel sorry for me, and don't blame yourself. I have had a wonderful, full life, in spite of its short duration. I have provided for you, and made you independent of your family. I want you to be happy, and my fondest hope is that someday you will be able to be with the man you truly love.

With Great Respect and Love,

Owen

Chapter Ten

August–September, 1936

Paris

There was no question that Owen's letter changed my life. While he told me not to feel guilty, nor to feel sorry for him, it was impossible not to do so. The letter haunted me, and I would have given anything if he had only come to me and talked, as he had pledged. However, in time I had to face the realisation that Owen made a choice, and I had no right to question it. He was not delusional. Thus, if what he chose to do was his true desire, then I had to accept it.

The next few months were surreal. Shortly after the funeral, Edwina and I arrived in Paris. I was dressed in a black linen suit, with a flowing coat, my dark curls tied back with a black and white taffeta ribbon. Edwina was wearing the latest rage….. A pajama ensemble, with broad silk pants and matching shirt, falling loosely to her hips. Of course, the look was marvelous on her. We gathered our luggage and hailed a taxicab.

"I was surprised that your Mum didn't give you more difficulty about this trip," Edwina said, as she rolled down the window to let in some fresh air. It was a very warm summer day. Even though we had been together over the past several days, we'd scarcely had time to talk at length, because of the funeral, and my responsibilities as a hostess. I was exhausted and had slept on the train and ferry trip from London to Dover, Dover to Calais and on to Paris, so this was the first real opportunity we'd had to chat.

"I think both of my parents were just glad to see me go. Mummy shows remarkably little interest in the baby. Didn't you notice that?"

"Yes, now that you mention it, I did. Strange. I thought she'd simply want to take over."

"She just doesn't seem very involved."

"Perhaps that's for the best. Certainly in terms of her letting you out of her sight."

"No question about that. The next few weeks will be the hardest part of this whole scheme. I don't think my parents will make any fuss until September nears, but then they're very likely to grow perturbed when I tell them I'm not returning to England yet."

"We'll deal with that later," Edwina smiled. "I know this isn't easy for you," she said, with a sympathetic expression, patting me on the knee.

"I'm *terrified* at the prospect of the birth," I admitted. "I'll be so relieved when this is all over."

"I'll be here with you every moment, I promise," Edwina said, hugging me again. I felt so fortunate to have her beside me during such a time. I certainly could *never* have told my parents the truth, and I could never have gone through all of the maneuvering involved in such a scheme, by myself. As it was, I'd been uncomfortable being around my parents ever since announcement of the pregnancy. Mummy was not a fool, and she tended to be quite distrustful and vigilant. *Yes, paranoid.* It would not have surprised me if she had reached the conclusion that I had wanted to marry Owen so quickly because I was pregnant, which was, of course, the truth. Although it had not been discussed, I knew Mummy had never forgotten that only a short while before my marriage to Owen, I'd been desperately in love with Spence. I knew that it was possible my mother might suspect that Spence was the father of my baby. Of course, knowing the truth about Owen, it was equally possible that Mummy blamed the poor baby for having what she would term a '*queer*' for a father. That would also explain why she had little interest in her prospective grandchild.

Our car crept its way through the congested streets of Paris. Finally we arrived in the Ninth Arrondissment, with its narrow streets, lined with tiny galleries, selling 'about to be discovered' art works. The area had preserved its nineteenth century architecture, charming courtyards and timeless Parisian air. That was where Edwina lived, as well as where her school was located, on Rue de la Rouchfouchuod. In rather short order we pulled up in front of a building, which had clearly known better days. Still, the neighborhood possessed a certain charm. It was populated with young people, living the quintessential Bohemian existence. We extricated ourselves from the taxicab, and while I paid the driver, Edwina took the baggage, continuing toward the entrance to the building on Rue Blues. The flat was on the fifth floor, with a lift. The building dated to the 1840's. Once we reached her floor, we were required to walk down a narrow corridor. Edwina maneuvered round, and produced a key ring, which opened the door to the flat.

Upon entering, I couldn't help but be amazed at how Edwina's unique, creative style had brought elegance, and panache to what would normally have been a rather cramped, small living space. There was a living room, two bedrooms and a bath. A balcony overlooked a Louis Philippe style courtyard. The floors were wooden and there was even a small, marble fireplace. It was decorated in black and white, which was unusual, and perhaps daring at that time. There was a feeling of clean, geometric precision in the furnishings, and the only objects' d'art were crystal. The entire effect was opposite of the Queen Anne and Chippendale that surrounded me at *Willow Grove Abbey* and *Winnsborough Hall*. While it was not what I might have chosen, I rather liked it. It *fit* Edwina's personality. There were glass shelves on one wall, with mirrors behind them, creating an illusion of space. In front of those stood a chrome and glass teacart, where a silver ice bucket rested, along with a cocktail shaker and a variety of crystal glasses.

"I'm going to have a martini. I'll fix you up with a smashing glass of milk, my dearest friend," Edwina exclaimed, with a laugh. She moved to the bar and began to pour gin into a glass.

"How kind," I laughed, making a face. "But, never mind, I'm only teasing. My baby is much more important to me than a cocktail. I've never had a martini though. Once the baby comes, I really must try one. Remember when we had our first pink gin together?"

Edwina arched an eyebrow and made a little moue with her mouth. "Such a long time ago, Lady Sophia. I do not believe it was *my* first, but I may have led you to believe so. I'm no longer that *'jeune fille'*."

I laughed again. "Martinis are all the rage in America, aren't they?"

"And on the Continent. Everyone in Paris is drinking them. I don't want to boast, but I've been told that I concoct the world's perfect martini," she pronounced, airily.

"Ah…After the baby comes, we'll toast its arrival," I smiled.

Edwina poured a glass of milk from a bottle in the small icebox, and we sat in her tiny parlor. It was good to be away from all of the stress and upheaval of the past weeks. "A boy or a girl?" she asked.

"It doesn't matter, as long as the baby is healthy."

"You do have an actual due date, don't you?"

"Yes …. Oh, yes. August second. It isn't that far away, Edwina. Have you made arrangements for me to see a physician here?"

"Yes, and he's supposed to be very fine. Several people recommended him. He speaks English too. You have an appointment in the morning."

"Perfect. I shall feel better when I've established myself with a good medical person. This is all a bit overwhelming." I placed my hand on my enlarged mid-section.

"Of course it is, Sophia. Nevertheless, everything is prepared. Come, I need to show you where the baby will sleep." She reached out her hand, helping me to stand. We walked into one of the three small bedrooms. In the corner was a beautiful bassinet, festooned in white lace. It was exquisite. I was extremely touched that Edwina had gone to such trouble. There was a small table piled with nappies, lotion, and every other necessity one collects in preparation for a birth.

"Edwina! You've thought of everything! How wonderful you are. And so organized."

"I knew there wouldn't be a lot of time after you arrived. I wanted you to be able to relax as much as possible. After all, this has been the most beastly year for you, in so many ways. I do so want this to be a happy event, in spite of the circumstances."

I was so choked up, I could scarcely speak, so I simply reached out, put my arms round Edwina, and buried my head on her shoulder. It didn't take much to make me weep in those days.

During the following weeks, I familiarized myself with Edwina's neighborhood. I did not venture far away from the flat, as I tired easily and had no desire to socialize. Edwina was free from classes for the summer months, so we lazed about, sleeping late and taking our meals at small neighborhood bistros, such as *Au Petit Cafe*, and *La Petite Invalides*. I visited the physician, Dr. Dupree once a week, and felt I was in excellent hands. He pronounced that I was in fine health, and predicted an easy birth. My parents rang once weekly, and I reported upon my lovely, restful visit, keeping them unaware of what was really happening. On 5 August, as Edwina and I were sitting in *Au Petit Cafe* finishing a lovely meal, I felt cramping in my lower abdomen. There was no doubt what it was.

"Oh…Oh my Gosh, Edwina. I think I'm having a labor pain," I cried.

"Oh…. Oh Goodness, Sophia. Shall I fetch an ambulance?"

"No, no. However, I think we had better return to your flat. I shall ring Dr. Dupree and tell him what's happening. He'll tell me what to do."

We immediately returned to Edwina's flat, and rang the doctor. Thank goodness, there was not a long delay reaching him. He was very calm, telling me that he wanted me to time the contractions, and to ring him back when my water broke. Edwina told me to have a lie down, which I gladly did. We proceeded to wait. It seemed an interminable length of time, although in reality it was not. Less than two hours later, I felt a rush of wetness, and immediately rang Dr. Dupree again. That time he told me to take a taxicab and meet him at hospital. I had prepared a small travel bag ahead of time, so we were able to depart immediately. There was no difficulty finding a taxi, and while I was anxious to get there, it didn't seem an unduly long ride. By then the pains were much more intense, and I was growing fearful.

Edwina was a Godsend. She stayed very serene and that, in turn, helped me to keep sane. She checked me in, and the nurse took me by chair to the maternity floor. I was settled into a room, dressed in a white, sterile gown, and the doctor came in. He examined me and said that it would still be awhile. I wanted it to be over at once. However, no matter what I wanted, the baby had its own ideas.

Finally, at three o'clock on the morning of 6 August 1936, I gave birth to a healthy five pound, three ounce baby girl…. . '*Isabella Chloe*

Winnsborough'. From the moment of her arrival, she was the absolute light of my life. She had dark hair and Spence's gorgeous blue eyes, along with a tiny rosebud mouth. How I wished that I might have shared the joy of her birth with him. When the nurse brought her to me, she was wearing a tiny white baby gown, and her hair had been swirled into a minuscule curl. All of the nurses were raving about how long her lashes were. I reached down and touched her little hand, and Isabella grasped hold of my finger. At that instant, I lost my heart.

Chapter Eleven

LATE NOVEMBER, 1936
A CHANCE MEETING

Edwina was just as potty over Isabella as I was. Neither of us had much experience with babies, and we exclaimed repeatedly about her extremely tiny size. We examined her from head to toe, remarking about her extraordinary beauty. All of the trials and tribulations of the past months were inconsequential. Isabella was such a miracle, and each time I gazed at her beautiful face, I marveled at the fact that one weekend of passion had resulted in such a perfect little creature.

When we brought her home to Rue Blues, Edwina set about spoiling her unmercifully. Within the first three weeks of her life, she purchased eight tiny dresses, and then set about designing more. I bounced back very quickly, and by September on warm afternoons we took the baby for long walks in a lovely pram that I'd purchased. We would go to the Bois de Boulogne, sit on a bench eating ice cream, and enjoy sounds of children playing. Other mothers were there with their babies, and we compared them to Isabella. Of course, not a single one was as pretty.

No one in England knew of Isabella's arrival. I wanted to shout from the rooftops that God had blessed me with such a beautiful cherub. I continued to speak to my parents weekly, and as I'd feared, they began to badger me about returning home to have the baby. Finally, Edwina and I put into motion the final chapter of our campaign to ensure that Isabella be shielded from any truths that might cause her future pain. In early September, Edwina rang my parents, telling them that I was in hospital with labor, and that it appeared the baby was going to be born prematurely.

Twenty-four hours later, Edwina rang them back and said that Isabella had been born, on 16 September. Of course, Mummy was not at all pleased that her grandchild had been born in France, and proceeded to give Edwina a piece of her mind for not having insisted that I return to England sooner. Edwina handled the entire situation deftly, and by the time I spoke to Mummy she had calmed down considerably. I told her that everything was fine…that I intended to recuperate, allow the baby to gain strength, and then return to England. My family immediately sent two dozen pink roses. Edwina convinced them to send them to the flat, saying that I was sharing a room at hospital, and that it would be rude to put on such a show in front of a stranger. Mummy was infuriated that I was sharing a room, but no matter. That was only a minor blip.

At first, Mummy and Papa were determined to travel to Paris at once to bring Isabella and me home. I was horrified at the mere thought that they might actually do so, and begged them to not even consider such a thing. I told them that everything was wonderful; that I felt splendid, and that all I needed was a bit of time for recuperation before I could travel back to England. In addition, I explained that the baby was definitely too tiny to travel yet. Edwina told them that it would upset me greatly if they were to make such a trip. The protestations finally seemed to satisfy every-one concerned. I breathed a tremendous sigh of relief. There had been such a large number of instances over the past nine months when I'd not been at all certain that everything would work out so well. It had required a great deal of strength not to fall apart at so many junctures. Now, it was over. I had the baby, and Isabella was all that I had imagined she might be.

I lingered on through the fall, and into the start of winter. I'd had no intention of staying such a long time. It irritated my parents no end, but I was always prepared with an answer for them. One of the best was that I had no husband to return to, and that it would depress me greatly to return to England. They didn't argue about that. In mid-November, I finally began to make plans for my return. Isabella was healthy and robust, but still very small, so I was not overly concerned that anyone would think she looked older than she should. This meant that I still had a couple of weeks left in Paris. Classes had resumed at the end of September, and Edwina had more or less returned to her normal life. I'd not let Isabella out of my sight since her birth, but finally I grew to trust the girl who lived in the flat above Edwina.... .A ballet dancer of Russian extraction, named Kira Brunkow. She was a lovely girl, but I had difficulty communicating with her. Edwina had become quite fluent in French, and she and Kira were able to converse in that language. Edwina, in turn, acted as an interpreter for me. Kira was completely enamored of Isabella and continually begged me to allow her to baby sit. Finally, one night Edwina and I decided that it was time to re-join the world. Kira offered to sit with Isabella, and I knew that I could trust her. Therefore, I relented and Edwina and I planned an outing. I fed Isabella and placed her in her bassinet. I probably still wouldn't have left, had the baby not been sleeping soundly. By that time, I had weaned Isabella from nursing, and she was perfectly content with her bottle.

Edwina mixed two of her famous martinis, and I finally sampled one. It was divine. We were feeling marvelously giddy by the time we crawled into a taxicab, and headed to Edwina's favorite haunt, *Les Deux Magots*, that well-known café on the corner of Place St. Germain-des-Pres. Seated at a corner table, we settled into the comfortable camaraderie that can only be associated with close friends. Being together again, just the two of us, was nice. We were free, and able to talk at length without the interruption of a baby's grizzle. We felt young. It had been a long, long time since I'd felt young, though I was still only nineteen. It was obvious that Edwina was very much at home at *Deux Magots*. The waiters knew her by name and several patrons acknowledged her upon our arrival. This was usual, for Edwina had a way of drawing people to her. It was her *joie de vivre*..... An indefinable charisma that set her apart from others. We ordered a bottle of Pouly Fuisse, and began to chatter and gossip, just as we had at *Ashwick Park*.

"Sophia, how do you feel now about your decision not to tell Spence about Isabella?" Edwina asked me. "Now that she's actually here, I've wondered if you've had misgivings, but haven't wanted to bring up anything that might upset you."

"I made the correct decision, Edwina. Not that I don't still think about him. On the contrary, especially since Isabella's birth, I think about him constantly."

"Do you think you'll ever really get over him?"

"Oh, I'll move on. I guess I already have, really. I cannot imagine falling in love that way again. Everything about Spence was my absolute ideal. If someone had given me paper and pen, and asked me to list all of the traits I was searching for in a mate, my completed list would describe him.

"Well, I must admit that he *is* an attractive man. Of course, I never knew him well, but he seemedsmashing. I would probably change only one thing about him, if he were to match *my* ideal man."

What would that be?" I asked. "Spence is so perfect in my eyes, I cannot imagine changing anything about him."

"He'd be older. I prefer older men."

"But, Spence *is* older. He's seven years older than I am."

"No. I mean quite considerably older. Perhaps twenty or even thirty years older.

"I've never known that about you, Edwina. You have never been *involved* with someone that much older. Or *have* you?" I grinned.

"No, not really. I've had crushes. You know what I mean. Sometimes there are impediments that cause difficulties."

"What sort of impediments?"

Edwina looked down at the table and her eyes darted to the right and left. I'd never felt that she kept secrets from me, but the thought crossed my mind just for an instant.

"Oh just things," Edwina answered, twirling her glass in her fingers.

"An older man will sometimes think that a younger woman shouldn't become involved with him. Sometimes he will be too set in his ways.... Or married.... Or something."

I laughed. "Edwina. If I know you, there isn't *any* impediment that you couldn't overcome."

Well, there really *are* some," she smiled.

Next, we moved to the topic of the moment. People in cafes all across the globe were obsessed with England's new King Edward the Eighth, and his paramour Mrs. Simpson. It was fast becoming the most astonishing story. Apparently, the couple had embarked on an eastern Mediterranean cruise aboard a yacht called the *Lady Nahlin*. Photographs of the King, who looked like a young boy with his untidy golden locks and a tanned, bare chest, flanked by the notorious American divorcee, were appearing daily in newspapers and magazines worldwide. I was astonished at how little I actually knew of the story. Paris whispered appalling and titillating tales, and Edwina was the perfect person from whom to learn all of the details. Because she had recently returned to classes at *Esmod International,* she was up-to-date on all of the gossip. She described how, at a remote spot near Dubrovnik, visited on the cruise, the local militia had been summoned to handle the crowds. I was enthralled by the story. In fact, I was so wrapped up in Edwina's recitation that I was completely unaware that we were no longer a party of two. A third person was standing next to my chair. Edwina stopped speaking and her face drained of color.

"Edwina, what in heaven's name is the matter? You look as though you've seen a ghost," I remarked, while turning my head in the direction toward which Edwina's eyes were riveted. Then, my heart felt as if it were doing a somersault, and I literally gasped for air. As difficult as it was to believe, *there stood Spence.* I was speechless.

He spoke first. "Well, Sophia and Edwina. I thought that looked like you, and yet it seemed inconceivable that it could be. Don't the damnedest things happen? I'm in Paris for a two-day medical meeting. I don't normally attend these fool things. Now, who should I meet but the two of you. This is incredible."

"Yes…incredible," I echoed.

"Unbelievable," repeated Edwina.

"Serendipity?" Spence stated.

"What?" Edwina asked.

"Serendipity. That's what this impromptu meeting is. It refers to something that's meant to be…predestined…fate. I believe we spoke of this once, Sophia," he answered, looking at me with those flinty, direct blue eyes.

"That's an interesting word," Edwina said. "I'll have to remember it." She smiled and played with a lock of her hair.

"How are you Spence?" I asked, almost frightened to look at him, for fear my feelings would show.

"I'm quite well, Sophia. And you? You're looking well." He smiled again, and my chest tightened. He turned to Edwina. "I assume you're still in school here, or have you finished by now?" he asked.

"This is my second year, Spence. I've just begun my second year." Edwina was repeating herself, which meant that she was as nervous as I was …. Something rare for my always-poised friend.

He turned back to face me. "And what brings you to Paris, Sophia?"

"I've been visiting Edwina….. On holiday….. Visiting…. Sightseeing." I sounded a fool. My thoughts were all a jumble, and I could not seem to regain my composure. I wanted to say to him that I was in Paris because I'd just borne his child ….. A beautiful, little girl named Isabella, who had his eyes and his mouth.

Edwina finally found her manners, but I wasn't at all certain how I felt about what happened next.

"Won't you join us, Spence?" she asked.

"Thank you, Edwina. Yes, I'd be delighted. I've a train to catch in a matter of hours, but I should love to buy you ladies a glass of wine." With that, he pulled out an empty chair at the table, and seated himself to my left. I was terribly conscious of his presence, and of the warmth spreading across my face. He ordered another bottle of wine, and I looked helplessly across the table at Edwina. The waiter brought the wine and poured it. Spence settled back into his chair.

"I heard that you'd married, Sophia," he commented, in an offhanded fashion.

"Yes, Last January, actually." My insides were churning.

"To Lord Owen Winnsborough, is it?"

"Yes….. Owen and I knew each other from childhood."

"I believe I read the announcement in the *Times*. So then, is your husband accompanying you on this visit?"

"No," I answered, almost too quickly. "No…. This is just a 'girls' get together."

Edwina interrupted at that juncture. "Sophia was widowed in July, Spence."

"Oh…. Oh, I *am* sorry, Sophia. I didn't know…. Hadn't heard."

"I figured everyone in Great Britain had heard," I replied, looking down at the table

"Was it an accident? He was so young," Spence asked.

Yes…. Well, we aren't certain. He was found in the Thames."

"My God..... I had no idea. What an awful turn of events."

"Yes," answered Edwina. That's why Sophia is here with me in Paris. Just getting away from all of the sadness and upset." I flashed her a look and kicked her under the table. I didn't want Spence to know of Isabella's birth. Thank goodness, she wisely understood, and said nothing more.

"Are you living in London, then?" he asked me.

"No, I'm at *Winnsborough Hall,* the family country estate. However, I do have a flat in London, and that's where I eventually plan to settle."

"I see. And when will you be returning to England?"

"I'll probably leave here sometime late this month or early in December. I suspect I shall spend the holidays at *Willow Grove Abbey* with my family, and then move up to London after the New Year. How are you doing Spence? I gather you're still practicing medicine in Twigbury?" I tried to smile, as I sipped my glass of wine, but it wasn't easy.

"Yes, still in Twigbury," he answered.

"Have you married?" Edwina asked, as I looked aghast.

"No Edwina, but I *am* engaged,"

When he gave that answer, I actually felt a pain shoot through my heart. I'd known I would hear those words one day.... It was just so dreadfully hard to hear them from Spence's own lips, and at such a time in my own life. I wanted to scream out that I still loved him.... That we shared a beautiful daughter, and that I'd made a beastly mistake. Nevertheless, none of that was possible. He had fallen in love with someone else, and that other woman would be his wife. I thought back to the night at the *Royal,* and the words he had spoken about what a special love we shared. How quickly that seemed to have been forgotten. It was exactly what I'd known would happen when I turned down his proposal of marriage, shattering both of our dreams. It was entirely my fault.

"I'm happy for you Spence," I lied. Edwina looked at me in amazement. She was surprised that I could utter the words. So was I.

"Thank you, Sophia." He didn't seem to radiate joy.

"So .... Who is the lucky woman, Spence? Do I know her? Or does Sophia?"

"I believe so, Edwina. I know Sophia is acquainted with her, and I should imagine you are, as well, since she too is an *Ashwick Park* girl. Her name is *Charlotte. Charlotte Ross* In fact, you were there when I met her, Sophia. That night at the *Royal Thames Room*, when she was with another fellow…. I believe William Young was his name."

I nearly fell off my chair. *Charlotte Ross? That manipulative little creature who clearly wanted to crawl all over Spence when we met at the Royal! How on Earth could he have become involved with her? Let alone engaged to her?*

Edwina responded before she'd had time to think clearly.

"Oh dear. I know Charlotte from *Ashwick Park*. She always wanted to be an actress. I didn't know her well, but I cannot say I liked much of what I did know.

"That was undoubtedly schoolgirl competitiveness. She's really a charming person. And she *is* an actress. I saw her last week at the Shakespearean festival. She was marvelous. I'm really quite proud of her."

"Spence, from what I know of Charlotte, I cannot imagine her wanting to settle down in Twigbury as a doctor's wife," I blurted out.

"We've discussed it, and she believes she'll be happy. We have a lot in common. She's of Irish heritage and is Catholic." There was complete silence after that remark. He clearly did not mean it to be vengeful, nor even to bring back painful memories. Rather, it was obvious that Spence had learned that commonalities in background and religion were important factors when one contemplated marriage. It was clear that he had decided not to become involved with another woman from a noble linage. I was profoundly hurt by his statement, only because I'd so foolishly led him to believe that any of those things truly mattered to me. My head was reeling as I thought of Charlotte Ross and Spence together.

"How did you and Charlotte end up together?" I asked. My curiosity was simply too great. I had to know. He had seemed rather disgusted with her that night at the *Royal*.

"I suppose you might say it was another *serendipitous* moment," he answered. "We ran into one another in all of places, Twigbury. She was apparently intrigued enough at my comments about how charming and quaint I found the village, and decided she had to see for herself. She drove over from London, on a Saturday, and I ran into her sitting by the Twig River where it babbles along near my office."

I was one hundred percent positive that Charlotte had planned the entire thing, so that she would 'accidently' run into Spence. She must have researched where his office was located, and then perched herself nearby, knowing full well she would eventually see him. It was amazing to me that he wasn't able to see how conniving she was. However, I didn't say what I was thinking, and just told him what a tremendous coincidence it seemed to be.

There was silence for a moment, as we three listened to the street sounds of Paris on an autumn evening.

Spence cleared his throat. "So..... .I couldn't help but overhear your discussion about our fair-haired King and his American woman. I'm sorry I interrupted. I gather that the relationship is causing quite a stir here on the Continent. All of Paris seems much more knowledgeable about it than those of us who rarely leave England." He was making a gargantuan effort to move to another topic. I appreciated his doing so. I felt a bit embarrassed that he'd overheard our silly, schoolgirl's conversation, but he didn't seem to be speaking in a condescending tone. "I've heard nothing but gossip about this cruise since my arrival in Paris," he continued. "There's actually talk of the King wanting to marry the lady. This is even being discussed in Court circles."

"How extraordinary," I remarked. "I don't believe that the English people will ever stand for a twice-divorced woman on the throne."

"That seems unlikely, doesn't it?" Spence answered, as I made every effort not to concentrate upon how handsome he was.

"Her divorce proceedings are soon to be heard at Ipswich, and Prime Minister Baldwin is even beginning to show concern. At least, that's what I'm hearing," Edwina added.

"Good Lord! Has Edward simply gone bonkers?" I exclaimed.

"It seems so," Spence replied, smiling. As he continued to speak of the Royal scandal, I allowed my mind to wander to lingering memories of the summer of 1935. How different my life was then. How much in love I'd been. That hadn't changed, of course. I still loved him, and knew nothing would ever alter those feelings. However, I knew that I could never say those words to him again. I could still feel his lips upon mine, as well as the warmth of his caresses. Indeed, I had a miracle child because of our love. I had to force myself back to the reality of the moment.

The conversation had turned to the alarming rumors of aggression and military build-up in Germany, master-minded and under the control of an odd little man, with wild eyes and a stubby moustache, named Adolph Hitler. Spence grew very serious when he brought up Herr Hitler's name. It was exceedingly clear that he was *not* joking when he said that such an evil man could alter the face of Europe, and perhaps the course of all of our lives. His words were chilling. I knew nothing of war or its horrors, other than stories I'd heard of the Great War of 1914, which was a year from its end when I was born in 1917. Papa served in that conflict, as had England's new King, when he was still a young Prince of Wales. There were members of the Somerville family who were lost in that conflict, and as a result, Mummy hated Germans out of all proportion to reason. Her elder brother, whom she had worshipped, died while defending the Maginot Line. There were horror stories about poison gas and indescribable destruction. *Willow Grove Abbey* had been commandeered by the military to serve as a hospital facility. I remembered those tales, and thought that surely such a thing couldn't happen again.

The wine bottle was empty and the crowd at *Les Deux Magots* had thinned, while a melancholy mood settled over the three of us. I was weary and it was late when Spence wisely chose to bring the evening to an end. "This has been a smashing reunion, ladies. I'm still shocked at having run into you here."

"Serendipity," Edwina repeated, smiling.

"Yes…. . Serendipity," he echoed. "Nevertheless, if I'm to make my train, I'd best be on my way. Edwina, you look marvelous, as always. Don't break too many hearts," he laughed, as he placed an arm about her and gave her a brotherly kiss on the forehead.

Edwina, in turn, wished him "Godspeed," and discreetly excused herself, saying that she needed to speak to some friends at another table. Spence turned to me, and his expression became very serious.

"Sophia, you're even more beautiful than I remembered. I'm so very sorry for your loss, and I truly wish you happiness …. . It's what you deserve." He took both of my hands in his, and it was all I could do to keep from trembling. "I've thought of you so often," he said.

My God. Does he still love me too? Then why is he marrying someone else? "I've thought of you too," I answered, almost afraid to speak.

"We shared something special, didn't we Sophia? I don't suppose one ever totally forgets that sort of thing. I surely haven't. However, one moves on," he said, as he looked directly into my eyes. I was mesmerized. I might have been back on the terrace of *Willow Grove Abbey*, or in that tiny cottage in Twigbury. I knew that I needed to respond to his words..... To let him know that I, too, still remembered. However, there was Isabella, and too many lies, and it was all so impossible. Tears were stinging my eyes. I was glad that it wasn't daylight.

"It's been wonderful to see you, Spence," I replied. I so hope that you will be happy in your marriage." There was a huge lump in my throat.

"If you should ever visit Twigbury, do look me up," he smiled. "And, if you should ever need a friend, please never hesitate to ring me."

"But, Spence, when do you plan on marrying?" I asked. *How could he be suggesting that I ring him up in Twigbury if he was to be married?*

"Not soon, Sophia. I'm being cautious this time round," he said, with a wry smile. A breeze blew up, ruffling his hair, and I remembered the day we picnicked in Hyde Park, when he'd kissed me for the first time. I could not think of anything to say. Or couldn't say the words that I *was* thinking.

"When you come up to London, I should love to see you," I finally managed, after finding my voice. I knew that I should not have said it. Certainly, no good could come of our seeing one another again. But, it was so difficult to say goodbye to him believing that I might never see him again. Parting seemed to be a bit easier if I pretended that we *would* see one other again in the future.

"I'll look forward to that," he replied. Then, he astounded me. He leaned down and put his lips on mine. His arms followed, wrapping around me in a warm, snug embrace. This was no brotherly kiss. I returned it with the same show of love that I always had. I wondered how Charlotte Ross would have felt about it, and did not care one whit. I was glad that Charlotte wasn't there, and was certain that I would remember that night in Paris for the rest of my life. And I have.

Later, on the ride home, Edwina was uncharacteristically quiet. She was certainly aware that I was thinking about Spence, and feeling anguish over the news of his engagement. Suddenly, she broke the silence.

"He doesn't love her."

"Who are you referring to? What do you mean? Are you speaking of the King and Mrs. Simpson?"

"No. No. The King is *potty* over *her*. I'm speaking of Spence. He doesn't love that obnoxious Charlotte Ross," she stated, in a supremely confident voice.

"How can you be so certain? After all, he's asked her to marry him."

"I don't care a mite whether he's proposed to her. One only has to look into his eyes when he speaks to you. He still loves *you*, Sophia."

"Oh, Edwina. I thought that for a moment too, but I think we're both seeing things that aren't there. I'd like to believe that's the truth, although I'm not altogether certain what difference it would make. Too much has happened. Still, I'd like to think that he does still love me. It truly makes me sick to think of him with Charlotte Ross. Remember? Neither of us could bear her at school? The night Spence is referring to is the night I broke it off with him. Before that took place, Charlotte and her beau were there in the *Thames Room,* and Spence asked them to join us for a drink. She practically slobbered all over Spence. She was obviously very taken with him..... Said he looked like a professional polo player, or a dashing RAF pilot."

"She doesn't seem his type. Not in the least," said Edwina.

"She's very taken with herself," I responded.

Lapsing into silence again, I pondered what I might do if that was truly the case. Things were vastly different. I was no longer dependent upon my parents. *What would happen if Spence still loved me?* Then, I remembered Isabella. It was impossible. Completely impossible. Spence didn't know that I had a child, and I was certain that he would be furious if he knew the truth. I allowed myself to speculate upon a renewed romance, but quickly reached the conclusion that such a dream was futile, and could only lead to more heartache. Much later that night, after tucking Isabella into her bassinet, following a particularly long session of rocking and lullabies, I had an odd feeling of uneasiness. I felt that something was about to happen that would tear my secure, comfortable world to shreds. I forced the feeling away, but didn't forget it. I was to remember that strange premonition many times in the coming years.

My remaining time in Paris flew by, and that sense of impending doom didn't return. Edwina and I were able to get out a bit more. Taking Isabella with us only added to the joy of our excursions. I finally met Edwina's German neighbor, Dieter Schoen, who seemed to have improved his command of the English language. I wondered how much his wishing to know Edwina better had influenced his language lessons. I didn't particularly care for him, but supposed that had more to do with my innate dislike and fear of Germans, which my mother had instilled. In truth, there was no reason to dislike him, In fact, he made every effort to be charming. He was typical of his race…practically white haired, and blue-eyed, with fair skin. He was tall, and erect, and looked as though he might click his heels together at any moment.

We visited the couture fashion houses, where I had a marvelous time. It seemed forever since I'd been able to purchase a frock with a waistline. Since I'd fully regained my figure, I indulged myself with several purchases. I ordered a stunning white *Worth* evening gown, a chic midnight blue cocktail dress of velvet and taffeta, designed by *Hattie Carnegie*, and a black and white satin -backed crepe *Chanel* suit. I knew that the coming season promised to be a festive one, with Edward the Eighth's coronation planned for May. I suspected that there would be several formal occasions and although I was still in mourning, I would be able to attend some of the functions. As a special 'thank you' to Edwina, I also told her to select any frock she desired. She chose an incredible Chanel gown, in pale butter -crème. We were young ladies on a spree that pretty day in Paris.

Chapter Twelve

2 December, 1936
Past the White Cliffs of Dover

Finally my self-imposed exile ended. I'd stayed much longer than planned. On 2 December, I bundled Isabella into a white, hand crocheted dress, which Edwina had purchased from an elderly nun outside of the Sacre Coeur, and said goodbye to my *shining friend*. There were tears, and promises to see one another in only a few weeks' time, when Edwina would be in London after her Christmas holiday visit to Bury St. Edmunds. I felt sad saying goodbye to her, and to Paris, but was also eager to be going home again.

Traveling with a small baby was a bit more difficult than I had imagined. It seemed that such a long time had passed since Edwina and I had left *Winnsborough Hall* in July. My entire life had changed so dramatically in such a short span. I'd arrived in France, anxious and frightened, still a young girl in so many ways. Sometime during that period, I'd left my girlhood behind. I was returning to England a more serious, mature woman, and a mother. Together, Isabella and I boarded the ferry at Calais, which would carry us across the English Channel, past the White Cliffs of Dover, and home to England.

As we settled into the First Class lounge, I picked up a copy of the *Daily Mirror*, which someone had discarded on the seat next to mine. I was astonished to see an enormous studio portrait of Mrs. Simpson gracing the front page. The British newspapers had finally broken their silence, and there was no doubt that all Hell was about to break loose. However, I had far greater things to occupy my mind, as Isabella was grizzling. I devoted my attention to making her comfortable, and settling her down. When we reached Dover, I was happy to board the train to London for the final leg of the journey. As I settled into my compartment, with Isabella snuggled securely in a basket next to me, I felt joyous to be back in Britain. I'd no idea what the future held, but I knew that I had weathered a great storm…. More than one great storm….. And that whatever lay ahead would be faced with a changed attitude and stronger self-confidence.

The train rolled swiftly through the English countryside as I glimpsed signs designating small villages. I adored the names of English hamlets… Wivenhoe…Frittenden…Appledore…Each had a special charm. No matter where I traveled, I always felt that England was a very distinct place. I thought about the things I wanted to teach Isabella someday about her ancestry…. About *Willow Grove Abbey*, and the Somervilles. For the first time it struck me that my daughter would undoubtedly want to know about her paternal heritage as well. That meant I'd have to recite the Winnsborough linage, as though it were Isabella's own. I was terribly glad that I wouldn't be faced with such a task until many years henceforth. I'd already learned that the best way to cope with life's twists and turns was to face them one day at a time. There was simply no point in worrying about things that might happen years or decades ahead, or perhaps never.

The train arrived at Victoria Station in the afternoon and I was exhausted. Rather than continue on to *Willow Grove* that evening, I decided to spend the night at the flat on Sumner Street, completing the trip to *Bedminster-with-Hartcliffe* the next day. I hadn't been back to Sumner Street since the nightmare encounter with Owen and his friend. I decided that it was time for me to face old ghosts. I was fortunate to find a porter on the train platform upon arrival. He retrieved the baggage and placed Isabella and me into an unoccupied taxicab. Within fifteen minutes, I found myself exiting the lift which deposited us into the foyer of the flat on Sumner Street. The door assistant helped with my bags, I tipped him appropriately, sighing with relief at my final arrival. I immediately set about undressing Isabella, and putting her into a nightsack. There was no baby cot in the flat, but there was the little basket she had travelled in. It served as an excellent substitute for a cot, cradle or bassinet. I took a soft quilt from the linen press in the hallway, folded it several times and placed it in the basket. With that in place, I gently settled Isabella into the center, where she seemed right at home. She quickly fell asleep. After I was certain that she was resting well and safely, I slipped out of my travelling clothes and into my own nightdress. Then, I padded to the parlor barefooted, and poured a small glass of Sherry from the decanter on the sideboard. Returning to the bedroom, I slipped between the smooth linen sheets. Placing the pillow against the headboard, I propped myself in the bed.

As I lay there relaxing, my thoughts turned again to Spence and our serendipitous meeting in Paris. *And the kiss.* Glancing over at the sleeping form of the child Spence and I had created, my eyes traced the outline of Isabella's face. I could see Spence's likeness. Isabella had only been in the world four months, yet I could scarcely remember an existence before her. She was the embodiment of everything that Spence and I had shared. A tangible reminder of our love. I wondered where he was on that December night. *Was he with Charlotte? Did he find her beautiful, and did she love him as much as I had? As much as I still did. More importantly, did he love her?* It was hard to imagine that he did, but over a year had passed since we had spoken our last true words of passion. I knew that I'd be a fool if I thought that Spence wouldn't or couldn't love again. I so clearly remembered our conversations about soulmates and wondered if he still believed that there was only one person for every other. My eyes began to grow heavy as I tried to recreate the conversation at *Les Deux Magots.* More than the conversation, I recalled the exact way he'd looked. Closing my eyes, I remembered the feel of his lips when he'd kissed me goodbye. As I continued with my memories, I drifted into a restless sleep, dreaming that Spence and I were about to be married. However, when I started my walk down the aisle, his face turned into that of a bloodhound. I awoke with a start, trembling. After checking on Isabella, I switched off the light, and finally fell asleep.

I awakened the next morning when Isabella began to grizzle for her breakfast. I checked her nappy, and indeed it needed changing. After taking care of that, I retrieved a bottle from the icebox, where I had placed it the night before. I warmed it, and brought Isabella into the large bed with me, holding her closely. She took her bottle with no fuss. *Gosh, I was getting very experienced at taking care of a baby.* I basked in the joy of motherhood. Sunlight splashed upon the crème colored duvet, creating tiny designs, as well as on the pale blue walls. It was a bright, day. I could hear birds singing in the square outside of my window. Isabella seemed very much at peace. She looked up at me with her wide blue eyes, which held a look of such innocence that they astonished me. I never stopped being overwhelmed at the realisation that this little creature's total existence was under my protection. I held her future in my hands. Reaching down, I put my finger into her hand, and she grasped it. I scrutinised her tiny face and vowed that nothing would ever hurt her, so long as it was in my power to prevent it. With a sigh, I placed her back into the basket, after she had finished the bottle, and I'd put her on my shoulder to burp her. Then, I rang my parents at *Willow Grove,* telling them that Isabella and I were in London. I spoke with Papa, who sounded delighted. He insisted that Joseph be sent with the car to retrieve us. I wasn't about to argue, as I'd already had my fill of travelling with a baby. Consequently, on 4 December, 1936, at almost precisely noon, my parents welcomed me and their new granddaughter to *Willow Grove Abbey.* They were more effusive than they had ever been in the past. Papa was particularly unrestrained when he first set eyes upon Isabella. Even Mummy was positively rhapsodic as she took the baby into her arms. I didn't remember her ever being so demonstrative. I've wondered since if Mummy was that enthusiastic about her own children when they were tiny. I believe she loved the fact that babies are so helpless, and therefore, she could impose total control. The first words out of her mouth were more characteristic of the mother I knew.

"Sophia, fortune has shined upon us. Thank the Good Lord. Isabella does not have one feature of Owen's. There is not a Winnsborough trait." I certainly could not deny that. "She is pure Somerville, through and through. Just look at that hair and those eyes. She is the spitting image of your father." I laughed to myself, as there was no question that Isabella was the absolute mirror image of Spence. However, it was my good fortune that Mummy didn't see the resemblance. I couldn't wait to tell Edwina about my mother's first reaction to seeing Isabella.

"No," I agreed, she doesn't look at all like Owen. She is a Somerville, except that she has your blue eyes, Mummy." I knew that would please her enormously. It was a fine way of explaining Spence's lovely blue eyes on the baby's face. Mummy and I entered the drawing room, still chattering about the baby. I was most relieved that neither of my parents seemed to think that she looked older than she should have. She *was* still small for her age and it would have been very difficult, if not impossible, for anyone to discern whether she was three or four months old. I planned to stay at *Willow Grove Abbey* until after the holidays. Then Isabella and I would settle in London. I was still very new at caring for a baby, and it was nice to have the support of others…. Even Mummy. I intended to take things slowly, as I'd never lived alone, and even with a nanny for Isabella, it was going to be a new experience. I'd placed the duty of hiring a nanny into my parents' hands, while still in Paris, and had to admit that they'd done a superb job. Her name was Martha Hunt. She was twenty-four years old, quite near my own age, had excellent credentials from a Swiss school, and was originally from a small hamlet north of London. She immediately adored Isabella. The nursery at *Willow Grove* had been refurbished, and a small sitting alcove next to that room made over as a sleeping chamber for Martha. It was very nice to be back in my old bedchamber, and to have Isabella securely ensconced in the lovely nursery where I'd slept and played as a child. I placed her into the cot, and then allowed Martha to look after her while I changed clothes. After that, I gave Isabella a quick kiss, and proceeded downstairs for luncheon.

The house was buzzing with the latest news of the Royal state of affairees, which at that point, had reached crisis proportions. As I seated myself at the table, Mummy was relating what she'd only just learned from Wallis Simpson's' confidante, '*Foxy Gwynne*.' Apparently the King, as far back as November 25, had provided the Prime Minister with the means to bring the situation to a head. He had suggested that he marry Wallis in what is known as a morganatic union. In such a marriage, Mrs. Simpson could be Edward's wife with certain restrictions. Most importantly, any children they might have would be denied the rights of succession. Mrs. Simpson was apparently in favor of that course. Edward asked that the proposition be brought before the Cabinet, but he also wanted to seek the advice of the various Prime Ministers of the Dominions. Telegrams were sent to the Dominions, requesting that a choice be made. The choice offered was between the King marrying Mrs. Simpson, upon which she would be recognized as Queen, or a morganatic marriage. Alternatively, the King would abdicate in favor of his brother, the Duke of York.

Nearly imprisoned at *Cumberland Terrace,* her home, which was also a Royal residence, with her Aunt Bessie, there were strangers hanging about on the pavement outside, and Mrs. Simpson apparently began to feel like a trapped animal. She received cruel, threatening letters. A rumor began that her house would be bombed. The King begged her to go to the seclusion of *Fort Belvedere*, his personal home. She did so, but as soon as she arrived, near a state of nervous breakdown, she began to feel that it was not at all the lovely home she'd once thought. She announced to her friend, Foxy Gwynne, that everything was terribly wrong. She felt she needed to leave England. She asked for a small get-a-way, to give everyone time to calm down. On the very day that I sat eating luncheon with my family, Baldwin confirmed that the Cabinet and the Dominions were unanimous in their rejection of the morganatic marriage. Having left the King with no alternative but to abdicate, Baldwin begged him to reconsider. His arguments fell upon deaf ears. Edwina had been right. The King was indeed *potty* over Wallis Simpson.

Later the evening of December the second, Edward returned to the *Fort* in a somber mood. He apparently explained to Mrs. Simpson what the outcome was for them. She decided to place a call to her dear friends Herman and Katherine Rogers who lived in Cannes, France, in a gorgeous villa named Lou Viei. After reaching them, she begged for a safe haven. She left her little dog, *Slipper,* behind as she traveled toward Newhaven, the cross-channel ferry, and the start of a horrendous journey, brought about by the scandal her romance with the King had created. When I heard that news, I felt a lump in my own throat. England was in the midst of one of the greatest Constitutional crisis in her history. Yet, I was weeping for a woman I had never met. The primary reason for my sadness was the fact that Mrs. Simpson had been forced to leave her beloved pet behind when she fled.

All of England waited expectantly to see what the outcome would be. Between the fourth and seventh of December, almost nothing else was talked about. The newspapers and wireless became the focus of all attention, as did Mummy's frequent telephone calls to and from Foxy Gwynne.

Of course, Papa had information from the official, governmental point of view, but only Foxy was able to provide the intimate details of conversations between the King and Mrs. Simpson. Although during that time the King's friends, including Foxy and Emerald Cunard, made rigorous efforts to turn the situation round, all was lost. The King made up his mind to abdicate on Sunday afternoon, December Fifth. England seemed to agree with Baldwin, his Cabinet, and the Dominions. Members of Parliament, including my father, listened to their Constituencies and then returned to London. They said that the people were against morganatic marriage, Edward the Eighth, and especially Mrs. Simpson.

Edward signed the Instrument of Abdication. Less than twenty-four hours later, he gave a heart-wrenching speech from Windsor Castle. My father returned from London exhausted, and the entire family congregated at *Willow Grove*. I wept, and everyone was caught up in the drama of the moment. My heart was with the newly abdicated King. On the other hand, Papa said that the King was a bloody fool, and my brothers naturally, concurred. The consensus among the men in my family was that the King was a weakling. Nevertheless, I tended to believe that it took immense courage and honour to renounce a Kingdom for the love of a woman. My perspective upon an individual sacrificing everything for the sake of love was to change greatly over the next decade. When I looked back years later, I was astounded by how much the various points of view held by my family in December, 1936, had altered.

After that momentous occasion, everything changed, but nothing was really very different. My life continued in 1937 much as it had before. There was, of course, my devotion to Isabella, as well as my enrolment at The University of London. On 12 May, 1937, Edward's brother, the Duke of York, was proclaimed King, as George the Sixth, and England set about restoring the dignity of the monarchy. George and his wife, Elizabeth, were definitely a much better choice. They gave off a very nice picture of domesticity, with their two little girls, Elizabeth and Margaret Rose. They seemed to be quite a normal family, especially for royalty. From a personal point of view, I thought them an immensely nice family, but I still had special feelings for the departed King Edward, thereafter known as the Duke of Windsor. On Thursday, 3 June, 1937, the Duke married Wallis Simpson at the Chateau de Cande at Tours, France. With their union, she became the Duchess of Windsor. The Royals never did accept her. They absolutely refused to allow her to use the title *Her Royal Highness*, which I thought was beastly.

Synonymous with Edward the Eighth's abdication, times became bleaker. It also seemed that life at *Willow Grove* became more problematic. I couldn't put my finger upon a precise incident....It was just a vague impression. There was tension and a feeling of unrest in the household. With the unsettled conditions in Europe, Papa became more involved with business on the Continent. There was concern that if Hitler didn't curb his aggressive tendencies, catastrophe could be waiting in the wings. Besides patriotic concerns, there was concern for my father from a business perspective. Most clients for the goods produced in the Somerville Mills were on the Continent, particularly France, Spain, Belgium, Italy and Germany, as well as the more eastern European nations, such as Austria and Poland. Therefore, it was no wonder that he was traveling more. He even made a trip to America during that period. He *did* ask Mummy to accompany him on several journeys, but she always refused, saying that both rail and steamship travel made her ill. Instead, she complained bitterly and often about his prolonged absences.

Isabella was thriving in the country air, and enjoying a comfortable, good life. I knew that I should set about making plans for the move to London. I'd already postponed our resettlement way beyond the initial deadline. But our circumstances were such that I wasn't terribly motivated to do so. So, instead of the move I'd planned for January, summer, my favorite season at *Willow Grove* arrived, and I was still there. I lay in my bedchamber in the mornings, with the windows cranked open, allowing me to sniff the newly mown grass, and the sweet, fragrant climbing roses whose tendrils reached to the second story. I played with Isabella, took long walks about the grounds, and read books under my favorite old knurled tree. I wasn't quite ready to leave.

Of course, Mummy aggravated me at times with her selfishness, nonstop complaining and biting criticisms, yet I couldn't help but feel sorry for her. She had so much and enjoyed it so little. I wished my mother could be joyful about her many blessings. Of course, her life was not perfect, but I didn't know anyone whose was. There was certainly nothing I could say or do to alter her moods, but when fall came, my college classes saved me from the unhappiness at *Willow Grove*. I made the decision to return to school, and began by enrolling in three classes a week at The University of London. This required a somewhat lengthy commute back and forth to London by train. While that was a bit tiring, I considered it only a temporary inconvenience, because I *did* eventually plan a move to Sumner Street. Isabella was well looked after, and deeply loved by Martha, so I did not feel guilty leaving her for those hours. I adored *Willow Grove*, and the magnificent countryside surrounding it, but also felt very isolated. I longed for the companionship of persons closer to my own age and University provided that outlet.

I was mad about my course work, and the academic environment, taking a special fancy to research. As time progressed, I became a protégé to one of my favorite professors, Dr. Richard Hausfater, who was the Chair of the Department of Psychology. A staunchly serious intellectual, with an impeccable reputation in academic circles, he was universally revered among his students and colleagues. I felt honoured and quite humbled when he took an interest in my educational endeavors. Time moved along swiftly, and I began to act as an Assistant in his office, correcting papers and performing mundane chores, which freed him to do important research. Sometimes he asked me to assist in his research, and those were my favorite assignments. I seemed to have a knack for finding just the proper citation needed, and spent untold happy hours sitting on the floor of the library, reading journal articles and dusty manuscripts.

The summer of 1937 turned to autumn, and Isabella was about to celebrate her first birthday. It was hard to believe that a year had gone by since I'd left for Paris and the impending birth of my child. Edwina was coming to England, and the Duke and Duchess of Winnsborough were driving down for the day. I hadn't seen them in ever so long. Not since Isabella and I had visited *Winnsborough Hall* the previous winter. It was kind of them to make the effort to come for Isabella's birthday, since they knew that she was not their true granddaughter. I genuinely enjoyed seeing them.

On Isabella's birthday, Mummy wanted to have a small celebration, which was the cause for visits from the Duke and Duchess and Edwina. Both of my brothers would be there too, from London and Scotland, respectively, and Edwina was bringing a beau from Paris. It was Dieter Schoen. His command of the language had apparently improved enough that he had become intimately involved with her. She mentioned him ever more frequently in her letters. However, it was difficult for me to believe that it was more serious than any of her multitude of other 'love affaireees'. Thus, the news that she was bringing him to England was unexpected. Nevertheless, I had learned early on never to be too surprised at anything Edwina did. I was probably much more surprised that Dieter had any desire to visit England.

As soon as the decision was made to have a birthday celebration, I immediately set about making plans. Edwina informed me that she would not be staying with our family at *Willow Grove,* which disappointed me. However, I agreed to whatever arrangements Edwina felt were suitable. I assumed that Edwina and Dieter were having an intimate relationship, and was certain that she did not want to place me into a situation that might prove untenable. It was a certainty that Mummy would have been aghast at the idea of an unmarried couple sharing a bed in her home. I didn't know if Dieter might have friends of his own in England, or if Edwina preferred a hotel. In all candor, I greatly wished that Dieter was not accompanying her to England. I selfishly feared that we weren't going to have any private time. We saw one another so seldom. In the end, Edwina and Dieter booked accommodations at *Easton Park,* a country hotel outside of Bath. I never asked if they booked one or two rooms.

I was also a bit nervous about the fact that Dieter was German. Sentiments in England were running rather counter to anything Teutonic. Everyone knew Mummy's views. In addition, I had invited Dr. Hausfater and his wife to the celebration. He'd not met any members of my family, with the exception of Isabella, for whom he had developed a special fondness. When I spent time helping in his office, I often brought Isabella along, and she charmed him. Because I'd decided to include Dr. and Mrs. Hausfater, the matter of Dieter's presence assumed more significance. The Hausfater's' had fled Germany just prior to the Great War, and were Jewish. I was well-aware of Hitler's anti-Semitism, and questioned whether I was making a mistake inviting Edwina and Dieter to Isabella's party. Immediately upon having such a thought, I was stricken with guilt. Edwina had been so good to me, and if it hadn't been for her, I might never have had Isabella. I knew that Edwina would never introduce someone into a social situation, if for one moment she thought that it might create tension. So, with a few lingering reservations, I pushed my fears of Dieter's nationality aside, and looked forward to a happy occasion.

I selected a special frock for Isabella to wear to the party. It was white taffeta, with ruffles at the collar and cuffs, and a wide yellow sash that ended in a bow at her back. Her hair, which was plentiful, fell softly into loose curls, and she wore a matching yellow bow on the top of her head. She looked adorable. I wore the black and white Chanel suit which I'd purchased in Paris, and it was delightful to dress for a joyful event, if only a child's birthday party. I planned an afternoon of fun for Isabella with little friends from surrounding estates. There were pony rides and games of all sorts, along with various 'goodies', including trifle and tiny iced cakes. Isabella had a wonderful time. She toddled among the guests, showing off her dress and creating a sensation when she dumped an entire bowl of ice cream on her puppy's head. That called for a change from her elaborate party frock to a more subdued corduroy romper, and a bath for her terrier, *Maggie*.

After Isabella's party ended, a second adult celebration began at eight o'clock. We all said goodnight to her, and gathered in the drawing room for cocktails and hors d'oevres. There were chicken livers in white wine, caviar on toast points, Roquefort cheese balls, Camembert biscuits, and exquisite pastry shells filed with Fondue au Gruyere. Edwina looked divine in black silk, and Dieter, whom I had remembered as rather pale and colorless, was actually very handsome. There was no question that his appearance was very Germanic. He had nearly white, blonde hair and glacial blue eyes, with finely chiseled features, along with a deep cleft in his chin. He and Edwina made a striking couple. One couldn't help but imagine what perfectly lovely children they might produce. Edwina also had a somewhat Nordic appearance, what with her pink and white complexion, somewhat prominent nose, and curvaceous silhouette. Dieter was extremely polite and hospitable, presenting Mummy with a nosegay of violets and a fine bottle of German wine. He kissed Mummy and me on both cheeks. Yet, for a reason I still can't precisely define, I didn't care for him. I saw no warmth in his eyes, and couldn't help but wonder how my fun-loving friend could find such a man remotely compatible.

I didn't have time to contemplate such thoughts however, as I was absorbed with hostess duties. Everything progressed enormously well, and it was a treat for me to be enjoying myself at a social gathering again. It was the first time in so long that I'd felt festive. I was relieved to see that my mother was being so cordial to Dieter, as I was acutely aware of her anti-German feelings. The Great War had left many of the British with ill-will toward the Germans. Many in my parents' generation had lost their lives in the trenches along the French border. Papa had served, and I had memories of his red Melton wool jacket, trimmed with navy blue velvet and gold braid at the cuffs and collar. Blake had played 'soldier' in it. Papa mustered out shortly before my birth in 1917. Many of his school chums lost their lives or limbs, and even their minds, due to that conflict. Therefore, it wasn't surprising that there remained a residue of ill will toward Germans. Those of my generation had largely put those hostilities to rest. Thus, it came as an enormous shock to hear the comment that Dieter made as we sat at the dining table, enjoying a sumptuous entrée of Fillet en Croute with Cognac and Shallot Sauce. His remarks came in response to a question put to Dieter by Dr. Hausfater.

"It is my understanding from many friends, who are in academia in your country, that a large number of German citizens are beginning to view the philosophy of Herr Hitler with increasing alarm. What initially appeared to be a re-awakening of national pride seems to be taking on a new dimension. What do you know of this?" Doctor Hausfater enquired.

"Men like Herr Hitler have a special destiny. His means cannot be questioned," Dieter responded, with a somewhat arrogant tone. Directing his icy gaze around the table, his eyes rested briefly on each guest. "Surely you, as Anglo Saxons, have an appreciation for Hitler's views on the purification of the white, Aryan race." His words hung in the air like icicles. There followed a stunned silence, after which my father was the first to speak.

"Dieter, I know of no Englishman who shares such a view. Indeed, I think I speak for my countrymen when I tell you that such beliefs are repugnant." I held my breath, expecting that Papa's retort had put Dieter firmly in his place, and that he would undoubtedly feel obliged to apologize for his offensive remark. That, however, was not to be.

"With all due respect, Somerville, Herr Hitler has a great vision for Germany, and for the world. Have you read *"Mein Kampf"*? It is a truly brilliant and inspired piece of literature."

"A piece of inflammatory, distorted trash, Sir," Dr. Hausfater replied, in a very strong voice.

Dieter turned his gaze upon Dr. Hausfater. "I would expect such a comment from you, Sir. I mean no offense, but you are not of white, Aryan descent, if I am not mistaken. May I ask Sir, what is your genetic heritage?"

Edwina gasped. "Dieter, that is an exceedingly rude question, and Dr. Hausfater should not dignify it with a reply," she said, in glacial tones.

Dr. Hausfater sat upright in his chair. "I should be pleased and proud to answer such a question. I am Polish by birth, and am of Jewish descent. I am also a British citizen. When we lived in Munich", we sensed feelings of coolness and disdain for those who were not fair- haired and blue-eyed. Rather like you, Sir. We were uncomfortable in your county. We finally made the decision to move to what we felt would be a more friendly environment. Thank God we left. I accepted a position at the University of London. When the Germans invaded France by trampling over Belgium, with no regard for prior agreements among nations, they proved what barbarians they were. Frankly, I do not trust your people. This Adolf Hitler is a worse barbarian than the Kaiser was. I fear his attitude toward any but those whom he considers the 'master race'. There is beginning to be real concern that there will be another war with your Hitler at the helm.'"

"The end will justify the means," Dieter replied.

I glanced in my mother's direction, and saw that she was clenching her teeth, as well as her hands. It was perfectly clear that the conversation was out of control, and indeed, headed for disaster. As the hostess, I knew that I had an obligation to put a halt to the exchange before it worsened. Yet, I was incapable of knowing what to say or do. It would have been an impossibility not to overhear a whispered conversation between my parents. Papa said to Mummy, "Now Pamela…. Please…. In response to something she murmured to him, but it was far too late. Mummy's face distorted with rage, as she stood to face Dieter. She was trembling, and her voice was an octave higher than usual. She threw her napkin on the table and began to shriek.

"How dare you? You absolute piece of filth! How dare you enter our home and make such remarks? You are typical of your kind, and your nationality. You and your bloody country! You are an arrogant horse's arse!" Papa continued with his pleas, which had no effect. I sat in motionless shock, as did all of the other guests. Naturally, I had seen this side of my mother before, but never in a social gathering. I even shared Mummy's outrage at Dieter's remarks, and in fact, silently agreed with the feelings she articulated, but could never agree with her method or timing. Dieter had managed to show his true colors, and everyone present saw him clearly, for what he was…. . A bigot and a fool. However, Mummy had just managed to lose complete control, for which I could find no justifiable defense. My brothers were equally aghast, and every bit as impotent in terms of being able to stop her tirade. The outburst continued until it culminated with the hurling of a silver candelabra in Dieter's direction. Had he not ducked very quickly, his white Aryan head might well have been badly or even permanently damaged.

That gesture galvanized the rest of those present into action. All stood, as Papa grabbed Mummy by the shoulders, and moved her toward the Great Hall and the staircase. She ceased the screaming and submitted to his urging that she retire to her bedchamber. Like the child she was emotionally, she allowed herself to be led away. I was not overly concerned about her, as I had witnessed far worse behaviour in the past. I knew that Papa would end up coaxing her back to reality with a stunning piece of jewelry, a fur wrap, or a priceless object d'art. In the end, she would manage to convince herself, and Papa, that her actions had been perfectly justified, and even admirable. I was very close to tears. My primary intent was to remove Dieter's offensive presence from *Willow Grove Abbey*. Edwina was openly weeping, and it seemed as though she did not know what to do. She was obviously desperate to be away from the sight of everyone who had witnessed the horrifying scene. Shortly after, Papa descended the staircase, having calmed Mummy, given her a sedative, and put her to bed. Then he turned his attention to Edwina. With great solicitude, he enquired as to whether she would like to be a guest for the night, and she immediately accepted. Dieter, who had been standing alone by the door, holding Edwina's white fur coat, looked astonished. He threw the coat upon the floor, turned on his heel, and departed. I was surprised that he didn't click his heels. Papa calmly walked over to where the coat lay in a crumpled heap, picked it up and hung it in the cupboard in the Great Hall.

Everyone was relieved to see Dieter depart. After a few moments, all seemed equally eager to leave themselves. Thus, there were multitudes of hasty departures, accompanied by half-hearted attempts at a show of good manners. Several guests even went so far as to murmur "*Thank you for a lovely evening*," which was, obviously, daft. Taking a deep breath of relief, I watched as the last guest disappeared down the circular driveway. I walked out of doors, and followed the ancient, well-worn pathway to the burying ground. I found myself next to the lynch gate. Leaning against it, I felt weak and quivery. Inside the house, I could hear the sounds of the cleaners, clearing away plates of half-eaten Fillet en Croute and unopened bottles of wine. I was certain that someone had discreetly removed the severely dented candelabra. Then I heard a sound, and glancing up, saw Edwina coming down the pathway toward me. Her head bent, she was weeping. It was so unlike Edwina. I knew the best thing I could do was to let her talk. Edwina had done that often enough for me. I needed to be loving, empathetic and supportive. Edwina knew the mistakes she'd made, and did not need to hear any more from me. When she reached the spot where I stood, I opened my arms and she walked straight into them. It was the first time I'd been the one to console her. Finally, when she seemed incapable of shedding another tear, I spoke.

"Edwina. This is not your fault. You couldn't possibly have known that he held such beastly views."

"No, I didn't Sophia. We never spoke of such things. Now I realize that we should have," she answered, still hiccoughing with sporadic sobs.

"I've learned a great lesson tonight. One cannot simply go through life skimming the surface, ignoring things like values and political beliefs. All I have ever really thought about was whether a man was attractive, attentive, and able to show me a wonderful time. Dieter had all of those qualities, and I never probed more deeply. Everyone must think me such a fool."

"No more a fool than any of a million people. Good Lord, Edwina, look at Papa," I replied. We stood there, looking at one another for a moment, and then the most amazing thing happened. We both were overcome with laughter. Gales and gales of laughter. It could only have happened between Edwina and me. The nightmare evening and all of its drama were not without humor, and it was undoubtedly healthy that both of us were able to see that. After all, we were still young girls, in spite of all we had weathered. Laughter had always been an integral part of our world. Especially in times of crisis.

Finally, we returned to the house, and I showed Edwina to her room. Then I checked on Isabella before retiring for the night. My little girl was sleeping soundly, with her thumb in her mouth, and her little terrier, *Maggie*, snuggled next to her bed. I was so glad that Isabella had not witnessed the scene in the dining room. However, I was suddenly keenly aware of the very real possibility that one of Mummy's outbursts would someday affect Isabella's life. That's when I knew that the time had come to make the move to London.

Chapter Thirteen

SEPTEMBER 1937 – FEBRUARY 1938
A MOVE

The more I thought about relocating to London, the more appealing the idea became. Therefore, the following week I travelled to the Capitol, and stayed at the Sumner Street flat. I left Isabella in the care of Martha, as there was a great deal to be done in preparation for permanent relocation. Edwina stayed on at *Willow Grove,* saying that she was exhausted from the horrid scene with Dieter, and wanted peace and tranquility for a few days. I understood her feelings, and didn't press for her to come to London. It was obvious that she had a lot of sorting out to do, and felt she could best accomplish that alone. Edwina always knew that she could come to me and talk, if she felt the need.

My primary task upon arrival in London was to convert one of the bedrooms into a nursery for Isabella. The flat was furnished in a heavy, Victorian style. While I found some of the pieces attractive, I felt that most of the colours were far too dark. So, I arranged to have the parlor done over with crème-colored, watered silk walls, and an Aubusson rug, woven with shades of rose and crème. The windows were covered in heavy, dark green damask, which I immediately tore down, and replaced with ivory taffeta. This lightened the room enormously. I was adamant about re-doing the master bedroom, as well. The present duvet cover was crème, and the walls were pale blue, but there was dark blue carpeting on the floor and the draperies were midnight blue velvet. I decided to do the entire room in white, with faint touches of rose as an accent colour. The comforter was replaced with a thick, white, goose down, and covered with a white Matillese duvet. Then, I filled the bed with gorgeous white decorative pillows, in delicate fabrics such as eyelet and organdy. White carpeting was ordered, as well as enormous fluffy, white curtains of lined handkerchief linen, draped into a bishop's sleeve.

Perhaps most importantly, was the room I planned for Isabella. I wanted it to be the quintessential little girl's room, predominantly pink and white. I selected a baby cot with a white organza canopy over the top. There was a comforter in a pink, white and taupe paisley print with matching curtains, as well as magnificent needlepoint carpeting, sporting a design of lambs and ducks.

Finally, I completely renovated the kitchen, borrowing from Edwina's décor, with black and white marble on the floors, and white marble countertops. Everything took time and I made many trips back and forth to *Willow Grove* during that period. I worked non-stop on the flat throughout the early winter of 1937, and grew well-acquainted with an entire crew of workmen. My plans were to begin living there on a permanent basis after 1 January, 1938. Isabella and I spent Christmas, 1937 at *Willow Grove, but* I was already looking ahead to sharing our own home, which had been so lovingly renovated. I'd taken leave from classes at the University, as well as duties with Dr. Hausfater, while arranging for the move. It was an immensely busy time.

Edwina finally *did* make the decision to return to Paris. I had truly begun to wonder if she would *ever* leave *Willow Grove Abbey*. After all, she'd been there since the ghastly party in September, and through the Holidays, with only a brief absence for a visit to her own family in Bury St. Edmunds for Christmas. However, my parents seemed content to have her there, so there seemed no reason for interference. Perhaps because I was spending less and less time at my family home, and had plans to move so soon, my parents found solace in the fact that Edwina was still an integral part of their lives. Finally, she came to London with plans to be my guest for three days en route to Paris. We spent most of our time at the newly renovated flat, catching up on chatter. Isabella was still at *Willow Grove,* so it was a nice time for us to be 'just girls', reminiscent of our time together in Paris.

When I look back now, Edwina seemed somewhat subdued, and more mature during that visit. She seemed softer. At any rate, it was clear that time in the country had been a nice respite for her.

"Will you return to school when you resume life in Paris?" I asked her one afternoon, as we enjoyed tea in the newly decorated parlor. We were both sitting cross-legged on the sofa.

"I think I'm ready to take on the design world, Sophia. I've had several offers to start in a beginner's capacity in some of the better houses. I contacted a few when I was at *Willow Grove,* and sent copies of my portfolio. If I get a final offer, I hoping to join *Vionnet.*"

"Oh Edwina, how exciting. Your dreams are coming true. Isn't that marvellous? *Vionnet* designed my Presentation Ball dress. Remember? The one with the appliqued swallows scattered across it. I adored that dress. I'm so very proud of you."

"Yes, I have to admit, I'm pretty darned proud of myself. Without a man in my life, this is the perfect time for me to really concentrate upon a career." She didn't sound at all upset about her newfound freedom.

"Edwina, I never knew you to base your future happiness on having a man in your life. That was my mother's dream for me. Remember? '*The suitable man* '. Honestly, the last thing I ever thought you wanted or needed was a man to muddy the waters. After all, you haven't fallen in love with your artist yet, and lived in his garret, I laughed."

"Well, dear heart," Edwina smiled, I just may have to skip that particular fantasy. I've found out a lot more about myself. It's been a very beneficial time. I've a much better perspective of what I want out of life…. Of what sort of man would be good for me. I've been all wrong in my choices." This was curious talk from Edwina. I had never heard her speak so seriously about men and love. It had always been a whimsical topic. I had undergone profound changes after Isabella's birth, and now it was evident that Edwina was experiencing something akin to what I'd experienced, albeit due to different circumstances.

"And what type of man have you decided would be your ideal?" I asked, genuinely interested.

"Defiantly someone more mature. Older than I am. I believe I told you that once before, when you were in Paris just after Isabella's birth. That I prefer older men. I suppose it isn't surprising, when one considers that my Dad is twenty-eight years older than Mum. I'm more secure, and feel more appreciated by older men. They aren't so apt to have foolish, radical thoughts, like Dieter."

"Edwina, doesn't the prospect of marrying a much older man frighten you a bit? It's almost a given that in such a case, you would be widowed, perhaps early in your life?"

"My Mum isn't widowed yet. And my father is sixty-eight, and neither is yours, and your Papa is sixty-five."

"Yes…. When you put it like that, it doesn't seem so far-fetched, does it? But…. Well, I guess we're just very different in that respect. I can't see what you would have in common with someone that much older. Especially you, Edwina. You're so full of life and so…. So…. Young." I laughed."

"I think once two people are adults, age difference really doesn't matter all that much."

Yes…. Perhaps you're right. You mentioned 'security'. Do you mean to say that you need a man to feel secure? Not you, Edwina."

"It would be lovely to never have to worry about money, or with having to support myself, if I didn't want to. Especially if I were to have a child, which I think I would like someday. After you had Isabella, I realized how important having a child can be."

"Well…. I'm certainly not going to argue about that. As you know, Isabella made my life *whole*. Is there someone in your life who puts you in this frame of mind?"

"No. No one in particular," she answered, after a moment's hesitation. I sensed that she might be holding something back, which was entirely out of character for her. We had always shared every secret, and it was hard for me to imagine why Edwina would decide not to tell me, if she had developed feelings for someone. I'd sensed something of a similar sort while in Paris, discussing the same topic. However, I certainly understood that it was my friend's prerogative to keep private emotions to herself.

Perhaps she wasn't yet certain of her feelings. Therefore, I let the matter drop, deciding that when and if the time was right, Edwina would tell me. I enjoyed my dear friend's company during those few days, and was sorry to see her depart.

I recall early 1938 as peaceful and content. At least, that was true of *my* life. Isabella, Martha and I made the transition to Sumner Street quite smoothly. Martha was thrilled with my request to have her join our household in London, as her parents had relocated to Lambeth, a somewhat 'down market' area of the city. They had originally lived in Lincolnshire. She would be able to see them much more frequently. She, too, would be living on Sumner Street, which could easily accommodate all of us, since there were three bedrooms. She was to see to the running of the house, while I devoted time to studies. I already knew that she and Isabella were very compatible. Isabella was fast developing into an exceptionally sweet child, and Martha had adored her from the beginning. There was a charm about Isabella that one didn't often encounter in children her age. She was thoughtful and had a desire to show affection. I wanted to foster all of those natural, God-given qualities. Isabella thought Martha was splendid, since she fussed over her so, and knew exactly how to satisfy my little girl's craving to absorb new things. From the beginning, it was clear that Martha had been the correct choice as someone who could assist with housekeeping chores, as well as perform the duties as Isabella's nanny. I would have been happy to add a true housekeeper, to take the load from Martha's shoulders, but she wouldn't hear of it. In no time at all, the flat was transformed into a light, airy, happy home, where the fragrance of pastries, pies and freshly baked bread continually drifted from the kitchen.

Dr. Hausfater rang me in February, asking that I meet him at one of my favorite pubs in London. His call somewhat puzzled me. I assumed that he wanted to speak about when I might be ready to resume classes and duties at University. He had taken such kind and special interest in me. I felt very fortunate to have him in my life. I looked forward to meeting with him, as we hadn't seen one other, nor spoken at length, for some time. We had engaged in a long talk following the scene at *Willow Grove Abbey* on Isabella's birthday, and I was greatly relieved that he didn't hold any resentment towards me or my family for what had turned out to be a ghastly evening. He'd become such a dear person to me. I would have felt dreadful if there had been animosity. I had no idea then, that the upcoming meeting with him would bring about a sea change in my life. I kissed Isabella goodbye, leaving her sitting at a small table in the kitchen helping Martha make cookies.

It was a bitterly cold February afternoon. I left Sumner Street wrapped snugly in a red cashmere coat, mittens, muffler, Wellington boots, and a red beret. There were dark clouds overhead, spitting a mixture of sleet and rain. In addition, there was still snow in the streets, serving as a reminder of the enormous winter storm that had roared through London and its' environs the previous week. I trudged along, taking care not to slip and fall on the many patches of ice still on the sidewalk. I lowered my head, as I walked into the biting wind blowing from the north. My newly styled, shorter curls were tucked beneath the red woolen beret. I'd felt as though I looked rather fetching when glancing into the foyer mirror upon my departure from Sumner Street. I could feel the cold, sharp wind bring roses to my cheeks, as I scurried across Sloan Square. Suddenly, I came to an abrupt halt. Noticing a familiar figure moving toward me from the opposite direction, I was knocked for six. It was Spence. It had been so long since that night at *Deux Magots,* yet I would have recognized his handsome face and tall, athletic frame no matter the time or distance. I wondered if he would notice me, and wasn't certain if I should acknowledge him if he didn't. *Should I continue on my way, looking down at the pavement as we passed?* Once again, my heart was in my throat. Fortunately, the dilemma resolved itself, for indeed, he *did* see me.

Well, I'll be damned. It's happened again. We just seem to continue running into one another," Spence exclaimed.

"Why, Hallo Spence," I replied, acting surprised to have come upon him so unexpectedly, pretending to have just seen him. He extended his leather-gloved hand, and I placed my own mitten-clad one into his. I so wished I'd chosen to wear my Italian kidskin gloves. I felt childish. He seemed, however, to be genuinely pleased at our accidental encounter.

"Serendipity," he smiled.

"Yes. You seem to have been on target," I replied, also smiling.

"Where are you rushing off to on such a dreadful day?" he asked. "I'm meeting a former professor of mine," I responded. "I'm not altogether certain what the meeting is about. We're fast friends and I respect him enormously, but he's never asked me to meet him away from University."

"Sounds intriguing," Spence grinned. "Is he a handsome, young chap fresh from Oxford or Cambridge?"

"Oh no, no," I protested. "Nothing of the sort. I daresay he's sixty at least. Perhaps older."

Well, you must be careful that you don't beguile the old gentleman with those eyes of yours," His tone was bantering, and it reminded me of our first meeting on the night of my debut.

"Oh my! I hardly think that's a concern," I smiled. He seemed about to initiate further conversation, but the arrival of a tall, svelte, posh redhead halted our brief exchange. I needn't add that it was Charlotte Ross.

"Spencer, darling, here you are! I've been waiting for what seems ages, and then I spied you over here, across from where you're supposed to meet me. Good Heavens, my dear, it's ghastly cold. How cruel of you to keep me waiting in this awful weather," she exclaimed, in her breathy, dramatic voice.

"Charlotte, I do apologize. I've just stumbled onto Sophia Somerville. You *know* we've known one another for eons. She's the sister of a former school chum. Sophia, you remember your former school mate, Charlotte Ross?" He made the introductions a bit awkwardly, and I could not help but wince when he referred to me as merely the sister of a school chum. He directed a look toward me that held a hint of apology for having to deny what we had once shared. Then, in what seemed an afterthought, he added that Charlotte was now his fiancée. His voice sounded reticent, but I have to admit that I could have been reading those feelings into the way he spoke. I knew that he hadn't yet married, as Drew had seen him over the Holidays at a gathering of former school chaps. He'd told me that Spence didn't seem in a great hurry to 'tie the knot'.

Charlotte wore gorgeous, elbow-length, black kid gloves, elegant open-toed high-heeled pumps, and a very chic hat with a black net veil covering the top half of her obviously breath-taking face. I hadn't remembered that she was so lovely. Her coat was fur. Black Seal, I thought. *I hated her.* She stood there in her posh elegance, possessively slipping her arm through Spence's.

"Hallo, Sophia. I haven't seen you since the night I met you and him at the *Thames Room.* Did you know that we're now engaged? Spence is just *too, too* much of a treasure. He's even changed my mind about living in a small Cotswold village. Isn't he utterly amazing?"

I knew that she meant to send the message that Spence cared only for her, and absolutely nobody but her. I did not know how Charlotte sensed that I wanted him too, but women have uncanny abilities. Of course, I had no idea what he had shared with her about our failed romance, but if they were planning on marriage, I image she knew quite a lot about me. I was aware of an intense feeling of jealousy, which was not a familiar emotion for me. It made me want to get away from both of them, as quickly as possible. I almost feared that Charlotte or Spence could read my thoughts. I managed to extend a few socially acceptable comments, and, as swiftly as possible, departed.

"It was lovely running into you, Spence, and so nice to see you again, Charlotte. I really must be on my way, as I'm late for an appointment. "Best wishes to you both," I murmured, moving on. I knew that Spence had to have seen the heartache in my eyes. I could only hope that he didn't understand my behaviour too well. I left them both standing in Sloan Square, as I dashed off to my destination, wishing I'd followed my original instincts and taken a taxicab from Sumner Street. In my haste, I hadn't even asked Spence what he was doing in London.

I arrived at *the pub* a few moments before my scheduled meeting, despite fears that I might be late. I visited the loo before being shown to a table, where Dr. Hausfater was already seated. He stood as I approached, and motioned to the chair opposite his, which the waiter held for me. I had removed my beret and mittens in the loo and now slipped out of my coat, placing it on the adjoining, empty chair.

"Lady Winnsborough. Sophia. How good of you to come. My apologies for bringing you out on such a day, but I really was most anxious to speak with you," my professor said."

"That's perfectly all right, Dr. Hausfater. I'm always glad to hear from you, although I must admit to being puzzled. There's nothing amiss, I hope?" The table was a very dark wood, polished to a high sheen. Before either of us could speak again, a waiter appeared and took our order, which consisted of a pint of bitters for him, and tea and biscuits for me. While he was ordering, I studied him. He was certainly not a young man, nor even middle-aged. His long face was heavily grooved, and craggy in appearance, topped with eyebrows that seemed to grow in a continuous line. They stretched across his very dark eyes and hawk-like nose, thereby creating a perpetually brooding look.

"No, my dear. Nothing amiss. So, Sophia, how have you been?" he enquired.

I was still somewhat embarrassed at the memory of the dreadful scene at *Willow Grove Abbey,* and Dieter's unspeakably rude remarks to Dr. Hausfater. "I'm been quite well, thank you, Sir. Keeping busy, what with our permanent move to London. We've finally settled in."

"And your little girl? Is she happy in London?"

"Oh, yes indeed. Isabella is happy anywhere, as long as she has people to pay non-stop attention to her. There is never a shortage of those," I laughed.

"Yes. She is a beautiful child." There was a pause as the waiter brought our order.

"So, yes, what are your plans now?" he asked in the quaint way he had of expressing himself, with his lingering foreign accent."

"I'm hoping that I'm going to be able to return to my work, assisting you, Sir, as I do plan on resuming my classes at University soon. Now that I'm actually living in London, it will be so much easier than in the past, when I had to travel back and forth. Have you been keeping busy, Sir?"

"Very much so. There is the excitement of a new project for me. This is the primary reason I brought you here today, so that I might have the discussion with you about it."

I placed my cup of tea back onto its saucer. "Really? And what would that be Professor?"

"Sophia, I come directly to the point. I would like to work in the partnership with you of the textbook writing." He made the statement in such a straightforward, but convoluted manner, and I wasn't certain that I understood what he meant.

"Are you saying that you want me to help you with the research on a textbook project?" I asked.

"No. No. I want you to be my collaborator. My co-author. It will be an Adolescent Psychology text. "

"Me? You want *me*? To collaborate on a textbook with *you*? Oh my, Dr. Hausfater, I'm extraordinarily honoured, but, well, Sir, I know nothing about Psychology. Only that which I've learned in your courses at University. I scarcely think that qualifies me to write on the subject."

"You are more the expert than you know, my dear. I fear you have *lived* the subject."

I was mortified. Obviously, he was referring to my mother, and the rage he had witnessed.

"Are you speaking of my mother's periodic odd behaviour?" I asked, looking down at the table, as I felt color rise in my cheeks.

Sophia, I do not ask that you reveal the matters of personal nature. We have spoken enough about the subject. I know what you have lived. I just mean to say that you know more about matters of a psychological nature than you think you do. Naturally, I was present when your mother displayed her remarkable lack of coping mechanisms, so yes that adds to the meaning of my comments."

I hadn't any idea, at the time, what *'coping mechanisms'* meant, and told him so.

"It is simply meaning that your mother has not ever learned to handle the stressful situation, and she loses all control. Sophia, I know the subject of Psychology up and down. However, you have a unique ability to speak to your peers. You have the marvelous ability to write, and this, I am certain, would make you an invaluable working partner."

"But, Sir, I've only just turned twenty-one. Surely you cannot believe that someone of my young years would be taken seriously?"

"And why not? My credentials are impeccable, and I am convinced that you have the rare gift for self-expression. You are going to do great things in life, Lady Sophia Winnsborough. Of that I have no doubt. As for your age, you may be merely twenty-one, but there are parts of you that are older than time. You have what I like to call the 'old soul'."

Oh, Goodness. He was saying almost the precise words Spence once spoke to me. Was there really something to what he was saying?

"How do you mean I have an *old soul*? I don't understand Dr. Hausfater."

"I speak of wisdom that goes beyond your years. I do not think that you have tapped into it yet, and undoubtedly still see yourself as a child, but you are already facing happenings in life that many people never do. One day you will develop the insight to know what I say. Trust me for now." He reached across the table, and patted my hand, in a fatherly gesture.

I was truly stunned. I wanted so badly to grasp such an opportunity. Dr. Hausfater was the first person in my life who had ever professed a strong belief in my capabilities. Besides, of course, for Spence. Here was a distinguished man of Letters, a well-respected Professor, offering to make all of my dreams reality. However, I was engaged in a powerful internal struggle. I could almost *hear* Mummy's voice admonishing me not to make a fool of myself.

Nevertheless, after a few moments of internal struggle, I took a deep breath and said "All Right, Sir. I shall have a go at it. I won't pretend to feel confident, and I am not at all certain that I won't turn out to be a disappointment to you. Nevertheless, I shall try very hard. It's a terribly exciting challenge, and I would be foolish not to pursue it."

He smiled broadly, and the single eyebrow gathered in the middle. "I'm very pleased. You have made the wise decision. I quite understand your fears, but in the final analysis you will see that I am correct." I too smiled, although my insides were quivering.

"Of course there is the matter of remuneration, he continued. "It will not be a large sum, but I have been awarded the grant of money from the private foundation for this project, so naturally you will receive the stipend."

"That never even crossed my mind," I gasped. "Just the privilege of working with you is compensation enough. I wouldn't dream of taking money"

He grinned openly. "My dear lady, you must learn to accept what you are entitled to. Of course, you will accept payment. I shall arrange for a bank draft and a contract to be drawn up, so that everything is kept neat and tidy."

"Oh how extraordinary." I brought my hands to my cheeks, which were now flushed deep crimson. "Thank you so much. I cannot put into words how delighted I am. How pleased and honoured." I had never actually *earned* any money in my life. None. What a lovely feeling it would be to actually be compensated for one's work.

"I have no idea of your schedule, but I should like to begin on the preliminary planning as soon as possible," he continued. I have compiled a file of notes with which you will need to acquaint yourself. I think they will provide a broad overview of subject matter I am wanting to cover. Then, I should be interested in your suggestions and opinions on an interesting format in presenting the material. I want this to be a readable text, Sophia. Not dry and boring, as so many are. Could you be so kind as to ring my office next week? We should be able to arrange to begin our work together by the end of the month. I shall have prepared for you by then. You will have the little space to call your own. "

"Do you mean I'll have an office?"

"Yes, Sophia, with a typing machine, telephone, and private door to shut out the world."

I was beyond exuberance. I couldn't wait to share the news with Edwina. And just for a moment, I wished I could share it with Spence. I knew he would be proud of me. Also, like a moth to a flame, I harboured my childish instinct to win approval from my parents. To prove to them that I had talent. To have them praise me. As soon as I arrived at the flat, I *did* ring them and told them of my wondrous good fortune. Mummy wanted to know what motive Doctor Hausfater might have for making such an offer, and Papa told me that he thought the money was a ludicrous pittance. I should have known what to expect. I probably did, but it never mattered. At no time in my life did I stop trying.

Chapter Fourteen

Spring, 1938

A Salutation

However detached my parents may have been from my joy over the offer to work with Dr. Hausfater, *I knew* that in the blink of an eye, my rather mundane existence had taken on an entirely new dimension. The work actually began in April, 1938 and it thoroughly captivated me. It consumed every spare moment. Together, Dr. Hausfater and I had decided upon a format which would include actual feature stories written by me, to accentuate the various disorders that were being discussed. I researched people who were hospitalized, or had recently been released, and then interviewed them, and wrote their stories for publication. One thrust of the book was an appeal for improvement of the Psychiatric system in general, and particularly for adolescents. And a total cessation of the word *'crazy'*!

Martha proved to be invaluable, for she kept things running smoothly on Sumner Street, freeing me to concentrate upon my work. Of course, I also spent as much time as possible with Isabella. I was always home in the mornings, when Isabella awakened, bathing, dressing and feeding her. At the end of the day, I made certain to be the one who tucked my little girl into bed, sang lullabies and read stories. In such a manner, we settled into a comfortable routine. My life was as peaceful and as busy as it had ever been. I still thought of Spence constantly. It would have been hard not to do so, as I had a continual reminder of our love. Occasionally some man or other would invite me to the theatre, opera or dinner, but I had no inclination to meet anyone new. I was content to live my life with my daughter and a job I adored. I was probably living in a bit of denial during that period, because I didn't ever think about what I would do once the textbook project was completed. I *did* want to complete my University studies and earn a degree, but that was about as far as I looked into the future. It never crossed my mind that I might re-marry. Overall, I was happy. Or as happy as I could be, with a heart filled with sad memories, and the longing I still embraced for Spence. No matter. That state of quasi-happiness continued for some time.

I suppose I should have known that such peacefulness could not last forever. After a quiet and relatively happy summer, in August, 1938, Adolph Hitler started making outrageous statements, hinting that he was going to send the German Army into Czechoslovakia. Neville Chamberlain had become Prime Minister in 1937, and the British government began to look ahead to a war with Nazi Germany. Chamberlain asked Parliament to pass the Emergency Powers Act and it passed on 28 August, 1938, giving the government permission to enact legislation which would ensure public safety. Over the next five days, around one hundred new regulations went into effect. All military reservists were called to mobilize. Hitler promised at Munich on 30 September, 1938 that he would make no more territorial claims in Europe. There was guarded relief when that occurred, but most persons of my acquaintance were still very fearful that there was worse to come.

The time between March and September of 1938 ended up being well remembered for a number of reasons. While everyone wanted very much to believe that all would be well'…. That peace would prevail…. There was a general feeling of impending doom amongst most people I knew. Working with Dr. Hausfater probably enhanced those feelings. He had grave anxiety about friends and relatives in the exact part of Europe which lay in the path of danger. Therefore, I was probably even more engrossed in what was occurring within the Third Reich than many of my acquaintances. Many still viewed countries such as Austria and Czeckslovakia as remote, distant, and far removed from our isolated island.

Blake and Drew were not fools. I knew that they worried, as did my father. Often I heard them discussing what they would do if war came. My brothers were of an age that meant, unequivocally, they would fight for their country. So was Spence. That thought frightened me enormously. Even though I had resigned myself to our never being together, I still had concerns for his welfare and happiness. The idea of Spence and my brothers fighting in some foreign land was enough to cause me overwhelming anxiety. Half of the summer months I tried to ignore the news coming out of Europe. The other half I was intensely concerned, which resulted in a sort-of limbo.

Then, something else happened that profoundly influenced my world, changing it forever. It was a rain-soaked Tuesday, in late August, 1938, and Papa was in London, having just returned from a trip to Paris and Milan. He meant to spend a day in the London office, before returning to *Willow Grove* and Mummy.

I always cherished the times when my father came to London alone. He *was* different when Mummy wasn't present. He spoke to me more about my life, and showed more interest in my thoughts and feelings. On that particular rainy morning, he rang me, and said that he had arrived on the night boat-train from Paris. He was in a suite at The Grande Hotel. He wondered if we might rendezvous for a quick breakfast, before he rushed off to a meeting with his bankers. The timing was perfect. I had a meeting with a person whom I planned to interview for my textbook project, and it was just a block from the hotel. Papa and I made plans to meet in the dining room of the Grande at eight o'clock a.m.

When I arrived, he was reading the *Times* at a corner table by a window, drinking a cup of tea. I shook out of my rainwear. I still remember that I wore a rain slicker with matching floppy hat and umbrella, all fashioned out of the same black oilcloth fabric, and sporting a bevy of brightly colored flowers. Papa seemed in good spirits when I joined him, in spite of the dreary weather. He asked if I preferred coffee or tea. I ordered a soft-boiled egg on toast, and a pot of Earl Grey. Then, I settled myself comfortably at the round table near the window. I could hear and see rain drops as they pelted the glass panes. We chatted about the weather, my book project and conditions on the Continent. I knew that he had been in Paris. Consequently, I enquired as to whether he'd found time to ring Edwina.

"Better than that," he smiled. "We were able to dine."

"Oh Papa, how lovely," I exclaimed.

"Yes, all quite unexpected. Edwina mentioned that she had spoken to you recently, and that you had told her of my forthcoming trip to Paris. Naturally, Edwina knows my habits, as well as any of you children. At any rate, she rang my hotel, and learned my arrival date. So who do you suppose was waiting in the lobby when I arrived to register?"

I clapped my hands! "How typical of Edwina." I thought it grand that she had surprised Papa in such a fashion. "How did she seem?" I enquired.

"Wonderful, as always" he smiled. "She seems very involved in her work. Seems to be making good progress, and feels that her talents are being recognized. Of course, she *is terribly* talented."

His comment about Edwina's talent couldn't help but scald me a bit. He had no difficulty proclaiming her *'talent,'* but when I'd announced the remarkable offer to co-author an adolescent psychology textbook, there had been absolutely no mention of my writing ability. No matter. I should have been used to it. "Did she speak of any new men in her life?" I asked.

"No. Nothing of that sort. I do not suppose she would speak to me about such things. We did discuss her friend, the German chap."

"Dieter? She isn't still seeing him?" I asked, appalled at the thought.

"Apparently so, but I don't believe there is any romantic attachment. She maintains that he feels beastly about the scene at *Willow Grove Abbey.*"

"I should think so. I cannot imagine that she would want anything further to do with *him*. She hasn't mentioned his name to me since her return to Paris, following that horrid evening."

"I have the impression that she believes she's managed to alter his views."

"Oh, surely that can't be so? He doesn't strike me as the sort who will ever be anything but what he is. A

ghastly bigot."

"Yes. Well, I daresay, I agree. But, Edwina is a grown woman, so we must respect her choices."

I would have liked to pursue the subject further, but we finished breakfast, and Papa was in a great rush to keep his appointment. As it happened, his engagement was scheduled for half after nine o'clock, and mine was not until one hour later. It seemed absurd to travel back to my flat, only to return to virtually the same locale in less than an hour's time. Normally, I might have enjoyed a rare shopping expedition, but since it was pouring rain, I wasn't inclined toward strolling Knightsbridge. The perfect solution lay in my waiting the three quarters of an hour or so in Papa's suite. He was leaving for *Willow Grove* after his meeting, but would be returning to the hotel for his luggage, so would not be vacating the room until later. We rode together in the lift to his suite, and after he collected his attaché case and various papers, we said our goodbyes.

After his departure, I found myself with little to do, save stare out of the window at the grey London morning. I watched the traffic creep its way through the narrow, wet, congested streets, while men and women scurried back and forth under mostly black umbrellas. I adored London even on such days, and never tired of looking across at the Houses of Parliament, Big Ben, and Tower Bridge. Even so, I found myself restless after a bit. I wandered over to the bedside table, where there was a wireless. I fooled with the control knob for a bit, trying to find some program of interest, but everything pertained to happenings in Germany, and I was not in the mood for depressing news.

Then, I turned to walk back towards the window, when I noticed a piece of paper on the floor. It was a standard sheet of business writing paper. I was surprised that I'd not spotted it earlier, since it stood out starkly against the dark grey carpeting. Without actually thinking, I bent to retrieve it, meaning to place it upon the bedside table. Mummy's teachings about tidiness and neatness were firmly entrenched. As I held the paper in my hand, I couldn't help but glance at its contents. It appeared to be the salutation on a letter, and it was plainly in my father's handwriting. There was only the beginning, followed by one, brief line;

'My Love,'
'No name. I learned that from you.'

How sweet. Papa still writes Mummy love letters when they are apart. That was my first thought. Of course, it was utterly ludicrous. Only a matter of seconds passed, before I adjusted to the true meaning of that beastly piece of paper. The salutation was obviously not meant for my mother, but for some other unknown female in Papa's life. I was stunned, shocked, and worried sick. Even though I knew that my parents' marriage was far from perfect, I'd *never* contemplated the idea that Papa was a cheater. That probably was utterly ridiculous. Certainly, I knew that they had problems, and yes, Mummy had *rages*, but Papa had always given the impression that he worshipped her. He seemed to have arranged himself to deal with her dark periods. Of course, I'd cut my teeth on the story of their glorious love story, and a part of me desperately clung to that fantasy. Crumpling up the offensive paper, I deposited it in the waste bin by the desk, as if by ridding it from my sight, I could return to my safe world of denial. However, the words were etched into my psyche.

'My Love. No name. I learned that from you.'

From whom did he learn what? What did that cryptic sentence mean? Had she told him that whenever he wrote her a love letter, he should use neither her name, nor his own? Who was she?

I began to quiver from head to toe. I felt as though my entire world had turned upside down, along with everything that I believed. I didn't cry. Not then. I just continued the horrid trembling. Then I began to pace. I wanted desperately to talk to someone. However, who? My first and immediate thought was of my brothers. I suspected that they would be as surprised as I, at such a discovery. However, the topic did not seem the sort that I could simply ring up Blake or Drew about, blurting out the details. So, I continued to pace. *Edwina! I could talk to Edwina.* She had been part of my life since I was fourteen, and as dear to me as any sister. Edwina would definitely know how to handle such a shock. Even so, upon further reflection, I realized that Edwina would be at her workplace. It would be difficult, if not impossible, to talk for any length of time, especially about something so intimate. So, the quivering and pacing continued. In the course of my well-worn path, I wandered into the adjoining bath. Glancing at the ornate gold waste-bin under the washbasin, I saw another piece of the same sort of paper. I reached down, and retrieved it, smoothing it with both hands, so that I might clearly read the words written upon it. My heart was pounding so loudly that I could feel it in my ears. There, again, was my father's handwriting, with nearly the identical words

I'd observed only a few moments before. However, there was one, distinct difference. It began with a name.

'Edwina, my love'.

I froze. I felt as though I had a lump of ice in my chest, or that someone had punched me in the stomach. "Oh my God! This could not be happening. *Edwina. There could be only one Edwina. My Edwina. Our Edwina. My father could not do such a thing to me…. To Mummy. Edwina could not…. Would not…. Not to me, nor to Mummy. Yes, Mummy had problems. Everyone acknowledged that, and Edwina knew them as well as anyone else in the family.* Nevertheless, that did not mean Edwina would become involved with my father. He was practically her own father. My parents were like second parents to her. *It seemed incestuous.* There had to be some mistake. Some rational explanation for the bizarre note, which still rested in my trembling hand. *I* stuffed the offensive scrap of paper into the pocket of my skirt, ran cold water in the basin to cool my burning cheeks, and tried to calm myself. Then I drank a glass of water, and took a few deep breaths. I *had* to go to my scheduled interview, and to be in control. I brushed my hair, put on fresh lip rouge, and powdered my nose. I straightened my blouse, skirt and rain gear. Then, I left my father's room, with one last glance at his baggage. There was a second attaché case sitting in the corner. I had a momentary temptation to open it. I wanted to rummage about to see what secrets it might reveal. However, I was immediately ashamed of myself, and resisted the impulse. I wasn't certain that I could have absorbed any more shocks that morning anyway.

Somehow, I got through the interview. Later, I didn't remember a thing about it, nor of my journey back to Sumner Street. Thank goodness, when I arrived, Martha and Isabella were having a lie-down, and I don't believe they even knew that I had returned. The next thing I remember is sitting at my telephone table, ringing my father at the *Somerville Ltd.* London Offices. An office assistant put me through to him, although Papa was in a meeting. Obviously, I was not thinking or behaving in a rational manner, or I would have known that he couldn't speak openly or honestly while in a meeting. My primary concern was that he not leave London without allowing me the opportunity to discuss my beastly discovery. When I heard his voice on the line, I blurted out my question, with no preliminary niceties.

"Papa, what is going on between you and Edwina?"

At first, he was completely silent. Then, without ever knowing it, he revealed the truth, and incriminated himself beyond all redemption.

"Sophia, it is not an accident that I left that attaché case behind in the room," he replied.

The attaché case! That which I had been tempted to open, which obviously contained the completed letter or something equally incriminating. He thought I had opened and read it!

"Papa, I didn't open your attaché case," I answered, truthfully. "I found one piece of paper on the floor by the bed, and another in the waste bin in the loo."

More silence followed. "Sophia, I cannot discuss this at the moment. Let me ring you from the rail station before I leave for *Willow Grove.*"

I could not argue. Of course, he was correct. "All right, I understand, but just let me say one more thing. I expect you to tell me the truth, Papa. There is nothing in the world that you can tell me that I will not try to understand and forgive. However, I shall never understand if you choose to lie. Please remember that, Papa."

I hung up the receiver, and sat there, staring into space, watching the clock tick away the minutes. I never moved from the desk. After a very lengthy interval, the telephone rang.

"Sophia, Papa here," he began.

"Yes, Papa, I hoped it would be you. Have you an answer to my question?" I could hear trains being announced in the background and knew that he was trying to speak in low tones, yet was finding it difficult to hear me, with all of the noise in the giant station surrounding him.

"Sophia, it's not what you're thinking. Edwina knows nothing of my adolescent feelings," was his reply.

"I read the salutation on the letter! How can you possibly expect me to believe that?" I asked, incredulously.

"Sophia. I was lying in bed, composing a speech that I'm to give next week, when my mind began to wander. I diverted my attention to the memory of the lovely Parisian dinner with Edwina. I am terribly embarrassed to confess this. If Edwina knew, she would be horrified. I shall readily admit that I find her enchanting. What man, particularly a middle-aged, foolish one, would not? However, it is a schoolboy sort of thing. I would never presume to act upon those fantasies, and I should die if Edwina had the slightest notion."

"Then, what did you mean in the letter when you wrote '*No name, I learned that from you?*' It sounds to me as though Edwina instructed you never to use her name when writing to her, in case it might be read by a third party, which, of course, is exactly what has happened."

"I believe that Edwina *did* make some such reference during dinner, regarding never putting anything incriminating into writing, but she was speaking in general terms. Her comments were in no way associated with feelings of an intimate nature towards me. You must believe me."

Perhaps because I wanted so badly to believe his story, I made that choice. If I hadn't believed him, I'd be forced to face unspeakable feelings, and emotional conflicts that I just couldn't deal with. Yet, I harboured a sense of unease. Something did not seem right. I knew my father, and couldn't fathom his resorting to such fantasizing. Yet, I also couldn't fathom an involvement with Edwina. Then there was the inexplicable comment about the attaché case, and not leaving it behind by accident. Obviously, the briefcase contained *something.* How I wished I'd opened it. *Had it contained the completed 'fantasy' letter or a similar piece of correspondence from Edwina to Papa?* Before I could delve any further into the mystery, Papa announced that his train was posted, and that he had to ring off and board. There was little I could do but agree.

After I placed the receiver back into its cradle, I sat silently, studying a photograph on my desk. Taken at my wedding to Owen, it was one of the few mementoes remaining from that period in my life. I wasn't in the photo, nor was Owen. It featured Edwina in her primrose bridal frock, flanked by Papa, looking handsome and debonair in white tie and tails. They were both holding flutes of champagne, and smiling broadly. Edwina looked radiant, and they *did* make a handsome couple. *Was it conceivable that there could be more to the photo than appeared on the surface?* I suddenly remembered something Edwina said that night in Paris at *Deux Magots.*

And again, in London, one of the last times I'd seen her. It was that now profound comment that she *'found herself attracted to much older men'*.

I felt as though I desperately needed to talk to someone about my feelings. I was confused and hurt, and did not believe my father's story. Yet it was bewildering that he might be involved romantically with Edwina. Certainly Edwina could be alluring and desirable, if one preferred her type. There was no denying that. Nevertheless, I knew…. *I just knew*….That Edwina would never do anything to betray our friendship. Our entire relationship was based upon honesty. Always had been. In addition, I couldn't imagine that Edwina would betray Mummy. Of course she knew how dreadful Mummy's behaviour could be. She had witnessed it. Nevertheless, she'd always understood that Mummy had serious emotional problems. Edwina was not the sort of woman who would take advantage of such a sad situation. *Was she?* I remembered her voice, saying *'But, how sad that he can't marry her, if he loves her,'* when referring to Edward the Eighth and Wallis Simpson. *Was she also thinking of herself?*

I donned my coat, and went out, in spite of the dismal weather. I didn't care if I became soaked. I needed to walk and think, with no particular destination in mind…. Only a desire for fresh air and movement. Over blocks and blocks I wandered, trying to sort everything out. Nothing made any sense. Finally, I came upon the *Royal College of Surgeons* at *Lincoln's Inn Fields*. The building itself was enclosed with black iron fencing, but I spied a small, white marble bench sitting outside of the gates. I knew that Spence had received some of his medical training in that very place, and perhaps subconsciously, I felt as though I was closer to him. I sat down, feeling lonely and desolate. If what I suspected was true, then my friendship with Edwina had come to an end. I couldn't help but weep at the mere thought of losing my friend's presence in my life. As I sat there, lost in thought, without warning, I felt a tap on my shoulder.

"Sophia?" a voice asked. Incredulous as it may seem, it was Spence! There was no one in the world I might have wished to see more at that moment, and there he was. I *needed* to talk to him, to hear his sensible, intelligent voice, to help me sort out the muddle. He had told me that night in Paris to call, if I ever needed a friend, but I would never have done so.

"My Lord," I said, voicing the shock I felt at his unexpected appearance. "This is unbelievable." In spite of my emotional state, I was keenly aware that I must have looked gruesome. My hair was wet from the rain, my eyes were red and swollen from crying and my nose was running.

"Sophia. What is the problem? I almost didn't recognize you. You've been crying. What's happened?" he asked, concern in his voice.

"Spence, what…. What are you doing here?" I responded. "Why aren't you in Twigbury?" The coincidence of his finding me at that precise moment was uncanny.

"I've returned to London to take advanced courses in surgery. Have been here for several months. The chap I was filling in for returned from his travels. I could have stayed on, as his partner, but decided against it. I fear there is going to be another war. I want to be well prepared, if I re-enter the RAF. However, enough of that. What's wrong in your world that I find you crying on a park bench in the rain?" Had I been less upset, I would have realized that it was very foolhardy for me to pour out my troubles to him. He knew nothing about Isabella, and I wanted to keep it that way. The more communication we had, the more likely he was to learn of my daughter's existence. However, my mind was on the dreadful letter, and the subsequent conversations with my father.

"Oh Spence, it's such a demented story, I began…

Spence had been such an integral part of my life, and he was the one…. Perhaps the *only* one… With whom I could discuss my unsettling discovery. I was aware that he also possessed a dimension of objectivity of which I was incapable…. A desperately needed perspective. Therefore, I allowed him to lead me to a small, quiet pub, where we could sip a glass of ale and talk. I wasted no time describing the happenings of the morning at *Grande's Hotel*, as well as the conversations with my father, which had followed. Then I sat back and waited for Spence's response. He was silent for some time. When he did speak, it was obvious that he was choosing his words carefully. He must have felt as though he was tiptoeing his way through a minefield.

"Sophia," he began. "Your father has always seemed larger than life to you. Indeed, I suspect that's the case with most women and their fathers. Perhaps it's even more pronounced with you, because you've never been particularly close to your mother. That's also probably why you are so especially close with Edwina. In addition, I know you have mixed feelings for him."

"Spence, you're so right." As you said, I *do* have very mixed feelings about my father. In some ways, it's true…. I don't respect him at all for the way he has hurt me. Yet, I still love him, if that makes any sense. I don't know if I'm more upset at the idea of my *father* being involved with Edwina, or with the fact that *Edwina* would betray me…. And my mother…. In such a fashion. I've always thought of Edwina as the sister I never had.

Under the circumstances, I think the less Edwina knows about your life, the better. The *intimate* parts of your life, that is."

"Why do you say that?

"If there is…. And I stress the word *if*…. Something going on between your father and Edwina, then you don't want private details about *your* life becoming 'pillow talk', so to speak."

"Spence, I cannot fathom such a thing. That would mean Edwina is betraying our friendship and me. That simply couldn't be."

"Sophia, in spite of your marriage, and Owen's subsequent death, you are *still astonishingly naive*. It has always been a part of your charm. Nevertheless, in this instance, you cannot afford to be an innocent. Your father is not perfect, nor is Edwina."

"I haven't considered *him* perfect for a long time, Spence. I know he has flaws …. Some of them very pronounced…. Moreover, of course, I know that Edwina has her faults. But, goodness, it's a long way from admitting that one's father and best friend have faults, to accepting that they may be involved in a love affaireee."

"I understand that Sophia. You don't know anything with certainty. I admit that it looks suspicious. However, if that *is* the case, you must understand that you cannot control your father's or anyone else's behaviour. We both know that your mother has not always made life pleasant for your father. Would it be so strange then, if he turned elsewhere for the affection he doesn't receive at home?"

Of course, Spence knew of Mummy's *rages*, but my first reaction, resulting from years of denial, was to defend my mother. Then. I realized that I needed to be truthful, both with Spence and with myself. Still, was Spence suggesting that if there was any truth to the possibility that Papa and Edwina were involved romantically, it was justified because of Mummy's *rages?* I could *never* adopt such a perspective, and said as much.

"If Papa is so unhappy that he feels the need to step outside of his marriage for comfort, then divorce is always an option. I could never condone an extra-marital affairee, particularly with my former school roommate and best friend. There are a potful of women in the world. It wouldn't be difficult for a man like Papa, with heaps of money, and a seat in Parliament, besides a magnificent country house, to find himself a mistress. I'm not a fool, Spence, I know that it's done all of the time. But, Edwina....?"

"No, Sophia, I'm not suggesting such a thing. I just want you to be your loving and forgiving self. I, as well as anyone, know that you too, are human. I know the pain you have experienced at your father's hands. But, surely you of all people, can understand how it might be possible for two people to fall in love, even when there's an impediment to their having a future together?"

His words seared my soul. *How could I possibly have been so imprudent....? So foolish not to have recognized how grossly ridiculous it was to be reaching out to Spence at such a moment?* I looked down at the table and twirled my glass in my hands.

"Sophia, I can't bear to see you this unhappy. Please don't cry," he said, as he reached across and placed his hand over mine.

"Oh Spence.... I'm sorry. I'm just so confused. I shouldn't have burdened you with this. You're right....I should not assign one set of principles to my father and Edwina, and another to myself. Thank you for reminding me of that."

"Sophia, the hardest part of this is the realization that *if* there is any truth to this, Edwina is the 'other woman'. I believe you could accept an indiscretion on the part of your father, however painful that might be, if the female involved was a stranger. However, Edwina is your best friend. I know how you feel about her. I understand why you would view such an involvement as a betrayal of your friendship."

"*Of course it's a betrayal of our friendship!*" I nearly shouted. "The whole idea of Papa and Edwina makes me ill! Edwina is like family. It's.... It's.... *In essence, it's incestuous.*"

"Calm down, Sophia. I understand. You don't know anything with certainty. Perhaps your father is telling the truth. Perhaps it *is* just a fantasy on his part. Men *do* go through periods of odd behaviour. Especially at mid-life. You women don't have a lock on that, you know." He smiled that marvelous smile of his."

"Do you believe Papa's explanation?" I asked. It was impossible for me to imagine that he did.

"I believe he doesn't want to cause you pain. Whatever the *truth*, I'm virtually certain that he isn't going to tell you any more than he already has. Whether or not what he has told you *is* true, I can't really say. I don't know your father well enough. Well…. Let's face it, Sophia, I don't know him at all."

His comment made me realize how rather foolish it was for me to be asking Spence's advice about the motives and actions of a man whom he had never met. It also reminded me of the twists and turns our own relationship had taken, and of how much I wished Spence *did* know my parents. Perhaps, if I had braced myself long ago, and allowed the meeting to take place, I wouldn't be sitting with him now, having married a man I didn't love, and having given birth to Spence's daughter without his awareness. The entire tangled mess was horrifically complex.

"My God, Spence. If they're involved in an affaire, what if he leaves my mother and marries Edwina?"

"That's awfully hard to imagine, isn't it? It's a far cry from a dalliance outside of marriage to leaving your wife and marrying the other woman, whomever she might be."

"Spence, I think I'd lose my mind. That would just be too impossible. Things like that don't happen in the real world. Do they?"

"Unfortunately Sophia, things like that *do* happen in the real world, all too often. I could name you scores of families in Britain where precisely that sort of thing has occurred. I must say, however, even in families like the *Simpson's,'* I don't believe there has ever been a scandal involving a daughter's schoolmate. When I make reference to the *Simpson's*, you know I'm speaking of our former beloved Prince Edward and Wallis Simpson. One can go back as far as Henry VIII and clearly see how often divorce and remarriage has taken place on our Fair Isle. However, I think we're both getting ahead of ourselves. Right now, you don't even know that they really are involved in an affaire. Perhaps it's a bit of a flirtation, and that will be the end of it."

"Oh goodness, I hope you're right. I don't see that I have a lot of choice except to believe his explanation. There would be no point in confronting Edwina. I would only cause Papa embarrassment by telling Edwina about this, if it isn't true."

"Absolutely right. I think that's very wise thinking. I know you won't forget this has happened and I would suggest that you be somewhat guarded where both your father and Edwina are concerned, at least for a time. But, don't let it consume you."

"What do you mean *guarded*?"

"That's what I meant a moment ago. Don't tell Edwina something that you would prefer your father not know…. If there *is* anything of that nature in your life. That's where an involvement between your father and your friend could become sticky. Friends share secrets, as do lovers."

Isabella! My first thought was of my daughter. Edwina knew everything. She had been my salvation during the pregnancy and birth. Would she tell Papa that Isabella was not Owen's child? Obviously, that was a concern I couldn't discuss with Spence.

"Sophia, what is it? You look like you've seen a ghost," he said, with concern. "You're as white as a sheet."

What? Oh…nothing. I was just thinking of something. Your comment about friends sharing secrets reminded me of something."

"Nothing you want to share with me?"

"No, I'm afraid not, Spence. I'm sorry."

"Ah…. Far be it for me to interfere with the secrets of two *Ashwick Park* girls," he laughed.

That was the first bit of levity in what had been an otherwise solemn afternoon. I returned the smile. "Oh Spence, I'm so confused and frightened. What if my mother learns of this? She has always treated Edwina like a daughter…. Better than a daughter. And if she ever thinks that I knew…. Or that I even suspected…. Well, I just don't even want to think about what could happen."

"Since you've told your father what you found in his hotel room, he's going to be very circumspect. If nothing else, he's surely going to become less careless. I shouldn't overly worry that your mother will discover anything."

"My mother is totally capable of killing Edwina.... And Papa, and probably me. Most probably, me," I replied, with a half-hearted, watery smile.

"I'd forgotten what a beautiful smile you have," he said, suddenly changing the subject. The compliment unnerved me.

"How is Charlotte?" I blurted out.

"Charlotte? She's well. Just opened in a new West End play."

"How nice. You must be very proud of her." *That was one of the hardest sentences I have ever uttered.*

"Yes, she's quite a fine actress, actually."

He was now turning *his* glass round in his hands, looking as though he wasn't certain what to say next. It was unlike Spence.

"Have you set a date, then?" I asked.

"No.... No.... It's been, well.... Complicated."

"I suppose it's hard when she has an erratic schedule, what with rehearsals, openings, and so forth?"

"Yes.... Quite."

Spence looked distressed. He would not meet my eyes. A silence ensued.

"Oh, Hell Sophia. The truth is that there is not going to be any setting of a date. We have broken it off. It just didn't seem right. To be honest, after I saw you that night in Paris.... And then again in Sloan Square.... I realized that it was too soon after us. I don't know. I just couldn't go through with it. I'd allowed the engagement to go on for too long. I knew that I would never carry through on the marriage. Finally, I summoned up enough courage to admit I couldn't marry her."

My heart soared, even though I tried to make the requisite remarks about how sorry I was to hear about the end of his engagement to Charlotte.

"I'm sorry, Spence. But, I must be honest. I never thought Charlotte was the right girl for you. She's much taken with herself, and not at all 'down to earth'. She never struck me as a girl who would want to be a doctor's wife."

"Oh…. She's a bit different when one peels away the outer layers. She's really rather insecure. The difficulty wasn't with her. To be honest, Sophia, I was somewhat surprised that you were able to move on so quickly after our relationship ended. You were married to Lord Winnsborough within a matter of months."

"Lord Winnsborough and I had known each other all of our lives, Spence."

"I know. Obviously, you were much better suited, but still…"

I couldn't bear the hurt that was so apparent in his eyes.

"Spence, I didn't love him as I loved you. That kind of love doesn't come along often. I married him because…. Because…. My voice trailed off.

"You married him because?"

"Well, because, I knew my parents would approve, and he was considered suitable. I knew I would never feel about anyone the way I felt about you, so I decided to settle for a life with Owen."

"Oh Sophia, what a muck we made of everything. In other words, you simply *settled*. Did it have to be that way?"

"I believed it did, Spence."

"Why did I always feel that there was something you weren't telling me? That you were holding back?"

I looked down at the table. My hands were clenched in my lap, and I was biting my cheek.

"I don't know," I murmured.

"Sophia, look at me. I think you *do* know. What is it you haven't told me?"

He reached across the table and put his finger under my chin, tilting it upward.

"Spence, can't we just leave it alone? What is done, is done. What difference does any of it make now?"

"It matters because I still love you." I jerked my head, and scrutinized him. I could not believe he had said those words. It was hard for me to believe that he was sitting there across from me, so strong, handsome and sensitive, when I had never even dared to hope that I would see him again, let alone hear such words from him. I began to blink back tears.

"Sophia, please tell me the truth. Whatever it is, it cannot hurt more than that which I've already endured."

"It's all so complicated."

"Just start at the beginning."

"Remember the night at *The Royal*, after I'd seen my parents and spoken with them about us?"

"Of course. How could I ever forget?"

"Well, two days before that I went through absolute horror. I told my parents of my feelings for you, and Mummy went mad. I have never seen her in such a state. She was thoroughly out of her mind. Completely irrational."

"Because I wasn't of the gentry?"

"Yes, partly. However, I think even more because you are Irish and Catholic. She is demented on both subjects. She threatened horrible retribution if I continued to see you."

"What sort of retribution? What sort of revenge could she possibly enact upon me?"

"She said that she was prepared to pay a prostitute to say that you had performed an abortion, thus ruining your career, and possibly causing you to be sent to prison."

"And you believed she would do such a thing?"

"Yes. Definitely. She would have, Spence. It could have ruined you. Don't you see, I couldn't allow that to happen?"

"Why didn't you come to me with the truth?"

"Because I knew that you would want to try to talk to her. I knew that would be futile. It would only have caused more pain. I didn't want to expose you to her verbal abuse. She can be so biting and cruel."

"What of your father? Was he content to stand by and watch this debacle, without acting to stop it?"

"Not content, but helpless. That's the way things have always been in our family. There is nothing he could do to change her mind. Had he intervened, she simply would have turned on him too. Actually, she did anyway."

"Sophia, don't you know that nothing she could have said would have mattered to me? The only thing I cared about was you."

"Yes. You say that now, Spence, but do you really think you would have married me if my mother and father had registered such harsh disapproval?"

"I think it could have been sorted out. I have believed for some time that your mother needs someone strong to stand up to her. She has gone through life browbeating her children and husband into submission, and in general, acting like a tyrant. I think she has been crying out for someone to take a stance with her. Once that was done, I believe we actually might have come to an understanding. We might even have gotten along quite nicely."

"I simply couldn't take that chance."

"And so, instead, you chose to lie to me, and marry a man you didn't love."

"Yes."

Spence cleared his throat, and lighted a cigarette. There was silence for a moment.

"Sophia, I've heard rumors about your marriage. I've tried not to listen, but I would really like to know. Did Owen commit suicide?

"To be honest, Spence, yes, he did. He left a note with his solicitor, which was solely meant for my eyes. Only my parents and family, and his parents know, besides me. Well, and Edwina. The last time Owen and I spoke, I thought everything was all right. I thought that we had come to an understanding about our marriage. It was going to be annulled.

"Annulled? On what grounds?"

"I'd learned some shocking truths. Owen was homosexual, Spence."

"Oh, dear God! Poor Sophia. How astounding!"

"Sometimes it's difficult for me to believe that I ever married him."

"I'm surprised that under the circumstances you didn't revert back to your maiden name?"

"I'm certain that I would have, but for Isabella."

I absolutely had not planned to tell him about my daughter. It just uncontrollably slipped out. Nevertheless, perhaps the time for secrets was over. At least the time for *most* secrets. I still didn't intend to tell him that he was Isabella's father. Nevertheless, I certainly couldn't hide my baby's existence from Spence if, as I fervently hoped, he was about to become a part of my life again.

"And who is Isabella?" he asked.

"My daughter," I replied.

"Your daughter? You have a child? But, I had no idea. When was she born?"

"I became pregnant shortly after Owen and I married in January, 1936. She was born on the 6th of September, 1936. In fact, she was born while I was visiting Edwina in Paris, shortly before we ran into you at *Deux Magots*. She was actually due in October, but she was premature. I had become so adept at lying about Isabella's birth, that I, myself, almost believed that her birthday was in September instead of August.

"My God. I'm speechless. So much has happened." He sat back in his chair, and looked as though someone had just delivered a blow to him.

"Spence. You look upset. Does it matter about Isabella? Does it cause you to feel differently about me?"

"No, of course not. I'm just surprised. It's none of my business, but did you plan a baby so quickly after your marriage?"

"No. In fact, Owen didn't want children so soon. Of course, now I understand why. I'm not certain he ever planned children. He did, of course, want an heir. But, Isabella was conceived on our wedding night."

"I see." he replied. It was clear that he didn't like to think of me in someone else's bed.

"Actually, it was the one and only time," I added.

"The one and only time?" he echoed, looking perplexed.

"The one and only time he touched me. I suppose he felt it was his duty on our wedding night, but it never happened again."

"Amazing. Moreover, as a result, you are a mother. I should like to meet your little girl. Let's see, she would be about two years old now. Is that right?"

"Well..... one and a half.... She'll be two in September. She's a little darling. I absolutely worship her. Spence, she is so advanced. She already has a vocabulary. She's like a miniature adult."

"And how do you manage to work at University and be a mother, as well?" he asked.

"I've an indispensable woman who keeps things running smoothly at the flat. A housekeeper, who also acts as nanny. Isabella adores her, and so do I. Dr. Hausfater, the professor I work for, is terribly considerate about my obligations at home. He adores Isabella. I even bring her along to work with me some days, if she's not feeling well…. Has the sniffles or something…. Or sometimes he tells me to work at home on that sort of day. I'm very fortunate."

"Well, I'll certainly look forward to meeting this remarkable child," he smiled. "I want her to become well-acquainted with me, as I hope you're going to allow me back into your life, Sophia."

"Spence, I'm not sure that much has changed."

"Sophia, everything has changed. There will be no more lies. I'm assuming that the objections you voiced regarding Catholicism and Class were simply fabrications in order to avoid the truth. On the other hand, I could be wrong. Are those topics still a problem for you? "

"No. They truly aren't, Spence. They never were. I still don't know much about Catholicism, but I wouldn't have any problem learning. But, now, I have Isabella to consider too."

"Naturally. And what of your parents?"

"I don't know? I'm independent of my parents now, in terms of finances Nonetheless, I wouldn't be totally honest if I didn't admit that I'm still tied to them emotionally. For such a long, long time, I very nearly had no identity, Spence. My mother is *such* a dominating individual. I've spent my life trying to satisfy her. Even now that I'm a mother myself, I find myself reverting to that behaviour. She can still frighten and intimidate me. Papa doesn't frighten me so, but I crave his approval as badly. I don't know why that is, because, frankly, I think of them both as children."

"It's going to take you a lifetime to overcome the damage they've both done, Sophia.

"I know that, Spence." But, in terms of a relationship with you, or any man for that matter, I believe my mother would be less inclined to voice objections toward whomever I might become involved with," I smiled. "I think she now believes that I'm damaged, and that I'd be fortunate to have *any* man pay attention to me. Also, I've made it perfectly clear that I intend upon earning a University degree. Mummy is concerned that I won't *ever* remarry. She thinks I'm bonkers to want an education.…That I'm going to turn into a *blue-stocking*, and that no man will ever want me."

Spence burst out laughing. It was good to hear him laugh. "

What rubbish. Well then, perhaps we won't have to worry so much about *Mummy*, and her threats this time."

"Oh Spence. I bungled things so badly. Do you really think we might overcome all that's happened?"

"I only know that I meant it when I told you that I've never loved anyone the way I love you. I still feel like that. You have said that you feel the same way. Surely that means we mustn't walk away from one another again, without trying very hard to find solutions to whatever obstacles exist. I *do* think we should act quietly on our feelings for a time. Only because we don't need the aggravation of attempted interference from your mother. In addition, we need to go slowly with Isabella. She adds a new dimension to the whole scenario. I want her to learn to know…to trust…and to love me. That will take time."

"Thank you for being so understanding. I'm so happy that my heart literally feels as though it could burst. I never dreamed that today would turn out this way. I've almost forgotten what brought us here in the first place."

"Sophia, you're still such a precious girl," he smiled. He reached over and covered my hand with his. "Please remember that whatever is going on with your father and Edwina is going to have to resolve itself in its own way. You have to let them lead their own lives. I know it's hard, and that it could irrevocably alter your relationship with both of them. There's little you can do now but wait. At least you know more than you did. You can stay vigilant. Perhaps the opportunity to speak with Edwina will present itself. Maybe *she* will come to you. I truly believe, as close as the two of you have been, that if there's anything to this, she *will* come to you and tell the truth."

I believed he was correct, and his words comforted me. It would have been exceptionally difficult to remain upset when the rest of my world was bathed in a radiant glow. The only discomfort I felt at that moment was a gnawing sensation somewhere in the pit of my stomach when I thought about Spence meeting Isabella, and the secret I still harboured.

Chapter Fifteen

AUGUST 1938– SEPTEMBER 1939
THE TRUTH COMES OUT

The happenings of the next year diverted my attention from the shock concerning Papa's possible involvement with Edwina. To begin with, Edwina's own actions completely obliterated any lingering feelings of unrest and suspicion that I had. In September, 1938, Edwina announced her intention to marry Dieter Schoen! I was aghast at the news. It required a tremendous amount of effort to show even a minuscule amount of joy at my dear friend's engagement. There'd been no mention of Dieter since the deplorable incident at *Willow Grove*, but for the brief conversation I'd had with my father. I assumed that Edwina had severed all ties with Dieter. Certainly all *romantic* ties. I couldn't fathom Edwina becoming Dieter's wife. Even if I had not witnessed his abhorrent behaviour at Isabella's birthday party, I would still have found it difficult to profess true happiness at the prospect of Edwina spending her life as 'Frau Schoen'.

Edwina made the announcement via long distance telephone, probably because she knew that my reaction would not be overwhelmingly positive. In one respect, however, the news came as something of a relief. I certainly felt that it leant more credence to my father's explanation of the deplorable letter salutation I'd discovered. It seemed unlikely that Edwina would commit to marrying a man who had been seen behaving in such a rude fashion, unless she truly loved him. Certainly she would not have done so if there were any sort of love affaire taking place. However, I was still intensely dismayed.

Sentiments in England were becoming ever more negative toward Germans. Dieter had done nothing to endear himself to my family or friends. I found his political views repugnant, and could not fathom Edwina feeling any differently. No argument, however, seemed to phase my friend. Her mind was made up. I correctly sensed that too much negativity would only serve to damage our friendship irrevocably. Edwina maintained that a fellow traveler had treated Dieter shabbily on their trip from Paris to England for Isabella's party. This, then had caused him to feel resentful and ill at ease upon arrival at *Willow Grove Abbey*. However much Edwina protested, I found it hard to view him in a favorable light. Although I made every attempt not to be critical, and to give the impression that I was happy for her, I simply could not bring myself to attend the wedding, scheduled for May, 1939 in Paris. They planned a small affaire with little elaboration. There was not even to be a church ceremony, which surprised me greatly, as I'd always assumed Edwina would want an enormous amount of glitter and splendor. I *did* know that Edwina's father was not well. It was possible that the stress of an elaborate event would be too physically demanding for him. I also believed that Edwina was sensitive to the prevailing anti-German feelings in Great Britain. Perhaps she felt that it would be uncomfortable for those in Bury St. Edmunds if she brought Dieter Schoen to the local parish church for the nuptials.

Before I could turn my attention to Edwina and her upcoming marriage, I encountered more trauma in my relationship with Spence. Following our meeting in August, our bond continued to develop. We didn't rush headlong into a torrid love affaire, as we were both wary of being too impetuous. When the time was right, we knew it would be a lifelong commitment. The second time around we would allow nothing and no one to come between us. Because we felt so fortunate to have another chance, we wanted to savor every moment. And then, there was the very real consideration of Isabella. I had no intention of introducing a strange man into her life one moment, and making him her father the next. Isabella was not used to sharing her Mummy with anyone. I knew that I needed to ease her into the idea of having another person in her life.

As a result, I didn't immediately introduce my little girl to Spence. I took her to *Willow Grove* for the Christmas holidays, and he and I had a quiet celebration later. When I finally felt the time was right for an introduction, it was early April of 1939, eight months after our reconciliation. Spence had been gently pressuring me for months. Though the event was well planned, I was still somewhat nervous, as it was the first time that I'd introduced a man to my daughter. Spence came to the flat at six o'clock on a Saturday evening. Martha prepared a simple dinner of roast beef, browned potatoes, Yorkshire pudding, and green beans….Isabella's favorite. When Spence arrived, he was carrying a large box, clearly meant as a gift for Isabella. She was still in her nursery, being dressed by Martha, and it was a few moments before she made her appearance in the parlor. She emerged, wearing a white plisse' dress, trimmed with green ribbon. There was a green bow in her hair and her long, black curls were brushed back from her face. She was such a beautiful child that sometimes she literally took my breath away. It was apparent that Spence was instantly smitten.

"Well, well, so you are Isabella. What a lovely young lady you are," he said.

She smiled shyly, and then spied the box sitting next to him on the sofa.

"Ith that for Bella?" she asked. She had quite a pronounced lisp, which the doctors told me she would outgrow. I thought it added to her charm, and wasn't the least concerned about it.

"Yes, yes, it is. Would you like to open it?"

"Oh yeth." She clapped her hands in delight, and looked at me for permission.

"Yes of course, darling. Let Doctor Stanton help you with the wrapping."

Spence began removing the wrapping paper and ribbon. Isabella helped. Together they lifted the lid off the box, and there lay a magnificent doll, made in the likeness of the Princess Elizabeth. She wore a white satin dress, and on her head was a tiny tiara of rhinestones. Isabella was enchanted.

"Oh. Oh…. Mummy, look!"

"Would you like to hold her?" Spence asked, placing the doll in Isabella's arms.

"Do be careful of her darling," I reminded. "And do thank Doctor Stanton for such a lovely gift."

"Thank you" she said, shyly.

"You're very welcome. When I saw her in the shop window, I knew she needed a little girl just like you to take care of her."

"She's booful," said Isabella.

"So are you," Spence answered, smiling at her mispronunciation.

Isabella settled down in a corner of the room and began to play with the doll, exploring her clothing and hair. Spence and I enjoyed a cocktail before dinner, watching my precious daughter. It was a delightful evening. I couldn't help but think that this was what life would be like when we married. Martha called us to the dining room, and Isabella made certain that her dolly came with us. We made a great fuss about placing *Elizabeth* in the place of honour. The conversation was dominated by talk of the games Isabella liked to play, and she chattered on about kings and queens. Spence seemed very impressed. He alternated between utter fascination with her and speechlessness. He gave her his undivided attention and I was glad. After the meal, we returned to the parlor and relaxed with an after dinner liqueur, while Isabella continued to arrange *Elizabeth's* hair.

"How thoughtful of you to have brought her the doll. She loves it. What a perfect gift," I commented.

"I'm glad she likes it," he answered, taking a sip of his drink. "She really is a little beauty, Sophia. Where did she get those eyes? They're an unusual shade of blue?"

I felt uneasy. Isabella's eyes *were* a gorgeous sapphire blue. I knew that Spence had been told all of his life how unusual the color of his eyes was. My own eyes were green.

"Were Owen's eye's blue?" he asked." I met him at your Ball, but don't remember much about him."

I suppose I could have lied, but knowing that he had met Owen, I wanted to be as truthful as I possibly could be.

"Yes, but rather lighter than hers…. Somewhat 'washed out'. I haven't figured from whom Isabella inherited hers….. Possibly Mummy, although hers are more icey blue. Probably a Winnsborough. I've never really known many of them."

"Does she see them often?"

"Not frequently. They travel a great deal. I try to make certain they see her at special times, such as holidays. Nannies' primarily raised Owen. He was at boarding school early. Therefore, they're not accustomed to lavishing attention on children or grandchildren. No matter. I think it causes less confusion for Isabella"

"She has an engaging way about her. She reminds me of someone."

"Isabella reminds you of someone? Who on Earth would she remind you of?" I asked.

Spence didn't answer right away. He took another sip of his drink. It seemed as though he was taking some time to decide upon how to proceed or what to say next. The silence lengthened and it began to make me anxious.

"Spence is something the matter?" I finally asked, breaking the stillness.

"I think perhaps you should ask Martha to take Isabella to her room," he responded.

"Why? Whatever is wrong?" My throat felt dry.

"Please, just do as I ask, Sophia. I'll explain as soon as we're alone." Reluctantly, I complied, and instructed Martha to take Isabella to the nursery to prepare for bedtime. My little girl took her new dolly and, grasping Martha's hand, toddled down the corridor to her bedchamber.

I turned to Spence with a puzzled expression. "What is this about?" I asked.

"It's about the fact that Isabella is *my* child."

"I beg your pardon?"

"You heard me, Sophia, and there's no point in pretending or lying to me. She is my child. My daughter!

I felt panicky, but tried to maintain a semblance of control.

"Why would you think such a thing?"

"Because she's a replica of my mother when she was a child, right down to the tiny birthmark on her arm, the cleft in her chin, and the color of her eyes. I have portraits of my mother at Isabella's age. You would think it was the same person. I've watched her throughout dinner..... Her mannerisms...the expression in her eyes.... . Even the slight tilt of one eyebrow."

"Spence, this is your imagination."

"Stop it, Sophia! This is *not* my imagination. Isabella is my child. You must have become pregnant that weekend in Twigbury. The timing would fit perfectly. I don't believe she was born in September. Nine months would put it at August. Edwina must have been in on the entire scheme. She must have helped you. This is beyond comprehension, Sophia. How could you have lied to me this way, and kept me from my own child?"

There was no point in continuing the artifice. I was sick inside, and all of a sudden, there seemed no logical explanation for why I had ever attempted such a ploy.

"Spence, how can I make you understand?" I began.

"You can't. Not in a thousand years. I loved you Sophia. I wanted to marry you. You knew that. I even believed it when you told me that you ended our relationship because you were afraid of what your mother might do to me, and to my reputation. When you learned that you were expecting my child, how could you not have come to me? Was I not good enough to be Isabella's father? Did Lord Winnsborough seem a better choice, with his lineage and title?"

"Oh Spence, no. It was nothing like that. My parents would have sent me away. They would never have allowed a marriage. I would have had to adopt out Isabella."

"Over my dead body! Rubbish. I am bloody sick and tired of you using your parents as an excuse for your own weakness. Nothing on earth would have kept me from marrying you, and giving our daughter her rightful name. Nothing! Certainly not your foolish, fatuous mother nor your spineless father. This is complete poppycock. I will not sit here and listen to such gibberish. You lied, Sophia. You schemed and robbed me of something precious."

"I didn't feel I had an alternative."

"Then you were a bloody, little fool!" He slammed his glass down so hard on the tea table that it broke, and I was surprised that it didn't cut his hand. I ran into the kitchen and grabbed a towel. While sopping up the mess on the table, I continued pleading with him.

"Spence, please, please listen to me."

"No Sophia. You have had more than one opportunity to tell the truth, but you didn't intend to ever do so. Even as recently as last August, when we were promising one another that there'd be no more secrets or lies, you were prepared to continue this deception."

"I didn't know how to tell you."

"*You didn't know how to tell me?* I cannot imagine such a rotten, vile, cursed thing. You are not the woman I fell in love with. You're a silly little piece of fluff, and I'll never forgive what you have done."

I threw the towel down. I was weeping, but Spence was far too angry to care about my tears. I couldn't blame him. He was correct, and I knew it. There was nothing left to say. It was perfectly obvious that no amount of pleading on my part was going to undo the hurt I had caused. Nothing could bring back the three years of Isabella's life he had missed, nor make up for the fact that she wouldn't be raised as her father's daughter. To the world, she would always be Isabella Winnsborough.

"I need to get some air, Sophia. I don't recall ever being this bloody angry. When I have had a chance to think, I shall be in touch with you. Not because I want anything more to do with you, but because I *do* intend to have *some* part in my daughter's life. I just cannot think how that can be arranged. I can't think logically about anything right now."

He stood up and walked to the lift, and in a matter of moments, he was gone, before I had a chance to say another word. I sat on the sofa sobbing, feeling horrendous anguish. How could I have been so stupid? Spence was right. I should have told him. Everything would have been all right. Why had I been such a fool?

"Mummy, why are you crying?" Isabella's voice penetrated my thoughts. She was standing in front of me, still holding her doll, dressed in a white night dress, her black curls shining.

"Oh darling. Mummy's just had an upsetting conversation. It will be all right. Don't fret about it. Come here and let me hold you. That'll make me feel better." Isabella crawled onto my lap, and buried her head on my shoulder.

"Is Mummy thad?" she asked.

"I'm all right, sweetheart. Everything will be fine."

"That man made you cry."

"No, he's a nice man, Isabella. He didn't do anything. I did something silly and it made him sad. That's why I'm crying."

"Then thay you're sorry."

"Perhaps, baby." I kissed the top of Isabella's head. "Mummy's very tired now. Would you like to come and sleep in my bed with me?"

"Yeth. May I?" It was one of her favorite, special things to do.

"Yes, you may," I answered. I carried her to the bedroom, tucked her under the down comforter, and prepared myself for bed. Turning out the light, I snuggled next to my little girl's warm body, and thanked God for blessing me with such a treasure. However, even the comfort of Isabella couldn't erase Spence's words from my memory. I finally drifted into restless sleep with a heavy heart.

Chapter Sixteen

September 3, 1939

War

I did not hear from him for a week. When he finally called, I had almost willed myself to believe that everything would be all right. I tried to imagine that when he'd had time to think it through, he would see that there'd been justification for my behaviour. He would forgive me. Needless to say, that was fantasy. While he seemed subdued, and much more controlled, it was apparent that he was every bit as angry as he had been. His feelings hadn't changed.

"Sophia," he began. "I want to talk to you about the decision I've reached regarding Isabella, and my place in her life."

"All right," I answered. I was hopeful that, at least if he wanted to be a part of Isabella's life, I would be able to see him. *Perhaps, in time, he would mellow. After all, he could not have stopped loving me so abruptly.* I knew that he was terribly hurt, and I understood why. However I had always been an incurable believer that time was a healer.

"I don't intend to see her again," he flatly stated.

"What?" I replied, astonished.

"I don't intend to see Isabella. I don't think it's fair to her, and it's terribly painful for me. She is not old enough to understand all of this. I have no wish to cause her confusion. Perhaps someday when she's older, and can better comprehend."

"But, Spence, don't you think she deserves to know her father?"

"I think you've a bloody lot of nerve making *that* statement. If you'd been concerned about Isabella knowing her father, we wouldn't be in this predicament."

"All right, Spence. I know I was wrong. I cannot do anything to change that now. I have said I'm sorry. I know it's not enough. But, does Isabella have to pay for my mistakes the rest of her life?"

"Sophia. If you and Owen had remained married, would you *ever* have told Isabella the truth? Would *I ever* have known the truth? Would *Owen ever* have known the truth? I do not think so. You were perfectly prepared to make Isabella pay for your mistakes the rest of her life, until you got caught in your lies."

"I *did* tell Owen the truth. He knew about the entire, sordid scheme. He understood.... Better than you do. Why do you want to go back over the past repeatedly? Why can't we start from today with the truth?"

"Because I'll never trust you again. Now you tell me that Owen knew. Perhaps that bit of knowledge contributed to his suicide. Has that crossed your mind, *Lady Winnsborough?*"

"The knowledge that Isabella wasn't his child had *nothing....* ..Absolutely *nothing.....* . To do with Owen's decision to end his life. He even wanted to give the baby his name, and there was no animosity."

"Well, that's just delightful," Spence, responded, in a sarcastic tone. "I'm so glad that everyone was so civil about the fact that I was being shut of my own child's life."

"I accept your anger. I accept any rotten words you want to throw at my head. But, I still don't see why you don't want to know and love your daughter now that you have the chance."

"Sophia, are you *unable* to think about what is best for Isabella..... . Instead of yourself? You are only twenty-one years old. You will be married again someday. I have no doubt of that. When that time comes, Isabella will become someone else's daughter once again. She cannot *truly* be my daughter. It would be a delusion to think so. All I would do is cause her heartache by muddying the waters. It is far more kind to let her go on thinking that she's Lord Winnsborough's only child, until she has to learn to accept a step-father. It's the kindest thing to do for her now."

"I don't agree, Spence, but I'll do whatever you ask."

"That's what I'm asking."

"Shall I have any contact with you at all?"

"No, unless of course Isabella is ever ill or should need anything. I'll always want to help her in any way I can, if she needs me."

I was holding back tears as I answered. "All right, Spence. I understand. I won't bother you."

"All right. Goodbye, Sophia. I wish it could have been different," he said, as he rang off quite abruptly.

I was devastated. Everything I'd dreamed had ended. The world crashed about me, with nothing remaining except memories and empty promises. I had managed once before to pick myself up, and move on, accepting that Spence wouldn't be a part of my life, but I wondered if I could do so a second time. Thank God, I had Isabella. Just as my precious little girl had provided a reason to go on when she was still in my womb, the need to care for and protect her would have to sustain me again. I knew that there was no one to blame but myself, and repeatedly I tried to analyze why I had lied. Doctor Hausfater could have helped me to sort out the entire muddle. I knew that he would surely have helped me to understand my abhorrent behaviour, but I couldn't imagine telling him the truth either. I was truly heartsick. But responsibilities at home, as well as my work at *University*, didn't allow for a fall into the abyss of self-pity. Between what I perceived as the loss of my best friend to the enemy, and the loss of the great love of my life, it was difficult not to sink into a deep depression.

I *was* somewhat relieved when Edwina rang me, and said that she and Dieter would not be living in Germany. They were to remain in Paris, and Edwina would not be giving up her British citizenship. Dieter was assigned as an Attaché to the German Embassy in Paris, and they planned to move to a larger flat, near the Place de la Concorde. At least I was not going to have to relinquish Edwina completely to the Rhineland. I hoped that perhaps in time, Edwina might return to England. It was foolish to think that Dieter could be persuaded that England was a lovely land, but it was easier than facing reality.

Frightening headlines in the newspapers, on 19 March, 1939 made everyone realize that it was probably only a matter of time before whatever peace we enjoyed would be shattered. Hitler took over most of

Czeckslovakia. Hoping to save Poland from a similar fate, Britain joined with France in guaranteeing Poland's independence. Many believed that war between England and Germany was inevitable. I could not imagine Edwina married to a man who might soon *truly* be the *enemy*. I tried to convince Edwina to return to England, at least until the unrest eased, but her resolve was steadfast. I had never known her to be quite so stubborn and closed-minded, and feared that Dieter was already having a negative effect upon her. On the other hand, she did seem to be sincerely in love. I had terribly conflicting feelings, as she had been such a loyal friend. A part of me wanted to defend her choice, and share in her happiness. However, whenever I thought of Dieter, the memory of his cold stare and seemingly fanatic bigotry reappeared in my memories. Whatever my feelings, the marriage became a *fait accompli* in May. I sent a massive floral arrangement, accompanied by a *Western Union Wire,* wishing them great happiness, but I silently sat in the flat on Sumner Street weeping. I knew that Edwina and I would never again be such close friends, and another chapter in my life had closed.

Summer was horribly sad and dismal. Usually my very favorite season, it only seemed to resurrect memories of that other unforgettable summer with Spence. That and fear of a war with Germany created a lot of stress. Only Isabella and work saved me. The textbook project progressed beautifully. I was proud of the work I was doing. Doctor Hausfater praised me repeatedly, which helped to heal the wounds of the past few months. Isabella continued to blossom, and as her third birthday approached, I enrolled her in a nursery school at a nearby Parish. She was to begin in September, and was terribly excited about meeting other children. She was such a bright child. I knew that an early start on schooling would undoubtedly be superb for her hungry, little mind.

That first day of school in 1939 never became a reality, for on the first of September Hitler's army marched into Poland. Two days later, Britain and France declared War. From that moment on, nobody's life was the same. On Sunday, 3 September, 1939 I had just returned from church services, looking forward to an afternoon relaxing in front of the fire, reading the *Times,* and sharing some special moments with Isabella. I turned on the wireless, and began to enjoy a *BBC* Broadcast of classical music, while reading.

Suddenly, there was an interruption in the programing, and an announcer's voice came over the airwaves. With a strong note of gravity, he proclaimed that since eleven o'clock, Britain had been at war with Germany. Martha joined me in the parlor, and we sat in shocked silence. I had known in my heart that such a moment could well be imminent, as there had been rumors all summer long. They had definitely increased during the days following the invasion of Poland. Nevertheless, like so many others, I had desperately wanted to believe that something would happen to avert such a catastrophe. Now, there would be no turning back. The future appeared ominous and terrifying. Isabella sensed that something was amiss and came to stand by me, grasping my hand. We listened, as the announcer went on to state all of the changes our country now faced. It was surreal and beastly. I wondered how, while sitting in a safe, secure London parlor, sipping tea, there could be such horror-taking place on the European continent. The telephone rang and it was Mummy. Naturally, she too had heard the broadcast, which was what had prompted the call.

"Sophia, you must come home at once," she asserted. "London will become a very dangerous place. Everyone will want to evacuate to the country. You are fortunate that you have *Willow Grove Abbey* to come to."

"Mummy, wait," I, implored. "I haven't had time to think about what I'm going to do. I am rather inclined not to make any hasty decisions. I appreciate your offer, but London is my home. I'm not certain I should want to leave, unless it becomes absolutely necessary."

"For Heaven's sake, Sophia. Do not be obtuse. You cannot remain in a city that in all likelihood will be bombed. Your father agrees with me. I cannot and shall not allow it."

"Mummy, I'm an adult. I shall make this decision. Please trust me to do what I think is right."

I glanced at Martha, and made a wry face. Martha smiled ruefully in return.

"Mummy, I'll ring you back in a bit. Thank you for calling and I promise to give your suggestion serious thought."

That seemed to pacify her for the moment, but as I rang off, I suddenly felt very young and alone. I spent the remainder of the day trying to glean more details from the radio, and making several telephone calls, to my brothers, Dr. Hausfater and other friends. Blake and Susan, who happened to be in London from Scotland, stopped by about five o'clock, followed by Drew and Annie afterwards. We were together when we learned that France, too, had declared war against Germany. That evening, we all sat in a circle round the radio as King George broadcast an emotional and heartfelt message to the nation. None of our eyes was dry, as the broadcast came to its conclusion. I remembered how a similar scene had played out when Edward the Eighth abdicated. This time, even Blake, who seldom showed emotion, was profoundly moved. Annie, Susan and I excused ourselves and went to the kitchen, on the pretense of making tea. I asked Martha to prepare Isabella for bed, as I wanted to be able to speak freely to my sister's-in-law, and did not want to alarm my child. I could tell that Annie was having a difficult time accepting that Drew would undoubtedly be a member of the military before months' end. I had spoken with Blake and Susan earlier in the day, and he was already certain that he would be enlisting immediately.

"What will you do?" I asked.

"I'm not certain, Sophia. I'll probably wait to see if Drew remains in London or is posted elsewhere. Then, I shall make my decision. It's an awful thing to say, but I'm actually grateful that we don't have children to consider. I'm sorry if that isn't a thoughtful thing to say to you. I don't mean it in a hateful way, Sophia. You know that I adore Isabella. It's just that in our case, since we don't have children, I won't have to worry about their welfare."

Drew and Annie had been trying for years to have a child, but had met with beastly luck. Blake and Susan were not yet parents either. Of course, he had the two children by Elizabeth..... Blake, Jr. and Pippin, but I was certain they would remain with their mother, Elizabeth, in the country. She lived just outside of *Bedminster- with -Hartcliffe*. So I was the lone one among my siblings who had a small child to consider in the entire muddle. I needed their advice, as it was difficult not having a husband to speak with about such important matters.

"I understand what you mean," I replied. "It's perfectly understandable. I am so confused now, Annie. I can't believe this has happened,"

"What do you think will happen to Edwina?" Annie asked, placing into words other fears that I had been holding inside.

"Oh dear, Annie, I don't know. Will she have special protection because she's a British citizen? Do you suppose she'll be allowed to return to England, without Dieter, of course? After all, she *is* still a citizen, and we're not at war with France. However, I should think he would have to leave Paris and return to Berlin. Surely, he wouldn't expect her to accompany him. Would he?"

"Oh good Lord, Sophia. Edwina doesn't belong in Germany. She belongs here, with her friends and family. What a horrible mess," Annie exclaimed.

"Yes, isn't it just?" Susan joined in, nodding her head in agreement. "Do you think we would have any luck if we tried to ring her?" She wondered aloud.

"What a smashing idea," Annie answered. "Let's put a call through and let her at least know that we're thinking of her."

We returned to the parlor where Drew, who was seated in front of the fire, was discussing various branches of the armed services with Martha, whose father had served in the Royal Navy. Drew was leaning in that direction. I knew that Blake would undoubtedly enter flight training, and for a moment, I thought of Spence. I was certain that he would re-join the Royal Air Force. He had already mentioned that those were his plans, if war broke out. I had a fleeting memory of Blake as a child, running across the green lawns at *Willow Grove Abbey*, excitedly pointing to an aeroplane as it passed overhead. That was in the very early days of aviation, and the whole notion of flying was filled with adventure and risk, both of which held tremendous appeal for Blake. Not for him the muddy trenches, nor the decks of a battleship.

After repeated tries on the telephone that evening, we were finally able to make a connection to Paris. I was terribly happy to hear Edwina's voice. As ever, she seemed in good spirits, and there was not the slightest hint of fear in her voice. If anything, she sounded exhilarated.

"Edwina, is that you?" I shouted through the crackling on the telephone line. The connection was terrible, and Edwina's voice kept fading in and out. "Edwina, Edwina, are you there?" I shouted through the static.

"Sophia, do stop wailing," Edwina laughed, "I'm here in Paris, and I'm fine. Everything is a bit strange. They say we're at war, but no one is particularly acting like it."

"What do you mean, Edwina?"

"Just that. Oh, there are soldiers and uniforms already, and talk of rationing on certain items…Butter, Sugar and the like, but basically, Paris is as lively as ever."

"Nevertheless, Edwina, what of you? Moreover, what of Dieter? Isn't there a problem, since you're married to a German?" I asked.

"Dieter is going to have to leave, as the Embassy is being closed. I'll probably remain in Paris for the present. I haven't any great desire to accompany him to Berlin. We were on holiday in Italy in August, and I have scarcely recuperated from that yet. Really splendid, but I certainly haven't any desire for more travel at the moment."

"Edwina," I continued, "I'm not talking about a holiday. You are British. How can you and Dieter be all right, when your country is at war with his country?"

I couldn't believe we were having such a mindless conversation. I couldn't imagine that Edwina was even *speaking* to her husband, let alone, "getting along" with him.

"Sophia, Dieter and I have an agreement that we simply don't discuss political issues. I don't care to know about the German point of view, and I keep my opinions to myself."

"Edwina, that's patently absurd," I responded. "Do you honestly believe that you're going to live through a war with your husband on one side and you on the other?"

"Well Sophia, we shall have to."

"Please. Please return to England as soon as you can, before things get any worse. Do you want to end up in Germany, for God's sake?"

"Sophia, I'm *married* to a German. I shall have to do whatever he thinks best. I imagine that if this thing really becomes beastly, he will allow me to return to England for the duration. Honestly, we have not discussed anything of the sort yet. I think that too much is being made of this. Please don't worry. I shall be fine. Now, what of you?" she asked. I began to tell her about Drew and Blake, but then thought better of it, as a ghastly thought crossed my mind. Much as I tried, I couldn't dismiss it. Edwina was married to a German. She was therefore married to an enemy of Great Britain. From that point on, I could not openly discuss anything of a military nature with her, much less the facts of my brothers' branches of service or deployments. Our correspondence would be censored, and we would not be able to speak freely. Edwina did not seem to grasp the gravity of the situation, but I certainly did. It weighed heavily. Before we terminated our conversation, Edwina lowered her voice. I could scarcely hear her.

"Sophia, there's one other detail. I'm going to have a baby," she whispered.

"You're going to have a baby? Why are you whispering? Oh God. Doesn't Dieter know?"

"No, I haven't told him. I don't intend to. If I do, he'll make me go to Berlin."

"But, Edwina, he has to know. You can't stay in Paris and have the baby alone."

"Please don't worry. I've not thought it all out yet. I'll figure a way to come home to England."

Chapter Seventeen

3 September 1939 to 4 September 1939
A Papa

I crawled into bed the night of 3 September, weary and anxious. I brought Isabella in with me, as she too seemed frightened and confused. I wondered how in the world it would be possible to explain the concept of war to a three year old. I knew that Isabella had to be told the rudimentary facts as, indeed, her life would be changing dramatically. Yet I also felt that I needed to try to make her understand why those changes would be coming, and to do so age appropriately. She was filled with questions, and sensed that there was a somber mood in the household.

"Mummy, what doth war mean?" She asked.

"Well, Isabella, it's a nasty state of affaires. In another part of the world, a country named Germany wants to have power and control over others, and will do anything to get their way. England needs to keep that from happening."

"How will they do that?"

"We don't know for certain, darling. It depends upon what the Germans do to try and get their way. If necessary, our brave men will have to fight them in battle. Many people could be harmed."

"Could they be hurt really bad?"

"Yes, darling, I'm afraid so. That's what is so beastly about war. But, we must hope and pray that this will all be over quickly, and that no one we love will be harmed".

"Will you be harmed?"

"Oh, I shouldn't think so, dear heart. I'll take great care to protect myself, and of course to protect you."

"What about Martha?"

"Yes, of course, Martha too. If necessary, we'll leave London and go to stay with Grand'Mere and Grand' Pere Somerville in the country. You mustn't worry about such things. I promise that I'll always be honest with you about everything that's happening, and I want you to promise that you'll try to be a brave girl."

"I'll be brave, Mummy, and I'll take good care of you too."

"I know you will, Isabella. We'll take care of each other, like we always have".

It was difficult not to weep, yet I didn't want to upset her. I read her a story, tucked her down, listened to her prayers, and asked her to promise that she would come to me with any fears she had. After a bit, she settled down, and drifted off to sleep. I gazed at her sweet face, and prayed that all would be well. I tried to read for a while, but found I couldn't concentrate. I kept reading the same lines over and over again. Finally turning out the light near one o'clock, I tried to sleep, but awful thoughts and visions kept running through my mind. I tossed and turned, thinking about Edwina, my brothers, and what the turn of events would mean for everyone. Needless to say, I thought about Spence, and felt very much alone. At nearly two a.m., the telephone rang. It was the short ring, signaling that the doorman of the building was phoning from the lobby.

"Lady Winnsborough, sorry to disturb you Mam, but you have a visitor", he announced.

"Who on earth is calling on me at this hour?" I enquired.

"His name is Doctor Stanton, and he says that he must speak with you."

I was stunned. *What could bring Spence to my flat at such an hour?* Of course, I instructed the concierge to allow him toenter. I quickly threw on a dressing gown, but there was no time to brush my hair, or to do anything else to make myself presentable before I heard the lift ascending. I quickly glanced into the mirror, pinched my cheeks, and bit my lips to give them a bit of color. Then the doors opened, and Spence emerged into the foyer. I hadn't lain eyes upon him since April, 1938, some five months earlier. In spite of the circumstances surrounding our last conversation, as well as present happenings in England, I couldn't help but feel extreme pleasure at the sight of him. However, my first impression was that he looked solemn and weary, seeming to have lost much of his usual aplomb.

"Hallo Sophia", he said. "I'm dreadfully sorry to disturb you at this un–Godly hour. I felt I had to see and talk to you…… . Had to set some things straight…. To sort out this muddle".

"I understand, Spence. It's all right. I've not been able to sleep tonight anyway, what with the ghastly news we've had today. Would you like some coffee, or perhaps a brandy?"

"Yes, thanks, a drop of brandy would be nice. He smiled and looked more himself. While he settled himself in the parlor, I poured a snifter of brandy from a decanter on the sideboard. After pouring myself a small glass of Port, I moved to a club chair next to the sofa where he sat. I felt anxious in his presence, and was puzzled as to why he was there.

"I've come to see Isabella, he suddenly stated.

My heart lurched. "Oh Spence, I've had such a time getting her to sleep. I'm very reluctant to awaken her. Is it absolutely necessary?"

"Sophia, I'll be leaving on the morrow. I've been at High Wycombe, at The Royal Military College, training to be a flight surgeon for the past several weeks."

"What is a flight surgeon?" I asked, astonished at his revelation.

"It's a relatively new branch of medicine that was used for the first time in the last war. Doctors are termed flight surgeons. We'll sometimes accompany the men on operational flights…… . Will fly at least four hours a month. But, most importantly, flight surgeons will organize the most efficient system of getting aid to the wounded men in the planes…. And to get that aid to them as soon as the plane lands…. You've known that I've suspected England was going to find herself in a war, sooner or later. I hoped it wouldn't come to this, but the signs have been there. I feel I'm needed…… . Want to help. That's why I initially joined the RAF before I went on to medical school. I'm already a Flight Commander…… . Have got my pilot credentials, so it has merely involved flight surgeon training. God knows what the future holds for the lot of us. So then, I simply have an overwhelming need to see my daughter before I leave".

I knew that I would probably begin to tremble. It seemed such a lot of information to take in. Spence would be leaving. England was at war. Spence could be injured…. Could be killed.

"Good Heavens, Spence, why so soon?" I managed to ask. "Couldn't you have waited a bit, until things sorted themselves out?"

"No, Sophia. That's why I've been training during this time. I wanted to be ready if and when the time came. My training is complete, and now I'm ready to take up a post. I would have gone anyway. Men with my training will be needed."

"Where will you be posted?" I asked.

"I'm posted to the 19th Fighter Squadron at Duxford, Cambridgeshire. I'll be training with Spitfire pilots. She's the finest fighter ever built. I'll be just about an hour from London".

"What will your duties be? "Just as I said…..A physician and pilot."

"Spence, this is just too overwhelming. Will you be placed into danger? "

"Anyone serving in the military will be in danger, Sophia. I'll probably be in less danger than many. I'll fly operational missions, but I'll mostly be based here in England to attend to fliers when they return from operations."

I was quiet for some time, trying to digest the new information. It was obvious that I would have to allow him to see Isabella before he left.

"Well certainly, under the circumstances, I don't suppose it will do any harm to awaken Isabella. I want you to see her before you leave. I just don't want her to be unnecessarily upset."

"I have no intention of upsetting Isabella. I simply want to see her. She is, after all, my daughter. I don't know when or if I'll ever have this chance again."

"Oh Spence, please. Don't say such a thing. Don't even think it?"

"Sophia, no one knows what the future holds. This dreadful business has turned the world on its head. I've been thinking for hours, ever since I learned that war has been declared. I need to see my child before I leave, and I need her to know that I'm her father."

Ice water traveled down my spine. This was a totally different turn of events. He planned on telling my baby that he was her father. *Oh Lord, what was I to do?*

"What do you intend to say to Isabella?" I asked, trying not to let my voice break.

"I intend to gently, and without any drama, tell her that I'm her true father. I won't make you out to be a villain or anything of that sort".

"I'm not against your telling her, Spence. Perhaps if the circumstances were different…. If she were a bit older and able to understand….I don't want my baby to suffer," I cried. "You told me when we last spoke that you had no intention of becoming involved in Isabella's life."

'That was before tonight, Sophia. I've done a lot of thinking. I was extremely angry and hurt when we last spoke. Perhaps I was unfair. I don't know. I only know that now I'm more concerned than angry. I'm not concerned for my own welfare, but for Isabella's…. And for what will become of you both."

"You needn't worry about Isabella's future. She'll always be loved and well-cared for. I've already contemplated taking her to *Willow Grove Abbey* if things get rough in London. Of course, I'll be fine. I want to keep Isabella's life normal for as long as possible."

"I don't want my little girl to think that she's Lord Owen Winnsborough's daughter for the rest of her life," Spence said emphatically. "Of course I know that she'll be well-taken care of and provided for. That isn't what I worry about. If I don't tell her the truth now, she may never know who she truly is."

"Spence, I've made the decision to tell Isabella the truth about her paternity in the weeks since our last disastrous conversation. I just want her to be old enough, so that she's able to understand the complexities of the situation."

"And, how many years away would that be? Forgive me Sophia, but I haven't been given any good reason to trust that you would keep to that intention."

His words stung, but I had to admit that they were based on accuracy. I *had* been less than truthful with him, and was responsible for this horrible mess.

Sighing deeply, I answered. "All right, Spence. I'll awaken her, and you have my permission to say whatever you wish. May I at least ask that you allow me to be present when you reveal the truth about her paternity?"

"Of course. I want you to be present", he answered.

I excused myself, and proceeded to awaken Isabella. She was sleeping soundly. Leaning over her bed, I kissed her on the forehead. Isabella stirred, and turned on her side.

"Isabella, darling, you must wake up," I whispered gently. "Someone special is here to see you." Sleepily, she opened her eyes and murmured that she didn't want to get up. "I know it's late, darling, and I wouldn't ask you to wake up if it weren't important. Please try to sit up. That's a good girl. Let me wash your face and put on your pretty, pink dressing gown."

She came more fully awake and sat up in bed, rubbing her eyes. "Who hath come to vithit me?" she asked.

"Do you remember Doctor Stanton, who brought you Elizabeth?" I answered.

"Yeth, I member him. He made you cry.'"

"Oh no, no sweetheart, he didn't make me cry. Remember, I told you that I had done something foolish that hurt his feelings? I was crying because I'd made him unhappy."

"Yeth, I member. Are you made up now? "

"We aren't angry at one another. He's come here to tell you something very important. Something I think you're old enough to hear. Do you remember the talk we had before you fell asleep, about war?"

"Yeth," she murmured.

"Well, Doctor Stanton is going to have to go away to help England fight against Germany, the country that is causing so much trouble. He's going to try to protect all of us from harm, just as your uncles are going to do. But, before he leaves, he wants to talk to you. Mummy will stay with you, and there's no need to be afraid. He's a nice man, Isabella. I want you to listen very carefully to what he has to say. Try hard to understand him. If you have any questions after he's spoken with you, both Doctor Stanton and I shall try to answer them."

I was quaking with anxiety as I tried to reassure my daughter that there was nothing untoward about the conversation which she was about to have. I was also furious with myself for placing my precious baby into such a morass. If I had only been honest from the beginning, none of this would have been necessary. And Spence wouldn't be struggling with lack of trust for me. Isabella seemed satisfied with my brief explanation. Fully awake, she crawled out of bed, and let me help her into a dressing gown. Then, she fetched *Elizabeth*, and taking my hand we made our way to the parlor. Spence was still sitting on the sofa, smoking a cigarette, and staring into the fire with a sorrowful look. Nevertheless, his face lighted when he saw Isabella.

"Well, look who's here," he began, "and I see you've been taking splendid care of *Elizabeth*, just as I knew you would."

"I love her very much." Isabella replied.

"I'm sure she loves you just as much. She's very pretty, isn't she? Almost as pretty as you are. You've grown in just the short while since I last saw you, haven't you?"

"Yeth. Everyone tellth me I'm quite pretty." She smiled shyly, looking at the floor.

"Indeed you are," Spence laughed. "Could you come over here and sit by me on the sofa, while we talk about something rather important?"

Isabella looked at me for permission, and I took her over to the sofa settling her between Spence and me. I was extremely apprehensive.

"Mummy told me you're going away to fight in the war, Isabella said.

If I'm lucky, I won't have to do too much fighting. Because I'm a doctor, I'll try to save lives and help people who get hurt. That will be my job. I'll be called a flight surgeon, which means that sometimes I'll go along on the airplanes with the men who are flying them, and sometimes I'll fly them myself. I'll help them if they find themselves in trouble or injured."

"Oh…I thee" she answered.

Of course, she didn't.

"When will you come back?"

I'm not exactly certain, Isabella. That's why I wanted to see you tonight. It might be a long time before I can see you again."

Isabella's face took on a puzzled expression. A tiny line formed between her brows as she asked, "But why did you want to thee me?"

"Because you're very important to me, Isabella."

Why am I 'portent to you?

"Isabella, it's a very long story, and your Mummy will help you to understand it better at a later time. It isn't important right now that you understand all of the details. There's only one, really big and important part of the story that I want you to know."

"Doth it have a happy ending?" She asked.

"I think it's a very happy ending. I hope you'll think so too, sweet girl."

"What ith the sthory about?"

"It's about you, your Mummy and me, and about how I got a huge surprise not too long ago when I learned something wonderful."

"What did you learn?'

"Isabella, I learned that I'm your real Papa." *There. He'd said it. It was out in the open.*

Isabella was completely silent, and her eyes grew very large. Finally, she spoke. "But, my Papa lived at Winnthsborough Hall and he died. His name was Lord Winnsthsborough." It was hard not to smile at the lisp with which she pronounced 'Winnsborough', but it was important that we keep the conversation serious.

Yes…. Well…. That's what I thought too, but it turns out it was a mistake." Spence glanced over at me. "Lord Winnsborough was a fine man, and he was proud to have you for a daughter, just as I am. But, it turns out that I am your *true* Papa. I know that's hard to understand. You see, I knew your Mummy before she married Lord Winnsborough, and we fell very much in love. When two people love each other very much, sometimes they're lucky enough to be able to make a baby together. That's what happened with your Mummy and me. We made you."

Isabella looked confused. "What makth a baby?"

Oh Goodness. Now we're really in deep muck. How do we explain this to her?

"A man and a woman start off loving each other a lot, and then a beautiful and mysterious thing happens. God plants a seed inside the Mummy, and it becomes a baby. When it grows big enough to live outside of the Mummy's body, it is born. The baby we made was you."

"Oh…now I thee," she replied."

There was no question that she didn't see at all, and I only hoped that Isabella would accept Spence's simple explanation until she was old enough to understand the biologic details.

"How do you feel about this news, Isabella?" I intervened.

"Did god put Doctor Sthanton's theed in your tummy, Mummy?"

"Yes, darling, he did. And I was very happy to know that I was going to have his baby."

Isabella turned to Spence "But if you are my Papa, why did I think my Papa wath Lord Winnthsborough?"

Spence answered in a sad voice. "Because, sweetheart, it was a giant mistake. I didn't know your Mummy and I had made a baby. If I'd known, I would have been a part of your life from the very beginning."

I felt horribly guilty. Because of my stupidity, Isabella now had to adjust to this astonishing news at three years of age, instead of having securely known her Papa from birth.

"Did *you* know, Mummy? She asked, turning to look at me.

This was the question I had dreaded. "Yes, Isabella. I knew. It's all very complicated. Mummy made an awful mistake. I didn't tell Dr. Stanton that we had made a baby."

"But, why?" She turned back to Spence, with eyes that were wise beyond her years. "Didn't you want me to be your baby?"

"Oh, Isabella. I should have wanted you more than anything in the world. Don't ever, ever think that I wouldn't have wanted you. And please don't feel angry toward your Mummy. She did what she thought was right at the time. Someday she'll explain it to you in more detail. The important thing is that you and I both know now. I hope and pray that you'll be happy that I'm your Papa"

She smiled at him, and reached out to take his hand. "Yeth, and you can bring me prethents and we can play together. I think it would be nice having you for a Papa"

I was so relieved. I sensed that Spence was holding back tears. He cleared his throat several times.

"Well…. So…. . Then, that settles it, doesn't it? At least for now. I'm going to have to leave to help with the war, but I'll come back to see you as often as possible, and will write you long letters, and send you presents."

"May I call you Papa," she asked?

"That would make me the happiest man alive," he replied, smiling broadly.

Isabella crawled onto his lap, and put her arms about his neck, hugging him fiercely. "Papa, I think you are very nice," she murmured.

"Oh, Isabella, I think you're very nice too, and I promise I'll try to be the best Papa in the world." She disengaged herself from him, and pulled back a bit, looking up into his eyes.

"When you come back, will you live with me and Mummy forever?"

I quickly intervened. "I don't know about that, Isabella. But, you *will* see a lot of your Papa, just as soon as it's possible."

She looked at me with her old soul eyes. "I would like all of uth to live together. She crawled down off Spence's lap, and stood in front of us. *You, Papa, Martha and me,* she stated in a stern, little voice. Then she put her hands upon her hips, and pronounced fiercely, "*Papasth live in the thame houthes where the Mummy'sth and little girl'sth live.*"

"Well, we'll just have to think on that," Spence answered. He couldn't help but laugh. "You feel quite strongly about this, don't you, Isabella?"

"Yeth, I do.

"I can see that," Spence answered.

"I know you would love that darling," I broke in. Let's just take one thing at a time, shall we? Would you like Papa to tuck you back into bed? I promise we'll talk more about this tomorrow."

"Yeth, I'd like that very much. Do you think you could read me a sthory?" She asked, looking at Spence searchingly.

"Of course I'll read you a story," he replied, as he stood up and took her by the hand. I was hesitant about whether I should accompany them, but quickly decided that if Isabella wanted me, she would ask. I watched as she marched down the hallway, with *Elizabeth* in her right hand and Spence's hand in her left. I heard her tell him that she wanted to show him her nursery, which I interpreted as a good sign, as she obviously wasn't feeling the need to assuage feelings of insecurity by returning to my bed. I sat alone in the parlor, contemplating everything that had happened. The relief at having the truth out in the open was overwhelming. I knew that I would have to brace myself to tell my parents and brothers the truth also. Amazingly, that seemed like a minor hurdle. I felt terribly grateful to Spence for handling such a difficult situation in the manner he had. Although I had no idea what, if any, impact this would have upon our relationship, I knew that it was going to have a very positive influence upon Isabella's life. After nearly an hour, Spence returned, looking much less solemn, and very relieved. "She's sleeping. Children are amazing, aren't they?" He said.

"Yes. So resilient. Thank you, Spence. I do think this was a terribly wise decision. You've obviously made her very happy"

"It has made me happy, too. I feel better than in a long time. Anger is so unhealthy. It eats away at a person, until they wonder if they can bear another moment of pain."

"I'm sorry for everything, Spence. I was a stupid, immature fool." I began to weep. He was standing by the fireplace, with an unreadable expression on his face. He turned, as though in preparation to leave, but then stopped in the foyer. Striding over to where I sat, half-slumped over the arm of the sofa with my head buried in a cushion, he reached out and placed his arms about my waist, pulling me to my feet. Then, he swept me into his arms, and kissed me with fierce passion. But, as quickly as the embrace began it ended, and he dropped his arms to his sides.

"Spence, what is it? Why did you stop? You know how I feel about you…..That I've always loved you. Can't you forgive my foolishness? You just said that you aren't angry anymore."

"Sophia, Sophia. No, I'm not angry, and yes, I've forgiven you. My reluctance to renew our relationship has nothing to do with forgiveness."

What does it have to do with, then?"

"Trust, Sophia. Without trust, there's no hope for a relationship. I want to trust you, but I'm just not certain that I can. Don't you understand what your lies did to me? How can I be certain that the next time you're faced with a crisis, you won't revert to dishonesty?"

"Spence, I know what I did was wrong. I would never, ever do anything so foolish again. I'll never let my parents rule my life like that again"

"Sophia, it isn't just my being able to trust you. I need to believe that you trust *me*. If you had trusted me before, when you learned you were pregnant, you would have come to *me*, not to *Edwina*. You would have trusted that I would have known what to do, and how to handle it"

"I realize that, Spence. I acted like a frightened child. But, I've grown and changed. Please believe me"

"Sophia, now is not the time to begin anew. We're at war and no one knows how long it will last. We haven't the time necessary to learn to trust again. I'm not ready to make that sort of commitment, and certainly not in the midst of war. Too many people have made rash decisions in times of war, only to regret them later. I'm not going to start something that I cannot finish. Let's just leave it as it is for now."

"I remember another time when we said that to one another," I said, through my tears. That beautiful, innocent summer when first we met. Only that time I said it to you."

"Yes. I remember. Do you think I've forgotten one moment of that splendid summer? I've ached with memories of those times."

"So have I, Spence. And for all of your talk tonight of rationality and trust, I believe…. No…. I'm certain, that you still love me. And I know I still love you. Nothing you can say, and no amount of time is ever going to change that."

He looked at me with those piercing, blue eyes, and I felt that he could see my soul.

"Sophia, I once told you that I believed we'd known each other forever. I still truly feel that we were destined to be part of one another's lives. I cannot deny that I love you. I'll probably always love you. But, I don't believe that love, by itself, is enough. You said those same words at the *Royal* that last night. I can't believe I'm saying them now. In many ways, Sophia, you're still a child. Still believing that love conquers all. You were right that night at the *Thames Room*, though you didn't really mean what you were saying. Life isn't so romantic. Love does not conquer all. I simply don't intend to start something anew with you. I'm sorry if I gave you that impression."

I was terribly wounded. Openly weeping again, I cried out to him. "Why do you want to be unhappy? Why? Perhaps I *am* still a child, but I know one thing with absolute certainty. It doesn't matter who is right and who is wrong. What matters is who lets go of the anger first. No, I don't believe that love conquers all. But, I'm certain that when two people love each other, they can work through just about anything. I made a mistake, Spence, and in spite of your calm, reasonable words, I think you're still harbouring anger towards me. Now it's you who are making a mistake. I think you're punishing me for being such a little nit, and if that's the case then there is nothing…. Nothing at all…. That I can do about it." There was silence in the room, and I could hear him breathing. The embers in the fireplace were dying, and the wind outside on Sumner Street caused a branch to brush against the window pane. I was praying that he would take me into his arms again. But, then, he spoke.

"I don't want to be unhappy, Sophia and I'm not punishing you. Please believe that. Nevertheless, an awfully lot has happened. I'm sorry, but I can't shrug it all off. The timing is all wrong." He cupped my chin in his hand, and tipped my face up toward his. "Pray for me and keep your optimism. This isn't the last time we'll see one another. God willing, we'll meet again." He kissed me….A long, lingering kiss, filled with passion and longing.….A kiss to last a lifetime, as it seemed too many in our lives had already been.

"Spence, I'll pray for you every night," I sobbed. May I write to you? Wouldn't you at least like to have news of Isabella?"

"Of course, I would. I want news of you too. I won't promise I'll have much time to answer your letters, but I'll try. You're so young and beautiful, and we live in a tumultuous world. If you can find someone whom you feel will be good to you….Will be good to Isabella….Then give him your love. I'm not in a position to deal with a love relationship now."

His words were cold and harsh, and I was wounded to my core. I also didn't believe him. But, I refused to continue making a fool of myself. If he didn't want me, then I had no choice but to accept that as fact. *Or pretend that I did.*

"Now, I really must go. I've a long day tomorrow. Actually, today," he smiled. "I didn't plan on being here tonight at all, let alone so terribly late. I'll post you as soon as I reach Duxford, and send my address. I need you to be strong for Isabella." I took a deep breath. He was right. I did need to be strong. Those of us who were left behind would have to keep a stiff upper lip for those who were defending us.

"I'll be all right, Spence. Please don't worry about me. Of course I'll worry for you, but I'll keep busy. Just take care of yourself."

He took his coat from the foyer, and pressed the button for the lift. The creaking of the cage as it ascended pierced the silence. When it reached the flat, Spence pulled open the brass grille-work on the door and stepped inside. Then, he turned toward me once more.

"Take care of Isabella." he said. And he was gone.

Chapter Eighteen

4 September 1939
An Admission

I scarcely slept all of that night. The next morning was one of those inexplicable English days, when the sky was azure blue without a cloud. I rose early and immediately went to Isabella's room. My daughter was also just waking. I wanted to make certain that the conversation of the previous night had made sense to her, and that there was nothing further I could say to help her understand. Isabella was her usual ebullient self, smiling and sweet. "Do you remember everything that happened last night?" I asked her.

"Yeth I member. Dr. Stanton is my Papa. I have a real, live Papa who loveth me. Can I tell my friendsth? Now I have a wonderful, new Papa, and he ith *very handthome* and *very* nithe."

"Yes, dear, he is all of those things," I replied. "And, of course you may tell anyone you wish. There will be no more secrets. Mummy is going to tell Grand Mere and Grand Pere Somerville today. They don't even know yet. Will you mind if I leave you with Martha, while I drive to *Willow Grove* to tell them our happy news?"

"Will they be ath happy ath me?"

"I don't know, darling. But, it doesn't 'matter, does it? What matters is that your Papa, you and I are very happy, indeed."

"I don't mind if you go to tell them. They thould know.

"Thank you, baby. I won't be gone the whole day. Would you like Martha to take you to the park?

"Oh, thank you, Mummy. That would be justh wonderful," she said, jumping up and down on the balls of her bare feet. I couldn't help but laugh at her mature vocabulary. Surrounded by adults, she had begun to sound as though she were a miniature grownup, albeit one with a lisp. I'd made the decision to ring my parents and enquire as to a convenient time for a visit. I had no intention of waiting any longer to tell them the truth about Isabella's paternity. It was part of the vow I'd made to myself.....That trust would be reestablished between Spence and me. Whether he wanted me or not, there was no question that the first step was to open the door to the past, and let the sun shine in on our dark, murky history.

I can't say that I wasn't a bit nervous when I rang my parents. Mummy, of course, thought I had come to my senses, and was ringing to say that I wished to move back to *Willow Grove Abbey* for the duration of the war. Clearly, the last thing that my mother envisioned was the announcement I was about to make. I asked if there was a possibility that both of my brothers and their wives might be present too, since I wanted to make the truth known to the entire family in one sweep. It turned out that they'd arranged a trip to see our parents anyway, as plans were being set into motion for Blake and Drew's enlistments. They undoubtedly wouldn't be home again for a long spell. Mummy seemed genuinely pleased that I was going to join in the family gathering. I don't believe she attached any particular significance to my visit.

And so, I arrived at *Willow Grove Abbey* on a Monday afternoon, having left Isabella in the care of Martha. I'd sold Owen's *Pierce Arrow* automobile, and had purchased my own little auto, a 1938 *Ford Prefect*. I adored the freedom it afforded. Thus, I drove down to the *Abbey*, enjoying the late summer scenery. Roses were still blooming along the hedgerows, and the rolling land was a soft green, dotted with tiny white fluffs of sheep in the far distance. In such beautiful pastoral surroundings, it seemed impossible to believe that our country was truly at war. My short, tussled curls whipped in the wind, and I breathed in the lovely fresh county air. My spirits were high when I arrived at my beloved family home. I was firmly committed to not allowing anything to deter me from my chosen path. Mummy and Papa both met me in the Great Hall, and they too seemed in a rare, happy mood. Mummy was acting witty and charming, and Papa seemed relaxed as he followed us into the drawing room where cocktails were waiting to be served. My brothers and their wives were already there, seated comfortably on the various sofas scattered about, and I made a round of the room, greeting and kissing each person.

A grand piano dominated one end of the room, covered with Sterling frames which held photos of the family. A Cecil Beaten portrait of the family hung above the fireplace. I remembered being about four years of age when the portrait was commissioned. I'd always felt that my eyes held a sad expression. Annie noticed that I was studying the portrait, and commented upon it. It seemed a lifetime since I'd faced off with my parents in that very room, in the fall of 1935. So much had happened since that beastly day.

"What a handsome family, Sophia. You were such a beautiful child," Annie said, glancing at me fondly.

"Thank you, Annie. That's a lovely thing to say," I murmured.

"Yes, Sophia's eyes have always been spectacular," Papa concurred, as he handed me a gin and tonic.

"When the nurses brought her to me after her birth I remember their comments about her long lashes," added Mummy. *How ironical that her words were almost identical to those that were spoken to me about Isabella's lashes, after her birth.* I was taken aback by such uncharacteristic compliments. My mother generally had extreme difficulty praising *anyone*, let alone me. I seated myself comfortably beside Annie and sipped my drink. At such times I was almost able to delude myself into believing that we Somervilles were a normal family, which was totally daft.

"So, Sophia, we've been discussing the ghastly war events. Drew and Blake have just told us that they're enlisting, but I suppose you've already suspected that," said Papa.

"Yes. We spoke about it yesterday. It's beastly, isn't it? But, I can't help but be proud of them," I added.

"And what of you, Sophia? Have you had time to make any decisions?"

"Well.....Yes and no. Quite a lot has happened, actually. That's one of the reasons that I'm here today. I wanted this chance to talk to the entire family."

"Have you decided to move back here?" Mummy asked.

"No, I haven't reached any decision about that yet. I prefer as little change for Isabella as possible. If things become difficult in London, of course, I'll strongly consider relocating."

"Then, whatever did you come to speak to the family about?" she questioned.

"I'm not exactly certain where to begin. I need to tell you something that has weighed upon me for a long, long while. It's been a horrific burden, and a difficult secret for me to keep. It should never have been a secret." I leaned forward in my chair.

"I daresay you're confusing us, Sophia," Papa responded, with a frown.

"Well, to begin with, I need to tell you that Isabella is not..... Is not.... Owen's child."

Mummy gasped and put her hand to her breast. "What are you saying? How on earth can she not be Owen's child?"

"Quite simply, Mummy. I was pregnant before I married Owen. Isabella is Spencer Stanton's daughter." I leaned back.

Both of my brothers let out a huge guffaw, and their wives smiled. But, Mummy and Papa looked ashen.

"Spencer Stanton? The Irish-Catholic physician?"

"Yes, Mummy. The man you forbade me to marry. I didn't' know when I asked for your permission to marry him that I was expecting his child. When I found out, I would have married him in a heart's beat, as I loved him so deeply and knew he loved me. But, you'd threatened such beastly reprisals against him, if I went against your wishes that I was terribly afraid for him. I'm not here to chastise you now, but if I'm to explain the facts. Then you must understand the 'whys' and 'wherefores.'

"Sophia, had we known about a baby we would most certainly have viewed the situation in a different light," said Papa.

"Perhaps, Papa. But, I was afraid to take that chance. I was terribly frightened that you would send me away somewhere, and force me to adopt the baby out. I could never, ever have done such a thing. Mummy made it very clear that she would never accept Spence into this family"

"Well. He is, after all, Catholic and Irish ..... And hasn't a thing to offer you," she retorted.

"Except love," Drew interjected.

Pamela whirled around and glared at her son. "Well, love is not enough. Nigel and I did not feel that Doctor Stanton was a proper choice for Sophia."

"I suppose Owen was?" Blake asked.

"He seemed, at the time, to be a much better choice. Did Owen know the truth about Isabella?" Mummy asked, turning back to me.

"No, Mummy. He didn't when I married him. It was wrong of me, I know. But, I did tell him later. When he confessed that he was homosexual, the truth was told about everything. I don't have any ill will towards Owen, and he had none towards me."

"*You have no ill will towards him*? Have you lost your mind? Look what he did to your life? Didn't he care what people would think? He went and killed himself." She picked up a framed photo of Owen in his riding habit. Studying it for a moment, she continued; "Look at his mouth. I can always tell from the mouth. I should have paid attention to it. Well, he didn't' get away with it, did he?" She threw the photo down, and the glass shattered.

"Mummy, calm down. I mean it. I am going to leave and return to London. I'll not come back if you're going to continue in a tirade," I said, shocking myself with such courage. To my amazement, Mummy *did* calm down. Perhaps Spence had been correct, about taking a firm upper hand with her.

"No, I do not have any ill feelings towards Owen, and if I honestly look at what he did to my life, his largesse made it possible for me to be truly independent."

"Continue with what you were telling us," said Papa, trying to avoid any new confrontation.

"Right. Well, Edwina helped me. I went to Paris and had Isabella. She was actually born in August, but we waited and told you that she was born in September."

"My God! I never even suspected, and I don't believe any of us did." Papa looked round the room at the gathering of faces.

"No. I *did* notice the lack of resemblance to any of the Winnboroughs, but I simply thought that Isabella was a Somerville, through and through. Now that I think of it, from what I recall of Dr. Stanton, she does seem to resemble him," Mummy mused. "I only saw him once, when he attended your debut Ball, and came through the receiving line, but it would be hard to forget him." I was truly amazed that my parents seemed to be handling the news so well, and except for the one, brief episode, I'd not seen signs of rage. I felt that my brothers and their wives' presence helped enormously.

"Does Spence know the truth?" Blake asked.

"Yes, he does now. He didn't for the longest time. I'd made the decision not to ever tell him. He seemed to have gone forward with his life, and I saw no reason to interrupt that. I still cared for him, but thought he'd forgotten all about me. However, things changed last spring. I saw him again, quite by accident. We talked at length. It's taken much longer than it should have, but he finally knows that Isabella is his daughter. More importantly, Isabella knows the truth. I'm greatly relieved, and Spence is deliriously happy. Isabella is thrilled, as well."

"Good show, Sophia!" shouted Drew.

"Sophia, that is really splendid, added Annie. "I always knew you never stopped caring for Spence."

"So what now?" asked Papa?

"I don't know. Don't jump to hasty conclusions. Spence is not ready to resume any sort of relationship with me. He was dreadfully angry at my not telling him the truth initially. I kept Isabella from him for a long time, after all. I understand his wariness. I've lied to him three times. Once when I told him I wouldn't marry him because we weren't of the same Class and because of his religion, both of which were horribly untrue; once when I learned I was pregnant; and once when we resumed our friendship last year, and swore we would always be honest with one another. I didn't tell him the truth then. He's not brimming over with trust for me. He's trained to be an RAF flight surgeon, and is already off to his post. But, I do still care for him greatly, and it's impossible not to have hope. However I'm also trying to be realistic. The important thing right now is that Isabella knows that he is her father, and hopefully will see him from time to time. I suppose a lot depends upon the war. Isabella needs to adjust to the news at this point."

My parents were silent. Finally Mummy spoke. "Can he support you?"

"Pamela, that's hardly an issue, considering Sophia's settlement from Owen."

"Mummy, he can support me very nicely, but even if he couldn't, I love him," I stated, in a firm voice. "However, again, I must ask that you please don't rush to hasty assumptions. Spence has not asked me to marry him. And, I can tell you one thing with certainty. Spence would *never* even consider allowing Owen's money be a part of our income."

"Well, it seems to me that if he loved you so much that the two of you created a child, he might be decent enough to marry you," Mummy said, cynically.

"He loved me and wanted desperately to marry me, when you threatened to ruin him", I answered, between clenched teeth. "He did not deserve to be lied to. I acted like a child."

"Oh for God's sake, Sophia. Doesn't he understand that all women play little games where men are concerned? What is a tiny lie here and there?"

"No, Mummy, he does not understand that, and he doesn't expect it, and you are wrong. All women do not act in such a manner. I'm just learning that. There will never be anything but honesty between Spence and me from this day forward, whatever happens."

"Well…Yes, I can see where that sort of lying might have created a problem. He certainly *is* charming, and really quite alarmingly handsome," she replied. "I do so wish he had a better lineage. Of course, the Catholic thing is devastating to me."

"It isn't the least devastating to me, and I'm the person who would be accepting it," I replied.

"Do you mean to say that you would convert to Catholicism?" Mummy spoke in a tone of utter disbelief.

"Yes, Mummy."

"Never," she shouted! There was silence in the room, but for the clinking of ice cubes in glasses, and the occasional shifting of positions. Papa cleared his throat, but said nothing.

Finally, Drew stood up. "Oh, for the love of God, Mother. Sophia has been through enough. If Spence makes her happy, let it be. I know him well. He's a fine chap…A decent, warm human being. You should be hoping that your interference hasn't ruined any chance for their happiness, permanently. Stop meddling in Sophia's life." I could literally have wept with joy. Drew's words galvanized the others.

"Pamela. Drew is correct. Enough is enough. Sophia and Spence have waited long enough to be together. They need the support of her family in order to work out the muddle that the past has created. I gladly offer my support," exclaimed Papa.

"I second that," said Blake. Susan and I are delighted, Sophia."

Mummy sat silently, perhaps in shock. Finally, after several minutes, she spoke. "I suppose we must take into account the fact that in some circles Sophia is damaged goods, so to speak. After all, Sophia, you *have* been married, not to mention having borne a child. However odd your marriage turns out to have been, many gentlemen of quality would not think of marrying someone with such a past. I'm very much aware of the way some people judge others. I know how *men* think, and as a mother myself, I know that I wouldn't be thrilled if *my* son announced an intention to marry a woman with these stains upon her background. It's indeed fortunate that Spence's parents are deceased, so we needn't face that obstacle." *Oh God, Mummy was absolutely insufferable.*

Out of the blue, Susan stood up, looking radiant in a peach silk day dress, which nearly matched her hair. "Well, Countess Somerville, I believe it's time that I made you aware that I became pregnant before I met Blake. I was forced to undergo an abortion because of the same sort of attitude that you espouse. Are you then saying that knowing such a truth about me, makes me no longer acceptable as your daughter-in-law?" Mummy was speechless. We all were. Blake had a wide grin on his face, as he had obviously known the truth before his marriage.

I stood and went to Susan, hugging her closely. "Susan, dear, it wasn't necessary to reveal that. Thank you so much for your support. I'm dreadfully sorry you felt the need to tell that."

"No, no, Sophia. I'm glad to have it out. Blake has always known about it, and he's *never* been judgmental. That's all that's ever mattered to me." The angry reaction from the various members of my family, coupled with Susan's revelation, was, at last, too much for Mummy to bear. It was the first time in my memory that we had all united in defense of one another. I couldn't, for the life of me, understand why we hadn't done so long before.

"Mother, I think this conversation has gone far enough," stated Drew. "Obviously Spence knows everything there is to know about Sophia's past pain, and he certainly doesn't consider her damaged goods", nor does anyone else. Spence is a top-drawer gentleman, and I hope we have the chance to welcome him warmly into the family."

"Quite right, I think, murmured Mummy, in a subdued tone. "I was only trying to say that, under the circumstances, we should feel very fortunate that Spencer, even though lacking a title, and carrying the burden of being an Irish Catholic, may want to marry Sophia'."

"Once again", I replied, you are all getting ahead of yourselves. I am not at all certain that Spence and I can ever put this thing back together. I chose to tell you the truth today because I have made a vow to myself that there will be no more lies in my life or in Isabella's. That's why I'm here and nothing more. "It was on that day that I came to a startling realization. By intently listening.to my mother, it was exceedingly clear that whenever she made denigrating remarks about another, she was actually describing the way she felt about herself. It even made me wonder if Mummy herself had either had an abortion, or worse still, had an out-of-wedlock child before she married Papa?

Chapter Nineteen

SEPTEMBER 1939 TO DECEMBER 1939
A STRAINED FRIENDSHIP

And so, Spence was off to Duxford, and both of my brothers had enlisted. Blake, too, went with the RAF and Drew chose the Royal Navy. Blake was sent to flight training at Cramwell, and I heard nothing but talk of Vickers, Wellingtons, and Spitfires, which were the types of bombers and fighters he was learning to fly. Drew was sent to Portsmouth, to train as a naval Chaplain.

Spence wrote much more often than I might have hoped. His letters were always addressed to Isabella, and they were absolutely proper, with no romantic overtones, nor any mention of feelings towards me. I wrote to him too, sending pictures of Isabella, and telling him the latest news from London. But, I too kept my feelings to myself. Having been rejected so frequently as a child by my own family, I was particularly sensitive to not opening myself up to such a possibility again.

During that period, which was later referred to as the *'Phony War'*, relatively little of import happened. It was a quiescent period, after the fall of Poland, and there was talk of pathetic leadership and poor tactical design. It seemed as though there would not *really* be a war and everyone prayed that would be the case. The Polish army surrendered in Warsaw on 27 September, and Franklin D. Roosevelt, the President of the United States, announced that the USA would remain neutral in the European war. On 14 October, the Russian army became involved when Joseph Stalin formally took control of Poland. All was quiet in England. So quiet, in fact that my anxiety was largely put aside. I occupied myself with my work with Dr. Hausfater, as well as my pleasing life with Isabella. Dr. Hausfater was not naive, and he showed great alarm when, in October, the first Jewish ghetto was established in Piotrkow, Poland. It was during that period that another startling and overwhelming event occurred. It carried the power to wipe all thoughts of war, at least temporarily, from my mind.

It began when Papa was in London, for a round of his usual meetings, and I wanted very much to speak with him, as I needed and wanted his advice on some investments. I rang him at his hotel about nine o'clock in the evening, but continually received a busy signal. This went on for literally hours. Finally, when it was approaching midnight, I gave up, and assumed that something must have been wrong with the connection. Instead, in a mellow mood, after sipping two glasses of Sherry, while writing a letter to Spence, I decided to place a call to Edwina in Paris. It was always easier to get through to her during late night hours, and Edwina never minded. It would have been highly unlikely that she would have been sleeping. However, something strange happened when I was put through to her number by the operator. *Her* telephone line was *also* busy. I asked the operator to ring me back when the line was free, and that occurred shortly after I had given up on ringing Papa. The thought flitted through my mind that Papa had been talking to Edwina. Then, of course, I immediately remembered the salutation to that beastly letter, which I'd found in his hotel room. It was never far from my mind. I didn't say anything about my suspicions when I spoke to Edwina, but made a mental note to pay attention to anything of a similar nature that might occur in the future. I recalled Spence telling me to be careful of what I said to Edwina, in case there was, indeed, something to my intuition

We chatted about inconsequential things. It was nice to have a long talk. Dieter was back in Berlin, and she didn't seem to particularly miss him. The conversation primarily revolved around the fact that she was pregnant, just a bit over a month. Of course, I was happy for her, although I had to admit to a small, fleeting fear that the baby might not be Dieter's. I didn't even want to think such a thing. Edwina said that she felt splendid. We discussed the fashion market, and she said that it had been very slow because of the war footing. As a result, she hadn't been working much. I asked if there was any chance that she might come to England, at least for a visit, but she hemmed and hawed, and never directly answered the question. By the time we rang off, it was near two in the morning, and I was more than ready for sleep. I tried to put my disturbed thoughts about Papa and Edwina aside, and snuggled into bed.

My suspicions couldn't be quieted indefinitely. The next thing that alerted me was a trip Papa took to Paris. Of course, it was under the auspices of business. But, I spoke with my mother by telephone while he was abroad, and Mummy said that he had rung her asking if she would mind his staying over the weekend in Paris. He supposedly wanted to attend a new stage play that had just opened. I couldn't believe that my mother gave her assent. I also found it improbable to believe that my father would have the slightest interest in altering his schedule to attend a stage production. That was completely and utterly out of character for him. He had never shown a whit of interest in *any* of the arts.

Shortly after that, I had a letter from Edwina, telling me that *she* had attended the same theater production. She made no mention of my father.... Didn't say she had seen him during his visit.... But, I was certain that she had. In fact, I was certain that *Edwina* had been the reason for his visit. And so, I rang her once again, with a very definite purpose in mind. The conversation began in our usual friendly manner. I really didn't know how I was going to broach the subject. I just knew that I was, indeed, going to bring it to her attention. As we talked, I told her that I'd run into a chap whom we had both known while at *Ashwick Park*. It was true that I'd seen our mutual acquaintance at University, where he was now a professor. He rang me shortly thereafter, and, although I suspected that he was married, he asked me to dine with him. I declined. With that, Edwina said something that opened the door for me.

"Oh Sophia, whatever you do, don't become involved with a married man," she exclaimed.

Without missing a beat, I answered. "Are we speaking of you and Papa now, Edwina, or are we speaking of me?" My heart was racing, as I waited to see what her reaction would be to my comment

Edwina was mute, while seconds ticked by. I didn't rush an answer, and just sat at my desk listening to the traffic outside on Sumner Street. At last she spoke.

"Whatever do you mean? Why would you say such a thing?" I could tell by the tone of her voice that she was nervous.

"Edwina, I'm not a fool. I've put two and two together. I believe that you and Papa are having some sort of relationship."

"Well, your father and I are good friends. You know that. I think of him as a mentor. We have a friendship. It's nothing more than that. I can't imagine that you would think otherwise."

"If that's all it is, then there's nothing amiss, is there?" I answered.

"I won't be concerned, and I'm sorry if I upset you. I couldn't imagine that you would betray our friendship in such a manner, but..... Well..... I suppose anything is possible."

We chatted for a few more minutes about nothing terribly important, and then rang off. I apologized again. It wasn't but five minutes before the telephone rang again. It was Edwina and she was weeping.

"Oh God, Sophia, I'm not being honest with you. We *are* having an affaire. A full-blown, head-over-heels love affaire."

There it was. I had known. I had known from the day that I found the beginning of the letter in Papa's hotel room. Her words only confirmed what I had known. Although I hadn't thought that I would be surprised if my hunch turned out to be correct, I was. How could I assimilate the fact that my best friend, and former school roommate, was involved in a love affaire with my own father? How was I to deal with *it?* I tried to remember what Spence had told me when we'd spoken of such a possibility. Everything was a jumble, and all I could really think was that I neither wanted to lose Edwina's friendship, nor my hard won closeness to my father. I also couldn't help but wonder if my hard-won closeness with my father had anything to do with his romance with Edwina? Were they using me? I didn't want to see Mummy destroyed, and knew that she would be, if she ever learned of the affaire. Mummy was so precariously perched emotionally, and I couldn't imagine what such a revelation would do to her. I was furious. The fact that Edwina and my father were engaged in a physical relationship made my stomach churn. But, I didn't make Edwina aware of my emotions. Instead, I fought desperately to maintain a calm I didn't feel. If I had been in a rational frame of mind, I would have remembered the vow I'd made to Spence not to ever let lies be a part of my life again. But this was such an untenable situation, and it didn't allow for such a black and white decision.

"How can this be happening when you've just married Dieter? When you're expecting a baby? How long has this been going on? Why did you marry Dieter?" Questions were pouring forth, coming one after the other.

"Sophia, I married Dieter because I was trying to make your father jealous. I thought if I announced that I was going to marry Dieter, it would cause your father to realize that he had better leave your mother and marry me, or he might lose me forever. I didn't think I would really *have* to marry Dieter. I just thought Nigel would stop me, before it got that far. I know now that my actions were daft. Nigel was horrified, but he didn't do anything. So, we just continued the affaire after I married Dieter. It had begun in earnest long before that, when I was in England with Dieter for Isabella's first birthday."

"How can that be? You weren't even married to Dieter then?" I was stunned and confused.

"No, but the way Dieter acted threw me into your father's arms. Nigel was so kind…. So compassionate, that awful night, when Dieter acted a fool. Do you remember that I spent so much time at Willow Grove? Well, of course, you do. Nigel came to me that same night, after that ghastly scene with Dieter. He came to my room, simply to talk, and we *did* talk. But, then something else happened. As we shared thoughts and feelings with each other, he told me that he had watched me grow from a young girl into a beautiful woman. He told me that he'd harboured feelings for me in secret…. . Had wanted me to know how he felt for so long. He kissed me that night, and it was then that I stopped pretending about the feelings that I'd also hidden. We'd flirted before. Do you remember the time I surprised him when he was checking into his hotel in Paris?"

"Yes, Edwina. Most definitely," I answered.

"Well, on that night we both had feelings that were more than casual for one another"

So the salutation on the letter I'd found in Papa's hotel room did have more meaning than simple fantasizing.

"Edwina, I was still at *Willow Grove Abbey* the night you are speaking of. I even remember showing you to your room, after we spoke out near the cemetery. When did Papa come to your room?"

"Much later. I'd had a bath, and was in bed, still feeling just horrible. He tapped on my door."

"Did the fact that we were practically sisters mean anything to either one of you?" I asked.

"Sophia. Don't you understand? I was in love. I wasn't thinking. I was in love."

It was the most selfish, inane answer to a question that I'd ever heard. *'She was in love'*. And what about the other people who would be greatly affected by such *'love'*?

"Edwina, if your father had come to me professing love, I would have told him that I was flattered, but that you were my dearest friend on earth, and that would have been that."

"You don't know that, Sophia. You don't know what you might do in such a situation, if you were in love."

"I know that I would never, ever have betrayed your trust."

"I didn't think of it that way. I honestly thought you might be happy that your dearest friend and your father were in love. I didn't know what I was going to do at that point. I asked Nigel to give me time to think."

"And…."

"And the next night I went to bed with him," she said, rather calmly.

"My, my. You thought about it a long time," I countered.

"I was in love, Sophia. I'm sorry if you're hurt, but I'm not sorry I fell in love with him"

"What of my mother," I asked?

"What of her? I don't respect her. Never have. She's beastly to your father. She's beastly to you. Pamela doesn't deserve him. If she truly loved him, she'd let him go. She would want him to be with someone who could make him happy, and be a better wife to him."

"Are you daft? Even a more stable woman than my mother wouldn't think that way. Never in my life have I heard of a wife who would willingly give up her husband to his mistress, because she believed that the 'other woman' would make him happier! This is all pure poppycock!"

"No, no Sophia. I'm talking here about unconditional love. If she loved him…. Really loved him… Then she would love him unconditionally.

That means that she would want him to be happy, no matter what. Don't you understand that?"

"No, Edwina, I don't. That is *not* love. What about the vows they made to one another when they married, and pledged to spend the rest of their lives with one another? For better or worse?"

"Well, your mother didn't turn out to be the person he thought she was. She put on a huge act to get him. She saw a good thing and went after it. Well, she got him, and she's made his life miserable ever since."

"And I'm beginning to wonder if *he* didn't have something to do with that. It *wasn't* Mummy who went after Papa. He had inherited *Willow Grove Abbey* and had learned that the estate was almost totally insolvent. He had to find a wife very quickly, who could provide a large dowry. Mummy met all of his qualifications."

"Sophia, naturally she did. Any woman of means would have been more than happy to give him whatever she had, if it solved his problems and made him happy. That *is* unconditional love."

"No, Edwina, I don't know that. And there are things about him that you don't know. Your foolish comments about so-called 'unconditional love' are so much drivel. If Papa was simply looking for love, why did he make certain that the wife he chose could provide him with heaps of money? Perhaps Mummy has always felt, deep down, that Papa never really loved her, but only married her for money he so desperately needed. Perhaps that accounts for her behaviour. Who knows how differently she might have been, if she had truly felt loved? At any rate, I don't think that you are in a position to be telling *me* about *my* father."

"I think I know him a bit better than you do," she shouted.

"I'm sure you do, in certain ways. But, I have known him *and my mother* for a lifetime."

This wasn't the Edwina I had always known. It was true that she'd always had some values that were different from mine, but we could never have been as close as we'd been, if our values were so divergent. I couldn't think what direction I should take. I knew Edwina would call Papa the moment our conversation ended, and if he was as taken with her as she implied, he would not be supportive of me in any way.

"Are you going to tell your mother," Edwina asked? I had a grave suspicion that Edwina hoped I *would* tell my mother. I believe that she thought all of her problems might be solved if Mummy knew the truth, as she assumed that there would undoubtedly be a divorce if the affaire became known. That would leave Papa free to marry her. But, what about Dieter, and what about the baby?

"I don't know. I don't think I'm going to tell her," I answered. "It would probably kill her." I did not know what else to say. "I need time, Edwina. This is a tremendous shock. I don't see how we can continue on, as though nothing has happened, and yet I don't know how to do anything else. I've always loved you so, and of course I love Papa. But, I cannot imagine the two of you involved in a relationship. I don't know how I can bear this. We cannot just go back to our old ways, Edwina. That simply isn't possible."

"Please think very hard about it. We need to talk more. I need you to understand my feelings."

"It would help if you tried to understand *my* feelings, as well, Edwina," I answered. "And whose baby are you carrying?" I blurted out. There was a sinking feeling in my heart. *My God! Was Edwina carrying a brother or sister of mine?*

"No…No, Sophia. The baby is Dieter's. At least *I think* it is. I don't want Dieter to know, because I'm not certain what I'm going to do. I wish I didn't have to go through with the pregnancy. On the other hand, if the baby is *Nigel's*, I'd want it very much. This is very much like what you went through with Isabella."

"Edwina, you really have lost your mind. In the first place, Spence was not married. Secondly, I had only had sexual relations with one man, when I married Owen. Thirdly, I knew who the baby's father was. Yes, I *did* lie to Owen, and that was wicked of me. If I could turn the clock back, I would never have done so. But, all in all, there is absolutely no resemblance between my situation with Owen, and yours. Edwina, I do not understand how you can't be certain who the father of your child is?"

"Oh, Sophia, don't be obtuse. You know exactly how it would be possible for me not to be certain."

"In other words, you had relations with both of them at about the same time. Right?"

"Yes. And, if it *is* Nigel's child, then I know he would leave your mother and marry me. I just know it. If a woman loves a man unconditionally, then she wants him to be happy, no matter what. You mother couldn't possibly stand by and watch your poor father be labeled the father of a bastard. Not if she truly loves him. And if *you* loved him unconditionally, as a daughter ought to, then you should want him to be with me instead of your mother. I am praying that this child is Nigel's. Nothing would thrill me more. Don't you see that this baby would be your half-brother or sister?"

"Oh yes, Edwina. I understand that all too well. And you expect me to be happy about such a thing? My God, Edwina, what do you intend to do about your marriage? Are you going to let Dieter think that this is his child, when it may not be? Are you going to divorce him? Or, does he know of your affaire? Does he even know about the child?"

She answered in an exasperated tone. "Sophia. I haven't the slightest notion what I'm going to do about my marriage, other than of course, I don't intend for it to continue past the birth of my baby. I have no intention of letting my child be called a 'bastard,' I want Dieter's name on the birth certificate, unless of course, Nigel leaves your mother and we are either married or about to be, when the child is born. Then, I would put 'Somerville' on the Certificate. Yes, if I must let Dieter think he is the father, I shall. You weren't above doing that when you married Owen to give Isabella a father."

She was correct about that. "Yes, I'm well aware of that. It was a ghastly thing to have done. I was acting like a child, and I never, ever should have done what I did. I shall spend my whole life trying to make up for doing such a rotten, vile thing."

"Well, haven't you turned into a little Saint? I wonder if you'd be saying that if Spence weren't back in your life, and you weren't hoping to snag him and make him the legitimate father of Isabella."

"Edwina that is an unkind and unnecessary comment. Spence *is* Isabella's legitimate father. You know that I have loved Spence from the moment I laid eyes upon him. Of course I'd love to see my precious little girl have the father she should have had since birth. But, that has nothing to do with my feelings regarding whether it was right or wrong for me to have done what I did when I married Owen."

"No matter, Sophia. Believe whatever you wish. I have my own problems to deal with. My only concern at present is whether or not I can marry your father before I give birth."

"I think you're being terribly narcissistic, Edwina, and terribly irrational. I'm telling you right now that I don't believe Papa will ever leave my mother. They have a history together ..... A long history. They have raised three children together."

She laughed. She actually laughed. "I think I know him a bit better than Pamela does."

"You may know him in a different way than she does, Edwina, but not necessarily better," I retorted, in outrage.

"Ha! I had my first *orgasm* with him," Edwina shouted.

I was aghast. This was beyond the pale. No daughter should ever have to hear such a thing about her father and her best friend. There were not words to express my fury.

"Edwina, I cannot discuss this with you any further. I'm thoroughly disgusted with you at the moment. Please don't try to contact me. I need to ring off. I shall think, and try to be fair. I'll try to see this as I would if I'd just learned that my father was engaged in an affaire, but that the other woman wasn't you."

"Yes.... Yes.... That's a good way to think of it, Sophia. We can get through this. Think of all that we've weathered in the past."

"I *am* thinking about everything we've been through together. The problem, Edwina, is that my father *is* engaged in an affaire with my best friend. I don't see how I can just pretend that isn't true."

Edwina had been the best.... The dearest friend any girl could ever have been blessed with. If I concentrated upon the past, perhaps I could survive the shock. Nevertheless, it was the present that I couldn't cope with.

"I need time to think," I shouted, slamming down the receiver. Our conversation ended, but my upset didn't. I had no idea what the future held, and was surely in a state of shock. What I'd always done when placed into a position where I felt unable to cope, was retreat into denial. And, looking back, that's exactly what I did. In a pathetic attempt to retain my closeness, both with Edwina and with my father, I decided to live with the knowledge of their involvement, as though nothing had changed. It was a repeat of my old need to win my parent's approval. With a new twist. I thought that if I gave my blessing to the illicit affaire, Papa would be forever grateful, and his approval of me would skyrocket. And it actually worked, for a while, until I had to face the fact that it wasn't a game. It wasn't pretend. Edwina and I were no longer school girls, giggling over crushes. There were *real* persons involved. . . . . . My mother, father, my school roommate, and me. It was absurd for me to believe that it could ever end in anything but heartache.

Papa rang early the following morning. Naturally, I'd been expecting his call. I was already up and dressed, and Isabella had been fed. Martha had taken her for an outing.

"I gather you had a rather disquieting conversation with Edwina last night," he began. He sounded somewhat ashamed, but one could never tell with Papa. He was so terribly good at playing any role he was thrust into.

"Quite," I answered. "Are you able to speak openly?"

"Yes. Your mother is still sleeping. Sophia, I'm sorry if this has upset you. This isn't how I planned to tell you."

"Did you plan to tell me at all?" I'm certain he could hear the anger in my voice. I didn't make any attempt to hide it. I was still simmering over Edwina's comments of the night before.

"Eventually, I suppose I would have told you. I don't know, Sophia. I've been swept away in a storm of emotion. Just completely swept away."

"That's rather obvious Papa. And, it seems that Edwina has been swept right along with you. I am having a very difficult time understanding how you could have initiated such folly. And before you say anything more, I understand about things like this," I continued, as I my thoughts turned to Spence and me. "But, Papa, the person you're swept away by is *Edwina*. Did it not matter to you that she was my dearest friend?"

"Sophia, Edwina needs you. Don't abandon her now. She is frightened and alone. And, please don't forget she's pregnant. "

"Papa, don't you realize that there are other people involved in this besides merely you and Edwina?"

"Yes, of course I do."

"What are your intentions? Do you plan on leaving Mummy for Edwina? What of Edwina's marriage?" There was complete silence. "Again, I'm asking what you intend to do about *your* marriage, Papa."

"I shall never leave the mother of my children. I've told Edwina that." I had a tremendous sense of relief. However, knowing what Papa's intentions were worried me less than knowing what Edwina's were. And Edwina's were to manipulate Papa into marriage.

"I believe Edwina has hopes that you'll change your mind. She thinks she can convince you in time that she would be a better wife for you."

"She probably *would* be a better wife for me, but I don't have the strength to go through the horror of a divorce with your mother."

I felt somewhat better when he told me that. Perhaps the affaire would simply run its course. Edwina would soon tire of being the other woman. In my opinion, she was definitely not suited to a back-street existence. While I had always adored Edwina, I felt strongly that, like my mother, the aura of power that surrounded Papa, due to his position in the nobility, was a strong attraction. I also couldn't forget that Edwina's own father was twenty-eight years older than her mother. I thought of some of the theories I'd learned in my studies with Dr. Hausfater. How patterns in one's past tend to repeat themselves..... . How people try to get right as adults the things they aren't able to get right as children. *Was Edwina seeking a father figure? And was Papa simply going through a mid-life crisis, or was there deeper meaning to his actions? Was he playing out fantasies with someone whom he thought of as a daughter?* There *were* no answers to those questions. There was only speculation, fueled by the small amount of knowledge which I had about the human psyche. That same theory made me think about my relationship with Spence. Was I, too, seeking a father figure? Certainly, I relied heavily upon Spence for advice, and if there was one or the other of us that was more the child, it was certainly me. It was Spence whom I ran to for advice, and rational thinking, when I found myself faced with some trauma or other. I needed to think more on that subject, and begin to work harder on becoming more mature.

"Papa, I don't know what to say to you. I'm stunned by all of this. I love you, and I don't want to create trouble between us. However, I'm not certain that I can live with this knowledge, and keep silent. Do Blake and Drew know about this?"

"Blake does. Andrew does not."

"And what is Blake's view?"

"He's perfectly all right with it. You know that he doesn't especially feel that Pamela is a good wife or mother. I suppose he feels sorry for me. He wants me to be happy. He has his own life, and feels I should make my own decisions about what makes me happy. Of course, he has been divorced and re-married, and apparently has no regrets."

"Yes. Well, I certainly wouldn't cite Blake as a role model. I'm not one bit certain that he doesn't wish he'd stayed married to Elizabeth. Susan doesn't fight back with him, as Elizabeth did. She just takes what he dishes out, and then does exactly as she wishes. She is devious. Anyway, Papa, I don't really care what Blake thinks. Your *mistress* isn't *Blake's'* best friend. There's a distinct difference. Also he's *never* had the relationship with Mummy that I've had. I know she's been beastly to me....To all of us. But, she is *still* my mother. I respect that. I think I understand her better than any of the other family members. Beneath her facade of dominance, there is a wounded soul. I believe she craves your love, but is frightened of letting you know that she needs it. If I feel sorry for anyone in this muddle, I feel sorry for Mummy. As I have grown, and studied, I have begun to understand how very much one's upbringing plays a part in future behaviour. I've never known a lot about Mummy's parents, but I *do* remember her speaking of what a total shrew her mother was. Perhaps she simply copied her own mother's behaviour. All I know is that she must have a great deal of pain inside of her, and I wish we had all tried harder to let her know that she is loved."

"You have too kind a heart, Sophia. Do you intend to tell your mother what you've learned?"

"No. I've thought and thought about it. I cannot be the one to cause her that sort of heartbreak. I'm going to hope that you mean it when you say that you'll never leave her. I'm going to hope that this is a passing fancy. I'll to try to understand, and be a friend to Edwina, as well as a loving daughter to you."

"Thank you, my dear. Thank you so much."

"Don't thank me yet, Papa. I'm going to *try*, but I'm not at all certain I can do it. And, this doesn't mean that I'm condoning the affaire. I'm not."

"Just knowing that you'll try means the world to me. You're an incredible woman."

I am chagrined, even today, to admit that I was thrilled to hear those words, and I am still humiliated for being so needy. I was bowing to his wishes in order to gain his approval and praise, and I was well aware of it. Over the years, I have regretted my actions a thousand times over, and have never forgotten that beastly conversation.

Chapter Twenty

DECEMBER, 1939 – SUMMER, 1940
WILLOW GROVE AND FRANCE

Spence returned to London for Christmas, and I had never been so happy to see anyone in my life. He came straight to Sumner Street, and Isabella and I made a great fuss over him. He was wearing his Royal Air Force dress uniform, and I couldn't take my eyes from him. I wanted to memorize every detail, knowing we would soon be parted again. While he was warm and loving to Isabella, he was distinctly distant with me. He wasn't in any way mean or hurtful, but made it clear that he did not want anything to be misunderstood. We sat in the parlor and sipped tea in front of a roaring fire. There was a clear, blue sky outside, but it was beastly cold. There was a forecast of snow. I had a small Christmas tree in the corner, which Isabella and I had decorated with popcorn strings, cranberries and chains made of colored paper. Isabella was so thrilled to see Spence that she wore herself to a frazzle, chattering about all of the things that had happened in her life since she'd last seen him, and playing with the small models of 'Spitfire' airplanes that he brought to her.

After she'd gone to bed and he was preparing to leave, I immediately told him what I'd learned about my father and Edwina. He was calm and thoughtful about my news, as I knew he would be. It was his nature. When I told him that I felt hideous, pretending that everything was all right in front of my mother, he helped me to analyze the situation in more depth.

"Sophia, what precisely are your choices?" he asked.

"Well, I could end my friendship with Edwina. If that's even what you could call it anymore. Or, I could refuse to listen to anything Papa has to say about her, nor play any part in their illicit relationship. Or, I *could* tell my mother. I have thought most frequently about the latter."

"And, what do you suppose any of those things would accomplish?"

"Perhaps nothing, except any of those actions might make *me* feel better, since I'd be living up to my standards. I absolutely hate this subterfuge, Spence. You know that I promised that I would not lie any more. Yet, here I am in the worst position I've ever been in..... Well, perhaps not the worst..... The worst was with you and Isabella, but still, this is pretty horrific."

"I agree. It is a ghastly position to be in. I do think you can take off the hair shirt though, in this instance. If you were to take any of the actions you just cited they would accomplish more than just the obvious. If you cut off your friendship with Edwina, sooner or later, your mother will want to know why. Another lie will have to be told, to explain yourself. If you refuse to communicate with your father about this, you will lose any hope that he will *hear* what you are saying, and end this thing before there is more hurt. Lastly, if you tell your mother, you are surely courting disaster. I don't think you will be thanked. I think she will turn on you with vengeance. She will blame you for everything. That's your mother's nature. *She* certainly wouldn't look to herself, and ask the hard questions about what part she might have played in this. Frankly, Sophia, I don't think you really have a lot of options here. "

"But Spence, you are the one who so detests lying. You are the one who lost all trust for me because of the lies I told. Now you're saying that it's better for me to continue on in such a vein?"

"They are two entirely different situations. I don't want to rake up everything that happened between us, Owen, and Isabella. But, you didn't start out committing adultery or planning to hurt anyone. You were a young girl, who panicked and made a terribly unwise choice. That isn't the case in this instance. In this case, you father and Edwina seem to be acting like selfish children. They are betraying your mother, you, Dieter, and the child she is carrying. You played no part in their decisions. Now, you are the one who is left with trying to stop the heartache."

I saw that he was right, and it helped to assuage my guilt. But, it was so terribly hard for me to be around my mother, or even to speak to her on the telephone, when I knew the lies she was being told on a daily basis. In only a few days, I was planning a Christmas trip to *Willow Grove Abbey,* and was dreading it. I didn't know if I could face it, and told Spence as much.

"Would you like me to accompany you?" he asked.

I was completely thrilled. "Of course, I would. Isabella would be ecstatic. It would just help so much if I felt that I had someone there who knew the whole truth and was on my side."

"I want you to be utterly clear about why I would do so," he replied. I don't want any misconceptions. Since I haven't anywhere else to be for Christmas, and have no family to spend it with, I should love to spend it with my daughter. And with you. But, I don't want your family, or you, to get ideas about us. I've told you how I feel Sophia. You know that I respect you, and care for you, but I don't want any other relationship. Not now. Please don't feel that I'm being selfish. It's just the reverse, in my mind. I'm trying to save both of us from future heartache." His words hurt, but I swallowed my pride, and told him that I understood completely.

And so we went to *Willow Grove Abbey* for Christmas. I was so proud of him. He wore his uniform and the gold wings that signified his rank as an RAF Flight Surgeon. His finely chiseled features gave him an air of masculine refinement, and I would have given anything if I could have announced that we were going to be married. We entered through the Great Hall, and then proceeded to the drawing room, where the family was already gathered. Everyone stood, with kisses all round for me, and handshakes for Spence. He immediately went to Mummy and kissed her on the cheek, which brought a flush to her face. Papa clapped his hand on Spence's shoulder. "Right. Shall we call you Doctor Stanton, or Group Captain Stanton?"

"Either is appropriate, but I'll settle for Spence, Sir."

"And I'll settle for Nigel," Papa replied. "Let me get you a drink," he added.

"Thanks. A spot of scotch and water would be nice," Spence replied.

"Well, this is indeed marvelous, Papa said, as he proceeded to gather refreshments. "It's wonderful to have all of my children here, and we're delighted that you could join us, Spencer."

"Yes. I'm delighted too. I'm especially delighted to be sharing this holiday with Isabella. Sophia has been so generous about that, and I can't thank your family enough for your hospitality."

"Of course you must be thrilled to be with your daughter on the holiday. You know that you're welcome in our home any time," Papa concurred. The men soon broke up into a small crowd, and began to discuss their military responsibilities, and concerns about the war. Annie, Susan, Mummy, and I sat down, and discussed our own concerns, but we tried not let our fears creep into what we meant to be a happy Christmas. Isabella ran off to her old bedchamber, to see if everything was still the same.

"What do you hear of Edwina," asked Susan.

I *did not want* to discuss Edwina, but it looked like the conversation was about to take that turn.

"Well, she's nearly four month's along in her pregnancy, and I have the impression that she's a bit undone by the thought of returning to England as the wife of a German."

"Well, I should think so. Gracious, Sophia, that girl needs her head examined. What in the world is she going to do now that there's a war? Why did she ever marry that disgusting Hun? He looks like an albino."

It was vintage Mummy. "I don't know, Mummy," I lied. Nonetheless, I couldn't help but laugh. My mother wasn't *always* wrong about *everything.*

"Dieter has been called back to Berlin, but Edwina steadfastly stays in Paris. It's beyond me how they deal with this muddle, but you know how she can be."

"Yes, I've never fully understood her," although I'm certainly fond of her. Dear Lord, Sophia, she's practically been a member of this family since you started at *Ashwick Park.*"

Her words sent chills down my spine. I knew that my mother was, indeed, fond of Edwina, and had often compared me to her, saying that she wished that I was more like my friend. I felt extremely uncomfortable with what was being said, but there was no way to tactfully change the topic. Oh, if she only knew the truth about Edwina!

"Perhaps she'll change her mind and return to England, once the reality of the war sets in, added Annie.

"It's unlikely," I responded. Edwina rarely does the sensible thing, I'm afraid."

"Surely Dieter doesn't want her to be in any danger?" Mummy speculated. "If *she* hasn't any sense, then I'd think he'd take it upon himself to look after her properly."

"Mummy, Dieter is German. What I fear is that he'll want to send her to Germany. To his family. He will assume that it's the safest place for her. After all, you *know* that he's absolutely convinced that there is no way Germany will be threatened by England in this war."

"What a dreadful state of affaires. Your father says that he'll try to speak with her when he's in Paris next week. Perhaps he can talk some sense into her."

I noticed that Susan was very quiet, and I looked at my sister-in-law more than once with an anxious expression. I knew that Blake was aware of the relationship between Edwina and Papa. Of course, he must have told his wife. However, to my knowledge, *she* wasn't aware that *I* knew anything about the mess. Susan raised her eyebrows slightly when Pamela mentioned that Papa was planning another trip to Paris. I desperately wanted to tell my mother that she should accompany him, but I knew there would be no point. She would never consider traveling with Papa on business... Never had.

"Will you be returning to Willow Grove?" Mummy interjected.

I thought we had covered that ground before. "No, Mummy, at least not for the foreseeable future. I feel that Isabella should have as little change as feasible, and I'd like to continue my studies at University and my work with Dr. Hausfater as long as possible

"I think that's wise," said Annie. "Drew and I are thinking along similar lines. We don't yet know where he'll be posted, either."

"And what of you and Blake, Susan?" I asked.

"The same, I'm afraid. He'll be going to Church Fenton, in North Yorkshire, but we're hoping for a permanent post at one of the bases in Scotland. He could be sent anywhere. I'll undoubtedly return to my family in Scotland if he is posted there, or if he is sent overseas."

Finally, the men came and joined our group, and we all went in to dinner to enjoy a sumptuous feast of Roast Beef, Yorkshire pudding and all the trimmings. The war seemed very far away on that last peaceful Christmas of 1939. Food rationing was about to begin, but Nan and the Rose had wisely planned. One would never have known that there was concern about quantities of foodstuffs. By the next year, of course, there was great anxiety.

The New Year began, and with it came the dreaded rationing we'd known was imminent. In January, 1940, bacon, butter and sugar were rationed. That was followed by meat, fish, tea, jam, biscuits, breakfast cereals, cheese, eggs, milk and canned fruit. Whew! As ghastly as it was, I actually heard very few complaints about the rationing scheme. People seemed happy to be able to sacrifice something for the sake of freedom and victory. Some began to buy black-market goods, and the open-air markets developed a reputation. Eggs, butter and milk could be obtained fairly easily, without coupons, in rural areas, such as *Bedminster-with-Hartcliffe*. We had all been issued gas masks over a year before, and one never went anywhere without one, oft times hanging about our necks. Blackouts were also a daily routine. Everyone had blackout curtains, which did not let a sliver of light through at night, and they made it much more difficult for German bombers to see after sunset. We kept only a few lights on, in any case.

I was much more concerned with what was happening to Spence and my brothers, as the war began to heat up in the New Year. In April the British army landed at Namsos in Norway, and a day later, the German army invaded Denmark. On 10 May, Adolph Hitler launched his Western Offensive and invaded France. That is what we all had feared. On the same day, Neville Chamberlain resigned as Prime Minister, and was replaced by Winston Churchill. By 14 May, the German tanks crossed the Meuse River, and opened up a fifty-mile gap in the allied front. Six days later they reached the Channel. Everyone one sat by the radio day and night, awaiting reports on the troops. There could be no denying that during such a frightening period I couldn't help but think of Edwina. She was in France, facing grave danger. I had heard nothing of her since our beastly conversation before Christmas, but I believe I would have known if she had returned to England or worse, joined Dieter in Germany.

Between 27 May, and 4 June, one of the most valiant and gallant efforts of my countrymen took place. The British troops were trapped in Dunkirk, with no way to cross the English Channel. With either unbelievable luck, or what Spence later referred to as a 'serendipitous' happening, Adolph Hitler issued orders to his German troops in France and Belgium to halt their advance on 23 May. He did so because German infantry tanks needed to catch-up, allowing an orthodox assault on the allied troops. That decision stopped the Germans from being able to cut off the escape of the British and French soldiers. As a result, a total of 693 ships from England, ranging from destroyers, minesweepers, trawlers, yachts and a variety of other small craft picked up 338,226 soldiers. Of this number, 140,000 were members of the French army.

Later I learned that Spence had been in one of the Hurricane Fighters, which flew up and down the coastline near Dunkirk, scouting enemy planes. He was engaged in many dogfights with German bombers. He told me afterwards that the whole front was one long, unbroken line of flaming buildings. There was smoke pouring above the roofs. He was able to spot exhausted soldiers tramping their way along the meandering road, where dead bodies were strewn. 30,000 men were killed, wounded and missing. The British army could not defend their homeland. The army had left the majority of their weapons behind, on the battle-scarred land. There were nearly none to be had in reserve back in England. Spence told me all of these things when he returned home on furlough after Dunkirk. He felt strongly that France was going to fall to the Germans, and that England was about to be in the horrifying position of standing alone in the ghastly war effort. He believed that sooner or later London would become their target, and felt that the time was nearing when I needed to think about removing to *Willow Grove Abbey*. I detested the thought, but knew that I would heed his advice in the end. There had been consistent air raid sirens since September, 1939, and I'd become rather adept at knowing where to go, when I heard that dreadful wail. Most everyone I knew hated the Anderson shelters, but they did manage to keep a great number of us safe from harm. Sometimes we would sit in them for hours, crowded next to throngs of frightened adults, and crying children. It was beastly.

We spent Spence's last day of holiday furlough allowing Isabella to do whatever she chose. That resulted in a pony ride in the Park, an outing on a double-decker bus, and ice cream at her favorite restaurant. Included was a visit to Harrods, culminating in the purchase of a new doll. When we returned to Sumner Street, she was a tired little girl, and so were her parents. Spence made his usual promise to read her two stories before bedtime. After he left, I, too, retired for the night, flushed with the glow of happiness from a happy day with Spence and Isabella. The next morning he came to the flat, and we all had breakfast together. I splurged, and made Eggs Benedict, with Fried Chips, which I knew Spence adored. It was a memory I cherished through the years. His ominous words about the fight coming to our shores left me terribly anxious that harm could befall him. As far as I knew though, he would continue to be posted to Duxford for the foreseeable future. I was very happy about that, as it meant that he was able to come to London whenever he was given a few free days. Shortly before he left, and while Isabella was learning how to color, with Martha helping her in the nursery, he brought up the subject of Edwina.

"Do you have any news of her" He asked. "I haven't wanted to spoil this precious time with talk of unpleasant matters, but it *is* something I've thought about."

"No, I haven't heard a thing, and Papa says nothing. Of course, I'm certain that they're in touch. What will become of her Spence, if France falls?" Would there be any way for her to get back to England?"

"Not without a good deal of high level help. Even then, I should think it would be very difficult. Any Brits who're caught in France are going to be in a devil of a mess. Your father may be the best ally she has at this point. But, even Nigel can't pull off a bloody miracle."

"Do you think I should ask him about it?"

"That's entirely up to you. Just don't become too upset if you don't like his answer, or don't believe him. I'm not sure I know why you care very much what becomes of her."

"Spence, I don't know either, except that I have such dear memories of the past. No matter what, there is no way I would want anything to happen to her. But, I also don't want to get involved. Does that make sense? "

"It makes perfect sense to me, and you're a better person than I am," he smiled. After what she said to you the last time you spoke, I'm not certain that I could bear to ever hear her voice again."

"I know. I feel that way too. But, then I remember how good she was to me when I was pregnant with Isabella, and it's hard for me to believe that the Edwina I knew for all of those years has just vanished, and become a totally different person."

"Well, of course you know that I haven't the same warm feelings for Edwina. She may have been good to *you*, but I strongly feel that she should have come to me, and told me what was happening. I'm not certain I can ever completely forgive her for that."

"Spence, I understand your feelings. However, don't blame Edwina entirely. She suggested in the beginning that I come to you, and tell you the truth, but I wouldn't hear of it. I was too frightened that I would have to give up the baby, and of retribution towards you. Edwina really wasn't always so thoughtless. I don't know how she can have changed so."

"Perhaps the two of you have grown-up, and developed vastly different values. That can happen, you know. The adult one becomes is not necessarily as likeable as the child we remember."

"I think she's gone completely bonkers! She sounds so self-centered, caring only for herself and what *she* wants out of life, with no thought for anyone else, or about whom she might hurt."

Sophia, the trait of self-centeredness was always there in Edwina. Perhaps you weren't so keenly aware of it, because it didn't affect you in such an intimate way. But, I do remember that you told me once about how Edwina believed that if a person wanted something badly enough, she simply *made* it happen. She knew what she wanted and went after it, so to speak. Rather like a business plan."

"Yes, she has said that. And, in itself I suppose there's nothing wrong with that outlook, except when it fails to take into account that what one person wants may spell total heartbreak for another."

"That's the point. Let me know what you decide to do, and if you do talk with your father, try to keep calm. It isn't healthy for you to put yourself in an anxious way about this. I know you *are* anxious and tense, but talking with your father always seems to make it worse.

"I promise. I have my priorities straight. Isabella and me. The two of us. Anything that causes upset for our little twosome is not going to warrant my attention."

And then in the blink of an eye, Spence was gone again. However, that time it was very, very different than before. On 14 June, just two days after his departure, the Germans entered Paris. Paris had fallen! It was unimaginable. German soldiers were occupying that beautiful city. The German flag was flying over the Place de la Concorde! When I heard the news, it was mid-morning, and I telephoned my father at once. Without any preliminaries, I asked him what he knew of Edwina.

"Sophia, I can't speak of this on the telephone, he answered. But, I'm making a trip to London today, and if you're to be at home, I'll stop by and we can discuss it."

"Yes," I answered, that will be fine. About what time do you expect to arrive?"

"I should think somewhere in the early afternoon."

"Shall I have luncheon prepared for you?"

"No…No, I'll already have eaten."

"Right then, I'll look for you about two o'clock."

"Yes, perhaps even a bit earlier."

"And, Papa?"

"Yes?"

I'm assuming that you *do* know something regarding the person we're both concerned about?"

"Yes, I do, Sophia. I'll tell you everything when I see you."

Promptly at two-o'clock, I was standing at my window, looking out on Sumner Street, when I saw my father alight from our family's Rolls Royce. Joseph was driving, and he left, probably with the understanding that he would retrieve Papa at a certain time. In a matter of moments the doorman rang, and my father was in my parlor. I sent Isabella on a play-date with a little girl who lived in our building, and Martha took her. I wanted to be able to speak freely, without interruption. Papa hugged me as he came in the door, and hung his coat on the hall tree.

"It looks like we could have some rain," he commented.

"Yes. It's an awfully dreary day," I answered. "May I get you something? Coffee, tea, a drink?"

No, nothing, Sophia. I'm fine." We sat down across from one another, he on the sofa and I in the chintz chair. "So, what is the news of Edwina?" I asked, coming right to the point.

"Right. It is a bit complex."

"With Edwina, *everything* is a bit complex," I said, in a not altogether pleasant tone.

"Well. There's certainly some truth to that," he smiled, ruefully. "In a nutshell, I have arranged for her to evacuate Paris."

"How on Earth have you arranged *that*?" I questioned.

"I've made contact with a series of old acquaintances, who have agreed to help her. It's taken a bit of doing. But, at the moment she's in Madrid."

"Madrid?" I was very confused. "Why Madrid, and how?"

"Sophia, there were only two options left open. One was a sea passage, if we could find a ship, which seemed unlikely, and would be hazardous, and the second was overland to Spain, still neutral but unfriendly to the English, after the Spanish Civil War. Edwina was able to join a member of the British Embassy staff, in Nice, and she set off in a convoy heading for Spain, and then Portugal. I negotiated an entry permit for her. They traveled on to Barcelona, where they rested for the night, and the following morning headed on to Madrid. That was this morning."

"What are the plans from there?" I rolled my eyes. I should have known that Edwina would find safe passage home to England. The entire situation was just too amazing. How many times had I begged Edwina to come home to England before the war began, and she ended up trapped? Yet, she would not listen, and what I had predicted had come true.

"They will head for Portugal, where a high ranking government official has instructed that they should be picked up by flying boats off the Portuguese coast."

"My Lord, Papa. I'd say you've pulled off a miracle. How many people have high ranking officials in the government intervening on their behalf?"

"I'm just fortunate that it all seems to have worked out."

"I'd say Edwina is the fortunate one. And, what of Dieter? Does he know where his wife is, and what her intentions are?" How really cruel of her, if he doesn't. I know he's German, Papa, and you know I never liked him, but I still find it inconceivable that she would just abandon him like this."

"Well, he cannot know. It is extremely important that this be kept secret. Of course, he'll be livid when he learns that she is gone, but there's little he can do about it. Once she's safe on English soil, she'll be all right."

And where will she go, once she reaches England? She must have had the baby by now, for the Lord's Sake!"

"Yes. The baby was born in late May. It's a boy, and she's named him Christian. She calls him 'Kippy.' Rather a nice name, I think."

"For heaven's sake, Papa, who gives a whit what she's named her baby?" I replied, irritably. I didn't care if she'd named the baby 'Bubble and Squeak'. What a completely irrelevant bit of information that is.

"I just thought it a rather nice name, Sophia. Nothing to get upset about."

"That may or may not be true. Has she mentioned to you that this baby may be yours? There could be a great deal to be upset about."

"Mine? My baby?" A slow smile spread over his face. He obviously fancied the idea. "Wouldn't that be something?"

"Yes, it certainly would be, Papa. You look like the mere idea of such a thing makes you happy. It makes me sick to even think about something like that."

"Why Sophia? That would make the baby your little half brother or sister. Don't you think that would be lovely?"

"No, I do not, Papa. He or she would be my *illegitimate* half-brother or sister. You've always cared about what people think. Would you want to label your own son or daughter a bastard? Why on Earth would you imagine that I would be pleased about such a thing? Edwina being the mother of my half brother or sister? It's too disgusting, Papa. Where are your morals?"

"Let's not speak of this now, Sophia. I think the likelihood of that is slim, and I believe Edwina would have told me if that were the case. I'm certain the baby is Dieter's. But, I don't think she has any plans to stay married to him, and don't believe she's told him of the child."

"You know, I didn't particularly like Dieter, but I think it's sad, what she's doing to him. Does she just intend to leave France and disappear from his life, and never even tell him that he has a child?"

"She hasn't much choice at the moment, Sophia. Her husband is an officer in the German army. We are at war with his country. All of this will have to be sorted out after this ghastly war ends."

"So where are she and this child going to make a home?" I asked.

"I'm still working on that. She doesn't want to go back to Bury St. Edmunds. Says she prefers London, but I'm not certain how safe London is going to be."

"What difference does it make what Edwina prefers? Haven't you done enough, just getting her back here? Shouldn't she now go home to her own family?"

"Not necessarily, Sophia."

"But, why ever not?" And then it dawned on me. If Edwina were to return to Bury St. Edmunds, it would be much more difficult for him to see her, and to spend time alone with her. Also, Dieter might expect that she would return to her parents, and that could open another can of worms.

"Ahhh. I see. You want her nearby, so that you can see her whenever you wish. So, I suppose you're thinking of setting her up in a flat or house here in London?"

"Yes, I'm thinking of that, among other options."

"What other options?" I really was terribly afraid that I knew the answer to that question. I honestly

Wondered if Papa had gone totally bonkers, and I feared for his sanity.

"I've thought about bringing her to *Willow Grove Abbey.*"

"*I knew it*! Are you totally out of your mind?" I nearly screamed. "You cannot bring Edwina to the home you share with your wife. She's the woman with whom you're having an affaire. Have you no conscience whatsoever? I *know* she doesn't, but I gave you credit for more decency than this, Papa.

"I would not do anything improper while Edwina was under our roof. God knows there's plenty of empty space at *Willow Grove*. She could have an entire wing to herself, for that matter."

"I am aware that you have already 'christened' the house with your love, by sleeping with her when she was staying at *Willow Grove Abbey* after Isabella's first birthday, when your glorious love affaire began. Papa, you may be deluding yourself, but you're not deluding me. I don't care *what* you think you might or might not do, there is no way that the two of you could live under the same roof, without having secret rendezvous. In fact, knowing Edwina, I think she would rather like the idea of the intrigue. She would undoubtedly think it romantic."

"I haven't decided anything with certainty, Sophia. The primary reason I came to see you, was to ask if you could put Kippy and Edwina up for just one night.... Tonight. After they arrive in London. I *know* it's asking a lot of you. I'd be eternally grateful if you could find it in your heart to do so."

"Papa, you *must* be joking? Why can't she go to a hotel?"

"I don't want her to go to a hotel. I want to be able to see her, and cannot take the chance that someone might see us together entering or leaving a hotel. Also, I don't want her to be alone and frightened in a city where air raid sirens have become a way of life. She needs to *be* with someone."

"Why does that someone have to be me?"

"Because she loves you, Sophia. Always has."

"I have some awfully good cause to question that, Papa."

"I know that's what *you* think, but I also know how she feels. It *is* a muddled up situation. I'll admit that. But, it isn't all her fault. Please Sophia, I beg of you, just let her stay with you for one night. Then I'll have more permanent arrangements made."

"Why don't you take her to Drew and Annie's?"

"I don't feel comfortable speaking of this to Drew. Anyway, he's not there, and I don't think it would do to ask Annie to put her up. I'm sure that by now Drew knows of my relationship with Edwina, and of course, he's told Annie. Being a man of God, I sincerely doubt that he would lend his support."

"And why should I be any different?"

"Because you have always loved me unconditionally, Sophia."

"With the exception of Edwina, I suppose," I replied, sarcastically.

"In addition to Edwina," he answered." "Only two women in my life have ever loved me unconditionally. In that regard, you are the first. Edwina is the second."

"Papa don't start talking about 'unconditional love' to me. Edwina is potty on the subject. But, it seems to me that it's very one-sided. Where is the unconditional love for me? What if I said 'no'? I want no part in any of this? You know that I don't, Papa."

"I would love you just as much, Sophia. I would only be disappointed that you won't help an old man enjoy the company of the two women he loves." He was clearly enjoying the role of martyr, and he played it so exquisitely. I clearly recognized that he was being exceedingly manipulative. Even so, I finally gave in. I knew from the beginning that I would, and I'm sure he did too. In fact, I knew a lot of things I didn't want to admit, even to myself. For instance, I knew, beyond a shadow of a doubt, that Papa would be spending the night at my flat on Sumner Street too.

At four o'clock he left, and went to a pre-arranged destination, where he was to collect Edwina and her son. While he was gone, Isabella and Martha returned. I made the decision not to have Isabella in the flat when they arrived. I had no intention of muddying the waters by having to answer questions which I was totally unprepared for, from my three and a half-year-old daughter. In addition, there was the very real possibility that at some point in the future, Isabella might blurt out something about having seen Edwina and her Grand Pere at Sumner Street, to any number of persons, not the least of which could be her Grand Mere. But, where was I to send her? Then, I remembered Dr. Hausfater and his wife, both of whom adored Isabella. I knew I could count on them to help out. I rang them, and told them that I had a sort-of family emergency…Nothing to be alarmed about, but something that I would rather not have Isabella witness. I asked if they could have Isabella, and perhaps Martha, as overnight guests. They were only too happy to oblige. Within the hour, Dr. Hausfater arrived at Sumner Street and retrieved Isabella, Martha and an armload of toys. I thanked him profusely, and promised to collect them early the next morning. Isabella was delighted to be going on a sleep-over, and I felt immensely better about not having to be concerned about my little girl's questions.

Shortly before 8 o'clock, Papa, Edwina and Kippy arrived. I don't know what I expected. Perhaps a bedraggled and travel weary young woman, dragging along a tired and grizzling baby. However, such was not the case. Edwina was wearing an understated, but elegant dress, in midnight blue. The ensemble had two clips at the neck, set with sapphires, buttoned sleeves and a gathered waist detail. Alligator accessories completed the look. She even wore high-heeled pumps, and long gloves, both of which complemented a wide-brimmed hat. The dress was a Maggie Rougf and the hat a Carolina Reboux, both well-known and expensive couture designers. Apparently, her taste in clothing hadn't changed. She was carrying a beautiful baby boy, wrapped in a white cashmere blanket. He was very fair, with a good deal of hair, absolutely white in color, with Edwina's blue-green eyes. It was impossible to know whether this was Dieter's child, as he and Edwina had such similar coloring. I did not see anything of my father in the baby, but that could simply have meant that the baby was the image of Edwina. Papa entered the flat carrying two bags. "Where would you like us?" He asked. I was floored when he said 'us'. He wasn't making any pretense about the fact that he intended to spend the night at my flat, and to sleep in the same bedroom as Edwina. *Didn't either of them have any consideration for other people?* I swallowed hard… Swallowed the rage that I felt…. . But managed to recover my poise. I waved him toward my bedchamber. Then I quickly made the decision that I would move to Martha's room for the night. There was no other alternative, as the only other bedchamber was Isabella's. I would have left the flat completely, if there had been any place to go. I suppose I could have gone to a hotel, but I'm certain that would have been met with disapproval from my father, for my presence was definitely needed at Sumner Street, in case anyone were to drop by unexpectedly. Papa made straight-away for my bedroom, to unburden himself of the luggage, and I offered Edwina refreshment. She immediately said that she'd love a martini. I set about mixing it, and poured myself a glass of neat Scotch, which I seldom drank. Then I joined Edwina in the parlor.

"Right. So, I hear you've had quite a time of it," I said, sitting down near the fireplace.

"Yes.... Oh yes, Sophia. The roads were dreadful and packed with people, all trying to escape those damned Nazi's. It's pathetic to see what remains of the city of Madrid. The scars of the Spanish Civil War are still so evident. But, compared to Madrid, Lisbon was friendly and open, and there was plenty of food still, and very hospitable local people." I was astounded that she was talking so nonchalantly about trivial matters. Edwina made it sound more like she'd just returned from a holiday tour of the Continent, than an escape from a fallen Paris.

"I'm sorry you had to go through this, Edwina. I remember warning you a good while ago that you were taking chances staying in France. I don't know why you stayed as long as you did."

"I guess I just didn't' think it would happen...The unthinkable, you know. I never thought that Paris would fall. It's still hard to comprehend."

Yes, well it has, and we're truly at war, Edwina. What do you intend to do now you're back in England?"

"Norman Hartwell, Victor Stiebel, and Molyneux all have London design houses now. They've become part of a whole new generation of couturiers, and they're always looking for talented newcomers. I've developed a good reputation, so I might be able to find work in one of their establishments.'

"Yes, but Edwina, there's a war taking place. I'm not certain how much fashion matters at the moment. Rationing is in effect, and it is going to become more stringent.'

"Oh, darling, fashion will *always* be important to a certain class of women."

"I suppose," I answered, still finding it hard to understand Edwina's seeming inability to grasp what was going on around her.

"Where is Isabella, the darling of all London?" she asked airily, holding out her glass for a refill.

"I sent Martha and Isabella to friends for the night," I replied, as I got up and poured Edwina another martini out of a pitcher. "I thought it best, under the circumstances."

"What circumstances. What do you mean?"

"Edwina, quit acting so obtuse," I answered, sounding like Mummy. In an irritated fashion, I continued, "You know exactly what circumstances.

My father is about to spend the night here, in the same bedroom as my former school roommate. I don't want Isabella to question that."

"Oh, I see. Aren't you being a bit prim and proper?"

"Edwina, this isn't 1932 anymore. This is the real world. I am a mother, and so are you. A mother needs to think of things like that."

"Perhaps. I've not given it much thought."

"Do you nurse Kippy," I asked? Milk is in such short supply. Everyone I know with a baby is nursing."

Oh dear, no! What? And ruin the shape of my breasts with that little beast chomping at them? I wouldn't dream of it, "Edwina retorted. "Also, I wouldn't be able to drink any alcoholic beverages, and nine months was enough of that."

I was completely taken aback, but didn't really know why. The comment was very much in keeping with Edwina's narcissistic attitude. Edwina probably didn't even think it a bit crude.

"If I'd stayed in Paris I would have had a wet nurse. Anyway, I'll have your farther make arrangements for me to have the milk I need."

I was becoming livid with her smug, selfish attitude, but knew it wouldn't serve any good purpose if I were to show my irritation. She would, indeed, demand that Papa provide whatever she needed, and he would run her errands like a love-sick school-boy. At present, Kippy was soundly sleeping in Isabella's nursery. Isabella was three years old, and didn't used a cot anymore, so that is where we put Kippy, since my daughter's former canopied one was still up on one wall of the nursery. Isabella had her own little youth bed on the other wall.

Papa had mixed himself a drink, and was scanning the headlines in the *Times.* He put the paper down, looked at the two of us, and smiled. "Right, this pleases me greatly. I can't think of anything in the world I might enjoy more than sharing the evening with my two favorite women. "I smiled, although it wasn't easy.

"Oh Nigel, we've spoken so often of just such a thing. Isn't it lovely? Sophia, I *do* thank you so much for letting me stay here. It's so good of you."

"You were there when I needed you, Edwina. I suppose it's only right that I return the favor. "

"That's sweet," she answered. "Honestly, Sophia, I *do* know that this is difficult for you. It's a strange situation. Of course I know that. But, it will all work out. I'm just certain of that."

"I hope so Edwina. I just hope you both understand what you're doing," I said.

Papa stood up, and clapped his hands together, in what was an obvious effort to change the subject.

"What say we go out to a pub, have a few pints, and celebrate Edwina's being back on English soil?"

"Papa, Kippy is here and Martha is not. There would be no one to care for him." I replied.

"Aah, yes. I forgot. Sorry." He looked disappointed, but sat back down in his chair, taking another sip of his drink.

"Oh, Sophia what nonsense! Surely there must be someone we could ring and ask to stay with Kippy for a bit. He is a very good little baby…. . doesn't much grizzle at all. It would be fun to get out, and to be around people, but we couldn't go without you. If someone were to see us, it would be so much easier if you were in the party."

It was an unbelievably cheeky remark, but I kept still. I was growing rather used to cheeky remarks. I was a bit put out that they couldn't stay at home for one evening, but conversely, I felt that I'd rather be out in public, than sitting in my flat trying desperately to think of something to talk about. So, I rang a friend in my building, who'd taken care of Isabella in emergency situations. She was only too happy to come up to Number 7 and watch over Kippy while we went out.

We took a taxi to the *Café de Paris*, a favorite haunt of London's social set, but scarcely the pub Papa had spoken of so casually. Men and women were in full evening dress, wearing diamond bracelets, brooches and silk stockings. I felt sorely underdressed in a simple, classic summer ensemble, and also somewhat disgusted that there were so many people who didn't seem to understand that England was at war. Edwina didn't appear to mind her lack of formal attire, nor did Papa. When we entered, I saw several friends of mine from before my marriage. There were also persons I'd known during the time I was married to Owen. Some were those who'd made up the group with whom the former Prince of Wales ran. Lady

Therese Furnett was one of them. She motioned for us to come to her table. She was older than I was, by several years, but very nice. I'd always liked her. We all walked her way. Of course, Therese knew Nigel, but not Edwina. Naturally, the fact that we had roomed together at *Ashwick Park* took care of any awkward moments. How fortunate for Edwina that they had me for a cover, for otherwise everyone in London would have been whispering the next day about the beautiful young blonde who'd been seen at the *Café de Paris* with Nigel Somerville.

'Sophia Winnsborough! How splendid to see you. Where have you been hiding? It's been eons since I've seen you," Therese gushed.

"Therese. How nice to see you. I've been busy with my daughter and classes I'm taking at *The University of London*. I also have my school room-mate visiting. She's just been through the 'Fall of Paris' with her little boy."

"How ghastly." She smiled, referring to my classes. Then, turning to Edwina, she said, "You were at *Ashwick Park* with Sophia? I don't recall having seen you in London before..... Are you from here?"

"No," Edwina replied sweetly. I'm originally from Bury St. Edmunds, but I've been in Paris the last four years. I've only just returned, due to the ghastly happenings there."

"Oh my dear, isn't it *too* perfectly dreadful? Are you married?"

"I .....Ah..... Lost my husband quite recently. Edwina stammered, to my astonishment. "I have a two month old little boy."

"Yes, Papa chimed in. "Our family has known Edwina since 1932, when she and Sophia met at the *Ashwick Park* School. She's like a second daughter to us. When her husband was lost, I helped her return from France. She's going to become re-established here in London."

This was the first I had heard of Edwina's settlement in London, and her supposed widowhood. I didn't know if they had actually decided that she would settle in London, or if that was just a story. I assumed the widowhood story was invented to explain the possibility of someone seeing her with Kippy.

"Oh my sweet girl," Therese commiserated. "You are so young to be widowed..... And to have a baby, as well. You poor, poor dear. I suppose we're going to see a lot of this, now that the fighting has begun in earnest. Was your husband lost at Dunkirk?"

"Not at Dunkirk, but on the Continent," she answered. I had to admire her evasiveness. It *was* true that Dieter had been lost on the Continent. Nigel introduced her as Edwina Phillips, so it seemed obvious that she wasn't going to admit to having married a German.

"So, now you're going to re-locate to London? Do you know where you'll be, as yet?" Therese continued.

"I'll need to take a flat. I'm to begin looking tomorrow."

"I know just the place," Thelma said, clapping her hands together. "It's a town house in Mayfair. Really very smart, and perfect for a lady with a small child. The owners have removed to the country for the duration of the war. I know they'd like to let it, just to know there is somebody there to keep an eye on things."

"Well, that sounds splendid, Edwina replied. Is it terribly large?"

"No…. The usual. Three stories and narrow. Only three bedrooms, and a maid's alcove, on the third floor. Enough for you and your child, and a servant, of course."

Edwina glanced at Nigel out of the corner of her eye. He smiled, and nodded his head.

"Yes, yes. That sounds exactly like what Edwina has in mind. How would she go about seeing it?" He asked.

"I'll ring the owners, and make arrangements. Where are you staying, then"? Therese enquired.

"I'm at Sophia's flat at present. I can give you the number there, and you could ring me if that wouldn't be too much trouble. Or I could ring you, if you prefer. Therese took a small gold pen out of her evening bag, and wrote a number on the *Café de Paris* cocktail napkin in front of her. She slid it across the table to Edwina, saying, "This is my number. Please ring me tomorrow afternoon. I expect to be home until evening."

"Right. I cannot thank you enough. This is so nice of you. I'm just so touched. This could solve all of my problems. Really, Lady Furnett, I'm terribly grateful," Edwina went on.

"Not at all. I'm glad to be of help. Would you like to join our party?" She added, as an afterthought.

"No, I don't believe so, Nigel interjected. Thank you for asking, but these two," he said, waving his hand in Edwina's and my direction, "haven't had time to have a good chat, so I thought I'd give them that opportunity tonight," he smiled.

"Of course, Nigel. How nice to have a reunion of school friends. And Nigel, how delightful for you to accompany these two lovely, young ladies for the evening," she smiled.

"Yes," he replied. "It's always great fun to listen to Edwina and Sophia reminisce."

"Well, it was lovely seeing you Sophia and Nigel, and meeting you Edwina. I'll look forward to speaking with you tomorrow. Enjoy your evening," Therese said, as she waved us off.

I murmured the appropriate niceties, as we all did, and proceeded to our own table. I was simmering inside, as I *really* did not appreciate being used in such a manner, but then, what had I expected? That was exactly what made it so easy for my father and Edwina to be seen together in public. No one would think anything of it, because of the close friendship Edwina and I shared. Or had shared. It was shameful, but as ever I said nothing.

Chapter Twenty-One

1940
BACK TO WILLOW GROVE

When we returned to the Flat that evening, we wished one another a goodnight and I retreated to Martha's room. It was horrifically uncomfortable, knowing that my father and Edwina were down the hall in my room. I turned on the wireless, to drown out any sounds, and readied myself for bed. Then, I sat down at the desk in the corner, and wrote a long, letter to Spence, telling him of recent happenings. How I wished that he were there with me. As I crawled into bed, and pulled the comforter up, a well -known, popular wartime song was being sung, and I began to weep. It so reminded me of the last time Spence had kissed me, on that night when he came to my flat in 1939, wanting to see Sophia. He had said words to me about how we would meet again. My life had become so complex. All I'd ever wanted was the happiness and peace that accompanied a good marriage and a home of my own. Now, I lay in my *own* home, and in my *own* housekeeper's room, while my father was undoubtedly making love to my once best friend in my *own* room.

In the coming days, Edwina *did* take the house in Mayfair, and it *was* charming. There was no doubt in my mind about who was underwriting it. Edwina had no means of support, and certainly wasn't about to contact Dieter. I supposed she might have had some funds saved, but doubted that they'd have been sufficient to engage a property in Mayfair for any length of time. I was certain that the cost was dear. She also hired a Nanny/Housekeeper, by the name of Helen, who seemed competent, and set about making London her home. She didn't seek employment as a designer, and I didn't ask why. I had never believed it was a particularly good time to be seeking such employment. Most women of our class, who *were* working, had some connection to the war effort. Papa returned to *Willow Grove Abbey*, and I didn't see him frequently. I knew that he was in London often, as Edwina had no difficulty keeping me informed of that fact. Obviously, he stayed with her in Mayfair. It was very hard to speak with Mummy on the telephone during that time, knowing the many lies that were being told to her. It was equally hard to talk to Edwina, who didn't seem to understand the pain she was inflicting. She simply treated the whole affaire, as though she were involved with someone whom I casually knew.... Having a wonderful romance. Our conversations grew more strained as time wore on, and I became less and less able to tolerate such a duplicitous existence.

On 22 June, France signed an armistice with Nazi Germany, and was divided into two zones. Winston Churchill recognized Charles De Gaulle as leader of the Free French on 28 June, and on 3 July, the Royal Navy destroyed most of the French Navy at Mers-el-Kebir, to keep the German's from taking control of them. Then, madness reigned. On 10 July, 1940 the German Air Force began a massive bomber attack Temporarily, I stopped worrying about my father and Edwina, putting all of my energies into worry and prayer for Spence, and others engaged in the fight for their country, their lives, and their loved ones. Spence was in the thick of it. Every time the telephone rang, I jumped, my heart pounding with fear. I scoured newspapers, and listened to the wireless round the clock. Planes were lost and pilots killed by the score. I didn't hear from him for weeks, which nearly drove me bonkers, but I understood that he had scarce time for writing.

On 7 September, the German Air Force switched strategies. They started to bomb London. It became known as the Blitz. On the first day, 430 citizens were killed and 1600 were critically injured. The German bombers came back the next day and another 412 died. Every night, all night long, the Germans bombarded us. First we would hear the wail of the sirens; then the hideous sounds of German planes flying in from the sea. On a clear day, I could see their airplanes high up in the sky. On those days, I could also see our own British planes flying up to intercept them.

After the first siren, we were all supposed to go to the Anderson shelter. We were terribly afraid, and London took on a frightfully altered appearance. Eight Wren churches were destroyed in one night. Areas familiar to nearly everyone were unrecognizable. Streets were filled with burning buildings, broken, glass, and piles of rubble. On 10 September, I made the decision to leave London. I could no longer expose Isabella to such danger. It was apparent that we needed to evacuate to *Willow Grove Abbey*, where the war was more remote. The night before, innocent children asleep in their prams, and mothers with babies in their arms, were killed when a bomb exploded on a crowded shelter in an East London district. In one family, three children had died. The horror was unimaginable. I spoke with the Hausfater's, who were living in continual terror, and asked them if they wanted to move to a safe-haven in the country. They literally jumped at the opportunity. I assumed that Edwina would take Kippy and flee to Bury St. Edmunds, but instead, she announced that she, too, was going to re-locate to *Willow Grove Abbey.* I couldn't believe what I was hearing. I knew that it had to have been my father's suggestion, so I didn't even try to talk to him about it. I knew full well that anything I said would be met with stoic, stubborn resistance.

I asked Martha what her preference was. Did she want to leave Sumner Street and return to her own parent's home, or come with us to *Willow Grove?* She'd become so attached to Isabella, and of course was considered part of our family. Martha quickly decided that she wanted to remain with Isabella and me. With the sounds of sirens plaintively wailing about us, I hastily packed. The delicate and fragile items in the flat were sent to storage, including the chandeliers, as I had no illusions that Sumner Street might be fortunate enough to escape damage from the bombing. I hastily scribbled a letter to Spence, telling him of my plans, which I knew would relieve him. I was certain that he was well aware of the devastation taking place in London. He was surely worried sick about Isabella. In the letter I told him that after waiting so long and suffering such anxiety about what might happen if bombing came to London, now that it had finally arrived, I found myself too busy worrying about what needed to be packed to go to *Willow Grove*, and what would go into storage, that I didn't have time anymore for worry.

The people of London were bricks. They went on with their lives, in spite of the horror, and I never saw or heard anyone lose their heart or courage. I was proud to be a Londoner. King George and Queen Elizabeth were such incredible examples of bravery. They refused to leave Buckingham Palace. On the very day I decided to pack and evacuate, Buckingham Palace was hit by a delayed-action bomb, which fell outside of the north wing. No one was injured in the ensuing explosion, but the windows of the Royal apartments were shattered. The palace attack was on 13 September. The day was very cloudy, and it was raining hard. Six bombs made direct hits: two in the front courtyard, two in the quadrangle, one in the garden and one in the chapel, which was destroyed. Yet, the Queen and King held tightly to their determination to ride it out with their people.

Joseph drove up from the *Abbey*. He collected Isabella, Martha and me, and a separate car was sent for Edwina, Kippy and Helen. The Hausfater's drove my little *Ford* the following day. We left early in the morning, when bombing from the night before had ceased. After another night of terror and noise, with very little sleep, we made our way from the flat on Sumner Street to the waiting car. I could hear the sound of broken glass being cleared away, as we made our way through heart- wrenching streets. We would pass a building, which was no longer standing, but there would be two fireplaces straight up the wall. There was dust from brickwork in the air, and a strange odor from explosive materials which the bombs had contained. We could also smell domestic gas, seeping from broken pipes. My heart ached as I viewed the destruction. It was all so senseless. I knew that Spence would be actively involved in the battle. Britain was fighting for her life and all of the brave men who were defending her were struggling against horrific odds. The headlines in the *Times* kept everyone abreast of how many pilots and planes were lost. I prayed harder than I had ever prayed in my life, terrified that I would receive word that Spence was amongst those numbers.

The drive to *Willow Grove* Abbey was quiet. Each of us was terribly disturbed by the sights we'd seen. It was hard to leave, knowing that so many were left behind, to march on bravely. We all knew that there was more to come. And yet, I was so relieved to be escaping the horrible devastation. I wasn't so naive as to think that there wouldn't be bombing in the country, but it was far less dangerous at *Willow Grove* Abbey than in London proper. Isabella took it all so well. She was, after all, only four years old. She *did* show tremendous fear at the noise of the bombs, and the frightening concussions, but, Martha and I did our best to calm and reassure her that we were safe. I was extremely proud of the way my little girl displayed such bravery. We arrived at *Willow Grove* in the early afternoon, stopping only once for petrol and a quick pub lunch. Mummy was waiting in the Great Hall as we stepped out of the car, and made our way into the house. She seemed genuinely pleased to see everyone, and quickly set about directing us to our respective quarters. The *Abbey* was so immense, and there was certainly no lack of living space for additional numbers of people. Martha, Isabella and I were given a portion of one wing, consisting of a suite of rooms, which included a small parlor and two bedrooms with an adjoining loo. It was more than comfortable. Isabella's room had been transformed into a duplicate of her room on Sumner Street. Her bed had been moved, and everything was in its place, exactly as it had been in her own home. I was grateful for that, as it lessened the trauma of the move. Everything was ready, with fresh flowers in each room, and large, fluffy towels on the warmers in the baths.

Edwina was given a similar suite of rooms, in the same wing, and she was quickly able to settle with Kippy and her maid, Helen. Martha went to work unpacking Isabella's and my luggage, and the few boxes we'd managed to bring along. I took a long bath, although there was rationing in effect, regarding the level of water allowed. Then I changed into gray, flannel trousers and a cardigan sweater. My hair had grown quite long again, and I swept it up on the sides, securing it with combs, into what was known as a Victory Roll. Then, I went down the hallway to Edwina's rooms, to make certain that all was in order, and to offer any assistance that was needed. It wasn't an easy thing to do. I knocked on the doorway, and Edwina appeared at once. I couldn't help but be reminded of another time I had knocked on a door, waiting for Edwina to open it. That was on my first day at *Ashwick Park*. So much had happened since then. Who would ever have dreamed of the muddle that I was embroiled in?

Edwina was also dressed in trousers, but hers were topped by a bright blue tweed jacket with three pocket flaps at each side of the chest, and two below the waistline. It was nipped in at the waist, and I recognized it as a Jacques Helm original, which I'd seen in a fashion magazine. Edwina had no intention of letting a war interfere with her haute couture appearance. Her hair was longer too, and worn in a vamp style, with a deep wave over one eye, and a sleek page-boy in the back. She was bustling about her suite as I entered. Kippy was in his cot, and Helen was giving him a bottle.

"Thank goodness we're away from that horror," Edwina exclaimed, as she folded lingerie and placed it

into a drawer. "Lord, Sophia, whoever would've dreamed the world would come to this?"

"I don't know, Edwina. It's all so frightening....And sad. I wonder what will become of all of us."

"Dear heart, we'll survive this, and look back to laugh about it," she answered lightly.

"Do you really think so?" I replied. "Somehow I don't think we'll ever laugh about this. We are living

through a world changing event, Edwina. This war will change the course of history."

"Well, yes, I should imagine so. Wars generally do. But, life always goes on, doesn't it? People adapt to the changes. That's what we'll do. And, being here at *Willow Grove* isn't so very much different than our life has always been, but for these ugly blackout curtains", she said, pointing at the windows."

"Edwina, people are being killed. We can't just sit here in our insulated, privileged world and pretend that isn't happening."

"Well, what do you want to do? Roll bandages, or join the Women's Army Corps?" she said, with a brittle laugh.

"Perhaps that wouldn't be a bad idea. If I thought I could help, I'd consider it," I answered. "But, I also have a child to consider, and if, God forbid, her father doesn't return, she'll need me more than ever. I do intend to volunteer time to the Red Cross."

"Do you really?" Edwina answered, as if that were a novel idea.

"Aren't you in the least concerned about Kippy's father? I know that he's German, and an enemy, but how do you intend to explain to your son that you simply abandoned him? Don't you think Kippy will want to know about his father?"

"I'll worry about that when the time comes. I certainly wasn't going to sit in Paris, waiting for Dieter to come to the realization that he had a wife and child. And, I wasn't going to go to Germany. You know I never loved him, Edwina. I made a dreadful mistake. I'm just happy to have that behind me, and to be back in England safely with Nigel."

"But, Edwina, it isn't behind you. You have Dieter's child. And, how could he have come to the realization that he had a child, when he didn't even know you were pregnant?"You're still married to him. What do you intend to do about that?"

"I haven't thought much about it. Things have a way of working themselves out." She sounded irritated by Sophia's questions. "Anyway, don't you think you might be just a bit hypocritical, considering your own past?" she continued.

I was aghast. "My own past? You mean Owen? First of all, I didn't simply leave him, and didn't have his child. I told him the truth, and worked out what would have been an amicable solution to the whole mess. I wasn't having an affaire with a married man.... My best friend's father, no less. The circumstances were entirely different. The only comparison I can see is that neither of us loved our husbands. We've already had this conversation, Edwina. Why do you persist in saying things that you know are untrue, and are certain to upset me?"

"Because you always sound so judgmental, Sophia. *I'd* just appreciate it if you'd stop being so critical."

"Edwina, you're staying at my family home, while involved in an affaire with my father. The same home, I might add, where your affaire began, while my mother was under the same roof. My mother is under the same roof again, acting as your hostess. I *am* critical of that. It's beyond my comprehension. I've tried to keep quiet about my feelings. But, this is really over-the-top. I hope you and Papa have the decency not to engage in illicit acts *this time*, while here in this house."

Edwina turned on me, eyes blazing. "It's your father's home. I think I'll leave it up to him to decide how he wants this arrangement to proceed." She turned her back, peering into the vanity, touching up her lip color.

I was livid. "I'm warning you, Edwina. If I learn of anything untoward happening during your stay here, I'll not stand for it."

"Don't you threaten me, Sophia Somerville. If you make any trouble…… . And I mean *any,* it won't be *me* who'll be in danger of being put out. It will be you. Your father knows what he wants …… . And what he wants is me. So, deal with it."

I literally couldn't find words to voice what I was feeling. *How could Edwina possibly have been my dearest friend? I didn't even know the person standing in front of me.* It was at that moment that I knew our friendship was not going to survive such madness. I realized, in the blink of an eye, that I needed to start protecting myself. That Edwina meant to stop at nothing to get what she wanted. And what she wanted wasn't just my father. She wanted everything that being the Countess Somerville represented. Mummy's lifestyle, her riches, her name, and even her *home.* Edwina was single minded in the pursuit of her goals, and anyone or anything that got in her way would live to regret it. It was obvious that I had been a fool for a long, long time. It was clear that Edwina had been jealous of the Somervilles for a lengthy period. Perhaps from the very beginning of our friendship. Perhaps she *had* convinced herself that she was in love with Papa, but it wasn't just Papa she wanted. Without the trappings of wealth and power surrounding him, he wouldn't have been her *soulmate.* There was no doubt in my mind that she was correct about one thing. My father was totally under her spell. Talking to him would be of no use. For the first time since I'd learned all of the sordid details, I was absolutely certain that someone was going to be terribly hurt.

Chapter Twenty-Two

SEPTEMBER 1940 TO 27 DECEMBER 1940
"UNTIL DEATH DO US PART"

*P*apa had always harboured an interest in gardening, albeit roses were more to his liking. However, I vividly remember the next project undertaken by most of us, after our return to *Willow Grove*. It was the planting and tending of a garden. The government launched the 'Dig for Victory' campaign in 1940, and encouraged the cultivation of gardens and allotments. Everyone in England was asked to grow as much food as possible for the nation, to supplement the wartime food rations.

We began with great enthusiasm, and soon had a large plot near the duck pond. Papa enlisted the aid of everyone, but particularly Isabella, who became his most avid helper. We could all hear her marching around the garden area, pushing a small wheel barrow and singing the campaign song, by now very familiar to all English people: She had her own version.

"Dig! Dig! Dig!
Feel your muthles getting big,
Keep on puthing in the thpade,
Potatoeth, carrotth, beethroot and onionth,
Cannot thprout without your aid,
Never mind the wormth,
Just ignore their thquirmth,
And if your back achths, laugh with glee,

> And keep on digging,
> Till we give our toes a wigging,
> Dig! Dig! Dig! To victory"

We couldn't' help but laugh at her earnest efforts. She pronounced many words with th instead of 's', due to her lisp, and the word 'foes' became 'toes'. But she was a little trooper, and the garden did, indeed take shape. Nan was terribly happy at the prospect of having all of those homegrown vegetables, and as rationing became more stringent, the garden really did become a godsend.

Dr. and Mrs. Hausfater settled into the old caretaker's cottage, so they had a small place of their own. Thus, they were able to live their lives outside of the main house. I looked forward to visiting them in their cottage in the afternoons, where Dr. Hausfater and I continued with our textbook project, in spite of the fact that our lives had been up-ended. It was healthy to have something to concentrate upon, and to use my mind for something other than worry about Spence, my brothers, Edwina, and Papa. I never told the Hausfater's of the drama unfolding within the walls of the main house. I wouldn't have known where to begin.

I tried to maintain a facade that all was well between myself and Edwina, especially when Mummy was present. Otherwise, for the most part, I managed to ignore her. I didn't know whether Edwina had related our nasty conversation to Papa. He acted as though everything was fine, but that was his proverbial nature. Edwina devoted most of her time to sketching fashion designs, and talking of the career she would again take up, after the war ended. It never seemed to cross her mind that she might do something to aid in the war effort. I volunteered at the local military canteen two days a week, taught at the village school, part-time, and volunteered for a branch of the Red Cross. Edwina said that she would have considered the Red Cross, but that she wouldn't be caught dead in the *ghastly* shoes they wore.

Mummy was better than she'd been in a long, long time. She liked having a houseful of people, and of course, Papa was no longer running off on long, unexplained business trips. The war brought drama and purpose to her life. She seemed to dearly love having two small children to oversee. She'd always liked babies and small children......Was only when they developed their own identities that Mummy took umbrage. And so, the winter months fell upon us, and I waited with baited breath to see if Spence might receive a holiday furlough.

On 14 November, the Luftwaffe bombed Coventry, killing 380 people and injuring 865. The Nazi's claimed it was the biggest attack in the history of the air-war. There were apparently some fires still alight when dawn came, and the German bombers flew away to end a night of cruel bombing. The famous Cathedral was only a skeleton. Two hospitals, two other churches, hotels, clubs, cinemas, public shelters, public baths, the police station, and post office were also nothing but rubble. Coventry was a most important place in England, for it was a major center for the manufacture of airplane motors. Coventry would be manufacturing no more engines for many months to come. I felt teary, as I remembered that Spence and I had once spent a day there, exploring the lovely buildings. Many people around the world, including the Americans, began to express doubts as to whether England could hold on much longer.

And where was Spence? I knew that Duxford had been placed in a high state of readiness and to create space for additional units, 19th Squadron had been moved to nearby Fowlmere. Then came Hitler's attempt to dominate the skies over Britain. Duxford's first Hurricanes arrived in July with the formation of No.310 Squadron, made up of Czechoslovakian pilots who had escaped from France On 9 September, the Duxford squadrons successfully intercepted and turned back a large force of German bombers before they reached their targets. On the strength of this, two more squadrons were added to Wing No.302 (Polish) Squadron with Hurricanes, and the Spitfires of No.611 auxiliary Squadron, which had mobilized at Duxford a year before. Every day some sixty Spitfires and Hurricanes were dispersed around Duxford and Fowlmere. They were ready for action by 15 September, 1940, which became known as 'Battle of Britain Day'. On that historic day England twice took to the air to beat back Luftwaffe attacks aimed at London. That was right after we returned to *Willow Grove*. Thus, I knew that Duxford's squadrons had played a vital role in the victory, but since that time I'd had no real knowledge of Spence's whereabouts, or of the action he was seeing. I had the occasional letter, but portions were always cut away by the censors, so they didn't help to inform me of those unknown elements. The best purpose they served was to let me know that he was still alive, and was thinking of Isabella and me. I continued my daily writing, and fervently prayed for him.

One thing I liked about having returned to *Willow Grove* was my proximity to its attached chapel, and I began each day in that quiet sanctuary, with a morning prayer, and ended each day in the same Fshion.. Isabella always accompanied me on those occasions. I began to realize that I wanted more faith in my life, and started reading and studying religion, as well as teaching it to my daughter. Since Spence was such a devout Catholic, I wanted to learn more about his faith, whether or not he and I ever had a life together. I bought every book I could find on Catholicism, and as a result, my belief developed enormously. I also read other books written by esteemed theologians, such as C.S. Lewis, and tried to turn my problems over to God, putting my trust in His mercy, believing that good would prevail over evil. I began to understand much more clearly why Drew had chosen to become an Anglican vicar. It was really quite amazing considering that he and I had shared the same faithless upbringing. After reading so much theology, I was utterly amazed that there had been a world of information out there that I'd had no idea existed.

My prayers were answered, at least in part, because Spence came home for Christmas, 1940. *Oh Lord, how happy I was to see him.* I so desperately wanted to hold him, and to feel his arms about me, and yet it wasn't possible, as he continued his polite, kind, but distant relationship with me. I found myself becoming irritated and a bit hurt, but tried very hard not to show my feelings. I knew that if I lashed out at him, it would only drive him further away. Isabella was delirious with excitement, and my own emotions mirrored my daughter's. He sent a wire on December 21nd, informing me that he'd be arriving by train the next day. The entire family gathered at the station to welcome him, and I thought my heart would stop when he stepped from the railway carriage, dressed in his RAF blue uniform. He looked weary, and slightly thinner, but as handsome as ever. Isabella ran to him, and he swept her off the ground, holding her close to his heart. I so wished that he was greeting me in such a fashion.

"My darling, darling daughter …. . My Isabella. If you could only know how often I've dreamed of this moment," he cried, kissing her over and over. He swung her high into the air, while she screamed with delight, yelling "Papa, Papa." Then, with his arm about her, they walked to me, and Spence kissed me on the cheek, and gave me a nice hug. I wanted to grab hold, and never let him go. The three of us walked on to my parents, who were waiting on the platform, as well. Papa threw his arm about Spence's shoulder, while my mother gave him one of the most effusive hugs I'd ever witnessed. Edwina had stayed back at the house, for which I was grateful. There was so much to tell Spence about the entire beastly fiasco. He knew very little, as I'd not wasted precious space in my letters complaining of family strife, nor did I want to worry him about things he could do nothing about.

When we arrived at *Willow Grove Abbey*, he shed his uniform jacket, and Papa mixed him a drink. The house was decorated for the holidays, although not as elaborately as in times past, for the war was taking its toll in that arena. There were few decorations for sale in the stores, and no new ornaments were being manufactured. The tree, which had come from our property, and was technically against war regulations because of rationing on wood, was trimmed with strings of popcorn, cranberries and heirloom ornaments, which had been in the family for generations. There were a few packages under the tree, but nothing like the Christmas's I remembered from childhood. I'd spent the autumn and early winter months knitting a scarf for Spence, as well as an RAF blue sweater. Even my mother cro-cheted some lovely items. The wrapping paper was homemade, created and colored by Isabella, with added scribbling by Kippy. Bits of yarn acted as ribbon. Still, there was a wonderful fire roaring in the drawing room, and a giant wreath upon the door, as well as a pine garland wound about the stair railing. The *Victrola* was playing Carols.

Edwina made her appearance soon after we'd settled down and begun to chat. I heard her steps on the staircase, and looked up to see her enter the room, carrying Kippy in her arms. She looked beautiful, as she always did in those days. Dressed in a sky blue velvet dress, with a sweetheart neckline and three-quarter sleeves, reminiscent of a ballerina's gown, she sparkled, and rather resembled the Madonna, as she held Kippy. On her feet were matching blue velvet shoes. I, by contrast, was wearing a white angora jumper over black velvet trousers, with my pearls. Edwina went directly to Spence. She kissed him on both cheeks, warmly welcoming him home for the Holiday. Spence was his usually polite and gentlemanly self, but I detected a look in his eyes that signified a bit of annoyance. He turned his attention, at once, to Kippy, whom he made a great fuss about. Kippy *was* an adorable child, and it was not hard for one to be genuine when exclaiming that he was a delightful little boy. Papa immediately stood and offered his seat to Edwina, and then fetched her a cocktail. She smiled sweetly and thanked him.

"So, Spence, it's wonderful to have you here. How long will you be able to stay?" She asked.

"Just until the 29th, I'm afraid. I feel fortunate to have this short time. This damned war just goes on and on. We're holding our own, but it taking its toll."

"Can we hope for any respite?" my mother asked.

It's impossible to know. The Germans are giving us everything they've got. If the Americans would only join in, but so far Roosevelt is standing firm. They're sending guns and ammunition, but what we need are their boys. I'm so grateful that you've got out of London. Those poor souls…. Especially the people in the East End. It's bloody horrific."

"Yes," I said. I'm so glad we had an evacuation destination. Of course, many of the children and elderly have been billeted to country houses, but there are still so many others who're facing this horror. In the thick of it. Then there are those who were evacuated to the country early on, and thought there would be no bombing, so they've returned to London."

"I have friends whose entire families have been destroyed. It's beastly, and we *must* win," Spence said, in a forceful tone. He turned to Edwina. "What are your long-term plans?" He asked.

"I'm taking things one day at a time, at present. I haven't any definite plans. I'd hoped to do some design work, in London, but things are so precarious at present, I'm certainly not going to think along those terms, unless things settle down."

Of course Spence knew the secret of the affaire, and I could tell he was choosing his words carefully. "What of Dieter? I don't suppose you've had any news of him? Does he know of your whereabouts?"

"No…No, I'm fairly certain he has no idea where I've gotten off to. I certainly hope he doesn't. I don't think he could do anything, with a war between England and Germany, but I'd rather not chance it."

She ran her fingers through her long, sleek hair, and pushed one side behind her ear. "At some point, I suppose I'll have to make contact, and initiate divorce proceedings, but that's a very complex scheme to consider at the moment."

"Yes, I imagine it would be," Spence replied. "What of your family? Do you intend to rejoin them at some point?"

"I haven't given it a lot of thought. They know where I am, and are happy that I've been given such safe refuge. I'm in contact with them. I have their assurance that they won't divulge my whereabouts to Dieter, should he make an attempt to contact them. But, I've no great desire to return to Bury St. Edmunds."

"Edwina is welcome here for as long as she wishes to stay," Mummy chimed in. "We think of Edwina as another daughter, and adore having little Kippy here. You're no problem at all, dear," she said, smiling at Edwina, reaching over to pat her on the knee. Edwina returned her smile, and took a sip of her drink. *It was hard for me not to slap her."*

And what of Blake and Andrew," Spence asked.

"Both were given short furloughs, I answered. "And both went to their in-laws homes. Neither Annie nor Susan has been to their parent's homes since before the war started. They've been waiting in London to see where Blake and Andrew would be permanently posted. They were here for a bit, when things got rough. I would like to have seen my brothers, but it's perfectly understandable that their wives wanted time with their own families. We *have* been able to speak with them by telephone."

"Of course," Spence said. What do you know of the action they've seen?"

Blake has been flying bombers …. Hurricanes. He's been in some frightening scrapes. I suspect he's been over Germany. You know he can't talk of his operations, so we don't know with certainty. Andrew is doing Naval Chaplin duty. We aren't' certain exactly what that entails. Whether he's assigned ship duty, or on-base duty. Of course, I think we'd all prefer on-base."

"That's a bigger job than one might think," Spence added. "A bloody lot of emotional turmoil."

"Of course," Papa said. "I can't tell you how proud I am of all of you. It's a devil of a mess we're in, and we're fortunate to have such brave, young men to defend us. The country owes you a large debt of gratitude. I've joined the Home Guard in an attempt to do my bit. It's hard not to be able to do more to lend a hand."

"It's our job, Nigel. It seems every generation is faced with something like this. Just a bit over twenty years ago, everyone thought we were fighting the war to end all wars, yet here we are again. History simply repeats itself. You did your bit at Ypres."

There was silence in the room, as we all realized that it was a gloomy conversation for Christmas Eve. Yet, there was little else on our minds. The children were playing on the floor. Isabella was throwing a ball for Kippy, and we all turned our attention to them, commenting upon how adorable they were and how well they got on together. Our conversation continued until the Hausfater's arrival, and another round of kissing and hugs ensued. Then, it was time for all of us to go into the dining room to enjoy another of Rose's traditional Christmas feasts. Though there was a bit less of everything that year, due to rationing, she had still used the coupons wisely, and none of us could complain that we went away from the table hungry.

Spence stayed for only a short while in the drawing room following dinner. He obviously wanted desperately to rest, and to spend time alone with Isabella. It was all I could do to keep my hands from him. I continually found myself touching his sleeve, and wished I could snuggle up close to him as we sat together on the sofa. We both accompanied Isabella upstairs, and enjoyed some time reading to her, as well as readying her for bedtime. Martha had gone to her parents for the holidays, so Spence and I were alone together. At last Isabella became drowsy, after postponing the inevitable as long as possible. We yielded to her requests for an extra drink of water, an extra story, and an extra goodnight kiss. Then we turned down her light. Spence started to go to his own bed chamber, but Nan had turned back the bed covers in in my room, and there were fresh, white, monogrammed sheets. My white eyelet and organdy gown lay on the pillow, and on the nightstand was a bottle of champagne and two crystal flutes. It was obvious that she was trying to bring about some romance between us.

"You would think it was our wedding night," Spence laughed.

"Oh, that's just our silly Nan, being a bit of a matchmaker. Pay her no mind," I smiled. "We *could* sit in front of the fire and have a glass of champagne though. Would you like that, Spence?"

"Yes, that might be nice," he responded. It doesn't seem that I ever have time for such luxuries…Never time to just relax, and live a normal life. I wonder if that day will ever come."

"It will come, Spence. I know it has to be dreadfully hard for you. I wish there was something I could do to make things easier."

"You *have* made things easier, Sophia," he replied, as he accepted a glass of champagne and stretched his legs out. He'd removed his tunic, loosened his tie, and his hair was the slightest bit ruffled. *I wanted to run my hands through it.*

"It would be an awfully dreary Christmas if I didn't have Isabella, and if your family weren't so nice about accepting me as their guest. And, of course it goes without saying that I'm terribly grateful to you, for being a brick about everything. I'm not a fool, Sophia. I do know that this is an odd arrangement. There are times when I think that I should throw caution to the winds, and let myself feel the magic. But, the war never allows time for anything. I've seen several men in my RAF Group fall in love and marry on furlough, and six month later they regret their actions."

"We aren't exactly strangers, Spence," I replied. Those men probably met their brides, for the first time, while on leave. I don't exactly know what you're saying. Are you implying that you *do* still have feelings for me?" I asked, with trepidation.

"Of course I have feelings for you, Sophia. You know that. We share a daughter. But, do you realize how little actual time we've *ever spent* together? Since the summer of 1935, it's been virtually non-existent, but for the scant few months before I learned about Isabella."

"I realize that Spence, but I'm very confused at this point. You loved me enough to want to marry me that summer of 1935, before we had a daughter. You *still* loved me enough to want to marry me before you learned that Isabella was your child. *Now,* you seem to do everything possible to reign in your emotions. Not to show them. Or, perhaps they just aren't as strong. I certainly did enough harm to cause them to lessen. However, you say you have feelings for me, but what are they, exactly? Am I just someone you *used* to love? Have you been with other women since we last saw one another? Do you *want* to be with other women? You told me that I should get on with my life, and I'm doing that, as best I can. But, if I'm to be perfectly honest Spence, it's hard to do when you're still in my life. I never know but what there isn't a chance that our relationship might be rekindled." The champagne was giving me a modicum of courage, and at long last I was speaking my true feelings.

"Sophia, perhaps I haven't been fair with you. I've been giving this whole situation a lot of thought. I've been extremely critical of you in the past for not being honest with me, but I think that I'm guilty of the same crime."

"What do you mean?" I asked.

"I mean that I haven't been honest with you about *my* feelings. The truth is that I ache to hold you to make love to you… ..To be with you…. . But I've held back …. Not because I don't trust you, and not because I don't still love you, but because I've been trying not to be selfish. "

"How would expressing love for me be selfish? I asked, with a heart that was beating very quickly.

Oh God, Sophia. It's this bloody war. It could go on forever. Is it fair to become involved when there's so much uncertainty? I could be killed, and then you'd be a widow. You'd be alone for months at a time…… It wouldn't be a real marriage, if we were to do that. No long, lazy day's together, like we had in 1935. No cozy dinners, and hours of talking. Just rushed moments, here and there."

"Spence, for heaven's sake! This is pure poppycock! Aren't a few moments here and there better than none? And as far as my being a widow…. Well that's what I am now. I wouldn't want to think of such a thing happening, but I'd rather have had you for a short while than *never* to have had you. I've wanted to be your wife for such a long time. Please don't tell me that it would be a selfish thing if you were to marry me. It would be the most precious gift I've ever received. And, one other thing," I emphasized, "Just who in the world do you think I'd be spending time with? Every man over eighteen and under fifty is serving the country in some capacity, so I'd be alone, no matter. And, I don't want to be with anyone else. I never have. You know that,"

"You should have been a barrister, Sophia," he laughed. Turning towards me, he reached out and pulled me into his arms. I held my breath, for fear that he would change his mind, as he'd done before, but he only tightened his hold, and buried his face in my hair.

"I love you Sophia. I've always loved you. From the moment I saw you at your Presentation Ball. You were the prettiest thing I'd ever seen that night, and you're even lovelier now. Can you forgive me for being such a bloody fool? There's nothing I could want more in this world than to know that you're my wife, and that you and Isabella are waiting for me…. .waiting until this beastly war is over."

"Spence, did you just ask me to marry you?" I asked, as I pulled away from him just a bit, and looked up into his eyes.

"Yes, darling girl, that's what I did. Will you marry me Sophia?" He asked, as he kissed me with enormous longing and passion. I felt as though I must have been dreaming. After all of the nights I had spent alone, praying that someday we might work things out and be together again, it seemed surreal that it was finally happening.

"Of course I'll marry you, I replied. "Of course, of course." I was laughing and crying at the same time. "Do you know how happy this will make Isabella? She loves you so, Spence, and she wants us to be a real family. That's what I want more than anything too."

"I know, darling," he murmured, as he nibbled my ear, and covered my face with soft little kisses. "It's what we all want. Please, rest assured, I'll adopt Isabella immediately. No more 'Isabella Winnsborough'. She'll finally be 'Isabella Stanton', as she always should have been."

"Spence, when and how can we be married? How long will we have to wait? I don't want to wait any longer. Doesn't the Catholic Church require that banns be published, and other procedural rituals satisfied, and won't that take a lot of time?"

"Not necessarily. You don't have to convert, unless you want to. You just have to agree to be married by a priest, and to raise our children

Catholic. I think, in light of the war, banns could be dispensed with. We can be issued what it known as a 'special license'."

"I do want to convert, but can't I do that after we're married? Aren't there instructions I'd need to take?"

"Yes, there are, and yes, you can do that any time. How soon do you want to be married?"

"Now…This moment," I laughed.

"Well, I don't think I can arrange *that*, but give me twenty four hours, and I'll find a priest, probably in Bristol, but certainly in London. I promise that we'll be married before I have to leave." I was absolutely beside myself. Throwing my arms around him, I buried my cheek on the front of his crisp, blue shirt. I could smell the wonderful masculine scent of him, mixed with the spicy aftershave he always wore. I put my hand up, and ran it through his hair. "Do you know how much I've wanted this?" I asked. "Every time I've seen you it's taken all of my willpower not to throw my arms about you."

"I know, darling. I've felt the same way, and have been very foolish. But let's look ahead, not backward. We need to cherish every precious moment we have together."

"And I think we should begin right now," I said, with a sly grin. "Perhaps Nan's idea wasn't so bad after all." He crushed me in an embrace and I could feel that he was aroused. It had been such a long, long time, and I was surprised at the amount of passion that I felt, and at how my body responded instantly. He slipped his hand under my jumper, and unhooked my brasserie, allowing my breasts to fall free. Then, he leaned down and began to kiss them, as he continued to fondle me, and to trace the line of my leg and thigh with his other hand. I reached up and unbuttoned his shirt, and then shed my jumper, and when our bare skin touched, we both felt a jolt of passion. Our breath was coming in short gasps, and

Spence gently stood up, took me by the hand and led me to the bed. There, he slowly and sensually finished undressing me, and slipped out of his own clothing, all the while murmuring endearments. I only remember that we fell upon the bed at the same time, in one smooth movement, and continued with the kissing and touching. We had both waited such a long time. It was unthinkable that either of us could have delayed the consummation of our love. There was a feeling of completion…..A feeling that we'd finally found our way back to where we belonged. I knew that this time we would truly be one person for all time. We made love again repeatedly, languorously, until we were both fully sated and exhausted. Finally, Spence fell into a deep sleep, and I was glad to see him resting so peacefully. He looked happy.

I took a quick bath, and then slipped my gown and robe on. It was nearing three o'clock in the morning. Spence was sleeping soundly, and I knew that he needed the rest, so I tried to be as hushed as possible. After seeing that Isabella was also sleeping, I decided to make my way to the kitchen, as I suddenly had a mad hunger, and the thought of Rose's leftover Christmas Eve trifle beckoned me. Quietly opening the door, I entered the hallway and began to make my way toward the staircase, when I heard whispered voices. I flattened my back against a niche in the wall, and waited to see who was up and about at such an hour. Then I saw that the door to Edwina's suite of rooms was slightly ajar. Next I spied Papa, slipping through into the hallway. He turned and gave Edwina a lingering kiss, before tip-toeing in the direction of the opposite wing, where he and my mother's rooms were located. Edwina's door silently closed. I was dumbfounded, although I shouldn't have been. It had probably been going on since Edwina's arrival at *Willow Grove*. I had certainly worried about just such an occurrence. Waiting until I was certain that Papa had disappeared into the opposite wing, I then returned to my own bed chamber, since my appetite had disappeared.

I kept silent to Spence about what I'd seen. It was Christmas Day, and Isabella was bouncing on the bed at the crack of dawn, anxiously begging Spence and me to hurry so that she might see what Father Christmas had brought to her. She didn't seem in the least surprised to find that Spence was in my bed, and since Isabella didn't ask any questions, neither Spence nor I offered any explanations. We intended to announce our impending marriage at breakfast, and knew that Isabella would be beside herself. It wasn't the time to launch into a discussion about Papa and Edwina. The Somerville family had a tradition, whereby we met in the dining room on Christmas morning, ate a large breakfast, and then removed to the drawing room for gift exchange. When we arrived downstairs, but the only person present was Papa. I immediately asked where Mummy, Edwina and Kippy were, as of course the Isabella couldn't wait to get the meal behind so that the excitement could begin. I knew that the Hausfater's were due any moment.

"Pamela felt a bit under the weather this morning," Nigel said. "Nothing serious…probably taking a winter cold. She'll be down in time, but she's told us to go along and begin our breakfast without her. I'm having Nan send a tray up to her,"

"What of Edwina?" I then asked.

"Edwina's decided to join your mother for breakfast in Pamela's room. It was generous of her to not want Pamela dining alone," he added.

I was beyond furious. Edwina had obviously enjoyed a night of lovemaking with Papa and then, only a few hours later, was going to enjoy breakfast with Mummy in her bedroom! It was unbelievably cheeky. Unfathomable! *Could she have any conscience at all?* It was perfectly amazing that I didn't lose my composure and blurt out my rage. But it was Christmas, and Spence and I had such lovely news. I simply was not going to let anything ruin that happy occasion. So, I kept my mouth tightly buttoned, and never even said anything to Spence. God knows, he had all he could deal with, as he faced the loss of dearly loved RAF friends, companions and colleagues, not to mention fighting to protect our nation. He didn't need to hear about the foolishness of two very selfish people.

It wasn't long before both Mummy and Edwina appeared. Mummy was wearing a lovely white satin dressing gown, and Edwina was dressed in a pale yellow cashmere skirt and sweater, which matched her hair.

Soon the Hausfater's arrived, and we seated ourselves at the table, which was beautifully set with blue Wedgwood Queens Ware, Mummy's loveliest Sterling silver, and crystal champagne flutes. Once comfortably gathered, Spence stood up, and proposed a toast with his glass of champagne. He tapped on the edge of the crystal rim, and the glass tinkled prettily.

"Sophia and I have some very nice news to announce, which we hope will be a happy Christmas gift for the family, and especially for Isabella," he said, as he looked down at his daughter with loving eyes. Of course, the others had to have known what was coming, but it was still thrilling to hear him say the words.

"We've decided to be married as quickly as possible, while I'm still home on furlough. I'm going to be spending a good deal of time on the telephone in my quest to find a priest who'll marry us on short notice, but I'll succeed. I've promised Sophia."

The entire family, minus Mummy, reacted as I knew they would. There were kisses and shouts of glee from everyone, and Isabella jumped out of her chair and ran to me, clapping her hands.

"Oh Mummy. Is it true? You and Papa are going to get married? Does that mean that you'll be together forever and ever?"

"God willing, darling. We'll be promising that to each other. And, you'll be called 'Isabella Stanton', since Papa is going to make certain that your name is changed to what it should have been when you were born. As soon as we're married, you'll be 'Isabella Stanton'. Do you like the sound of that, precious?" I asked, smiling. Isabella hopped up and down like a little bird, and then danced a little jig. We all burst into laughter over her antics. Next, she ran upstairs to her grandmother's room, and fetched Mummy and Edwina. She told them that her Mummy and Papa had a grand Christmas present for everyone, and that they needed to join us. It wasn't long before both Mummy and Edwina appeared. Mummy was wearing a lovely white satin dressing gown, and Edwina was dressed in a pale yellow cashmere skirt and sweater, which matched her hair. Of course, Isabella had not been able to contain herself, and had already told them the news. For once, Mummy wasn't upset at having to leave her bed. She seemed genuinely happy, and said as much to Spence, and me.

"When are you going to be married?" Edwina asked. "Are you thinking of doing so before Spence has to leave on the 29th?"

"Spence intends to find a priest who'll perform a ceremony for us before his return to Fowlmere. He feels confident that he can do so," I replied.

"What will you wear, Sophia?" she asked.

"I haven't given it a whit of thought," I answered. "I don't care if I have to wear rags. It's just the ceremony that counts."

"Oh, but you must have a glorious outfit for this special day," Edwina replied. "I know, Sophia. I have a gorgeous white velvet suit, with gold braid at the cuffs and round the edges. It's a Chanel. I've never worn it. You're welcome to borrow it."

"That's awfully nice, Edwina, but anything of yours would fall to my toes." *I didn't add that it would also be about three sizes too large.*

"Couldn't Nan alter it? I'll wager that she could, with my help. Don't forget, I *am* a designer. I would love for you to wear it, Sophia," she added. There didn't seem to be any gracious way to say "No" to her generous offer. I was still harbouring anger over her antics of the previous night, and really wished there was a graceful way to decline her offer. However, I gave in, and said that I would accept Edwina's generosity. Edwina ran back up the stairs to retrieve the suit, and I couldn't help but think that there was a flash of the old Edwina in such a gesture. Perhaps I was being too hard on her, although the facts certainly made it a horrific situation. Edwina returned in scant minutes, with the magnificent suit, covered by a fabric dress-bag. It was truly lovely, and did look the perfect outfit for a wedding.

"Now, what shall I wear?" she continued, pursing her lips, and placing her finger upon them. "Since I'll obviously be the Matron of Honour, I'll need to look smashing. Do you have a coluor preference, Sophia?"

"Um…well…I hadn't even thought of an attendant," I answered, rather taken aback by Edwina's statement. Of course, I would need someone to stand up for me as a witness, but the last person alive whom I wanted was Edwina! Yet, how could I tell her that, without Mummy wondering why I was being so rude? It seemed I had been presented with a Matron of Honour. "Well…I guess anything you have that would blend with the style of the suit," I answered. "You know I prefer pastels, but if you don't have a dress like that, anything will do."

"Yes, I do have several pastels. A shell pink silk dress, and an ice blue satin suit, or a pale green moiré dress. I think the shell pink might be just the thing. You can carry a nosegay of pink and white roses, which will be lovely, and I'll carry a smaller version of the same." *It seemed that I had also been presented with a wedding planner.*

"How thoughtful of you," Edwina. Sophia, you are so fortunate that Edwina is here at this special time. She has such exquisite taste. Everything she has suggested sounds perfect," Mummy commented.

"Oh yes, I know I'm terribly fortunate to have her here," I replied, and no one seemed to notice the bit of sarcasm in my voice.

Spence wisely stayed out of that conversation, knowing that I would have to handle it as I saw fit, and of course, I realized that I had very little choice.

Spence laughed. "Well, thank God I don't have to worry about fashion. My RAF uniform will have to suffice. It makes things simple.'"

"I love your uniform," I replied. You will be the best looking groom in the world."

"What about me, Mummy? " Isabella asked. "What thall I wear? I want to look beautiful. It's a thpecial day for me too," she continued.

"I know it is darling, and we'll make certain that you're the most beautiful one of all. You have several lovely frocks. We can look them over, and decide which would be most suitable. And, you can carry a basket of flowers," I added, getting into the spirit of things. Isabella clapped her hands and jumped up and down some more.

"Come, sit down and eat your breakfast now though, darling, so that we can open the gifts that Father Christmas brought. I think there are quite a few under the tree with your name upon them," I said, coaxing my little girl, so that we might move the morning along. Isabella appeared to have forgotten that it was Christmas, as the wedding news temporarily erased everything else from her thoughts. But, once reminded, she scampered round the table, took her seat and began to eat a bowl of oatmeal.

"Where is Kippy?" I asked. "Surely he'll be opening gifts with us?"

"Oh yes. Helen is feeding and bathing him, and then she'll bring him down," Edwina answered. I'll have to pick out a precious little outfit for him to wear to your wedding too. Won't this all be fun?"

I answered that "it would, indeed, be fun", but there was very little time, so that we mustn't try to get too elaborate. "Besides, I want a very simple ceremony. Nothing flashy. Just quiet and meaningful." Everyone seemed to understand my wishes.

After we finished eating, Spence took me aside and asked whether I still had the engagement ring of long-ago. I told him that of course, I did, wrapped in velvet at the bottom of my jewel case. He kissed me. "Run upstairs and fetch it. It needs to be on your finger, where it should have been long ago." I almost burst with joy. I'd actually forgotten all about the ring in my excitement. I was so pleased that he had remembered. It took less than five minutes to retrieve it from my room, and when I returned, I was wearing it on my left hand. Everyone in the family oohed and aahed and told me it was one of the loveliest rings they'd ever seen. I thought it was too. I had forgotten how the emerald flashed in the light, and how the diamonds were such a perfect counterpoint to the deep, rich green of the square-cut stone.

"What shall we do about a wedding ring?" I asked? I suppose I can make do with this one, and use it for both. Otherwise, I would just want a simple, platinum band to go with this, but could we find one on such short notice? And with everything in such short supply because of war footing?"

"Sophia, I have the perfect ring for you," Mummy answered. It was your grandmother Somervilles'. It's exactly what you want. Just a simple, platinum band. I'll fetch it after breakfast, and you can decide if it will work."

I was deeply touched. It meant a lot that my mother was giving her wholehearted support to my marriage, and I truly loved the idea of an heirloom ring that had been in the family. I thanked Mummy profusely, and said that it sounded perfect. Finally, we all adjourned to the drawing room, and settled down to the business of exchanging gifts. The children were wild with excitement. It was fun to watch them, but I have to admit that I didn't concentrate on much else except the fact that I was going to be Mrs. Spencer Stanton at long last.

And two days later that is precisely who I became. Spence literally pulled off a miracle. He found a charming little Catholic Church in the small hamlet of *Witford,* not far from *Bedminster-with-Hartcliffe.* The priest was a warm, kindly man, who understood our dilemma completely. We drove to *Witford* and met with him on the day after Christmas, and he said that he would be pleased to marry us the following morning. A whirlwind of activity followed, with clothes being altered, pressed and cleaned, and miraculous flowers appearing from a floral shop in Bristol. Mummy had some connections where those were concerned. She produced the aforementioned ring, as well as my Grandfather's wedding band for Spence, a wide band of gold. Spence treasured it.

Isabella was dressed in a pink taffeta, full skirted dress, with a ruffled hemline and ruffled cuffs. She looked like a tiny Victorian princess. Even Kippy wore a black velvet baby romper, with a tiny white shirt beneath it. Everything was as perfect as could be, and it was truly an amazing feat, given the time constraints. There is no question that it was the happiest day of my life. I didn't have my father walk me down the aisle, and instead opted to enter the small chapel on Spence's arm. He looked splendid in his RAF dress uniform, and when the words "I now pronounce that you are husband and wife" were spoken, there were tears streaming down both of our faces.

Afterwards, Mummy rushed over and kissed me on both cheeks and told me that it was the prettiest wedding she'd ever attended, which was doubtful, but certainly gracious of her. "You know, Sophia, I was so surprised," she added, "The ceremony wasn't the least bit heathen. There was scarcely any difference between this ceremony and the Anglican, except of course for that beastly Latin," she commented, in the way that only Mummy could. I simply had to laugh, for I knew that Mummy honestly meant it as a compliment. I was much too happy to point out that my mother's words were very rude. I could tell that Spence was biting back his own laughter, when he heard her comments. Spence was so easy-going and mellow. I knew there couldn't have been much that might have upset him, unless it had been something that wounded me. He'd forgiven Mummy's threats of long ago. Sometimes he amazed me with his ability to forgive, and I vowed to try to be more like him.

After the ceremony, we returned to *Willow Grove, where* Nan had prepared a lovely champagne luncheon. Of course there'd been only a few guests at the ceremony..... .Mummy, Papa, The Hausfater's, Joseph, Nan, Martha, Helen, and a few of the family's old friends from the village and surrounding estates, whom I had known since childhood. When we were all settled in the drawing room, going over each detail of the morning,

Spence told Isabella that he had something to give her. Her eyes lighted, as they always did when her Papa presented her with a gift. I had no idea what he had come up with. Nonetheless, I knew it would be something she'd adore. Sure enough, Spence had done something extraordinarily thoughtful. He'd purchased a small ring for Isabella, which he placed on her hand. "This is to show that I became your official Papa today, darling," he said, kissing her on the cheek. It was a sweet ring, with a pearl center, and tiny chips of emeralds surrounding it. It was her first piece of jewelry, and she was nearly popping her buttons with pride. She ran through the house showing everyone her ring, and we all became tearful at Spence's lovely gesture.

When the last guest left, and Nan began clearing the remnants of the party, Spence and I decided to take a walk. We changed into comfortable clothes, and strolled about the property, ending up at the old burying ground, where I pointed out the resting places of various ancestors, and explained who they were and their significance to the family. He was genuinely interested. Not having had a family for so long; it was a gift for him to suddenly become a part of so much history.

"Sophia, I'm beginning to understand your deep love for *Willow Grove* as I spend more time here, and now that we're married, it's a good feeling to be a part of a family with such deep roots," he said, holding my hand, as he examined the quaint old epitaphs.

"I want you to love it as I do," I answered. "You know that I haven't always had a happy life here, but my memories of this house and its special setting are such a part of me. I wish we could live here someday, although that's probably a fantasy" I smiled.

"Well, one never knows," he answered. I promise you that we'll always visit frequently. Surely, your father plans on making certain that it remains in the family? He added.

"Oh, certainly. Actually the eldest son will be the one to inherit, according to the Law of Primogeniture, and that will be Blake, but he hasn't much interest in living here. His wife Susan is an only child, and she also comes from a family with an enormous estate in Scotland. I wouldn't be at all surprised if they inherit in Scotland, and he chooses that over *Willow Grove*. Drew will become the vicar at the Chapel someday, although there isn't much congregation to support such a position. People from the village still attend, and of course, family and staff, but there is a new church that was built shortly before the War. Blake will probably open a *Somerville, Ltd.* branch in Leith or Edinburgh. So, that leaves you and me. Of course, all of this is mere speculation, since Mummy and Papa are still very much alive. I certainly would never contemplate living here with them. Once the war ends, we can make our own home."

"The upkeep on an estate like this is vast, I'm sure," Spence commented. "I'd need to be a very successful physician to take on a property of this magnitude someday," he smiled.

"Spence, I have a good deal of money from Owen, you know. I hope you understand that anything I have is also yours, "I added.

"Darling, I know that. However, I feel strongly that I don't want Owen's money to be a part of our income or support. You know how I feel about that subject." I did know how he felt, as we had discussed it at length, and he'd made it exceedingly clear that Owen's money was not to be counted as income to support us. I understood his feelings, and didn't even think about arguing. Actually, I was proud that he felt the way he did. I would be completely content with whatever lifestyle Spence provided for us.

We strolled slowly back to the house, and went upstairs to what had become our bed chamber, instead of simply mine. Isabella was sleeping in Mummy and Papa's room, so that Spence and I might have an uninterrupted wedding night. We went directly to our room, where Nan had, once again, prepared everything as nicely as if we had been staying at the *Grande.* There was again a bottle of champagne and a tray of fruit, cheeses, and biscuits. I ran a hot bath, poured in some of my delicious lavender oil and disappeared for a good hour, while luxuriating and thinking about how differently this night would be than when I had married Owen. Although Spence and I hadn't been celibate since we'd rediscovered one another on Christmas Eve, the addition of marriage to the equation heightened my anticipation and love. When I stepped out of the bath, feeling warm and rosy all over, I brushed my hair until it shined, and slipped on my white satin, slip-style nightgown. I took pleasure in the fact that I was every bit as tiny as I had been in 1935, when we had first made love, yet my body was more fully developed, and more curvaceous. Finally, emerging from the bath, I found Spence sitting in front of the fire, reading the *Times*.

"So this is what men do to pass the time while waiting for their wives on their wedding night" I laughed, chidingly. Then, I leaned down and kissed him, and told him that I loved him madly. He reached up and pulled me down to him, and kissed me even more passionately. I could feel that he was aroused.

"Whoa, wait just a moment Mrs. Stanton." he grinned. "I want to bathe before I ravish your body. My God but you're beautiful Sophia."

"Then you'd better be off to the bath, because I don't want to wait more than a moment," I teased.

He kissed me again, and then disappeared behind the door of the loo. I heard the running of water. It wasn't long before he was back in the room, looking fresh and young, with his hair still damp, dressed in a pair of pale blue, crisp cotton pyjamas. We sat next to one another on the small loveseat in front of the fire, and he poured two glasses of champagne. Then, he raised his glass to mine and said "To my astonishingly beautiful wife, whom I promise to cherish every moment of our lives. "We both took a sip of the champagne, and then placed the glasses on the oval marble-topped table in front of the loveseat. He took me into his arms and began to kiss me with those little, nibbling motions, which he knew drove me wild. Our touching and caressing grew more and more intense, and we moved to the bed, where he made love to me in ways I had never imagined. I'd believed that I'd experienced every ounce of passion I was capable of, but it seemed that knowing we were husband and wife, and that nothing was forbidden, loosened any last inhibitions either one of us had. We were truly one, in every way, and the intensity of our love was overwhelming.

When it was over, Spence brought up the subject of more children. I'd hoped that he would do so, as I wanted another baby badly, and prayed that he would be in agreement. Knowing his feelings about the war, and our being apart, I wasn't certain that he would want to bring another child into the world at such a time. However, he surprised me by saying that he would like that more than anything, if I was in accord. So, we made the decision to dispense with all precautions, and let nature take its course. I knew that the time was promising for me to conceive, and hoped that we might mark that wonderful night with the creation of a new life.

We only had two nights together, and they passed so quickly. We spent our days with Isabella, and the nights without sleep, but we lazed about and slept late in the mornings. Still, it all ended much too quickly, and before I knew it, we were standing at the station again, holding one another, and saying goodbye. There were the usual words and endearments that lovers and spouses all over the globe were murmuring to one another about caution and care, and then he was gone again. I stood holding Isabella's hand, as his train disappeared into the distance.

Chapter Twenty-Three

10 February 1941 to 11 February 1941
An Unwelcome Letter

Things had been relatively quiet on the war front for that special holiday, but, it turned out to be only a lull before a storm. To begin with, on New Year's Eve, the Germans chose to launch one of the worst attacks yet upon London. Thinking that they would catch the Brits in a down time, during the period between Christmas and the New Year, they seized the opportunity and flew their beastly airplanes, dropping hundreds and hundreds of bombs onto that already devastated city. The Blitz just went on and on and on.

Also, in my personal life, as if the war weren't bad enough, it seemed that the Gods had much more in store. On 10 February, 1941 my father awakened in the middle of the night with chest pains. Mummy, naturally, fell to pieces. She ran to my bedchamber, screaming and crying. I groped in the darkness for a robe, and raced to the master suite. My father was conscious, but clammy, and his colour was pale. He was having trouble breathing, complaining of pain beginning in his chest, radiating down his left arm, and up into the jaw area. The symptoms were classic of a heart seizure. I knew that he needed immediate assistance and quickly telephoned for emergency help. An ambulance was sent from *Hartcliffe-with-Bedminster*. The medical workers were superb, and in short order, he was transferred to hospital in Bristol. Mummy rode with him, and I awakened Edwina, Nan, Helen and Martha. Then I dressed. Nan, Martha, and Helen stayed back at the house, to oversee the children, but Edwina and I took my auto and followed along to Bristol. We arrived at hospital about one o'clock in the morning, and then sat waiting for two more hours. Mummy was beside herself with hysteria, and acted dreadful about the amount of time that elapsed before we were able to see Papa. Finally, we spoke to his attending physician, and then Mummy and I were escorted into his room to see him. Extreme displeasure registered on Edwina's face when she realized that *she* wouldn't be treated as a member of the family. I didn't care a whit.

When we entered his room, the first thing I noticed was that his colour had vastly improved. There was a nurse, checking his pulse and other vital signs, and he seemed to be resting comfortably. I leaned over the bed and told him that I loved him, asking how he felt.

"Oh, not so foul, really," he replied. "Just very tired. No more pain."

"Oh Nigel, how could this possibly have happened? I'm so terribly upset. Just all undone," Mummy cried. "Please, please get better. I shouldn't know what to do without you."

"Mummy, please try to be calm," I whispered. "Hysteria is not going to help him. He needs peace and quiet."

"Oh, what the bloody Hell do you know, Sophia?" She shouted, turning on me with vengeance. "Just because you're married to a doctor does not mean that *you* are one too."

"No, that's true Mummy. I was just speaking what seems common sense," I responded. I knew that it would not be wise to argue with her. Whenever my mother was criticized, she turned on whomever was nearest. "I'm sorry if I upset you," I added. *It was always best to apologize. We didn't need a rage.*

"Pamela, please"…. Papa murmured from his bed.

"I want a private nurse in here for him" Mummy said. "I do not intend for him to be left alone for one moment. I surely cannot stay here day and night. There should be a private nurse here now. Where is she?"

"Mummy, I'd imagine that private duty nurses are in somewhat short supply, due to the war. So many nurses are serving. I think we can manage if we all take turns, until we make certain that Papa is out of danger."

At that moment, the doctor entered the room, and Mummy began to badger him. "My husband is The Earl Somerville. I expect him to be treated with respect, and I want him to have the best care."

"Countess Somerville, we like to think that all of our patients receive splendid care," he replied.

"Yes, yes, that's all well and good, but you and I both know it's not true. My husband is of the Peerage. That should count for something. To begin with, where is his private duty nurse?"

"Madame, the nurses in this wing of the hospital are all especially trained in the care of cardiac patients. He's not in need of another nurse. Actually, I'm very pleased with his progress, and over-all I think he is in excellent shape."

Mummy raised her voice an octave. "In excellent shape? Surely you are joshing? The man has just suffered a serious heart seizure."

"Somerville did *not* suffer a serious heart seizure. We have conducted tests, and as best I can determine, he has some heart damage, but it is on the back side of the heart, which, if one has to suffer such a problem, is undoubtedly the best place to sustain damage"

"My God almighty! Heart damage is heart damage, you damned fool. I want a private duty nurse. Period." She was now shrieking. Next, she ran over to a bureau on the wall opposite the bed, and picking up a lamp, threw it. It smashed onto the floor. "Pamela, please…. ," Papa moaned again. Then, he leaned over to the table by his bed, and yelled "Vomit." I reached over and placed a curved basin under his mouth.

"Countess Somerville, I'm going to have to ask you to leave," the doctor stated firmly. "I cannot tolerate these antics, and you are upsetting your husband." He took her by the arm, which was a huge error. She pulled away from him violently, and slapped him across the face. I jumped, pulling her away, and pushing her out of the doorway. Mummy was screaming and had deteriorated to complete irrationality. Several nurses came running down the hallway. I motioned them away with a wave of my hand, and steered her to a bench. Edwina was sitting nearby, and her face paled when she saw what was taking place.

"Mummy, you *must* calm down, this instant. Stop this right now," I demanded, nearly as strongly as I'd ever spoken to her. One of the nurses ran over, offering me a glass of water to give to my mother, in an attempt to calm her. Mummy reached her arm out, and swept the glass to the floor. More shattered glass. Then, she rummaged around in her pocketbook and pulled out a small comb. She jumped up and literally attacked the nurse, digging the comb into her scalp, like a knife. It actually drew blood. The nurse screamed and drew back. "I am quitting this position," she shouted, as she ran toward the nurse's station in the hallway. At that point, Edwina bounded over, and taking Mummy's arms, pinned them to her sides.

"Countess Somerville, that is quite enough," she shouted. Mummy began to weep. I was delighted to see the tears, knowing that they signaled the end of her frenzied rage-state. Of course she didn't apologize for her behaviour, but at least she lowered her voice.

"I cannot take this, Sophia. I cannot bear it. I must go home. You will have to handle this."

"Yes, Mummy. I understand." I'll stay here with Papa all night, if necessary. Edwina will take you home." I gave Edwina a severe look, making it clear that I didn't want any argument from her.

"Will you make certain that he has a private nurse by tomorrow?" Mummy continued.

"Yes, yes. I'll make some sort of arrangement. Just go on home and get some rest yourself." With that, Mummy leaned against Edwina and the two of them disappeared down the pale green hallway. I re-entered Papa's room, and sat down in the chair by the bed. The doctor was still there, and I apologized profusely for my mother's deplorable behaviour. He was actually nicer than I might have been under such circumstances. He just patted my arm, saying that families were often overwrought when illness struck. He promised to do what he could about a special nurse, but said that it would probably be the next day before such arrangements could be made. I thanked him, and set about making myself as comfortable as possible for the remainder of the night. Most importantly, Papa was asleep.

At eleven o'clock, the morning of the next day, a private duty nurse arrived, who seemed highly competent. She was an older woman, which probably meant that she was unable to serve in the War effort. I felt fortunate that she was available and was terribly relieved when she entered the room. Finally, I would be able to go home and get some rest. I was exhausted. Papa was in quite good spirits, and the doctor who had visited him twice that morning, was optimistic. I kissed Papa goodbye, telling him that I would see him later in the day, and asked the nurse at the desk to call a taxicab for me. Naturally, I had already given my sincerest apologies to the injured nurse, who had gone home, but upon return said that she had reconsidered, and would not quit. She just would not have anything to do with Papa's case. I couldn't blame her. Things were settling into some sort of order and I allowed myself to relax a bit for the first time since Mummy had rushed into my room the previous night. Upon arrival at *Willow Grove Abbey*, I shed my coat in the hallway, and proceeded up the staircase, looking forward to a warm bath and soft bed. I encountered Edwina further down the hallway, toward her own suite of rooms.

"Ah ha, so you've returned. Thank God! How is Nigel," she asked.

"He's doing well. I feel optimistic. There've been no more chest pains. Of course the doctors are cautious, but things are much better," I answered. "How is Mummy? Did she finally get settled down?"

"Yes, as far as I know, she's still sleeping. She really is dreadful, Sophia. I don't know how Nigel has coped all of these years. It's a disgrace."

"Yes, Sophia answered. But one might say that it has been his choice, then, hasn't it?

"He feels sorry for her," Edwina replied.

"Edwina, don't be so naive," I snapped. "Papa hasn't left Mummy because it frightens him to think that secrets in our daft family would be let out for the world to see. It would also cost him an immense amount of money. He isn't about to have to divide his holdings with Mummy, and there would be a horrible battle if he fought her in Court. Ever since passage of the *Married Women's Property Act* in 1882, women are entitled to hold land and own property in their own right. Papa is well aware of that, believe me."

"Nigel cares nothing for money. He'd give it all up tomorrow if he could be free of her. She needs to be put into an insane asylum."

"That is probably true, Edwina. Mummy needs some sort of psychological help. But, no one in this family is going to commit her to anything like an asylum. It wouldn't do you much good, anyway, would it? He surely couldn't divorce her if she were to be ruled incompetent."

"Well, then she should have a round the clock mental health aide at *Willow Grove*. He could just get on with his life without concern for her."

"Edwina, I'm much too tired to get into a discussion about this. It's a completely inappropriate conversation for you and me to engage in, anyway. This entire fiasco is so demented, and I've got enough on my hands without adding this to it. You may find that Papa isn't so eager to continue his relationship with you, now that his health has been compromised"

"Are you accusing *me* of causing this attack?" She asked, incredulously.

"I'm not accusing you of anything, Edwina," I sighed. "I'm simply stating the obvious."

"I think the more obvious would be that Nigel may well re-evaluate whether he wants to spend his remaining years with such an evil, disgusting human being"

"Edwina, you are speaking of my mother, and I don't want to hear it. No one is more fully aware than I of her problems. I don't need to hear about them from you. You know only a small portion of the whole"

"Ha! Don't start that nonsense again. I think I know a lot more than you do."

"Edwina, I find you pathetic. Do you think an orgasm automatically opens your mind to everything there is to know about a man? Or his marriage?" I brushed past her, with the intention of continuing to my own room. I was very angry, and at my wits end. I wished Edwina would simply pack up Kippy and go to her own family. However, she stepped in front of me, causing me to stumble, and take quite a nasty fall.

"Damn you, Edwina" I cried. I started to get up, and felt a sharp pain in my abdomen. I'd told no one, but I knew that I was nearly two months pregnant, and the stabbing pain panicked me. I continued down the hallway to my own suite, and Edwina never said a word. She just stood there, looking angry because I had managed to withstand her wrath.

Once in my bed chamber, I quickly shed my skirt and sweater, which I'd hurriedly donned the night before, and Violet ran a nice, hot bath, while I had a lie-down. The pain subsided, and sinking into the warm water, I closed my eyes, letting my sore muscles be soothed. I was still shaken by the verbal confrontation with Edwina, but my mind was more appropriately drawn to my father and his illness. And of course, to my baby. I debated whether or not I should wire Spence and ask him to try to get a short furlough, and then immediately discarded the idea. It was really pure selfishness that even motivated such an idea, as it was I who desperately wished he could be at home with me. This was another time that I knew I had to act like a mature woman. I knew that this ordeal would have to be my burden. I'd not yet even told Spence that I was pregnant, as I'd wanted to wait until I was three months along.

After my bath, I changed into a pair of grey wool trousers and a blue jumper. The weather outside was dreary, with cold temperatures and mist. Of course the English heating, combined with war rationing, made for a chilly house, even though Nan and Perkins had fires roaring in all of the fireplaces. After I'd changed clothes, I went downstairs in search of Isabella, before I remembered that it was a Wednesday, and that my daughter was at school in the village. Thus, I changed direction, and headed for the kitchen for something to eat. I found Rose there, busily preparing a hearty stew for luncheon. She told me it would be about a half hour before she served. I grabbed a couple of biscuits and gobbled them down to stave off my hunger, and then wandered into the Great Hall where Mummy was sorting through the postal delivery.

"Why, hallo Sophia, I didn't realize that you were home," she said, as she glanced up and saw me in the dining hall entryway. "I've telephoned hospital several times. All reports are that your father is doing well. I thought I'd go to visit later today."

"Do you think that's wise, Mummy?" I asked.

"Why ever not?" Mummy retorted.

"Mummy, your behaviour last night was really not the 'done thing', you know. Perhaps it would be better to wait until things have settled a bit."

"My dear girl, I had every right to be uncommonly upset. Nigel should have had a private duty nurse. I don't intend to argue that point again. Sometimes one simply has to become upset in order to make certain that things are done properly."

"All right, Mummy. I'm not going to argue," I replied, knowing it was useless, and not wanting a repeat of the scene I'd endured only a few hours before.

"I should hope not," Pamela replied. It might behoove you to learn to speak up a bit more yourself, you know." I just nodded my head and changed the subject. Of course, I didn't mention the recent scene with Edwina or my fall.

"Are you planning on bringing Papa's post to hospital later," I asked.

"I am sorting it. He always receives a large envelope, forwarded from the London office, filled with correspondence addressed to him there, and I generally just toss it on his desk in the library. However, in this case, if something looks important, I'm pulling it out and making certain that it goes to him at hospital."

"That's a good idea." I stood and watched over my mother's shoulder as she flipped through the various envelopes, creating a large pile. I didn't know how she could tell what was and was not important, but I didn't ask. It appeared that she was pulling out anything that looked as though it might be correspondence of a more personal nature, probably assuming that his secretary would handle anything more business-related.

As I continued to observe, an envelope reached the top of the pile, upon which the address was clearly written in *Papa's own handwriting*. I looked at it closely, and immediately saw that it was addressed to Edwina, at a *Hotel* in *Madrid, Spain*. It was marked '*Hold for Arrival*', and had been posted during the time preceding Edwina's evacuation from France. My mind was racing. I knew at once what had occurred. Papa had obviously written to Edwina, assuming that she would receive the letter upon arrival in Madrid. For whatever reason, it hadn't reached her. After a protracted period of time, the hotel had sent it back across the Channel to the return address, which was Papa's office in London. In turn, it had been forwarded to him at '*Willow Grove*' by his office staff, and now rested in Mummy's hands! I felt as though I was watching my world collapse in slow-motion. I watched silently as Mummy turned the envelope over and over, examining it thoroughly.

"Whatever in the world is this? This is Nigel's own handwriting. Why would he have been writing to Edwina in Madrid? Why would he be writing to Edwina at all?"

"Well, you know he helped her escape from Paris after France fell. I imagine it was written during that time," I stammered.

Mummy ripped the seal and I stood by utterly helpless, continuing to look over Mummy's shoulder. She unfolded it:

'My Dearest,

As I write this, I know that you are en route from Barcelona to Madrid. Needless to say I am worried horribly about your welfare, and of course Kippy's. I know that everything which can be done to ensure your safety has been done. You are in good hands, and I am certain that you will come through this well.

I so look forward to seeing your lovely face, and holding you in my arms. If I knew precisely when you would be arriving, I would meet you. Once here, we have so much to discuss. The first order of business will be to find you a suitable address. The important thing is that you will be back on English soil. I know that your finances have to be depleted, which must be causing you consternation. Put your mind at rest on that score, for I shall transfer some of my assets to you as soon as you return. I am trying to curb my anxiousness to hold you in my arms, and to hug precious, little Kippy.

Be safe, darling.

Yours always,

Nigel

Chapter Twenty-Four

FEBRUARY, 1941

A TRAGEDY

If I had been through rages with Mummy before, absolutely nothing compared to the present one. While it may seem odd, my first fleeting thought was one of relief. Relief that my father had not referenced me, or the part I had played in his affaire. No matter how limited my participation, nor how horrifically distasteful it had been. After a minuscule pause to think of myself, I turned attention with full force to my mother's shock. Perhaps for the first time in my life, I didn't find blame with Mummy's reaction. She was experiencing unbearable pain. At first, her reaction *was* astonishment. Her face literally drained of all color, and I was concerned that she too might end up in hospital. I watched as the emotions worked their way across her features…Shock…Grief…Pain… finally, Anger. Heaps and heaps of anger.

"That horse's arse. That bastard. I should have let his heart stop beating. I should not have called for help. I wish I'd let him die. After all, I have done for him…. All we have shared…. That he would do this. Moreover, with Edwina! My God! What sort of a slut is she? She has been the recipient of my largesse. I brought her into this home as a guest. I treated her as a daughter. She is a tramp. A whore. I will slap her until she is black and blue. I'll slap the both of them."

I did not even attempt to interrupt. There would certainly have been no point. I simply stood immobile, looking at the ghastly letter, which I now held in my own hand. Mummy's tirade continued.

"I would never have known. Never! How long has this been going on? When did it start? That damned, scoundrel. Almighty God saw to it that this letter came to me at a time when Nigel could not prevent my seeing it. God wanted this filthy, abominable relationship to stop. This is *divine intervention*. Do you understand that, Sophia?"

"Yes, yes, Mummy, I understand that," I murmured. I had to admit to myself how ironical it was that the revolting letter had arrived when it did, and in such a strange manner. The chances of such a *thing occurring had to be extremely small. I thought of the word 'serendipity', which had so permeated important events in my past.*

"So many things make sense now. All of that travel he was doing," Mummy continued shrieking. "So much time spent in London. So many trips to Paris. My God! My God! What has she done to him that has caused him to forsake all of his Christian principals? Is that baby of hers your father's son? Sophia, could that be true?"

"Oh, I don't think so, Mummy. He looks an awfully lot like Dieter."

"That may be, but he also looks identical to Edwina, too. So who knows? Your father has not slept with me in eons. He told me he wasn't capable anymore!" she screamed. Then, Mummy began to throw things. She ran around the hallway, and into the drawing room, picking up framed photos of Papa and throwing them. Next came gifts hew had presented to her through the years…Collectibles…Silver. Figurines…Precious crystal items. Nothing was too valuable to escape her wrath. She had a collection of cobalt blue, Royal Copenhagen plates, sitting on a low rail encircling one wall of the morning room. She raced in there and began to systematically throw and smash each one. There were twenty-one in all, and each was in shattered slivers when she was through. Then, she ran back into the hallway, grabbed the letter opener, and began to gouge the furniture with it.

"And what is this drivel about transferring assets to her? Has he been supporting her? Of course, he has. That damned little whore."

Her eyes were wild. A small, inlaid table flew across the room. Finally, the inevitable happened. Edwina appeared on the staircase. She was dressed in a lovely ensemble, and was obviously on her way to hospital. When she heard the commotion, and saw the wreckage, she stopped, looking shocked and horrified. Before she had a chance to utter a sound, Mummy lunged toward her with the letter opener still in her hand. It is truly astonishing that Edwina escaped unharmed, for she dodged Mummy, and flattened herself against the curve in the stair wall.

I screamed, "Mummy, stop. You will kill her. Do you want to go to prison? For God's sake, think!" Mummy threw the letter opener aside, and began to pummel Edwina with her fists. "God Damn you! God Damn you! You will be fortunate if I do not kill you, you little whore. You slut… you…you trollop." I knew Mummy was well versed in curse words, and I wondered what new surprises she had in store. I did not have to wait very long.

"What have you been doing Edwina? *Blowing him off?* I was completely aghast, but Edwina only looked angry, not even frightened. In fact, she looked arrogant.

"It's none of your business what Nigel and I do," she said, as coolly and calmly as I could ever have imagined anyone reacting in such a situation. "I am sure you would be aghast at our methods of making love. Nigel has told me that you are an amazingly frigid woman."

Mummy slapped Edwina across the face. "I'm not a whore, if that's what he prefers", she shrieked. "Moreover, what do you mean it is none of my business? He is my husband, you idiotic piece of filth. If it isn't my business, whose is it?"

"He doesn't love you, Pamela. He loves me. I'm sorry you've learned the truth this way, but I really do think it's time you faced reality."

How could this be happening?

"Reality!" Mummy shrieked. "Reality!" I will tell you about reality. Reality is that you are about to take that brat of yours and get the Hell out of my home. Reality is that you will never see my husband again. Never! If I ever find that you have so much as spoken to him, I shall file an 'Alienation of Affection' lawsuit against you. I shall smear your name from here to Kingdom come. You will never be welcomed into any decent home again. In addition, you will never work again. Your child will be labelled a bastard. I will ruin you, Edwina. I will make it my life's mission to destroy you. There won't be a soul in Bury St. Edmunds who doesn't know what you are." Mummy was panting, and holding her hand to her chest.

Edwina actually smiled! "Pamela, you'd better calm down, or you're going to have a heart seizure yourself," she sneered. "I'm not at all certain that I'm ready to give up my friendship with Nigel. He'll have to be the one to make any decision of that sort."

"He'll not be making *this* decision, Edwina. Apparently, his decision-making capabilities are quite flawed. Now, you heard what I said. If I must, I shall call the local authorities, and have them remove you from these premises. Get out of my home, you God awful, disgusting tramp". Mummy moved again to attack Edwina physically, but I restrained her.

"Edwina, please…please just leave," I pleaded. "Surely you understand that you cannot stay here. Please. This is a nightmare. Don't make it any worse".

"All right. I shall go. However, do not count on Nigel backing you up, Pamela. As I said before, he loves me. He will choose me in the end. Just you wait." She turned on her heel and headed up the stairway, presumably to pack her bags and ready Kippy for a journey. Mummy and I stood at the bottom of the stairway. Mummy's immediate rage seemed spent, but I knew it was only a temporary lull.

"Mummy, you must have a lie-down. You must. I am going back to hospital to see Papa. I shall make certain that he is in a physical condition to absorb this news. I must talk with him. I also need to give orders to the nurses that they should not allow Edwina to see him. I suspect that's the first place she'll go."

"If she shows up at that hospital, I'll see that she is arrested," Mummy threatened.

I was not certain that such a thing was feasible, but did not say so.

"Will you let me take you to your room, give you a sedative, and then let me try to handle this by seeing and talking to Papa?" I begged.

"Yes. All right. However, I do not want you gone long. Moreover, I want Edwina away from here, before you leave. I'm not staying in this house with that slut."

"Yes, Mummy. I'll make certain that Edwina is gone, and when she leaves I'll come and tell you," I promised, as I gently guided my mother up the staircase and down the hallway to her rooms. She was sobbing by then, and was unsteady on her feet. No matter what heartache she had caused others in her life, there was no way I would have wished such pain upon her. I settled her in bed, and rang for Nan to bring some tea. When Nan arrived, I received yet another shock. Mummy was lying on the bed, and I intercepted our housekeeper in the doorway.

"Nan, we've had a beastly shock. It is bad enough that Papa is in hospital, but now Mummy has just learned that he has been carrying on some sort of secret romance with Edwina. Mummy is prostrate with shock and grief, as you can see. I must see to Edwina's immediate departure, and then go to hospital to see and speak with Papa. I do not want to leave Mummy unattended. Please watch over her until I can get these other things taken care of," I instructed.

Nan's hand flew to her mouth. "Oh, Miss Sophia, I knew she would find out. The Countess is no fool, Miss Sophia, no fool at all."

"What are you talking about, Nan? How did you know she would find out? What do you know?" I asked.

"Oh, Miss Sophia, I shouldn't say. It's not my place," she replied, looking at the floor, and twisting the top button on her uniform.

"It most certainly is your place, Nan. You have been a member of this family since I was born. If you know something about this, I need to know. Now please, tell me to what you are referring?"

"Well, way back…Clear to Miss Isabella's first birthday, when Miss Edwina were 'ere with that German, I saw something"

"You saw something? What did you see?"

"It was after the German left, and Miss Edwina was our guest. I was up at me usual 'our. Very early, Miss Sophia. The sun was just but up. I went to the rose garden, to gather me blooms, for yer table, like always. It was a fine day. I stayed a tad, enjoying the sunshine, yer understand?"

"Yes, of course, Nan. So what happened?"

Well, I heard a noise…Voices coming from the summer'ouse. Couldn't think who'd be in the summer'ouse at that 'our. I walked a bit closer, and saw 'is Grace and Miss Edwina. They was, well…..A man-woman way."

"What do you mean, Nan? Were they kissing? Having sex? Just say it, Nan."

"Yes, Mum. They was 'umpin."

"Oh, Nan, what a dreadful thing for you to have seen. Did they see you?"

"Oh no, Mum. They was much occupied with their business. I just turned, and run fast as these old legs could carry me, back to the 'ouse. Never said a word to no one. Lord Somerville been mighty good to me o'er the years."

Nan had tears in her eyes, and it was clear that she had conflicting feelings about the whole matter. Of course, I understood completely why she had kept silent. I was not in the least angry with Nan, but my level of ire toward Edwina and Papa rose substantially. To think that they would engage in sexual relations in the summerhouse at *Willow Grove Abbey,* while my mother slept on the premises, when anyone might have come upon them! It was utter and complete folly. I was ashamed of my father, who had reduced himself to the actions of a total fool, not to mention Edwina, whose behaviour was truly deplorable. I patted Nan on the arm, and told her that I was sorry she had witnessed such a scene. I also assured her that I would not tell Mummy, as I knew that Nan feared reprisals, because *she* had not told anyone. Nan promised she would see to Mummy. I left the bedchamber. I literally stormed down the hallway to the wing where Edwina's rooms were located. I did not knock when I came to her door. Instead, I threw it open with force. Edwina was packing a trunk, carefully folding each item, as if in no great rush. She turned when the door opened wide.

"Oh, Sophia. I *am* glad you have come. We do need to have a chat before I depart."

"A chat, Edwina? I responded, astounded at her poise."

"Yes, dear heart, a chat. I am truly sorry that you became a part of this. However, I shall never regret having fallen in love with Nigel. I have told you that before. The saddest part of this is that if the man involved in this were anyone but your father, you'd be happy that I'd found someone so wonderful to love."

"You're completely daft, Edwina. Why would I be happy? Even if he wasn't my father, why should I want you to be involved with any married man? How could you possibly believe that?"

"Oh, Sophia. Do not become righteous and moral. It is so tedious, and not the least becoming, you know. This is 1941. These things happen. You're sophisticated enough to know that."

"My God, Edwina, have you no conscious? We lived together for four years. We literally grew up together. I thought we believed the same things. Had the same values. What's happened to you?"

"I might ask you the same question, you know. What's become of you? Has this newly adopted Catholic religion of yours made you into a Saint?"

"Don't be absurd. I am flawed, just like every other human. Nevertheless, your reasoning is beyond the pale. Yes, I do believe in the Ten Commandments. You do not need to be a religious fanatic to believe in a simple blueprint for living. Do you believe in nothing?"

"I believe in love. I believe in being positive and thinking positively. I do not allow negative thoughts to enter into my life. Negativity causes sadness and illness. I keep my body in harmony. I concentrate upon what is good in my life. My relationship with your father is good."

"Love isn't destructive, Edwina. Love is kind. There is nothing kind about what you and Papa are doing and have done. You are hurting people. You may not believe in negativity, but you're causing other people to feel terrible pain and that is negative."

"What about your anger? Is that kind and loving," she shot back.

"Edwina, there is such a thing as 'righteous anger.' If there has ever been a time for righteous anger it is here and now."

"Who are Nigel and I hurting? Your mother? She deserves to be hurt. She's an evil person."

"I know you believe that, and I know better than anyone that Mummy can and has caused a lot of pain. Nevertheless, that does not mean that she is evil. I used to think as you do, but I do not any longer, because I have grown up and, apparently, you have not. I understand her immensely better, and know with certainty that she suffers from a personality disorder. And, even if it were true that she really is evil, that doesn't give you license to pass judgment upon her, nor to impose your own sentence upon her."

"You're speaking drivel, Sophia. I'm afraid our points of view differ greatly, and I really don't want to continue discussing this." She turned and resumed her packing, shaking her head, as though she could not fathom that a fool like me was trying to convince her of anything. *I wanted to slap her silly.*

"Edwina, I want the answer to one, final question," I continued.

Edwina gave an exasperated sigh. "What question?" she asked

"I want the truth about Kippy. Is he Papa's son?"

"Do you honestly think I'd tell you if he were?" she replied, with a catlike smile.

"I'd hope you'd be that decent, yes."

"You can wonder about Kippy's paternity until Hell freezes over," Edwina said, between clenched teeth.

"You told me a long while ago, on the telephone, when you were still in Paris, that you were certain that Kippy was Dieters child. Was that a lie too?"

"I guess you won't ever know, will you," she snickered.

Tears began to roll down my cheeks, and I brushed them aside in anger and frustration. "What on Earth did I ever do to deserve this from you, Edwina? What became of our friendship? Our loyalty to one another?"

"Oh stop being so dramatic and stop feeling sorry for yourself. No one has done anything to you. You have your precious Spence, Isabella and all off the money anyone could ever want. You do not have any idea what it's like to be on the outside looking in. Well, I do. And I don't ever intend to be in that position again."

"Edwina! You have never been on the outside looking in! You have wonderful parents. Had a happy upbringing. You have never wanted for anything. Your father is highly successful. This is idiotic talk."

"Oh yes, he's successful. However, not nobility. You think it never mattered that I couldn't be presented at Court. That I was not good enough to bow to the King. You think it didn't matter that I watched your life in this ages' old mansion and never compared it to my own home…That I did not look on with longing when I saw the way your family lives. The cars, hotels, gourmet restaurants, servants, chauffeurs, and on and on and on. You're so spoiled rotten that you have no idea that there are others who'd give anything to live as you do."

"So it's about money and status, is it?" I said, astounded

"Yes, quite…Well….Yes, and No. I do care about Nigel, and I am not giving him up. I need him. Nevertheless, I love everything about him, and that includes his title and his wealth. Moreover, if that makes me crass, then so be it. My son will never know what it is like not to be part of that revered class that you so take for granted. My son will have what I did not. I'll marry your father, and Kippy will have a title."

"Then you're saying that Kippy *is* Papa's son."

"I'm not saying anything. That is a private matter, and you will never know. Nevertheless, it has no importance.

"Well, Miss Edwina, you're showing your ignorance of English Law. Whether Papa adopts Kippy or not, Kippy will never have a title. Unless one is married to the titled individual at the time of the child's birth, then he cannot inherit the title, or any title. You are forgetting one other small detail. I have two brothers. Even if Kippy is Papa's son, there are two elder sons who take precedent, and you were not married at the time of Kippy's birth. Have you never heard of the Law of Primogeniture? It clearly states all of what I've just said."

"Yes, certainly I've heard of it. However, I do not think that either of your brothers has any desire to live at *Willow Grove Abbey*. Furthermore, you are the one who mentioned the *Married Women's Property Act*. Actually, that act more appropriately could apply to me. If Nigel ends up marrying me, and eventually I am widowed, I would have widow's rights. I would own all of the property, and could make my own decisions about whom it would be left to."

She had clearly researched all of her options carefully. "You've completely lost your mind, Edwina. On the other hand, perhaps I just never knew you. You have certainly planned this out rather well, haven't you? The only thing you didn't count on was the fact that Papa will not be leaving Mummy. Thus, your fantasy marriage will never take place. Please finish your packing and leave this house. I cannot stand the sight of you for one more moment. I consider your positive thoughts to be utter nonsense, for I do not believe there is a chance in Hell that my father will marry you. Goodbye, Edwina. I don't expect we'll see each another again in this life."

I turned and left the room before I had a chance to listen to any more foolishness from her. She was certainly no longer my 'shining girl'. I felt weak and sick to my stomach. I'd not slept for more than twenty-four hours, and had scarcely eaten. Moreover, I had undergone profound shock after shock, including taking a bad fall. The world seemed to be coming down upon my head. However, I knew that I could not let down. Not yet. I had to see Edwina off the property, and had to see Papa. I wondered if I could muster the strength needed, but there I had no choice.\

I continued to my own room and splashed cool water on my face. I was shaking from head to toe. What happened was unfathomable. I had no idea where it would all end. Oh God, how I wanted Spence! I needed his calm reason, and strong, reassuring presence, but, of course, that was out of the question. I tried to think what he would say to me if he were there. I knew he would try to make me understand that I could not control everything that happened, and that the fault was not mine, for feeling guilty. I *had* known of the affaire, and had not told Mummy. However, I still could not see what good could have come of such a confession. I had so hoped that the entire, ghastly fling would simply play itself out, but obviously, it had not, and it appeared that Edwina was adamant about getting what she wanted. Her single-minded obsession frightened me I ran a comb through my hair, dabbed on some lip rouge, and went back to my mother's rooms. Nan was sitting by the bed, a cold cloth on Mummy's head, trying to calm her. When I entered the room, Mummy sat up and started shrieking.

"Is that tramp gone from this house? Did you get her out of here? Sophia, I'm telling you right now, I shall kill her if she doesn't leave here at once."

"Mummy, please, please calm down. Edwina is packing. I should not think she'll be much longer. I am going to leave to go to hospital to talk with Papa. I want you to stay here and allow Nan to care for you until I return. I promise you that Edwina will be gone from this house, and will never return."

"I blame you for this, Sophia. I blame you for taking up with such a creature. You brought her into this house…. Into our family, and our lives. You should have had better judgement in your choice of friends. You knew she wasn't our kind," she screamed, accusingly.

"Oh Lord, Mummy. Do not start on that. I did not have a crystal ball. There's no way I could have known such a thing would happen.

You yourself have always been extremely fond of Edwina. You know that. There's no blame to be cast here, other than the obvious."

"What do you mean, 'the obvious?'"

"The blame should lie squarely on Papa and Edwina's shoulders. Do not leave Papa out of this. It takes two people to commit adultery."

"Men are weak. They are fools. She did things to tempt him. I do not excuse him. I shall never forgive him…. But, this wouldn't have happened if Edwina hadn't set her cap for him, and if it hadn't been so easy for her to insinuate herself into this family."

"I'm not going to argue this with you, Mummy. What is done is done. The question now is what we are to do about it. Do you even care if Papa wants a divorce? Do you intend to divorce him? You would, of course, have grounds."

"Divorce! I shall never divorce him. If you think I would set him free to marry that little trollop then you are daft. He'll be made to pay for what he's done to me, I can promise you that, but he'll not be given a divorce."

"All right, Mummy. I am going to leave now. Try to rest. I shall ring you from hospital after I have seen Papa. I turned to Nan and smiled, reassuringly. "Nan, thank you for being so caring. Everything is going to work out. Stay with Mummy, and help her to keep calm. I'll be back as quickly as possible."

Nan smiled back at me and nodded her head. "The Countess and me will be fine, Miss Sophia. You take care of yer duties, and me and her Ladyship will be fine." I kissed Mummy on the cheek, and patted Nan's arm. Then, with a deep sigh, I turned and left the room, dreading what I knew lay ahead.

Chapter Twenty-Five

11 February 1941 to 12 February 1941

Uproar

As I descended the stairway, I saw the Rolls Royce, with Joseph driving, and Edwina, Helen and Kippy in the backseat, pulling out of the circular drive. I breathed a sigh of relief that they had gone. I had no idea where they would go… Perhaps to her parents… Perhaps back to the leased house in London. It was February 11, 1941, and Edwina was gone from our lives. I did not care where she had gone, as long as it was far away from *Willow Grove Abbey*. I picked up the keys to my little auto and proceeded to the garages. In a matter of minutes, I was on the road leading to Bristol and hospital. As I drove, I went over in my mind exactly what I wished to ascertain from a talk with Papa.

Did he want to keep his marriage intact? Did he want to marry Edwina? (A hideous thought). Was Kippy his son? Just what did he intend to do?

I felt tremendous anger toward him for the muddled mess he'd created, and yet I also felt sorrow. There was no question that Mummy was telling the truth when she said he would pay for what he had done. There was not the slightest chance that Mummy could ever be made to see that she had contributed to all of this horror. If only Papa had been honest with her about his growing discontent in their marriage. If only he hadn't let her think that her intolerable behaviour was all right. Perhaps if they'd faced their problems openly and honestly, none of this would have happened. There was a lesson in it for me. I made a silent promise to myself that Spence and I would always share our deepest feelings with one another, and that honestly would be a cornerstone of our relationship. Hadn't I already learned that lying, hiding, and keeping secrets was never the correct way to deal with problems? My entire family had been rife with secrets and lies since before I'd been born. I had been criticized many times for being *too honest,* particularly by Papa and Blake, and even by Drew on one occasion, but after I'd lived through the miserable life that lies brought about, growing up in the Somerville family, and after nearly losing Spence forever, I'd made up my mind *never* to indulge in that sort of behaviour… Ever. I couldn't see what problem there was with being honest? If there was nothing to hide….. And nothing had been lied about….. Then, how could telling the truth be frowned upon?

Upon arrival at hospital, I made my way quickly to my father's room. Before entering, I spoke with a nurse, saying that I had some bad news to break to my father, and asking if she felt it would be safe to do so, or if he needed sedation before I spoke with him. The nurse assured me that he was doing very well, and that she didn't expect there'd be any difficulty. I opened the door, and found him sitting up in bed, reading the *Times.* The private duty nurse was reading a book in a chair. Papa smiled when he saw me, and put the paper aside. I felt tremendous sadness when I looked at him. It was another of the many times when it seemed that I was the parent and he was the child. He resembled a little boy, dressed in hospital gown, with white socks on his feet and wide, dark eyes looking innocent and vulnerable.

"Well, hallo Sophia? What a pleasant site you are this morning. I hope you've had some rest," he said.

"Not really," I replied. I turned to the nurse, and told her that I needed private time with my father, and that I would summon her when I was about to depart. The nurse laid her book aside, picked up a sweater that was folded over the back of the chair, and quietly exited the room. I turned back to Papa, and pulled up a chair to be closer to him.

"Papa, I have some beastly news that I'd give anything not to have to tell you, but I've no choice. Do you feel up to hearing upsetting information?"

"Yes, Sophia. I'm fine. What can be so terrible? Has something happened to Spence? Are Blake and Andrew all right?"

"Yes, yes….They're all fine, as far as I know. It's nothing like that, Papa."

"Well, Thank God. Then, what could possibly be so upsetting?"

"Mummy's learned of your affaire with Edwina," I replied.

His eyes grew wider, and then he slapped his hand down on the side of the bed. "Well, that's it, then," he said, in a resigned tone.

"What do you mean, 'That's it'? Is that all you have to say? Don't you want to know what happened?"

"Yes, of course, although it really doesn't matter very much then, does it?"

I explained about the letter..... How it had found its way back across the Channel and into Mummy's hands.

"Oh Bollacks! That's simply incredible. Quite remarkable, really. I suppose Pamela has gone into a

complete tirade."

You might say that, Papa. It's about as bad as I've ever seen. The question is, what do you intend to do now? Edwina has left *Willow Grove Abbey* with Kippy. Mummy literally threatened to kill her."

"Where has she gone?" he asked.

"I have no Earthly idea, and don't care," I nearly shouted. "Edwina is a totally self-absorbed, selfish, horrid person. I hope I never see her again."

"Oh, Sophia, no. This is not Edwina's fault. Sometimes things like this just happen between two people. It doesn't make Edwina a bad person."

"Papa, I've spoken with her, at length. She has absolutely no moral grounding. She doesn't feel even a minuscule amount of regret for the anguish she's caused. She's only interested in having what she wants, and what she wants is marriage to you."

"Well, I know that's what she wants." He chewed on the inside of his cheek.

"There's no possibility of that, whatsoever," I replied. "Mummy has already stated firmly that she will never, ever agree to a divorce." Papa did not answer and there was an uncomfortable silence in the room. "You had to know that if Mummy ever found out, the result would be unimaginable furor?"

"I suppose I never thought that far ahead. I was caught up in a storm, you know. Just lost in a storm," he murmured.

"Well, you're caught up in an even bigger storm, now, and I need to know what you intend to do."

"Much will depend upon Pamela, of course. In addition, I need to speak with Edwina. Where do you suppose she has gone?" he asked.

"To her parents, perhaps? Or back to London? I do not know, Papa. What do you need to discuss with her?"

"I'm concerned about her, of course. I'm concerned about Kippy."

"Yes. Kippy. I'm concerned about Kippy, too Papa. Edwina implied that Kippy might be your son. If that is true, I deserve to know. That would make him my half-brother. I need to know the truth."

"The truth is that I really don't know. It is a possibility. Edwina, herself, doesn't know for certain."

"How can that be?" I asked, incredulous.

"Ah Sophia, it's quite simple. Edwina and I had relations one hour after she had seen Dieter off to Berlin. Need I say more?"

"In other words, she was with Dieter the same day, so either of you could have fathered the child."

"Quite."

"I am sorry, Papa, but that is disgusting. Edwina is no better than a stray dog in heat. Did she even take a bath between the two of you?"

"Sophia! I do not ever want to hear you speak that way again. I understand that you are upset, and accept that I have caused great harm. But, there is no need for such talk."

"Do you mean that it's all right to act in a disgusting manner, but not to speak about it honestly?"

"This is getting us nowhere, Sophia. I have told you the truth. Kippy may or may not be my son. If there is even a remote possibility of that, I cannot and will not abandon Edwina."

"Aren't there tests that could prove whether he is or isn't your son?" I asked.

"None that I'm aware of, except something called Serological Testing which was begun in the 1930's. But, it only has a forty percent accuracy, so it's of little value. There is also blood typing. I already know Kippy's blood type. It is the same as Edwina's and mine. Moreover, Dieters for that matter. So, nothing is proven there." I have checked into all of that.

"I imagine Edwina has as well," I said bitterly. I felt my breath coming in small gasps. "Are you intending to give that child your name?" I asked.

"I do not know what I am going to do, Sophia. I have not had time to think this through. In any case, it will not affect you in any way."

"Not affect me? Are you mad? Of course it affects me! Edwina means for him to have *Willow Grove Abbey*. It means nothing to her that I have two older brothers. It means nothing that *Willow Grove Abbey* has been our home forever. She means to have it all."

"That's rubbish. Blake, Andrew and you are my heirs, and always will be. I can make provisions for Kippy, without your being affected in any way. I assure you, Sophia. *Willow Grove Abbey* will always be your home, if you want it to be. I promise you that. As for your mother, well that is another story. She need not know about Kippy...About the possibility that he is mine. It would only cause her further anguish. I shall take care of any obligations I have without involving Pamela."

"Are you willing to put that in writing? I asked.

"You mean that you, Andrew and Blake will inherit *Willow Grove Abbey'?*"

"Yes. I don't feel comfortable without some proof that you won't change your mind."

"Oh Sophia. That is cruel, and beneath you. I have never cheated you out of anything and never would. You will have to trust me on this." His words were somewhat reassuring to me, but I would have felt better if he'd agreed to place something into writing. At least he was not saying that he intended to be with Edwina at any cost. At that moment, a nurse tapped upon the door, and entered the room. She held a yellow envelope in her hand.

"Earl Somerville, a wire has been delivered for you," she said, as she placed it on the table by his bed. Then, she straightened his covers, took his pulse, and departed, smiling. Apparently, the upsetting news had not caused an alarming physical reaction. Papa took the telegram and opened it. He read it through and then passed it to me.

"HAVE TAKEN ROOMS. STOP. BERKELEY SQUARE
HOTEL. STOP. BRISTOL.
CALL SOON AS POSSIBLE. STOP.
EDWINA."

"Well, then, I guess we know where she's gone off to," I commented. "Not nearly far enough to suit me."

"Sophia, I knew she wouldn't leave the vicinity without speaking to me first. I shall speak with her as soon as the doctors allow me to make a call. I should think I could arrange it today. They'll bring a telephone to the room."

"And you'll say what to her, Papa?"

"I shall tell her what I told you. That, if Pamela will have me, I am going to hold fast, and stay with her. Edwina will be crushed, but, my first allegiance must be to the mother of my children. Sophia, I need your clear and sensible thinking and creative ideas."

"What do you want me to do?"

"I want you to try to contact Blake. See if he can procure an emergency furlough. Just for a few days. I shall need his help, for I do not think your mother will simply allow me to return to *Willow Grove Abbey* immediately. She is going to need a cooling off period, so to speak. I cannot begin to talk any sense in her present state. I want you to be with her. She is going to need you. But, I am going to need someone to check me out of hospital and stay with me for a bit."

"Where will you go?"

"There are several options. It depends on whether can come or not. We shall decide upon a destination after I know that. I feel beastly putting my own needs in front of a war, but there you have it. It's what has to be done."

"I'll try to reach Blake…. Shall send him a wire. I imagine he will ring me up. Nevertheless, is there no one else? Perhaps a friend you could stay with?"

"Sophia, this is a family matter. I'm not inclined to want to impose this difficulty upon outsiders."

"Oh no, Papa, we surely would never want to do that. It could cause irreparable harm to the family image," I replied, snidely.

"Sophia..... Please. I know you are angry with me, and I do not blame you. I am trying to do what I think is right. I am not abandoning my responsibility to your Mother, and I shall stay and pay the penalty for my behaviour. Nevertheless, please understand that in large part I am doing this for you. I know Pamela would lean on you to such an extent that you would never be able to get on with the life you and Spencer are trying to build. That would be unconscionable of me. So, please do not make disparaging remarks to me."

"And don't you try to make me feel guilty!" I cried. "I have every right to my feelings. I don't want you to stay with Mummy if you would rather be off. I have coped with Mummy's rages all of my life, and I'll do so now, if I must. I don't believe, for a moment, that you're making your decisions based upon my feelings. I suspect that you don't want a divorce because of the stain it would leave upon the family name, and the amount of money it would cost you "I was breathing rapidly, and my pulse was raging in anger. The sharp pain had returned to my abdomen.

"All right, all right, Sophia. Perhaps I am not even being honest with myself. I do not think I would have the energy to go through a divorce from Pamela. It would be excruciating."

"That it would be," I agreed. "And now, I must get back to her. I am seriously concerned for her sanity...For her very life. I am sure that she is quite capable of suicide. I shouldn't think any of us would want to see that happen."

"Of course not, Sophia. Of course not. Go then, and I will speak with you later. I will not try to ring the house, for it will only upset Pamela. However, do relate our conversation to her. The portions you feel she might want to hear. When she is ready to speak with me, I'll come to her."

"I shall never understand you, Papa. I love you, but I absolutely think you are daft." I felt the need to leave as rapidly as possible. I leaned over and kissed him on the cheek. "I love you, Papa. I don't like what you have done, but I *do* love you. I am sorry if I sound bitter and angry. It all just seems so unnecessary," I said, shaking my head.

"I know, dear. Go now, and take care of your mother," he said, patting me on the cheek.

I left hospital, feeling quite despondent. What could possibly be the outcome of such a fiasco? I couldn't help but think about how ridiculous it all seemed..... About our family's' many blessings and how foolishly they had been taken for granted. There had never really been any horrible crisis in the Somerville family No serious illness No children born with deformity or mental deficiency No financial woes. We were not even cursed with a family member addicted to drink. There was good health, wealth, prestige, and a higher than average level of intelligence. We really were a charmed circle. Why then, couldn't we be a happy family? Primarily, I thought, because the family was filed to the brim with lies. Certainly, Mummy's mental instability was a deep rent in the family fabric, but if it had been addressed properly, perhaps that too could have been improved. God had given us so much, and the appreciation had been so little. I thought of Spence, and of how his faith has always sustained him, and then I thought of the Somervilles, and the fact that there was never a religious foundation. My parents simply lived their lives according to instinct, searching out happiness where they could find it, seeking to control their world with money and power. Oh, there was a modicum of propriety, when it came to making certain that their lives were lived in the 'proper' manner. Appearances were vastly important, so there was no breaking of law or overt scandalous behaviour. Nevertheless, there was an abundance of sneaking and lying, and the now the secrets were finally spilling over. Shouldn't there be lines one never crosses? Wouldn't it have been far better if rules were followed? If marriage vows were kept? If truth *was* told?

We Somervilles treated ceremonies of life as mere rituals, performed in order to adhere to society's expectations. Baptism, Confirmation, Marriage. They were all ceremonious reasons for extravagant social affaires. Perhaps they should have been observed as the covenants that they were. Moreover, perhaps that was why Edwina and I had found ourselves on such divergent paths. Edwina's attitudes toward such milestones in life were precisely what my own had been, growing up in such a family. However, my conversion to Catholicism and simple maturity had changed all of that. Of course, I had not become a Saint, but I did have a far different perspective on life. I felt anger that my parents hadn't seen fit to teach their children the fundamental beliefs that all children have a right to know.

I knew that Edwina's mother, Thelma Phillips, was a Christian Scientist, and that her father was an atheist. Edwina tended to have a set of beliefs that reflected both of her parent's points of view. Her mother was the one who stressed positive and negative thoughts, and harmony. But Edwina didn't seem to have the intellectual capability to truly understand those concepts, and had bastardized such beliefs into an unrecognizable dogma of self-serving drivel. She was an apologist for her own dismal behaviour. I *knew* that she had never read the Bible, nor had she partaken of any spiritual education. Before I became a strong believer, even then, I never called myself an *Atheist*. In my own humble opinion, it is impossible to be an *Atheist* without being *extraordinarily* well educated in matters of Theology. How else can one have the necessary facts to make up one's mind? The more correct term would be *Agnostic*, which means 'doubter'. I am still a 'doubter' at times, and probably shall always be, but the greatest thing that religion had gave me was the clarity between right and wrong." My disappointment in my father was greater than my pain over what Edwina had done. It was so terribly troublesome to me that he could lie with such impunity. Usually, he was able to extricate himself from any sort of difficulty that might arise from impulsive actions, by exuding a strong dose of well-known charm and many untruths. I knew that he would do so in the present dilemma.... . Lie to Mummy and charm her. She would want to believe him, and that is what she would do.

I was so deep in thought that I almost missed the turn-off to *Willow Grove Abbey*. I veered my little car sharply to the right, made the turn and pulled into the graveled drive. I was so glad to be home. In need of rest, I wearily climbed from the auto and entered the Great Hall. The moment I set foot inside the doors, I met Nan, who was in tears, wringing her hands.

"Oh Miss Sophia. Thank the Lord you're 'ome. Your Mum is just beside 'erself. I cannot calm her. I fear for 'er, I surely do. Please, go to 'er," she begged.

I took the stairs two at a time. Upon entering Mummy's bedroom, I was astonished. There was a valise open on the floor, and she had begun to pack items in it. The room was in complete disarray. Mummy looked as though she had become an aged woman overnight. She was dressed in a robe, which tied at the waist, and the top portion was gaping open. She was sobbing, and it nearly broke my heart. I had never seen my mother in such a state. I was better equipped at dealing with her rages than her tears. Mummy put her head in her hands and tore at her hair, which was already standing up all over her head.

"Nigel should have died. I wish he had died," she screamed.

"No, no Mummy. You don't wish that. That's just your pain speaking. Things will be all right. I know you can't believe that now, but you'll see. Papa doesn't want to lose you. He knows he was foolish, and he wants to make it up to you."

"How can he make it up to me?" she asked, looking like a petulant child. "What ever could he do to make up for this?" *Memories of lovely jewels and furs were no doubt spinning through her mind.*

"Well, let's wait and find out what he says. I know that he doesn't want a divorce. That's very good news, I think. Don't you?"

"I don't care what he wants! He should be worried about what I want!"

I sighed deeply. "Of course, and he is. I am only saying that you need not fear that he has any desire to be with Edwina. To leave you and go to her."

Mummy leapt from the bed, and began, once again, to throw things haphazardly into the valise. I looked at the items already assembled and saw a strange conglomeration, ranging from one rhinestone encrusted evening slipper to, of all things, a jar of Nan's special homemade jam! It was clear that my mother was not thinking or behaving rationally. I feared tht she was having a complete nervous collapse.

"Mummy. Why you packing your luggage? Are you planning a trip?"

"Yes. Yes. I must get out of here. I'm going to the South of France…to Cap d'Antibe. I need sunshine and warmth, and the sea. Those things will help to clear my mind."

"Mummy, we are at war with France. No one is going to the South of France these days. It isn't allowed. There are Germans all over that area." She looked at me with a confused stare. "I'd forgotten that," she murmured.

"Mummy, I'm going to call the doctor. You need to speak with him. Don't you think it might help if he was to come and see you?"

"The doctor? Yes. Doctor Hardwick. Yes, I'd like to see him. He will be shocked to learn that Nigel would do such a thing. However, shall I tell him, Sophia? What might he think? Will he tell the entire village?"

"Mummy, doctors don't make judgments about such things. He'll understand and help you."

I rang Dr. Hardwick's office. It was late afternoon, and I suspected that he would still be at his dispensary. On the third ring, the young woman who worked with him answered, and I asked to speak with the doctor. Moments later, he was on the line, and I explained, as best I could, what was happening. He said he would be there as quickly as possible. I was greatly relieved. Hanging up the receiver, I turned to my mother and told her that Doctor Hardwick was on his way. That seemed to bring a sense of rationale back, as she suddenly became aware of her appearance. I helped her put on a long-sleeved gown and a more becoming robe. Then, I took her into the bath, and ran cool water on a cloth to wipe her face. We brushed her hair, and pinned it up. She looked infinitely better. Returning to the bedchamber, I helped her into the bed. She was still unsteady, but her appearance had vastly improved.

Shortly thereafter, Dr. Hardwick arrived. I heard his knock at the door, and then Nan opening it and greeting him. I excused myself from Mummy, and ran to the top of the stairway, where I met him as he made his way to the second floor.

"Ah, Sophia. It seems you've a mess on your hands, eh?" he said, smiling thinly. He was a tall, well-built, handsome man, with dark hair, combed to the side. I had always thought him terribly kind, and was grateful that he'd known our family for so long. He had very strong religious values, which I believed were needed at such a moment.

"Indeed, Dr. Hardwick. A Royal mess, one might say. I wanted to speak with you a moment before you go to Mummy. She is not in her right head ..... Shock, I suppose. I want you to know that what she suspects is true. There's no point in trying to convince her differently. I've known about this for some time, but she doesn't know that I have. Lord knows, I don't want her to know. I've spoken with Papa. He's promised that he'll stay with Mummy….. . Hasn't any thought of leaving and going with the other woman. Of course, Mummy's pride is wounded. He'll have to beg forgiveness, but at least he isn't intending to abandon her."

"Right. I'm glad to hear that. I shouldn't have thought Nigel would do that, but you never know. Men do some confounded things."

"Yes, I know. Anyway, I just wanted you to know the lay of the land. Papa won't come back here immediately, even when he's released from hospital. He says he'll wait until she's ready."

"Yes, splendid. I think he's on the right track. Well, let's go and pay Pamela a visit, shall we?"

Thus, we walked together down the hallway to Mummy's room. She seemed happy to see him, and much calmer. Once I was certain that things were under control, I excused myself and went to my own room. Dr. Hardwick said that he would come speak with me before he left. I was exhausted to the point of being ill. In addition, the pain in my abdomen had increased. I was glad that a doctor was present, as I was growing worried. I stepped out of my shoes, and threw myself upon the bed, closing my eyes while rubbing my temples. A throbbing headache had begun. I reached over and rang for Nan, asking her to bring a tray. In spite of my fatigue and pain, I knew I needed nourishment. The house was quiet, and it seemed strange that so much had transpired in such a short span of time. I remembered the need to send a wire to Blake, but decided to wait until I had eaten something. I also needed to write Spence. I hadn't written for two days, and he would be worried when my usual daily letter didn't arrive. What to tell him? Of course, I had to explain what had happened, but didn't want to alarm him. Nan knocked softly at the door, and entered carrying a tray. There was a bowl of steaming broth, two nice slices of freshly baked bread, a wedge of cheese, and some fruit. It looked wonderful, and I greedily sat up, taking the tray from her "Thank you so much, Nan. What would we do without you?"

"Miss Sophia, is the Countess all right? She seemed off in her 'ead. I didn't know what to do."

"She's going to be fine, Nan. She's had a shock, that's all. We all have, of course. Nevertheless, I'm certain that seeing Doctor Hardwick will help. I'm going to see him after he's spoken with her, and then I really must get some rest before I collapse. Can you keep things going while I have a lie-down for a bit?"

"Of course, Miss Sophia. You look tuckered out, and it's no wonder. You eat up what I brung you. I won't disturb you unless you ring for me. Don't you worry about your Mum. I'll see to it that she follows the doctor's orders."

I hugged her, and held her closely for a moment. There had been times in my life when Nan seemed more a mother to me than Pamela. I truly loved her.

"Oh Nan," I said, turning back to the tray. "One more thing. I need to send a wire to Blake. His address is in Papa's desk in the library…..The top drawer, in the green leather book. Here, let me scribble down what it needs to say. Could you please call it to the telegraph operator?"

"Yes, Miss Sophia, I'll be glad to," she answered.

I took a piece of stationery, and a pen from the drawer of my nightstand. Without hesitating, I wrote; 'We have emergency. Papa needs you. Can you come at once?" Then, I handed the paper to Nan, who tucked it into the pocket of her apron.

"I'll send it at once. Now, you rest, Miss Sophia." With a kiss on my cheek, Nan turned to leave the room. Suddenly the pain struck with alarming force. There was no mistaking what it was, and I cried out.

"Nan! Fetch Dr. Hardwick to my room at once. I think I'm having a miscarriage!"

Doctor Hardwick arrived in mere seconds, although it seemed much longer. My water had broken, and I had severe cramping. I knew with certainty what was happening. The Doctor quickly examined me, and verified that I was in the midst of a spontaneous abortion.

"Isn't there anything that can be done to stop it?" I cried. I want the child so terribly much."

,"No Sophia, I'm afraid not. Your water has already broken. I can perform a Dilation and Curettage, or we can wait until you expel the fetus on your own, but you are going to lose this child."

"Will this affect my ability to have other babies?" I asked.

"It shouldn't, my dear. I recommend that we do a D & C. It will make certain that everything is cleaned out and sterile, and will lessen the chances of infection." Nan was standing in the background, with tears streaming down her face. "How can I 'elp?" she sobbed.

"Call the ambulance lads, please," Dr. Hardwick said. "We shall need to get Sophia to hospital so that I have surgical facilities. The cramps were coming closer together and I was truly in agony. I felt as though my insides were being torn apart. I was crying and moaning, biting down on the corner of the bed sheet. "I'm going to wash my hands, my dear. I'll just be a moment", the doctor said.

"Please don't leave me," I begged.

"I'm not leaving, he insisted, as he went into the adjoining bath, and ran the water. He was back by my side very quickly, with a cool cloth, which he placed upon my head. "Try to breathe deeply and slowly.

Try to relax. I know it's hard," he encouraged. We continued in such a vein for what seemed like hours. In reality, it was but a few minutes. The ambulance arrived and took me to the same hospital where Papa was currently residing, albeit to a different floor. I was given ether, and the next thing I knew I was in a private room, trying to adjust to what had happened. Dr. Hardwick was sitting next to the bed, and he had a solemn expression on his face.

"Sophia, dear, I've some bad news for you," he said, reaching over and taking my hand.

"What?" I asked.

"This was more complex than I originally thought. It was not a simple miscarriage. Did you have a fall or some sort of accident?"

"I had a fall..... In the hallway, but it wasn't terribly bad."

"Well, apparently it caused severe damage. It tore the placenta. You had internal bleeding, and in the end I had to perform a hysterectomy."

"Hysterectomy? You mean you have taken away my ability to have children! Oh God, no. Tell me that isn't true." I turned my face into the pillow, as tears began to fall.

"I know it seems ghastly. However, you *do* have Isabella. Thank God for that."

"But, I wanted a lot of babies," I sobbed. "Spence and I had decided on a large family." I was crying hysterically.

"I understand that this is a shock, Sophia. We're fortunate that you're alive. The internal bleeding was severe. You must have been in that state for some time. Your husband would rather have you than a million babies. You need rest. Try not to blame this upon what was happening with your parents. You will be fine, but you're weak. We had to transfuse you with two pints of blood. Do you want me to tell your parents?"

"I suppose they must know. But, if Mummy is sleeping, don't awaken her," I managed, between sobs. "Also, don't disturb Papa here at hospital until morning, please," I said. I felt utterly alone.

"What about your husband? Shall I wire him?"

I thought for a moment, and then said, "Yes. Yes. I need him. I want him with me."

"Of course you do, Sophia. I shall make certain that he is notified immediately. Now, you're young and strong dear. I have lived long enough to know that these things have a way of sorting themselves out. It will be all right. Try to calm your mind, and quit worrying about your mother. She seems fragile, but Pamela is one of the strongest women I've ever known. It will take more than this to stop her. You need to think about getting your own strength back."

Chapter Twenty-Six

FEBRUARY 1941 TO MARCH 1941
A CALL TO NIGEL

I have always prided myself upon my excellent memory. Nevertheless, the weeks following Edwina's departure from *Willow Grove Abbey* and my hysterectomy are still a blur in my mind. I remember bits and pieces of the loss of my baby quite clearly, but there are long stretches where my mind is completely blank. The first few days after the surgery, I had tasks to occupy my time. I was weak and unable to do much more than get through the necessary. Spence procured emergency furlough, and came home to a wife who could scarcely do more than weep. He held and kissed me, trying to soothe my grief, but it was impossible. We both knew it. He was as grief stricken as I was, but tried to remain strong, so that I might have the luxury of falling apart. To Mummy's credit, for a short period after the disaster she turned her attention to me, as did my father.

After Spence left, I wanted to return to my bed and stay there, with the covers pulled up over my head. That wasn't possible. I had a child and she needed me. It had been a loss for her too, and the atmosphere in the house wasn't settled. Mummy calmed down until the physicians announced that Papa was ready to leave hospital. When I gave Mummy that news, she said that there was no way, whatsoever, that she was going to allow him to return home. My parents hadn't really spoken at length since the whole nightmare began. Papa tried on two occasions to ring her up, but she slammed the telephone down when she realized it was him. I talked with him daily, trying to glean some idea of his plans should Mummy not opt for a divorce, and instead press for separation. Papa said that he would agree to whatever Mummy wanted. Would even give her *Willow Grove Abbey*. Would make certain that she was well provided for. He said he just wanted peace in his life, and was willing to live simply. Somehow, I couldn't imagine such a change. I knew that eventually she would give in, and I am sure he knew that too. So, he was in no real danger of losing his home or fortune.

Blake was able to procure a furlough. He arrived on the day Papa was being discharged, which was five days after I'd been sent home from hospital. Spence had left, I was terribly grateful that my brother had arrived. Until then, the burden had been completely upon my shoulders. I knew that Blake could be relied upon to be levelheaded. He'd known about the affaire, so of course that was no major surprise. He arranged to have Susan take the train from Scotland to Bristol in order to meet him. The two of them then set about taking rooms in a hotel. On the day that Papa left hospital, I drove to the hotel, as I needed to speak with him about financial matters pertaining to *Willow Grove Abbey*, as well as Mummy's state of mind. I was still weak, but not infirm, and having something to occupy my thoughts seemed beneficial. Susan answered the door to the room, and I was happy to see her. We had grown closer, ever since her revelation to Mummy about her abortion, and the support she'd shown toward my fight for acceptance of Spence. It had been a long time, and so much had happened. Of course, it was not an occasion for a nice, friendly chat, but we hugged one another, and rolled our eyes over the mess that had brought about our reunion. Then, she hugged me again, saying, "Sophia, darling, I'm so sorry for your loss. It is the most horrific thing. I can imagine your pain."

"I'm all right, Susan. This isn't something that one ever recovers from. You know that. Once simply goes on." I answered, while entering the room, where I saw Papa sitting at a table with Blake beside him. Blake looked at me with a grin on his face. It struck me as peculiar that he could find humor under such tragic circumstances.

"This isn't humorous, Blake. There's absolutely nothing funny about it," I said. He never mentioned the loss of my baby or my hysterectomy. The smile on his face disappeared, and a look of anger replaced it.

"Don't you come in here and start any sort of row. Dad's just been released from hospital, and I'm not about to have him upset," he said, in a commanding voice. Turning to Papa, he said, "Dad, I want you to go into the bedroom and lie down." Just as instructed, Papa stood, and shuffled off toward the hallway and the bedroom.

"And don't *you* think that you're going to come here and start issuing orders," I shot back. "I've had all of this dumped upon me for months now. I've tried to keep you, Drew and Spence out of it, because each of you has all he can cope with, fighting this war. You aren't really completely aware of what has taken place. You haven't seen Mummy, who has come near to having a complete collapse. Papa knows that I love him, but I'm also very angry with him at present."

"Dad has to make a decision about the rest of his life," Blake continued. "I think he should leave our mother and marry Edwina."

"And just exactly what is Mummy supposed to do if that happens?"

"Our mother will have to decide what she wants to do with the rest of her life."

"Are you daft? Mummy is nearing forty-eight years of age. She's lived with Papa for over thirty years. Just what do you suggest that she do at this stage of her life?"

"She'll have to decide that for herself," Blake replied, coldly. His mouth was set in a firm line. I was absolutely enraged. This wasn't really unusual for Blake. He'd never in his life thought of anyone but himself, and I don't know if he was even capable of understanding the pain that our mother was going through.

"Has Papa changed his mind about leaving Mummy?" I asked.

"He doesn't know what he's going to do. He cannot go back to our mother and let her kill him. He has a weak heart. He can't take the uproar that will ensue if he returns to living with that shrew." I was nearly one hundred percent certain that Blake had been working on Daddy to make the decision to leave Mummy from the moment that he had arrived.

"And what about Edwina?" I asked.

"I've spoken with Edwina. Of course, she wants Dad to come to her, but I have told her that he won't do that at this juncture. He needs time to think. I've tried to speak to Mother, but she refuses my calls."

"Blake, she's horribly wounded. Not just wounded. Shocked. She truly *did* trust him, as well as Edwina. She never dreamed that such a thing could happen. You shouldn't wonder that Mummy is beside herself. Dr. Hardwick is treating her, and I spend as much time as possible with her. Please remember that I've been ill myself. She seems to be dealing better with all of it, but she has a lot to get through."

"Our mother has been a shrew all of her life. It's about time she found out what it's like to have someone treat her the way she's always treated others."

"Oh Blake, how childish. Mummy has *never* been well. We have all known that for a long time, but have simply gone about pretending it wasn't so. She should have had help years and years ago. You don't just abandon someone when they're sick and frightened," I replied. "Instead of getting her help, Papa never mentioned her behaviour to any doctor, and pretended that she was absolutely normal, when we all knew she wasn't."

"You can feel sorry for her if you want to. This study of psychology that you've undertaken has softened your brain. You've had all of this education about mentally ill people and you still haven't a clue as to what's wrong with our mother."

"I have more than a clue, Blake. To be exact, our mother suffers from what is known as *"Borderline Personality Disorder."* There are nine criteria for its diagnosis, and an individual needs only two to be diagnosed. As far as I'm able to gather, Mummy suffers from all nine, to one degree or another. I'm not going to go through each and every symptom. But, trust me, I have focused upon this for a long time, in an attempt to understand Mummy. It has always been clear that there is something the matter with her. You know as well as I do that normal people don't behave as she does. Daddy knows that too. But, instead of trying to learn what might be wrong, he has simply helped her to cover up the symptoms, and lied for her, which has just exasperated the illness. Instead of being so beastly critical of her, why don't you try to learn why she is the way she is?"

"I think psychology is a bunch of mumbo-jumbo. When a person acts like a horse's arse, then the psychiatrists label them with some disorder. I label them as a 'horse's arse'. I don't feel sorry for her. I feel sorry for Dad.

I want to see him happy, and if Edwina makes him happy, then so be it." Blake was adamant that Papa not go back to Mummy.

"Well, I think this conversation is premature anyway, because at the moment, Mummy has given no indication that she even *wants* Papa back. However, I suspect that is pride talking, and when she's really faced with the idea of losing him forever, she'll completely fall apart .Fear of abandonment is one of the greatest issues that a person with *Borderline Personality* faces. I don't believe she could cope without him. She certainly could never cope alone. She doesn't do very well when she *isn't* alone." Obviously, I would be the one to take her under my wing, and I'll do so, as she *is* my mother, no matter what things she has done to hurt me. Nevertheless, I'm not going to lie and say that I don't think this entire thing is beastly unfair. I didn't decide to have an affaire with anybody, and didn't create this nightmare. Yet, if Mummy and Papa separate, I'll have to pick up the pieces. I think I've already paid a high enough price."

You're right about that Sophia. None of this is fair. Dad should have thought about such things before he ever got involved with Edwina. Actually, he should have thought before he ever got involved with our mother. Sometimes it's easier to get into things than it is to get out of them. Dad told me that, himself. But, I still can't say I blame him."

"Well, I think for the time being, things should be left as they are until Mummy has a chance to think things through a bit more. She's certainly in no condition to do that now. However, he can't stay in a hotel in Bristol indefinitely, so where will he go if this drags on?

"Susan is willing to take Dad back up to Leith with a car and driver. We can get a medical petrol ration. There's plenty of room at the house in Scotland, and it'll be a quiet place for Dad to recuperate. I'm going to put in for a transfer to a base in Scotland so I'll be able to get home occasionally.

And what of Edwina? Is she still here in Bristol?" I was afraid to know.

"Edwina has returned to London. Even with the Blitz, I think she feels better there. Of course he'll keep in touch with her, but he has no plans to see her," Blake answered. "Edwina has even mentioned taking Kippy and going to America, She has that sister in Connecticut, which is near to New York, and she thinks she could get work there. But, in my opinion he's a bloody fool if he allows her to do that. She would need his help with a passport. Also with funds. If he loves her, and she loves him, then he should do what his heart tells him. He's given our mother more chances than any ten women. How he can feel any allegiance to her is beyond me." Blake was shouting.

"This is so typical of you Blake," I shouted back. "You've never given the slightest thought to the feelings of others. You don't feel sorry for Mummy. Instead, you seem to hate her. *I am* the one who knows Edwina better than anyone in this family, *and that includes Papa!* She has no morals, no sense of right and wrong, and no empathy for the terrible pain that her actions have caused. She's so terribly much in love with Papa because of his wealth and title. I wonder how long that will last if Papa and Mummy divorce, and Papa doesn't have the vast amount he's always had."

"Oh this is sodding idiocy! Edwina is a perfectly fine girl. She doesn't want Dad for his money. I've even spoken with her on that very subject. The money means nothing at all to her. She loves Dad, unconditionally, rich or poor."

"Blake, you are a dimwit if you believe that! I too have spoken with her, and she made it exceedingly clear that wealth and title hold great meaning for her. She wants to be Countess Somerville as badly as she's ever wanted anything in her life."

"Well, I'm all for it," Blake again responded. Susan was quiet, looking at me with a worried expression on her face. I knew that she agreed with my point of view, but I also knew that she would never break rank with Blake.

"Sophia, I'd expect you to take Mummy's side in this. You were always her favourite. What are your expectations? Do you think that if they divorce, and I take Dad's side, as I believe Drew will too, you'll end up her only heir? Wouldn't that be nice for you?" Blake said, accusingly.

"My God! I cannot believe that you'd even say such a thing! I 'was always her favorite'? Are you daft? It's obvious that you have a rotten memory. As for my being 'money motivated', that has never entered my mind. You know I'm not like that. Never have been. I fell in love with and married a doctor, much to Mummy's chagrin. I certainly wasn't worried about money or title then. I'm studying for a University degree, and upon completion, I plan on taking a job. I look forward to work. I do not need Papa's money. In addition, I was left a sizable inheritance when Owen died." I raised my voice at least two octaves.

"Please lower your voice. Do you want the people in the next room to hear this discussion," Blake said, in his most authoritative manner.

I really don't know what happened to me. I had no plans to say the words that came out of my mouth. I suppose a human being can take just so much in a lifetime, and I'd certainly taken my share from Blake and from my father. I was terribly angry, had a beastly headache, felt weak, shaken, and wondered if I could go on coping with everything that was happening. In any event, without even thinking, I turned to Blake and blurted out words that could never be taken back.

"Oh how very, very typical. We're supposed to worry about whether or not the people in the next room hear our conversation, but as long as things are done privately and secretively, then that's just fine! You are exactly like Papa. It was fine for you to know that Papa did evil, wicked things to me when I was only a child of eleven. You were seventeen years old, Blake, and you didn't care a whit what was happening to your little sister. I ran to *you*, Blake, after what Papa did while bathing me. I told you everything. And your answer to me was to get out of your room. Your exact words were, "*Ahhh, the poor guy…he never gets any affection.*" In today's world, Papa would be labelled a sexual abuser."

Susan's face drained of color. Turning to her husband she said, "Blake, what is she talking about?"

"Ah, she's just trying to get back at Dad and me. She's crazy. Don't pay her any mind, Susan. It's a pack of lies. "

Susan had a stunned look, as though she didn't know what to believe. It hadn't been my intent to hurt anyone. I'd never confronted Blake, and certainly not Papa about the hurt inflicted upon me. Yet, I had also never forgotten it. It had been with me every step of the way growing up, and had festered for a long time. At that moment, when emotions were running high, I erupted. Turning my attention to Susan, I apologized. I said it had nothing to do with her, and wished she could forget what I'd said. Of course, she couldn't. I knew beyond any doubt, that I'd lost Blake for all time. He was so much like Mummy, and he worshipped the ground

Papa walked upon. Making such an accusation toward Papa was as bad as making it about Blake. One simply *did not* confront him in such a fashion and then go back to having a normal relationship, as though it had never taken place. Even though he knew what I'd said was true, he would never admit it was so. If I hadn't said it in front of his wife, we might have gotten beyond it, but I doubt it.

Susan ran from the room, and Blake muttered that he would never forgive me if it ruined his marriage. I told him that I did not think there was any way that would happen. Susan loved him, and Papa's sins were no reflection upon Blake's character. The only thing I was criticizing Blake for was my having pleaded for him to help me, and his treating me like I was nothing but a bother to him. Because of the way he had reacted on that long ago evening, which was still seared in my soul, I never approached him or anyone else about the several other incidents I suffered at my father's hands. It was abundantly clear that no one cared.

You're crazy, just like your mother," he screamed. Then, he strode out of the room, leaving me alone. I marched down the hall to one of the bedrooms, and gently knocked. Papa's voice told me to come in. Blake must have been in the other bedroom with Susan, for Papa was alone. There was no way he hadn't overheard the furor. *The expression 'crazy' was so completely overused, especially in our home, and it was so absurd. In truth, what he was really saying was that he didn't like what I was saying.*

"Well, this appears to be a fine kettle of fish. I'm sorry, Papa. I should not have said what I did, but it *is* the truth. You know that. I would never lie about something like this. Edwina loves to wax-on eloquently about 'unconditional love." Well, Papa, if there has ever been an example of unconditional love, then it is my actions toward you. In spite of what you did to me, I have *never* confronted you with it, and have always shown great love for you. I've protected you, and kept your secrets. You know that's true."

"I know that, Sophia. I know," he murmured.

"Did you think because I was such a young girl, that I had forgotten about it? Or had buried the memories?"

I suppose I hoped so, Sophia. You never gave any indication that you remembered."

"No, I didn't. And if you remember the incident, when it occurred, Mummy was out in the hallway when I screamed out *'Papa Stop'*. I quickly *lied* to keep you from Mummy's wrath, and called back to her, lying, telling her that everything was all right. I said that you had only been scrubbing my back too hard. How utterly amazing that at such a tender age, I would have been more concerned with protecting you, then in protecting myself. Do you remember that, Papa?"

"Yes, Sophia. I don't like to remember it, but I do. I always hoped that it would never be brought up."

"Well, I'm sorry, but it *has* been brought up. I don't intend to tell Mummy, or to mention it again. But If I know Blake, he is going to try to turn the entire family against me, and tell all of the others that I am *crazy*, which they will be only too ready to accept. Papa, you know precisely what you did to me as a child. I pray to God that you will be decent enough to stand up to the rest of the family on my behalf, and for once in your life tell the truth. You needn't get into specific details. I just want you to make it clear that Blake is the one who is lying. He is embarrassed now, and doesn't want people to know that it was in his power to put a stop to it, and he chose to act as if it didn't matter what was done to me. The only thing that mattered to him was that you were protected."

"I cannot take sides against my children".

"Oh Papa, how sad," I continued. You are willing to let me be called a liar and a crazy person rather than admit that I'm merely being honest? Isn't that taking Blake's side? "

"I just want to have a relationship with all of my children. I can't take sides."

"You can't take sides? Can you tell the truth? There is a difference. You made me into a victim once, Papa, and now you want to do so again. You know that everyone in the family adores you…even Mummy, in spite of present circumstances. Whatever you say has always been the Gospel truth. And in this situation, if this is to….. *And it will be*….. It will find its way to Drew and Annie and undoubtedly even to Blake Jr. and Pippin. If you don't admit that what I've said is true, there is no question that I will be shunned by my entire family. No one will believe that *I'm* telling the truth. Everyone will be carrying on about what an evil person I am to make such an accusation about you…… . And about Blake. How could you do such a thing to me?"

"Because I am a survivor, Sophia. Sometimes survivors have to say and do things that go against their grain?"

"*Survivor!* Perhaps more correctly a *sociopath,* with no conscious. In other words you would do anything to survive and keep your reputation intact, including lie about your own daughter, and if necessary let her be thrown out of her family? *'That* is your definition of a survivor? In other words, you would rather put yourself first at all costs, and if that means stepping all over me, and ruining me, so be it"

"Sophia, all you need to do, to stop any of this from occurring, is to say that you were angry, and said things that weren't true. Tell Blake that what you implied about me is not true, and that it never happened. Then, apologize."

"In other words, lie! Apologize? What am I apologizing for? Telling the truth? Being honest? Having feelings? Finally blurting out the truth after a lifetime of holding it in, and letting Blake treat me like a piece of garbage? Oh. Papa, no. There was a time you probably could have talked me into something so vile. But, no more. I didn't do anything wrong. Not when I was eleven years old, and not now."

I shook my head from side to side, as tears fell from my eyes. It hurt a great deal to know that my own father would not defend me. I don't know why it surprised me as much as it did. After all, wasn't that what he had always done? *No matter the issue.* All scales fell from my eyes. It was a devastating moment. I gathered my handbag, and put the papers I'd brought on the table, all the while shaking.

"Well Papa, I'm sorry about all of this. If this family weren't so thickly tangled in a web of lies, perhaps we wouldn't have rows like this. Perhaps we might even have been a normal family. I'm beginning to wonder, Papa, if this affaire with Edwina was the first in your life? Perhaps it's just the first time you were ever caught? In which case, perhaps Mummy senses that, or has even known it all along, but her fear of abandonment has placed her in an untenable situation."

"Sometimes it's better not to be honest, Sophia. What is the sense in hurting people?

"Is that an answer to my suspicions? *Have* there been other affaires? I suspect that I even know who some of them may have been. When I look back on your life, I see a pattern. You and Mummy would become very friendly with some couple or other. That couple was usually very unhappily married. Thus, the woman was extremely vulnerable to someone like you…. A supposed fine man, handsome and titled, saying loving things to her. And I think it always worked. When you told them you wouldn't leave Mummy and marry them, they eventually broke it off, or if they were too infatuated, *you* ended it. It was the same pattern with Edwina, only you got in way over your head."

There was complete silence from Papa. It was clear to me that I was correct

"Why not just love people unconditionally?" Papa responded?

"Oh Bollocks, Papa! Stop it! Unconditional love has nothing whatsoever to do with this. You know what you did to me, and I suspect what you've done to others. The amazing thing is that I *do* love Blake and I do love you, Papa. In spite of the ghastly situation you have caused due to your cheating and lying and… yes…abuse. My silence, and my protection of you, *is* unconditional love. Now, it is exceedingly clear that you will lie for Blake, and make me out to be a *crazy* person. God, I hate that word. It is so childish. Where is my unconditional love?"

I was trembling from head to toe, and could feel perspiration break out on my forehead. I wondered if I might faint. I needed to end the conversation and get away from there. "You and Blake don't have to worry, Papa. I have no desire to tell any of your secrets to the world." I kissed him on the cheek, and told him to try to get some rest. "Our entire family has always suffered from so many secrets and lies. I am rather adept at keeping secrets," I added. Without saying another word, I got up, and left the room to begin my journey back to *Willow Grove Abbey*.

When I arrived home, Mummy was sleeping soundly, and everything seemed in good order, as contrasted with the melee I had been through. Isabella was home from school, and I went to the nursery to play with her. She was filled with chatter about school, and friends, and I was glad that her world seemed so unaffected by happenings around our home. She was nearly five years, still small for her age. Still a beautiful child. Her hair was very long, reaching to her waist. It was a mass of ringlets. There were also wavy bangs scattered above her perfectly shaped brows, enhancing her wide, dark blue eyes. Her beauty always took my breath away. She looked so much like Spence.

"Mama, Mama, we've had a letter from Papa. I've been waiting ever so long for you to come home so that we can open it," she cried as she came bouncing to me. She was dressed in a checked gingham play dress, with a pink bow in her hair, looking like a cherub.

"Well, bring it to me, darling. Let's see what Papa has to tell us today," I said, sitting her upon my lap. Together we opened the letter, and I read it aloud to her.

"Now let's see," I said. It begins *'Dear Sophia and Isabella,'*
Isabella clapped her hands together in glee. Then, I continued;

"There is a shortage of pilots and, I have been flying more than I thought I would be, since my return. I can't tell you where I've been, as it would only be cut by the censors. Just know that I am taking good care, and that I have painted both of your names on the side of my Spitfire. The other chaps joke with me, asking who 'Sophella" is. I just laugh. I am already so lonely for both of you. It is hard to believe that I only said goodbye to you such a short time ago.

Isabella, I miss you very, very much and think about you every day. Every night when I go to sleep, I say a special, little prayer that God will keep you safe from harm. Sophia, my darling, never forget that you are in my thoughts day and night, and that I only live for the day I can hold you in my arms again. Your letters are wonderful, and help so much to keep my morale high. They give meaning to why I am here. Keep writing darling, and take very good care of yourself and Isabella. You are both my world, and are all I need.

I Love You.

I wiped tears from my eyes, and held the letter close to my breast, as if by doing so I could somehow bring him nearer to me. Isabella traced her finger over the handwriting on the envelope, and said that she had the most wonderful Papa in the world. I certainly didn't argue with that remark. Spence knew the trauma I was enduring, but I didn't intend to tell him of the latest chapter in the saga. He'd endured enough pain, and he was trying to tell me that it was all right that we wouldn't have more children. If possible, I loved him even more for that. I had told him of Papa's inappropriate behaviour toward years before, when we were together in his charming office in Twigbury. After we had made love for the first time. But, I certainly had no intention of telling him what had happened now, while he was risking his life for his country.

Two days later, while I was out in the garden, preparing beds for spring planting, Mummy came running out of the house in a frenzy. She'd been snooping in Papa's desk, and discovered telephone records covering a period of nearly three years. Waving them in her hand, and screaming at the top of her lungs, she ran across the lawn. Her hair had been hastily pinned up, and tendrils fell about her face. She was out of breath when she reached me, so the papers were simply thrust into my hands. I took off my gardening gloves and scanned them. They astounded me! Over a three-year period, Papa had placed hundreds and hundreds of calls to Edwina in Paris. Then, after Edwina's return to London, often the calls were just moments apart. They would talk for ninety minutes, and then hang up. He would ring her back ten minutes later. Even on the Christmas when Spence came to *Willow Grove* for the first time, there was a 47-minute call to Edwina. Clearly, he was obsessed. Of course, I understood immediately why Mummy was beside herself. I tried my best to calm her.

"Mummy, the affaire may not have been going on all of this time. You know that she considered him her mentor. Perhaps he was giving her business advice?" I ventured.

"Oh Fiddle! He was not giving her advice of any sort, and you know that. You know very well what he was giving her..... *And* what she was giving *him*. He was bonkers over her. These calls prove it. I could show them in any court in the land and be divorced at once."

"Is that what you want?" I asked.

Mummy began to cry

"I don't know what I want. Where will he go if we divorce? Will he still be nearby, so that I can lean on him as I always have?"

"No Mummy, I doubt that very much. I think he would stay in Scotland, where he is now. He says he just wants a peaceful, simple life."

"Well, that isn't what he'll have if he marries Edwina," she sobbed.

"I'm sure that's true," I answered.

"I always thought that he would be nearby. I can't imagine that I would never see him. He has been my whole life for nearly thirty years. I don't want to lose him. I'm too old to start again."

This was an admission of gargantuan proportions.

"Are you telling me that you want him to come home?"

"Yes. Will you call him at Susan's and tell him I want him here with me at *Willow Grove* Abbey?"

"Are you saying that you feel you can forgive him?"

"Well…. No…. But, I'll try. I can't just forgive him overnight. It will take time. But, I don't want our marriage to end."

I put my arms around my mother, something rarely done in our family.

"I'm so glad you've reached this decision. It's the right thing to do. One doesn't throw out the baby with the bath water, you know. You and Papa have shared a lifetime together. You can work this out. When shall I call him?"

"Right away, before I change my mind," she smiled, feebly. It was the first smile I had seen on Mummy's face in weeks.

Therefore, I went up to the house and placed a call to Susan and Blake's number in Scotland. Susan answered and I asked to speak to Papa. When he came on the line, I was quite succinct with my message.

"Your wife wants you to come home," I said.

There was a moment of silence, followed by a sigh, and then he said,

"I'll catch the next through train to London, and from there to *Bedminster-with-Hartcliffe.*"

"I'd meet your train in London, but the rationing has made it just about impossible for me to get enough petrol to drive that distance, round-trip," I told him. "I could send Joseph, but the same problem exists."

"That's fine, Sophia. I'll be just fine. It will be a nice, quiet ride. Give me time to think."

Yes, indeed, I imagined there would be a great deal of thinking on his pending journey.

Chapter Twenty-Seven

May 1941 to February 1942
Captured

My father came home. I spent hours preparing my mother, in an attempt to keep her from driving him off permanently. If Mummy had a *rage* the moment Papa walked into the house, he'd have an excellent excuse to leave forever. I suspected that was the advice that Blake had given him. I patiently explained that if Papa truly had deep feelings for Edwina, Mummy would be playing right into his hands if she was out of control when he returned. I told my mother that such behaviour would give him a perfect excuse to turn and walk away, saying that his health wouldn't permit him to live with her. Mummy nodded her head, and actually seemed to be listening to me, for the first time in her life. Once again, roles reversed, with me acting the parent and Mummy, the child. I was certain that my father was expecting my mother to attack him the moment he arrived. Mummy was instructed to do exactly the opposite. I told her that she needed to be kind, solicitous, and concerned for his health. She should ask if he was tired from the long journey, tell him his bed was turned down, and that a tray was ready. Mummy promised that she would do all of those things.

An hour before his arrival, Mummy decided that there should be roaring fires in all of the rooms. She had Nan, Violet, Rose and me scurrying about laying the proper kindling. Joseph had gone to the depot to collect Papa, and Perkins had the day off. They were the ones who normally would have seen to such chores. Unfortunately, the chimney flue in the master bedchamber was closed, unbeknownst to any of us. Thus, when the fire was lighted, smoke began to billow out in large clouds. The room quickly filled. I ran to the telephone, rang the firehouse, and requested that they immediately dispatch a truck. It arrived at almost the exact time that Joseph pulled up in front of the house with Papa in the car. It was a strange homecoming. By then, Mummy had lost all composure and forgotten everything that I had told her. As Papa entered the house, Mummy ran to him and started beating him on his chest.

"Damn you, Nigel. This is entirely your fault. If I hadn't been worn to a frazzle over what you've done to me, I would have remembered to check the fireplace flue. You're the one who always does such things. It wasn't my responsibility. You..... You..... *Arse!* Now, we'll have to have the entire bedroom wing redecorated. The damage is horrific."

"Calm down, Pamela," he said, in his usual stoic manner. "That sort of language doesn't become you at all. The fire lads will take care of it. It's nothing that can't be fixed".

He looked somewhat pale, but otherwise seemed to be his usual self. Shrugging out of his overcoat and hat, he handed them to Nan, and climbed the stairway, presumably to survey the damage. I reminded my mother of the topic we had discussed earlier.

"Oh Bugger off, Sophia," Mummy shrieked. This isn't my fault. I would have been fine if that terrible flue had been open. This is your father's fault..... All of it."

I threw up my hands in surrender, gave a deep sigh, and headed toward the stairs to write a letter to Spence. There was nothing else to do. It was time to turn my attention to what was important in my life.... My husband and our little girl. As I walked toward my rooms, I remembered what Dr. Hausfater had said long ago, about Mummy's lack of 'coping skills.' *Oh, wasn't he too right!* After I finished my letter, I rang for Nan, and asked that she bring a tray for dinner, so that Isabella and I could dine in our rooms. It seemed best to let Mummy and Papa fend for themselves. From time to time during the hours Isabella and I were ensconced in our rooms, I could hear their voices..... Mostly Mummy's..... risen in anger. I knew that it would not end soon. There was no way the muddle could be sorted out in any sensible or calm manner. However, I also knew that I couldn't continue to be a referee in their God-awful battles. Isabella asked me, during our en suite meal, whether her grandparents were having a row. She was old enough to know that there was something very wrong. I didn't lie.

"Yes, I'm afraid they are. I think we must let them try to work it out, as best they can, without our interference. Sometimes married people go through rough patches."

"It theemth like Grandmother is mad at Grandfather," she said, wisely.

"Yes, that's the way it is," I replied. "But, she's been angry before, and I imagine she'll get over it."

"Did he do thomething bad?"

"You might say that," I answered. "But, it's nothing for you to worry about." She was silent for a moment.

"Where did Aunt Edwina and Kippy go? I liked having Kippy here. It was fun to have a baby."

"Well, sweetheart, they had to leave. They weren't going to stay here forever. It was just a temporary place to be until Edwina decided where to settle."

"But, where are Kippy and Aunt Edwina *going*?"

"I'm not really certain. I think they've gone to Bristol for a few days, and then perhaps back to London."

"I wish they could have sthayed," she said, looking rather sad.

"Darling you have your little friends at school, and isn't it nice to be just the two of us again?"

"Yes, I sth'pose. But I wish Papa could be here too."

"Of course, darling. I wish so too, and won't that be a wonderful day? Oh Isabella, he'll be so happy to see you. To see how much you've grown, and how beautiful you've become."

"Yeth, and to sthee how beautiful you are too, Mummy."

I laughed. "You are such a precious, little girl. I'm so lucky to have you and to have Papa. We're a very lucky threesome."

There was a quiet knock at the door, and I opened it to find my father standing there, looking rather pathetic. I invited him in, and asked Isabella to go and play in her room for a bit, while I spoke with him. Papa sat down in the chintz chair by the fireplace.

"So how is it to be home again?" I asked, rather snidely.

"Frankly, I'd rather be almost anywhere else on Earth. Nevertheless, I'm taking my punishment. Pamela needs to get all of the anger out. There's a lot of it, and it will take time."

"Yes, I've no doubt that's true," I frowned. "You can scarcely blame her, Papa."

"No. I don't. My God, we men can do stupid things, can't we?" he mused.

"What can I say, Papa? You know how I feel about this whole mess. I'll never understand why you got involved with Edwina. Of all the people in the world, why Edwina?"

"Sophia, she was there. She made it easy. I don't mean to place the blame upon her, but that's the truth. She was right there under my nose. Moreover, she listened to me. She hung on my every word. Treated me as if I am some sort of God. Made me feel special. God knows, Pamela has never done much of that."

"I know that, Papa, and I'm sorry for what you've missed in your marriage. But, I can't condone the affaire with Edwina."

"I understand," he answered, but continued, as though he had a vast need to unburden himself. "It wasn't just the attention she paid me, either. It was more than that. Sophia, I don't know if Edwina never had much sex in her life, or just what, but she was an absolute wild woman in bed."

"Oh, I can assure you, she had plenty of sex in her life," I laughed. However, Papa you shouldn't be telling me this. I don't want to hear about you and Edwina in bed."

Yes, I understand. I'm only trying to explain what the attraction was. She isn't really beautiful, you know. I wouldn't have thought that I would find her type attractive. Her bosoms are much too large and she's actually a bit plump for my taste. But, still, there is something…"

"Papa, the only thing I care about now is whether or not I can trust you to have ended it? I absolutely cannot go through any more of this. I'm still terribly disturbed that Kippy may be your child, and I don't understand how you aren't sick with worry about that possibility."

"I care very much about the truth of Kippy's paternity, but there's nothing I can do. Whether Kippy existed or not, I would still feel obligated to provide financially for Edwina. After all, I certainly brought her life to shambles."

"Papa, she had a choice! She's not a child. We've discussed this before. You act like she's a twelve-year old."

"I'm much older than she is, and should have been the one to put a stop to it before it got out of hand."

"I think Edwina wanted it to get out of hand. She set her cap for you, Papa. Can't you see that? Didn't it ever cross your mind that Edwina had to have learned her 'wild ways in bed' from someone else along the line?"

"Perhaps. However, I owe her something and intend to see to my obligation. Particularly since I feel the only course of action that can be taken with your mother is to make *her* believe that it wasn't a full-blown affaire.... . That Edwina was totally at fault. It's what Pamela *wants* to believe. She needs to believe that, in order to stay with me."

"Are you saying that you're *still* not going to tell Mummy the entire truth?" I asked, with great annoyance.

"I can't, Sophia. It would destroy her. She already believes that Edwina seduced and tried to entrap me."

"What exactly have you told her?"

"Well, I told her that there was only one physical encounter. That I took Edwina to dinner in Paris, and we drank too much wine. She thinks that's disgusting enough, but it's *much* better than her knowing that this has gone on for years."

"You honestly think she believes you? She's *seen* the list of telephone conversations, and read the letter you wrote. Mummy isn't stupid, Papa On top of that, Edwina herself indicated to Mummy that you and she had numerous and varied sexual experiences."

I can brush that aside by saying that Edwina was only trying to hurt her. I know she isn't a fool, but because Edwina has been such a part of this family for so long, she believes that the telephone conversations *were* about business matters. And also about her marriage to Dieter. That I was giving her advice."

"Oh, Lord help me! So, now we're going to have to live with another layer of lies in this family? Papa, why? Why is it so impossible for anyone to tell the truth in this family?"

"I don't like to hurt people," he replied. "I hate confrontation."

"Oh, Papa! Did you ever think about not doing the things that cause the hurt to begin with?" I asked, in exasperation. I want an answer to the question I asked of you back at the hotel in Bristol. Have you been involved with other women during your marriage to Mummy? "

He sat there, silent for a minute, and it was very clear that he was debating whether or not to tell me the truth. Finally he answered.

"Not while you children were small. But, later, yes. They were simply affaires. They didn't mean anything to me. It was just a way to escape my unhappiness. Edwina is the only one who really meant anything to me." He fiddled with the glasses he was holding. Then, he ran his fingers through his thick, dark hair. Sophia, I'm going to tell you something that I have never shared with a living soul. I'm going to tell you the truth about how my marriage to your mother came about."

"I'm not certain I even want to hear this. I believe all of us have wondered why in the world you married her, if you had the slightest inkling that she suffered from such mental problems."

"I met your mother in 1910. She was absolutely gorgeous. I had never known anyone like her. Of course, I had been a bachelor for a good many years. I was thirty-nine when I met her. Since my school days, I had become well-versed in knowing the proper thing to say to women....what you young people today would call a 'line'. I knew them all. The first outing we had, I escorted her to a Ball. As I was gliding across the dance floor with her, I said something I had probably said a thousand times to other girls. I said, 'My mother told me that there would be nights like this.'" Papa laughed. "The truth, Sophia, is that my mother died when I was only eight years old. Of course, Pamela didn't know that then. There was nothing terribly evil about it. I was just having a bit of fun."

I smiled. What he was telling me wasn't terribly unusual, even by 1940's standards.

"I followed that 'line' up with another of my favorites," he continued. I said, 'Pamela dear, what would you say if I asked you to marry me?' I'd asked that same question of hundreds of girls, feeling perfectly safe, because no girl in her right mind would accept a proposal on a second outing. Well, Pamela was different. She said, 'Why don't you ask me and see?' I was only flirting. Certainly not serious. But, she had carried it that far, so I answered her. 'Pamela, will you marry me?' I asked, smiling, but certainly not in a serious tone of voice. My God, Sophia, she said 'yes'.

The next thing I knew, she had run to her father and mother and told them that I had proposed to her, and that she had accepted! *I was literally trapped.* In 1910, to have backed out of a proposal might well have been cause for a duel! I know you've heard the story that my father had recently died, and I'd discovered that the Estate was nearly insolvent. That is true. But, there were many, many women whom I knew much better than Pamela that I might have married. Ladies of my own class. Pamela had what many people today would call a 'past'. She had run off to *Gretna Green* when only sixteen, and married. Of course, her parents were apoplectic, and had it annulled. However, she was already with child, by the time they found out. The baby was adopted out, and we have no idea where she went. It was a girl. I didn't know all of this until I married her. Anyway, before I knew what had happened, I was engaged to be married. Her father actually bought the ring that I gave her! The whole fiasco was most peculiar. He immediately also gave me her dowry, which was very extensive. However, she was lovely, and seemed to be well-bred, if not noble, plus she did have that large dowry, which I sorely needed, so I went ahead with the marriage. Not long after I learned why her parents and she had been so anxious for her to walk down the aisle. On the morning after our wedding night, she threw her first tantrum."

"What could bring on a tantrum on one's first day of marriage," I asked.

"I wanted to make love to her. I awakened before she did, and I lay there looking at her, and admiring her beauty. Finally, I leaned over and kissed her, and put my hand under her night dress. She roared up out of the bed and shouted "Let's get one thing straight, right now. There will be none of this *shit* in the mornings! Sophia, I had never heard a lady use such a foul word. I called her on it......Told her it was most unbecoming..... . And she threw herself onto the floor, kicking and screaming. That was the beginning of over thirty years of pure Hell."

"Papa. This is amazing. You mean to tell me that Mummy has another daughter somewhere? That she was married before? It practically sounds as though her father *bought* her a husband. Surely they knew that she threw these ghastly tantrums. That must be why they were anxious to get her married quickly, before any poor man learned the truth. Why did you stay with her? Surely there must have been grounds for divorce."

"It wasn't at all easy for a man to obtain a divorce in those days. Really, it would have been her word against mine. She was so terribly peculiar. Occasionally, at night, she seemed to enjoy sexual relations. But, never, never in the daytime hours. At any rate, before I had a chance to even think about the whole mess and how I should handle it, she became pregnant with Blake. I would never have left a child of mine. Never. I should have been stronger with her. Should have forced her to grow up. But, I've never been a terribly strong-willed person. So, I just tolerated her behaviour, and went my own way, when it came to finding affection. It was easier that way."

"Well, this certainly explains a lot, Papa. I'm sorry you spent so much of your life in such a sad way. No wonder you worried about who I might end up marrying. But, none of this explains to me why you did foul things to me. As you just said, if you wanted or needed affection, I'm sure there was plenty of it to be had.'"

There was silence again. With a sigh, he stood and said he would be sleeping in one of the guests' bedrooms. "Thank you for listening to me, Sophia. I'm glad you're here. We'll get through this, you know. Everything will be fine."

I stood too, and kissed him on the cheek. "Yes, Papa, we'll get through this," I replied, sighing deeply. He turned back to me before he left the room.

"Sophia, you asked me why, of all the women in the world, I chose Edwina?"

"Yes, Papa. I did. I'll still never understand it."

"Perhaps it was because it was the closest I could get to you.

He left the room, and I could hear his footsteps retreating down the hallway. There was total silence. Suddenly, it all made perfect, if completely irrational, sense. And it was very, very sick.

Mummy refused to let go of the affaire with Edwina. It was as though it had a hold over her. She had draped herself in a mantle of martyrdom, from which she couldn't escape. There was a wounded look in her eyes. Whenever I found myself alone with her, every iota of information regarding the affaire was gone over with a fine-toothed comb. It was pure torture, because I had to keep straight in my mind the story that Papa had told her. I had to be mindful not to say anything that might signal that I'd had knowledge of the affaire before her interception of the letter. She carried the list of telephone calls with her wherever she went. It was always in her pocket or handbag. She loved to study it. I occasionally wondered what had become of Edwina and Kippy, although I never asked. I was certain that my father knew, and was undoubtedly still in communication with her. Doing so, however, had to be extremely difficult with Mummy monitoring all of his telephone calls, as well as his correspondence. Still, he *did* have to travel occasionally, and there were also the Somerville offices in London through which correspondence could be routed. I knew that where there was a will, there was a way. I also knew that, at least on Edwina's part, there was *very* strong will. I had almost no opportunity to speak with my father about Edwina, since he pointedly avoided me like the plague. I believe he was apprehensive about what the conversation might turn to if the chance for a private chat presented itself. He very much wanted to avoid any such discussion. I also thought that he strongly regretted saying what he had to me about the reason he'd succumbed to Edwina's charms, as well as his involvement with other women, and his reasons for marrying Mummy. It was probably one of the very few times in his life that he was honest with me.

Blake returned to his RAF base. I knew that he corresponded with Papa, but I never heard a word from him. Nor did he attempt to communicate with Mummy. As far as Mummy was concerned, Blake had been permanently erased from the family, because of assistance rendered to Papa after he checked out of hospital. Of course, that was foolishness, but then so was a great deal of what went on in our family. Susan, by extension, was also ex-communicated by Mummy. *I* didn't know what Blake had told her, but I stopped receiving letters from her as well. They had two children of their own by then.…. Gabrielle and Emma.

It hurt the most not to hear from Elizabeth's two children, Blake Jr. and Pippin. I truly loved them dearly, and would never have done anything to destroy my relationship with them. Susan or Blake must have told them that I was a liar, or crazy, or God knows what. Their loss nearly broke my heart. I wished that I could have turned the clock back to a time before I'd blurted out the intemperate comment about Papa's behaviour. I could have cut my tongue out for having lost control. Nevertheless, it was too late for self-recrimination. What had been said, had been said, and in spite of my remorse, it was the truth.

I knew that there was no way Papa would *ever* own up to it, and defend me. After Papa had told me the entire story of his marriage to Mummy, I couldn't help but feel sorry for him. But, it sickened my heart that the father I had always adored, in spite of his behaviour, had never really loved *me* in a healthy manner. I hated to spend time thinking about it, as it could make me very angry. I felt as though I'd been victimized in a cruel fashion, and that I was being re-victimized again by a conspiracy of silence. Therefore, I decided to pick up and move on. Papa could have solved all problems by admitting the truth to everyone, but he chose not to do so. I *did* hear from Drew, and it was apparent that he did not yet know of the confrontation between Blake and me. I hoped it stayed that way. Because he was a minister of God, the entire family tended to keep unpleasant subjects from him.

I had a daughter and husband who needed me, and there was a war on, which seemed to grow more intense and widespread every day. I lay awake far into the nights, thinking and wishing that Isabella and I were far away from *Willow Grove.* That, of course, was impossible. If the Luftwaffe hadn't still been bombing London day and night, I would have returned to Sumner Street, but there was no way I could place Isabella in harm's way. My thoughts were continually with Spence. I wondered where he was each moment. Later I realized that if I'd truly known the answer to that question, I might not have endured. At nearly the exact time that I was thinking of Spence's whereabouts, on an evening in May, 1941, he was in a Spitfire, somewhere over the Channel Coast of France. I didn't know that at the time. Later, I learned that his aircraft, while engaged in a dreadful skirmish with a German airplane, literally exploded in mid-air. It fragmented into a thousand pieces. Spence was ejected, unconscious into the skies. When he awakened, he was on the ground, his open parachute beside him. That was only the beginning of the worst nightmare ever.

I had no knowledge of this until much, much later, when I was able to obtain further details. A wire was received from the War Department three days later, informing me that Spence was missing in action. I was absolutely beside myself. Such dire news served to return a semblance of normalcy to *Willow Grove,* as attention turned to attempts at obtaining additional information. Since Papa was influential in government, I assumed that he would have access to information the average airman's family did not have. I badgered my father unmercifully to contact anyone who could tell me something…. . Anything. Unfortunately, my assumption was incorrect. There was absolutely no way that he was able to garner any information about Spence's whereabouts, or even if he was alive or dead.

I alternated between being certain that Spence was dead, to absolute belief that he had survived and was, even then, making his way back to England, with the help of the underground. None of my fantasies came true. Day after day, week after week, month after month, I prayed, and hoped that I would receive some word about my darling husband. But, it never happened. It was as though he had evaporated into thin air. I continued with my volunteer work at the Red Cross, and the canteen, but my heart was not really in it. Nothing much mattered to me anymore, except Isabella, whom I told the truth to about her father, and each night we made our trip to the chapel, lighting candles and saying prayers for Spence. In those days, none of us had any idea how long the war would last. The RAF had done such a spectacular job trying to gain air supremacy over the skies of London, and the Germans had turned their attention to bombing other major cities in the country, including Birmingham, Bristol, Bath, Manchester, and of course, Coventry. Everyone said that their plan was to soften up our airfields and beaches, before they made their supreme effort…. . To invade England with infantry troops. We all lived in deathly fear of coming face to face with a German. There were always rumors floating about that a German had been cited parachuting into a small village, or on the property of some estate. Thus far, all had proven to be false. However, in August of 1941, we experienced a very frightening occurrence.

Mummy was in her bedchamber, with the lights turned out, and all of the blackout curtains in place. Papa was not at *Willow Grove Abbey,* as he was on a short trip to London. Of course Isabella and I were there, as well as the servants, but we had all retired for the night. Mummy awakened in the darkness, at about two o'clock in the morning. She heard sounds in her room, and slowly opened her eyes. There, not ten feet from her bed, was a man.....a German Paratrooper, we were later to learn. He was rummaging through her jewel box, which sat atop of the dresser. Amazingly, she did not fall to pieces, and she did not scream. Instead, she slowly, and soundlessly, scooted across the bed and reached for a cane that was resting next to Papa's side of the nightstand. Papa did not use the cane very often, but occasionally he had difficulty with lumbago, and so it was always at the ready, to help him get around when he arose in the mornings, stiff and in pain. Mummy grabbed hold of the wooden cane, and then slowly crawled out of the bed. The German soldier's back was to her, and by now her eyes had adjusted to the darkness enough that she was able to see that it was a German. No one and nothing infuriated Mummy like the presence of a Hun! Particularly a Hun in her own bedchamber! She must not even have thought for a moment of the fact that the soldier was surely armed, and that her life was in danger. Her volatile temper had once again taken control of all reason.

Creeping bravely up behind his erect back, she hit him squarely on the head with the cane. Whack! He roared in pain, and went down on the floor. He'd had a pistol in his hand, but when he was hit, he dropped it, and it flew across the room. He was a large man.....At least six feet, two inches, and broad shouldered. But, that didn't stop Mummy As he went to try to pick himself up, she began to beat him unmercifully again with the cane. She battered him all over, from head to foot. Each time he made a move to steady himself, he received a whack in the head. All of the while, Mummy was shrieking in a tirade.

"Just who do you think you are, you disgusting Hun, showing up in a lady's bedchamber at this hour? Only a dirty Hun would do such a thing." Whack! "There, how do you like that? One of your kind killed my dear brother in the last war. Don't think for one moment that you will get out of here alive." Whack! "I've waited a lot of years to avenge my brother's death. Well, now is my chance." Whack. Whack. Whack. Finally I heard the uproar, and I was immediately wide awake. I threw on a robe, and ran to Mummy's room. There in the corner, huddled into a ball, like a fetus, was the German soldier, trying to shield himself with his hands, as Mummy continued hitting him. As I walked in, she was whacking him in the crotch, and he was howling like a wounded dog.

"Mummy, I screamed. "Stop. I'm ringing the police. They will take care of him. If you continue on, you will kill him." His face was bruised black and blue, and there were several teeth missing. One arm hung at his side, as though it was broken.

"I fully intend to kill him. That is my wish," she screamed. Whack! Another hit in the crotch. Now he was begging her for mercy. I quickly rang the police, and in no time at all they were with us in the bedchamber. I suspect that no German had ever been so happy to see an English policeman in his life.

The police took him away, and as he was being led out of the doorway, Mummy screamed "There! Now you go back to your filthy country and tell your Hun friends that this is what they'll face if they ever try to mess with a British Lady." Truthfully, we were all rather proud of Mummy. She was only disappointed that they wouldn't let her finish him off.

"Damn! I wanted to kill him, she shouted.

"Mummy, once you'd rendered him unable to do any harm" it would have been illegal to kill him."

"Why? We're at war with the bastards?"

"I know Mummy, but the rules of self-defense still apply."

"Well he won't be invading any other ladies' bedchambers, I can tell you that. I don't think he'll ever be able to do anything in a bedchamber, or anywhere else, ever again."

On 7 December 1941 The Japanese attacked Pearl Harbour in Hawaii. It was a ghastly blow. Catching the American naval men unaware on a Sunday morning, over 3000 lives were lost, and nearly the entire American fleet as well. Following that horror, the Germans declared War on America.

Of Course, America retaliated with a declaration of war against Germany and Japan. Before the beastly war was ended, the entire world would be engulfed in its madness. The declaration of war against Germany by America meant that finally the Yanks would be joining us in our fight and that England would no longer stand alone. The first of the Yanks arrived in England in January of 1942. Spence had been missing nearly eight months at that time. I had such strong hope that America's involvement would turn the tide, and that if Spence were alive, he would return home. I was virtually convinced that he was being protected by some wonderful French family, who were a part of the Resistance. I couldn't bear to think that he might be a prisoner of war in a German internment camp, and of course, I didn't allow myself to believe that he was dead.

The Blitz intensified in both England and Germany, with the first 1000 bomber air raid on Cologne. Finally, the second half of 1942 saw a reversal of German fortunes. British forces, under Montgomery, gained the initiative in North Africa at El Alamein and Russian forces counter-attacked at Stalingrad. The news of mass murders of Jewish people by the Nazis reached the Allies, and the U.S. pledged to avenge these crimes. In February of 1943, The Germans surrendered at Stalingrad, the first major defeat of Hitler's army. A combination of long-range aircraft, and the 'code-breakers' at Bletchley were inflicting enormous losses on the U-Boats. Toward the end of May, 1943 Admiral Donitz withdrew the German fleet from the contended areas. And the Battle of the Atlantic was effectively over. Allied bombers began to attack German cities in enormous daylight raids. The opening of a second front in Europe was being prepared for the following year, 1944.

During all of that time, I lived my life in a daze, and only thought of Spence. It was impossible to think ahead to what my life might be like if I lost him. I couldn't bear that thought. I knew, of course, that I would do what Spence would have wanted..... Get on with my life, and try to make Isabell's life as good as it could be. But, even the thought of such an existence made me terribly anxious and fearful, and so I tried to block all such notions from my mind. One evening, in late 1943, when Spence had already been missing well over two years, I made my regular visit to the USO canteen in Bristol. I arrived there at about seven o'clock, and greeted the other girls who were either just arriving for duty, or just leaving. We had all become good friends, after such a long time doing our bit for the soldiers. I put a fresh pot of coffee on, and hung up my coat. Not far from where I stood, I noticed an RAF officer, with the same emblem on his shirt as Spence wore, which signified that they shared the same squadron. My heart speeded up as I approached the young man.

"I couldn't help but notice that you are in the same squadron as my husband, "I said, and introduced myself as Mrs. Stanton."

"You must be his wife, Sophia," he answered. I was completely taken aback. "I'm Captain Ian French, and I know Spence well. He's been my wing man on several missions. Of course, I haven't seen him since May of 1941, when we were both shot down."

"You were both shot down? Where? Over France? Oh my God! Was Spence still alive when you last saw him?"

"I believe he survived, yes. Unless, of course, a Jerry came upon him later. Then, I suspect he would have been taken to a POW camp. His skills would make him too valuable for them to do away with him."

"Oh, please, please tell me everything that you know. Everything that happened to you and Spence. I've had no information since I learned he went missing in May of 1941. I've been almost mad with worry."

He sat down in a chair, and motioned for me to sit opposite of him. Then he began to speak. "There was a shortage of pilots. Had been for quite some time. Really, ever since Dunkirk. Spence and I both had been flying extra missions. Everyone was so confounded tired. We were getting by on almost no sleep. Yet, Spence is an excellent pilot, and I will never believe that fatigue had anything to do with his crash. We were both sent up on the same mission, to intercept German planes over France, which were headed for the coast. We spoke back and forth on the radio during the entire mission, and he seemed in fine fettle. There were many more German planes than British, so we were terribly outnumbered. Both of us knew that we would be lucky to get back home. I was hit first. The whole side of my spitfire was nothing but holes, and I had to ditch. My leg had taken a bullet too. I'd had communication with Spence just before that, and told him I was pitching it in. Shortly after I radioed my communication, he radioed back that he too had been hit. I asked him if he was all right, and he indicated that he was, and that he was preparing to parachute out. The next thing I remember is coming down into the English Channel, with my parachute open. Spence was not near me, but I had seen his parachute. I'm sure he wasn't injured when he jumped. As fine a soldier as Spence, it's highly unlikely that he would injure himself in a jump. He was over land when he was hit, so I am sure he wouldn't have landed in the water like I did.

I put on my Mae West, and floated for about forty five minutes, and then I was picked up by a British ship and returned to England. Since he wasn't injured, he may have tried to scout about the area, to see if there was a farm house, or a barn, or someplace where he could get out of the night air. Even though it was May, it was very cold, and damp. That's the last I saw of him, Ma'am."

"My God, My God! You've been the first person to give me any hope. Do you believe that he could still be alive?"

"I'd almost bet my life on it, Ma'am. Spence is one brave soldier. Plus, a smart one. If the Huns got him, and they learned he was a doctor, there's no way that they would want to lose him. He would be too valuable to them. So, my guess is that one of two things has happened. He is either being hidden by a French family, or he has been taken prisoner, and they're using his skills as a physician. Since it's been such a long time, I would put my money on the latter."

"So, you believe that he is a Prisoner of War?"

"Yes. That would be my best guess. Of course, I could be wrong. Don't put all of your trust in what I say. But, I know Spence pretty bloody… pardon me, ma'am'…pretty darned well, and I know he's a survivor."

My head was awhirl with this new news. Hope! I had finally been given a reason to hope. A concrete reason. I agreed with Captain French. If Spence had been captured, it seemed unlikely that they would not use his training and skills to their advantage. I poured Captain French a glass of soda, and then told him that I must excuse myself and go home to report this marvellous news to my daughter.

"That must be Isabella," he replied. "Spence talked about her constantly. He sure loves that little girl."

I had tears in my eyes. "Yes, I know he does. And she loves him so dearly. She will be thrilled to hear that he may still be with us. Thank you so much Captain French. Here, let me write down our address and telephone number. Please ring us up for anything at all. We would be glad to have you as a guest, if you get furlough, or simply come to dinner if you can. I'm so terribly grateful for the information you've provided."

"That's awfully thoughtful of you, ma'am. I just might take you up on that, if I get a chance. At any rate, I'm glad I could be of help, and I do hope to see you again."

With that, I quickly donned my coat, and got on my bicycle for the ride back to *Willow Grove Abbey*. I had stopped driving my car quite a long bit ago, as petrol was so dear. It was only there in case of dire emergency. As I peddled along, my heart was soaring. "Spence is alive! Spence is Alive!" That is all I could keep saying to myself, and sometimes I even shouted it aloud. It never once crossed my mind that he wasn't. I had a certain feeling deep inside that he was fine. That he would be coming home to us. How amazing that I had come upon Captain Ian French. Spence would definitely describe it as another 'serendipitous' moment. But, how long would this ungodly war keep on, and how long would it be before I could hold him in my arms again?

When I returned to *Willow Grove Abbey*, everyone was surprised to see that I had returned from the canteen so quickly, and wondered if I didn't feel well. That was so far from the truth. I ran into the drawing room, shouting out what I'd learned about Spence and the shooting down of his plane. For once, my parents listened, and didn't act like I was a fool for believing the best possible outcome. Isabella came running from the nursery upstairs, when she heard my voice, and we all sat in a circle while I went over word for word what Captain French had related to me. Papa agreed that the best and most likely scenario was that Spence was in a Prisoner of War camp, where the Nazi's were utilizing his medical skills. This new information gave us all more hope, and lightened the atmosphere in the house enormously.

Interestingly, almost overnight, Isabella's lisp cleared up. She just suddenly began to speak using the proper pronunciation for words with an "S" in them. The doctor thought that the lessening of the anxiety she had been carrying about her father had helped her to get beyond an infantile stage of development. Of course I was happy to have her speaking in a more adult manner, although I have to admit that I missed that sweet lisp.

And so, life continued on, but with more hope, and a different sort of waiting. On June 6, 1944 *Operation Overlord* got underway. It was what we had all been waiting for. Some 6,500 vessels landed over 130,000 Allied forces on five Normandy beaches codenamed Omaha, Utah, Gold, Juneau and Sword. Some 12,000 aircraft insured air superiority for the Allies, bombing German defenses and providing cover. Pessimistic predictions had been made of massive Allied causalities, but they were not borne out. On Utah Beach, 23,000 troops were landed, with only 127 causalities'. Most of the 4,649 American causalities that day occurred at Omaha Beach, where it was significantly more difficult to achieve the landing, and the Allies met with fierce German resistance. Overall it was a tremendous victory, catching the Germans by complete surprise. It still took however, a considerable amount of time for the Allied soldiers to make their way toward Paris, due to the thick overgrowth of hedgerows on French lanes. It was slow going. Finally Cherbourg was liberated by the end of June, and Paris followed two months later. I couldn't help but think of Edwina when Paris was liberated. It had been five years since she had escaped the dreadful German occupation, and Kippy had just been a newborn. It was strange to realize that so much time had elapsed and that Kippy would now be five years old. I wondered if Edwina would pack up her belongings and make way for a return to Paris and her designing dreams. I had no wish to see that happen. It would be much too close for comfort.

I was simply living out my dreary existence, expecting nothing of life, hoping for no more than solitude, and a lack of disarray. I was in a sort of limbo, a married woman, but not living the life of such, financially independent and fully adult, at twenty-five years of age, but still sequestered under my parent's roof. A mother, who oft times felt like a child. My parents were still limping along in their own limbo. By then, it was clearly a love-hate relationship, at least on Mummy's part. I could never ascertain with certainty what my father's true feelings were. Sometimes I thought that he, too, merely existed. Of Edwina, I knew little. I'd heard from former school mates that she had, indeed, immigrated to America, and I was vastly relieved at the news. I already had a hard time remembering her voice or the way she looked. I made a conscious effort to erase her from my mind. I still despised having to spend any time alone with my mother, as our only conversations at such moments were recitations of every detail concerning the affaire. And the never-ending scrutiny of the telephone bills.

Mummy *had* managed to convince herself that there had never been a *full-blown* affaire. In her fantasy, Edwina was the evil villain, and Papa the duped fool. Papa, *supposedly,* had tried to escape her clutches, and to remain faithful to his marriage vows, so the story went. Edwina's cunning had been too much for his weak, male ego. I listened and agreed. Papa pampered and spoiled my mother beyond imagination. He left small notes for her, even if he left the house for a quick errand, never forgetting to tell her how beautiful he thought she was, and how much he loved her. Her collection of jewels increased exponentially. At last, I believed that the relationship between Edwina and Papa was finished. There just seemed no way that they could have continued to see one another as the years progressed. Papa spent almost all of his time at home now, and he always asked Mummy to accompany him if he had to travel to London. He certainly never traveled to America.

There was one last battle of significance in Europe, when the Germans launched a counteroffensive in the Ardennes in France, where in December the Battle of the Bulge killed 19,000 Americans and delayed the Allied march into Germany. I spent another Christmas with just my parents and Isabella at *Willow Grove Abbey* in 1944. My initial thrill at learning that Spence was most likely alive, had dimmed somewhat, as the war just went on and on. There was no question that eventually the Allies were going to see a tremendous victory, both in Europe and in the Pacific theater, although both the Japanese and the Germans stubbornly refused to surrender. Shortly after the New Year, the Russians liberated Auschwitz, and the sickening revelation of the Holocaust was made. I thought of the unbearable *Dieter Schoen,* and his obscene comments about purification of the white Aryan race. I wondered how wonderful he thought Herr Hitler was now. Finally the bombing campaigns of the Blitz were over, but V1 and V2 rockets continued to drop on London. In the meantime, I simply existed. That is the way in which I view those months. I still don't think of that period as a time when I truly *lived.* I remember it as years of drifting on the surface. Treading water. If I went too deep, there would be pain, and I did not want to feel that pain, so I kept myself far above that plane. I did all of the things one was expected to do, which included being the best mother I could be, performing duties as a good and faithful daughter, and carrying out my volunteer work with the Red Cross and the canteen. I wasn't certain that I always excelled at any of those tasks. I reached the point where I hated living at *Willow Grove Abbey* with my parents, and longed for my own independence. Longed for friends and a *whole* life. Life at *Willow Grove* was anything but whole. It wasn't as vile as it had been before Mummy learned about Edwina, as her rages had, for the most part, ceased, but in their place was a continual, never-ending despair. No laughter. No happiness. There were times when I sank very, very low and there were other times when I felt like giving up completely. And yes, there were even times when I wondered if I had really ever known Spence. But, I held fast, as did nearly everyone. I wasn't unique, brave, or special in any way. Hundreds, even thousands of women had become war brides, only to spend years wondering whom they had married. Wondering whether there would ever really *be* a marriage. Thus, I was no exception. Isabella's existence was what kept me sane and focused upon the future. She was all I had. Her sweet face was the living embodiment of her father, and I owed it to him to raise her properly. To make certain that she had memories of him, in the event that he never returned. Moreover, assuming that he *did* return, I didn't want Isabella to wonder who he was, and why he'd suddenly appeared in her life again, after such a long absence.

There were many lonely soldiers and airmen who visited the local canteen where I helped out. Many tried to know me better, but I never yielded to any such temptation. Spence had been correct when he'd said on that long ago summer afternoon, in 1935, that we had known one another forever. I still believed that he was my soulmate, and if I hadn't believed that I couldn't have endured.

The Western Allies raced the Russians to be first into Berlin, and the Russians won. They reached the Capitol on 21 April, and three days later Hitler killed himself. That was two days after Mussolini had been captured and hung by the Italian partisans. Germany finally surrendered on 7 May, and the war in Europe was over. On 8 May, Victory in Europe Day was celebrated the world over. Throngs and throngs of people by the thousands crammed into London streets, shouting and singing. The King and Queen and their family came onto the balcony to receive the praises of their people. It was reported that the Princesses Elizabeth and Margaret were allowed to put head scarves on, and go out into the crowds to celebrate like any other ordinary young girls.

Chapter Twenty-Eight

JUNE, 1945
HOME

The question foremost in my mind in May 1945, was when or if Spence would be coming home. My whole life hung in the balance. I still had no certain confirmation that he had been a Prisoner of War. Then, finally, we received a wire from the war department informing us that Group Captain Spencer Ryan Stanton had been a Prisoner of War at a permanent camp for officers, south of Berlin. In close proximity was a nearby hospital that made use of captured doctors and medical corpsmen to treat wounded prisoners. So Captain Ian French had been correct. I was relieved to learn that this camp was considered a model of civilized internment. At that site, The Geneva Convention of 1929 was complied with. But, it was still a Prisoner of War Camp and had to be beastly. A second wire arrived saying that Captain Stanton had been liberated and would be setting foot on English soil again very soon. He was being flown to RAF Fowlmere, where he would be processed and allowed to proceed by train to his home. I didn't yet know the precise date, nor the train's timetable, but no matter. The vitally important elements were present. Spence was alive, well, and coming back to me. I felt a myriad of emotions. Elation, of course, quickly followed by apprehension. What if he'd changed? What if I had changed? I tried to push such fears aside, and concentrate upon the memories we'd made together, and those we would continue to make through the years that lay ahead.

The French were apparently the first prisoners to be flown out, as General Charles de Gaulle obtained first priority from General Dwight

Eisenhower. The Americans and the Brits waited, but finally were moved out to nearby German airfields and transported to Combat Personnel Replacement Depots on the French Channel Coast. From there they were taken to various bases throughout England. It was then that I finally learned the horrific story of what my husband had endured. I had a call from Captain Ian French, shortly after VE Day, asking if I could make time to see him. Of course I told him that I could see him at any time he wished. We made arrangements for him to come to *Willow Grove Abbey* for dinner and a sleep-over. When he arrived, Papa mixed him a drink and we settled into the drawing room, while he launched into the tale of Spence's last ordeal. He had already spoken to some of the other men who had been imprisoned with Spence, so he knew the entire story.

We learned that Spence had been seized almost immediately after his Spitfire had crashed. He had been taken first to the Luftwaffe Aircrew Interrogation Centre, where all Allied aviators were deposited after they were captured. There, each new soldier was put through horrific questioning, and then kept in solitary confinement. Subsequently they were moved to the camp south of Berlin. During the years he was there, he had been busy patching up wounded Germans, and sending them back out to their death. There was no question that he had been terribly glad to be able to use his medical skills. That probably kept him sane. Up until the end, the imprisonment was certainly no worse than that of many other captured soldiers, and probably much better than some, He was not beaten, and received an adequate diet. He was also allowed six hours of sleep a night, in order to be clear headed when he performed surgery. The end of his imprisonment was what brought the nightmare. In January of 1945, Hitler apparently wasn't ready to surrender just yet, although it was plainly clear for everyone to see that the Allies had conquered Germany, and kept the world free. It was only a matter of time until triumph was complete. Hitler issued an order to vacate Spence's camp in January of 1945. Apparently Hitler was worried that the Russians would free the over 11,000 Allied pilots in the camp and he wanted to detain them as hostages.

The prisoners were queued up outside in vicious weather, and remained there for hours while the piercing wind actually froze their uniforms. Beginning to move near midnight, they hadn't the slightest notion where they were destined. It was an evil, atrocious trek. They were in the midst of a savage snowstorm, and they staggered along in sleet and ice. There were seven Allied doctors, and they were given no medications or aid by the Germans. Spence was one of them. After trudging all day, they spent their nights giving assistance to those who were sick. They were on the march again when dawn broke. When no medication was available, their encouragement and wit helped men who thought they couldn't keep going.

Finally, on 29 January, they stumbled into a small German town, where all of them crumpled. They stayed in that place for nearly twenty-four hours, before they were ordered to make the sixteen mile trek to a bit larger village, where they were then crammed into railcars. Half stood, while the other half sat. The cars were designed to hold only forty people, but they were filled with nearly sixty. It was a three-day horror story. There was only one, small pail for use in relieving themselves, and it soon overflowed. There was nothing to eat. The odor of vomit and feces permeated the air. At long last, the train came to a halt, and the soldiers were then placed into a broken down complex, surrounded by barbed wire fencing, which encircled wooden billets. They were in deplorable condition, and had been erected to house other prisoners. There were fleas and the buildings were rat infested, and absolutely filthy. There, Spence spent the remaining days of World War II, knowing that the Allies were pressing forward, and praying for freedom, but still suffering from trauma, anxiety, and hunger.

On the morning of 29 April, 1945, elements of the 14-Armored Division of Patton's third Army attacked the SS troops guarding the camp where Spence was imprisoned. The prisoners all scrambled for safety. Some kissed the ground, while others crawled into open concrete incinerators. Bullets flew haphazardly, but finally the American's broke through. The first tank entered, taking the barbed wire fence with it. The prisoners went totally bonkers. They clambered to the top of the tanks in huge numbers, and nearly suffocated one another. They were free. Spence was at long last freed, and he would be coming home to England. Coming home to me, and his daughter, and a world that had changed in every way imaginable.

Captain French stayed as our guest two days, and he was so overcome with the comfort he found waiting for him at *Willow Grove* that he made us promise him he could bring his wife back to visit our splendid home someday. Naturally, we were more than happy to make such a pact. I told him that he could stay and greet Spence with us if he wanted, but he was most anxious to return to his own home, in Yorkshire, and said that he thought it would be inappropriate to intrude on such a private event.

The entire world had been engulfed in Adolph Hitler's insane desire to rule the globe. The War had stretched from Europe to North Africa, from the Philippines to Burma and Japan. When it was over, nearly 50 million people were dead, and hundreds of cities had been completely destroyed.

My brothers had come through those awful years, and of course we were all thankful for that. Blake had been at RAF Kinloss in Morayshire, Scotland, so had never been far from Susan. In fact, by that time, they had a little girl, Alexandra, of whom I knew little, since there was still an estrangement between my brother and me. I supposed that Blake and Susan would remain in Scotland, following the war, although it had always been planned that he would take over the London offices of Somerville Ltd. someday. Things seemed in a bit of a muddle as far as Blake was concerned. It had been so long since I had been close with him or even had any sort of conversation. I scarcely felt it mattered what he chose to do with his life.

Andrew had been posted to Scotland as well, at Scapa Flow Naval Base, where he'd performed the duties of Chaplin. While he'd seen no action at sea, he'd certainly experienced his share of sorrow in dealing with those men and women who'd faced the trauma and fear of battle. Annie had been with him throughout, and there's no question that, while happy for them, I also felt some envy at their togetherness. They too had become parents. In 1944 a little boy named Nigel, after his grandfather, was born. They came to *Willow Grove* Abbey on three occasions during the war, and it was lovely to see that they had formed such a nice family. Isabella thought it wonderful to have a cousin. I didn't know what their plans would be now that the madness had ended. Of course, my parents hoped that Andrew would choose to return to his home, and take up the clerical duties as vicar at St. Mary and St. Edward Chapel. That had always been the original plan, but so much seemed to have changed since the time when we'd been young, making plans for a future that hadn't included violent upheaval in all of our lives.

Finally, another wire came, telling me that Spence would be arriving on the 4:57 p.m. train at *Bedminster-with-Hartfcliffe*. Everything became chaotic. Mummy automatically expected that she and Papa would be accompanying me to the station. I, on the other hand, wasn't certain that I wanted them to be there. I would be seeing my husband for the first time in four, long years. In addition, there was the question of Isabella. Would it be better for me to greet Spence alone, and then let him become re-acquainted with his daughter in the natural surroundings of *Willow Grove*, or would he want her to be there, with me, at the station? Isabella solved that dilemma, for she insisted firmly that she *would indeed* be at the station to see her Papa come home from the war. Once I realized how strongly Isabella felt about the subject, there was no question that the two of us would be waiting for him on the platform. I finally decided, however, that my parents would have to wait to share in the joy of his homecoming. I simply chose, for once in my life, to selfishly savor the moment without the interference, and often-stressful presence, of my parents.

On June 6th, 1945, one year to the day that the Allied Forces had stormed the beaches of Normandy, turning the tide of the War, Isabella and I stood nervous and anxious at the small station house at *Bedminster-with-Hartcliffe*. There were no other persons waiting to meet the train. I was much too tense to sit down, so I paced up and down the platform peering as far as I could down the tracks to see if there was a locomotive in sight. I'd taken great care with my appearance although I'd had to make do with a not-so-new ensemble. Still it was a lovely summer dress, with a halter-top and nipped-in waistline, made of white cotton pique. I decided against gloves and hat, opting to let my hair, which had grown quite long, spill across my shoulders in a cascade of curls. I clipped it to the side with a pearl-encrusted barrette. Around my neck, I wore a simple, pearl cross. I was still only twenty-eight years old, although I had enough tragedy in my life to make me feel ninety. Isabella was also in white…starched cotton with pleated top and full skirt, and white Mary-Jane shoes with anklets. I held her hand as we waited, although at close to nine years of age, she was beginning to want more independence. She was still tiny for her age, a petite little girl, with long, dark curls and wide blue eyes. Finally, a train whistled in the distance, followed by the familiar roar of a diesel engine. My pulse was thumping, and I could scarcely contain myself. Isabella let go of my hand, and began to jump up and down, yelling. "Here comes my Papa." I wanted to shout along with her. The train came to a slow stop and suddenly there he was, standing between cars waiting to leap to the platform.

If I had been worried that I wouldn't know him, or that I'd think him a stranger, I quickly found that those fears were laid to rest. He was the Spence I had always known. My handsome, dear, dashing RAF pilot. Older yes, and weary, of course, looking thinner and somewhat gaunt, his dark hair flecked with silver. Nevertheless, his blue eyes still held their piercing quality, and he still flashed his wonderful dimpled smile. I ran to him as he leaped to the platform. In one quick movement I was in his arms. He kissed me hard and long, and I couldn't believe that it was finally happening. I buried my face in the rough fabric of his uniform, as I'd always loved to do, and rubbed my cheek against his, whispering how very much I had missed him, and how dearly I loved him. Isabella stood anxiously awaiting her turn, and while still holding an arm about my waist, he reached down and scooped his daughter up with his free arm.

"Oh, my beautiful daughter! You have gone and grown up while Papa has been away. But, you've grown more beautiful too," he laughed, giving her a big kiss.

She wrapped her arms around his neck, and said, "I love you Papa and I'm so glad you're home."

"Oh my precious, I'm so glad too," he smiled. We have so much time to make up for, don't we?"

We presented a lovely picture, standing there at the station. A father who hadn't seen his daughter in four years, a little girl who was so proud and happy that she was about to burst with joy, and a glowing, wife, whose love and happiness radiated from her being. Spence shook hands with Joseph, who had tears in his eyes. Bags were fetched, and in the blink of an eye we were in the car and headed back to *Willow Grove Abbey*. It felt so wonderful to have him there beside me. So right. Isabella kept up a constant stream of chatter about all of the things she wanted to show him, and the plans she had for him. Those included meeting all of her school chums, watching how well she played tennis, going for ice cream together in the village, playing chess with him, and his helping with her homework, just to name a few. Spence and I smiled at one another, and he reached over and put his arm over my shoulders, pulling me closely. Have I told you how utterly lovely you are?" he whispered to me.

Have I told you that you're still the most devastatingly handsome man I've ever known?" I replied. He squeezed my hand, and I felt the familiar tingle go down my spine. In that moment I knew that everything was going to be all right. The worst was behind us. We had weathered such an enormous storm…storms, really…and I knew that the future held many, many years of happiness. Finally we could look ahead to our own home. Finally, there was no more worry about Edwina. I could be independent again, with no more listening to the bickering of my parents. Spence and I would watch Isabella grow to be a young lady and woman, basking in our happiness. I couldn't imagine that anything on Earth could compare with what we had been through. I had no idea what lay ahead. However, there was no question that I believed with all of my heart that we were meant to be together, and we would face the future with that uppermost in our minds.

About The Author

Mary Christian Payne is an accomplished business woman, who has held high ranking, management positions with Fortune 500 companies, in New York City, St. Louis, Missouri, Orlando, Florida, and Tulsa, Oklahoma. She is a recipient of the Mayor's Pinnacle Award in Tulsa, for directing a highly successful program at The Women's Resource Center at the University of Tulsa. All of these positions involved significant amounts of writing. She has also acted as a speech writer for high profile political figures, and for executives of major corporations.

She is now a retired Career Psychologist. She was the founder and President of Transitions Counseling Center, in partnership with her father, the retired CEO of a four billion dollar retail organization. She has taught seminars throughout Oklahoma. Mary Christian is a world traveler, and has spent extensive time in England, thus creating an excellent foundation for writing novels set in Great Britain. The era of World War II has always held tremendous appeal for her, and she is a committed Anglophile. The daughter of an Army Major during World War II, she grew up hearing countless stories of that tumultuous and romantic time.

She lives with her husband, Jim, who is a Pharmacist, and their two beloved Maltese Terriers in Broken Arrow, Oklahoma. She is also the mother of two, adult children, and three-grandchildren.

One Last Thing...

If you enjoyed this book, I'd be very grateful if you'd post a short review. Your support really does make a difference and I read all the reviews personally.

Thanks again for your support!

www.ingramcontent.com/pod-product-compliance
Lightning Source LLC
Chambersburg PA
CBHW070756120726
47910CB00001B/190